MUNNARI
ASCENDING

NOVEL TWO

ML BELLANTE

Munnari Ascending: Novel Two

The Munnari Chronicles

ML Bellante

Copyright 2020 ML Bellante

BookWise Publishing, Riverton, Utah

www.bookwisepublishing.com

Editor, Interior Design, & Producer: K Christoffersen
Cover Illustrator: Brian Hailes
Graphics Illustrator: Juan Diego Dianderas
Cartographer: Hugo Solis

Library of Congress Control Number: 2020907263

ISBN 978-1-60645-248-6 Trade Paperback $16.99
ISBN 978-1-60645-249-3 eBook $7.99
ISBN 978-1-60645-250-9 Audiobook $17.99
10 9 8 7 6 5 4 3 2 1

Order online at Amazon.com
MunnariChronicles.com
MLBellanteBooks.com

5/21/2020 version

MUNNARI ASCENDING

NOVEL TWO

DEDICATION

To my loving sister as she struggles
through her health challenges.
My love and prayers are always with you.
—Brother Bear

TABLE OF CONTENTS

PROLOGUE

Coleman sat on a log, facing the warmth of his party's campfire. The Anterran's had retired to their tents for the night. Ayascho had just said goodnight and went to sleep under a cart. Coleman was now alone, so he retrieved his calendar stick from the other cart, returned to the campfire, and added another notch. He then counted fifty-four notches, each notch representing one day of travel. He gazed into the night sky and saw a gibbous Munnoga, the silvery moon, directly overhead. Munnari and Munnevo, the blue and red moons, were just clearing the trees. He watched in wonder as he often did, marveling at their splendor as they slowly rolled around each other. He recalled his shock the first night he had seen them, and the startling realization he wasn't on Earth. As he sat pondering his new life, he reviewed in his mind the many challenges he'd faced since his arrival on this unnamed world.

He was to be Earth's first dimensional traveler, using a recently developed mode of transport called Dimensional Harmonic Transference, commonly referred to as ripping. The scientists had successfully ripped many inanimate objects for years to the Moon, and recently, a monkey. When Coleman was ripped, he opened his eyes and found himself in a jungle. At first, he thought he was on Earth, but he soon learned he had been transported to another world. He had no idea of where he was, his own universe, or a different dimension of time and space.

All he had was the clothes on his back and the environmental suit he was required to wear for the rip. His first night became a harrowing experience when he was attacked by a ferocious beast. He survived only because of the toughness of his suit, although it had been destroyed during his life and death struggle. The next day, he was captured by a tribe of primitive natives. He was taken to their village where a clan council was held. Although Coleman couldn't understand the natives' language, he quickly deduced it was a debate for his life. Fortunately, the vote by the tusk-men, the village leaders, went in his favor, but just barely. The village taahso, a shaman and the clans' religious leader, told him his blue eyes, something no one else had ever seen, had saved him that night. The villagers considered the blue moon, Munnari, to be the good moon, and its influence blessed the People. The red moon, Munnevo, was considered the source of all evil. After the vote, Coleman was accepted into the tribe, and he was given the name Tondo, meaning the visitor. Besides his new name, the chief gave him the young woman, Atura, as a member of his family and a mentor to teach him the villagers' language.

Coleman was then given free reign in the village and soon learned how to communicate with the natives. Unexpectedly, he came down with a severe illness that nearly killed him. During his illness, he experienced a dis-

turbing vision that caused him worry and concern for the welfare of his adopted Batru family. After he recovered, Coleman
joined a hunt team and went looking for prey to feed the village. His hunt party was attacked by the most fearsome beast in
the jungle, the gorga, the same creature that had attacked him
during his first night on this world. With most of his hunt part-
ners down, Coleman called for Ayascho to help, but the young
man, in his terror-stricken panic, fled, climbing a nearby tree.
Coleman faced the gorga alone, baited it into chasing him in a
long run, and killed it when the beast was exhausted. During
a grand celebration in the village's great lodge, Coleman was
awarded the huge fang of the monster. He was then expected
to recount his epic battle with the gorga to the assembled villagers, which he did; however, he never shared with the others
Ayascho's cowardly retreat. Ayascho, never a fan of the outlander Tondo, only grew angrier because he felt he was now in
Tondo's debt, a debt he must somehow repay.

Coleman was also noticing that the taahso seemed to
possess what were seemingly magical abilities: healing
powers, the ability to help others learn faster, and the ability to control fire. It wasn't long before Coleman himself
began exhibiting some
of these same powers,
although he struggled
to control them. Nor
had he yet to determine
the extent of his in-
ner-power, but he knew
it was growing.

XII   ML BELLANTE

After he'd been with the clan for nearly a year, two other outlanders arrived at the village, a merchant, Myron by name, and his young-looking slave, Zoseemo, along with their three huge rasters, camel-like creatures with six legs. Myron's visit was enlightening for Coleman, for he learned that Myron came from a place he called the Ancient City. Coleman also learned that Myron was well over five-hundred years old, and Zoseemo was more than eighty. Myron was in a hurry and left the next day. Little did Coleman know that when Myron returned to the Ancient City, the Sutro Seer, the great

religious leader of the age, interviewed the merchant, and he sought the king's assistance in fetching the unusual man with the blue eyes, and bring him to the kingdom.

Nearly two years after his arrival, a detachment of warriors, sent by the king, arrived at Coleman's village. They had brought with them two large creatures that appeared to be triceratops, only smaller. The leader of the warriors, Titus, referred to them as thrice, and they pulled the two carts carrying the warriors' supplies. Titus wanted Coleman to return with him immediately, but the outlander would not comply. He told Titus that the rainy season was upon them, and they would have to delay until the rains abated or die in the muck due to disease and exhaustion.

Titus was in a hurry to return to the Ancient City and wouldn't wait. After a foolish attempt to take Coleman by force, he relented and resigned himself to the long wait. It was then that Titus revealed that what he called the Blessing of the City awaited them, granting everyone under its influence longevity. For every day they remained beyond its influence, they would age ten. Titus also told that the rumor was the Sutro Seer had warned the king of a rising threat in a distant land.

When the weather turned fair, Coleman informed Titus that it was time to leave. The men packed their gear into the carts and departed. After a few days' of travel, a couple of Titus's men caught a native following them. It was Ayascho. He had yet to unburden his debt to Tondo, and he would follow the outlander until the debt was paid. He was obstinate and wouldn't turn back. Coleman relented, and Ayascho was allowed to join Titus's party.

Toto, Coleman's pet betzoe, a huge dog-like creature with a convex headplate, dropped his head on Coleman's thigh and snorted. Coleman sighed and voiced aloud, "Yes, it has been a long day, my friend. It is time to turn in." He climbed into a cart and covered himself with a furry wrap. Toto joined him, and the two quickly fell asleep.

CHAPTER 1

On the fifty-fifth day of their travels to the Ancient City, sometime before dawn while it was still dark, Coleman awakened with a start, his trusty betzoe, Toto, was sitting up and sounding a low grumbling growl. Coleman grabbed his bow and poked his head above the sideboard of the cart, his eyes straining to see through the gloom. The moons had set, but the brightness of the stars gave a slight glow to the immediate area. Toto continued his bothered growl, but it was obvious it wasn't about something he saw; more likely, it was something he heard or smelled. Coleman placed his hand on the betzoe's back to comfort him, but he continued his grumble. Suddenly, the betzoe sounded his screechy bark; a signal Coleman knew meant danger. Through the brush, he could hear movement. He stood and fumbled for his quiver. Before he could nock an arrow, he saw a spear tip floating in the darkness, hovering just above his heart. In the dimness, he could see the whites of a pair of eyes staring back at him.

A warning voice came from the direction of the eyes, "Move no more, or I'll kill you!"

He then noticed bare-skinned men moving all around the camp. They looked like Batru hunters, but there were too many to be a typical hunting party. It soon became obvious, this was a carefully laid ambush. Titus and his men were quickly rounded up and ushered to the cart where Coleman was standing. Toto was growling wildly, and Coleman had to restrain him for fear of the invaders' weapons.

"Tondo, what's going on? Who are these savages?" Titus demanded.

"I have no idea. They appear to be men from a Batru clan I have never met before."

One of the Batru confidently walked up to the collection of men. He was clearly the leader of this band of captors. From his perch in the cart, Coleman stared down at him, waiting for the man to speak. Without saying a word, the Batru leader examined Titus and each of his men closely. He then pointed to Coleman, indicating he wanted him to step down from the cart. Coleman did so, and the man then examined him. He touched Coleman's beard and looked puzzled. By this time, dawn was beginning to break, and as the man looked into Coleman's blue eyes, he uttered his first word, "Munnari!"

A rustle was heard coming from under the cart, and a couple of the intruders darted to the sound, dragging Ayascho into the group and dropping him at the feet of their leader.

"You are Batru!" the man exclaimed.

"Yes, I am. Who are you?" Ayascho wondered as he stood and nervously faced him. He noticed a bataro tooth hanging from a leather cord around the leader's neck. Immediately he realized, this person was of some importance for he was a tusk-man.

"I am Zossi. I lead these men. Why are you here, and what is this?" he asked pointing at Coleman.

"I am traveling to a place called the Ancient City with these smelly men," Ayascho said as he pointed at Titus. "This is Tondo. They are taking him there," he told his captor in a voice that expressed his fear. Coleman smiled, but Titus and his men were not amused.

"Tondo? The visitor? I have never seen such a thing. Does it speak?" Zossi asked.

"Yes, I can speak and much more," Coleman barked as he touched the spear still aimed at his heart. The shaft burst into flames, causing its holder to drop it to the ground. Everyone but Coleman stepped back and gawked at the flaming lance. Individually, the Batru began to mutter the title taahso as they retreated a few steps more. Titus and his men kept looking back and forth between the flaming spear and Coleman. Amazement filling their eyes, also.

When Zossi shifted his gaze from the spear to Coleman, he noticed the gorga fang hanging from the beast-man's neck. "Gorga!" he cried while pointing at it.

"He killed it with knife and club, and alone," Ayascho boasted, taking everyone by surprise, especially Coleman.

Zossi found himself in a very unenviable position. This Tondo was definitely taahso, and no one to trifle with. For all he knew, the beast-man could kill them all in a flash of fiery death. The tusk-man was not accustomed to handling this kind of issue, so he decided it would be wise to tread lightly. He said, "Come with me and talk with my taahso."

Coleman looked at Titus and told him, "We had better go with them. If we resist, things could get really ugly, very fast." Titus simply nodded his reluctant approval. "We will go with you, but first, let us collect our things," Coleman told the Batru leader.

It took them only a few minutes to break camp, stow their gear in the carts, and start moving. The p´atezas was well overhead by the time the group reached the Batru village. It was much larger than the one he and Ayascho were from; at least twice as big, Coleman guessed. The villagers came out in droves and gaped at the awe-inspiring thrice and odd-looking men. As the group filed into the village, Coleman could hear villagers quietly utter, *Munnari* and *beast-man*, as fingers pointed at him. When they reached the center of the village, Zossi raised his arm, and the group stopped. The thrice stood chewing their cuds, seemingly bored by all the attention.

Two men stood before them, obviously the chief and the taahso. "I see the plan has worked, Zossi; well done. We can't have trespassers invading our lands," said the chief.

"He is taahso," Zossi said, pointing to the wild-looking Coleman. "He is Batru," he continued, pointing to Ayascho.

The chief examined Coleman more closely, marveling at the hair on his face. The chief spoke again, "You have the eyes of the blue moon. Can you speak? Has the great Batru sent you to us?"

"We are only passing through. We did not mean to trespass." Coleman's mind was racing, trying to find a way to extricate his party from this sticky situation. A thought popped into his head, "Ayascho, tell them your father's name."

"Why?"

"Just do it."

"My father was Ayoano. He was killed by the gorga."

"Who was his father, and his father's father, and so on?"

"Ayovi, then Ayundi, Ayagundi . . . " He continued rattling off name after name for some time, " . . . and before him, Ayashi . . . "

Suddenly the taahso's eyes widened, "Ayashi? Ayashi of the Great Separation?" he asked.

"Yes, he led my family."

The taahso gave a shout like a war cry, and it startled all the captives. "He is a son of Ayashi!" exclaimed the taahso. Many of the other villagers began shouting their glee and started dancing. The men beat their chests, and the women ululated, voicing their long wavering shriek of celebration and glee. Titus and his men shuddered in fear at the commotion. Coleman looked around and smiled at the joyous reunion.

From that moment on, his party was treated as honored guests, and the surprised Ayascho was the center of attention. As both guests and hosts relaxed, food was served. The chief, the taahso, Zossi, Ayascho, Titus, and Coleman, withdrew to a private meeting under a large shady tree with many air roots dangling from its branches. Zossi explained to the chief what he had seen Coleman do to the spear, and he made sure the chief noticed the gorga fang hanging from his neck.

"Ha! I believe Batru has sent you to us. We need your help," the chief said.

Titus angrily interrupted, "I don't want any more delays!" He was almost shouting.

Coleman quieted the man simply by raising his arm. "We are in a hurry, but what can we do to help?" he asked.

"A gorga has moved onto our lands. It has already killed

three hunters, also a young woman and her child. I see by the gorga fang hanging from your neck, you have killed one before. Can you save us by killing this one?" came the chief's desperate request.

"We don't have time for a hunting party. We need to get back to the city," Titus interposed, only slightly less panicked this time.

"If we kill the gorga, will you let us leave in peace?" Coleman asked.

"You may leave with my blessing any time you wish. Ayascho is of our clan, he is family, and you are his friends. We will not stop you."

"How many different gorga have you seen? If we kill this one, what about others? I'm sure it has a mate and offspring. We'll just be wasting our time," Titus grumbled.

"There's never more than one, I'm sure. Gorga's are always male, and they are the spawn of the red moon; my taasho says." Ayascho stated, leaving Titus perplexed and Coleman surprised.

"We will hunt it in the morning," Coleman announced, evoking huge smiles from the villagers.

The men in the impromptu council separated and went their separate ways. Coleman easily detected Ayascho's rising fear. When Sestardi Titus reported the news of another delay to his men, they grouched and cursed, but they knew there wasn't anything they could do about it. Coleman and the savages held all the power, so they would have to wait.

In the afternoon, Coleman organized his hunt team. He, Ayascho, and Toto would be the lead hunters. Zossi was invit-

ed and was told he could bring one other village hunter. Titus
was also invited, and he, too, could bring one of his soldiers.
The men spent the rest of the day preparing for the hunt.
Coleman made a few more arrows because his supply was getting low. Ayascho fashioned himself a new spear and lever.
Neither traveler had any time to make new weapons during
the journey because Titus had been driving the party so hard.

This is a good opportunity to rest both man and beast, Coleman
thought.

Dawn was beginning to break when the men assembled at
the soldier's camp. Zossi introduced Vihi, a scent man. Coleman smiled as he greeted the young hunter, for he supposed,
Vihi was in for a long and depressing day because he knew
Toto would be leading the party to the gorga. Titus introduced Gheedan, whom he said was very skilled with the metren, the soldiers' pike. Titus also carried one. Both warriors
were armed with short swords sheathed at their sides. The rest
of the village gathered around the camp and wished them a
successful hunt. The taahso blessed each hunter, just as was
done in the other Batru village, much to the consternation of
the two Anterran warriors. Then, all the hunters departed,
disappearing into the thick underbrush.

It took less than a half-hour for Vihi to find fresh gorga
scat. Coleman made sure Toto saw and sniffed it, and then
the huge betzoe was off at a trot. The men had a difficult
time keeping up. The betzoe moved silently, stopping to sniff

the ground in all directions when he lost the scent. Then he'd raise his head and dart off with the men hot on his heels.

As they followed Toto, the thought of facing a gorga again brought near panic to Coleman's mind. He had nearly been ripped to shreds by one during his first night on this world. Was his success in the second encounter pure luck? Self-doubt began to invade his thinking. He shook these thoughts from his mind and focused on the hunt. This time, he had a bow. He also had metrens and swords in the party. These weapons would be much more effective than an obsidian-tipped spear, he guessed.

In about an hour or so, the betzoe stopped at the edge of an open meadow. Through the waist-high grass and tall flowers, Coleman could see a lake far in the distance. He told the men to wait at the edge of the tree line, and then, with Ayascho and Toto, he walked into the tall grass.

After advancing about one-hundred feet or so from the others, he knelt and whispered to his betzoe, "Alright, boy, this is it. He is out there somewhere. Go find him and bring him to us." This was a gambit they had used before with other creatures of prey. Toto was the bait, Coleman, with his bow, was the trap. He gave the betzoe a pat on its haunches, and off Toto bounded, quickly disappearing through the tall grass. Coleman stood, then stuck three arrows into the soft dirt in front of himself. He nocked another and waited. He knew the gorga was an apex predator, and every lesser creature in its domain, including men, was a meal.

It wasn't long before the men heard the betzoe's snarls and his screechy bark of warning. The sound began to grow closer, and everyone became tense. Ayascho began looking from side to side, and then over his shoulder. Through clenched teeth, Coleman muttered, "If you run again, I will put this arrow in your backside!" Ayascho stiffened, drew forth the obsidian knife Coleman had given him, and he dropped it. He quickly picked it up, holding it in his left hand. In his right, he held his new levered spear, cocked over his shoulder, and ready to throw. From the corner of his eye, Coleman could see the young man shaking all over; however, Ayascho kept his eyes fixed on the field in front of them.

"Here comes Toto," Coleman said in as calm a voice as he could muster. Just then, Toto burst through the grass, running past the two men, turning and stopping halfway between the two groups. He began snarling and barking even louder, pacing from side to side, wanting to return to his master, yet too afraid to do so. A few seconds later, Coleman and Ayascho could see the enormous back of the gorga rising above the

grass a couple of hundred feet directly in front of them. The creature slowed its advance, raised its head high, and sniffed the air.

"He has our scent," Coleman whispered. A stifled cry of fear escaped Ayascho's closed mouth. They watched as the beast paraded back and forth, declaring its territory in a threatening display that would have caused any sane creature to flee for its life. The two men stood their ground. The beast was huge, even larger than the one Coleman had killed. Its shoulders reached a man's midchest. It had a huge head, full of razor-sharp teeth. Coleman couldn't see its feet, but he knew from experience, it had knife-like claws on all four. Even so, he couldn't help thinking about how majestic the brute looked. It reminded him of a bull as it prepared to charge a matador.

Angered by the impertinence of these creatures invading its territory, the beast lowered its head and rushed toward them with a grunt and a snarl. Coleman drew back his bowstring and fired his first arrow. It hit the gorga in the right shoulder and sank deep into its flesh. The gorga gave an agonized roar of pain but kept coming. Coleman snatched up another arrow, aimed, and loosed it. At about one-hundred feet distant, the arrow struck home and sank deep into the gorga's back. The beast stumbled, but it did not go down. As it resumed its gait, Coleman swiftly nocked another arrow and let it fly. Another hit, this time in the beast's left shoulder. This wound caused the creature to slow, yet it would not stop.

When the beast was only fifty feet away, Ayascho let his levered spear fly. It was an excellent shot, striking the beast in the head, just above the eyes. Coleman's elation was quickly dashed as the spear merely bounced off. The monster opened its mouth, exposing its huge, dagger-like teeth, preparing to tear into its tormentors. Coleman loosed his fourth arrow when the beast was little more than twenty-five feet away. It entered the gorga's mouth, piercing its skull from the underside, and ending its flight in the creature's brain. The gorga collapsed, sliding past the two men as Coleman jumped to the left, and Ayascho jumped to the right.

"Finish him!" Coleman shouted. Ayascho pounced on the convulsing beast and drove his obsidian knife into its neck. The last few beats of its pumping heart gushed blood all over Ayascho's arms and chest. Soon, the bleeding slowed to a trickle. The other hunters dashed to the fallen beast and began hacking and stabbing its carcass. Coleman took a deep breath, wiping sweat from his brow. "That was a bit too close for comfort!" he exclaimed.

Ayascho, Zossi, and Vihi began to dance and sing a song of victory; Ayascho raising his bloody knife and arm high into the air, the others doing the same with their bloody weapons. Gheedan soon joined them, much to the displeasure of his sestardi.

After the men had calmed down, Vihi dashed off to the village, returning an hour and a half later with a dozen village men. By this time, Coleman and Ayascho had weaved leafy baskets to hold the beast's choice innards, while the others skinned and dressed it. The victorious men marched back to the village and were greeted by shouts of, "P'oez! P'oez! P'oez!" They were indeed great hunters.

It was late in the day, and it was obvious to Titus that they would be going nowhere until the morning. He candidly resigned himself to yet another dawn away from his beloved city. The chief invited all the visitors to partake of the gorga's flesh, and he offered a portion of its raw heart to each hunt-er. Coleman took a bite, then, with great fanfare, gave the rest of his portion to the betzoe. Toto gobbled it down, then sniffed around for more.

That night, a fabulous celebration was held in the village's great lodge in honor of the hunters' suc-cess. There was much singing and dancing. Cole-man was awarded his second gorga fang, and Ayascho was awarded the other, much to his great surprise and unfeigned delight. Cole-man watched as Ayascho's pride and self-confidence grew. Coleman, too, was proud of the young man. He had been quaking in his bare feet, but he stood his ground this time. If they ever had to do something like that again, Coleman was certain he could count on him.

After the two lead hunters had received their trophies and returned to their places, Coleman started hearing the begin-nings of a familiar chant. "Oh, no!" he muttered under his breath in godspeak. But as more voices joined in, it became clear what the chant was, and what it was for.

"Tondo! Tondo! Tondo!" the villagers cried. It seemed to be his lot in this new life of his to keep telling a story of Tondo and the gorga. And so he did, over, and over, and over.

Early the next morning, Coleman awoke to the noise of Titus ordering his men to break camp. A soft, reddish-orange glow was beginning to brighten the horizon. Coleman and Toto quickly got up, soon followed by Ayascho. Many of the villagers had gathered at the camp. The tents were quickly downed, folded, and stored in the carts. The thrice were then hitched up, and the party was on their way long before the p´atezas's disk could be seen. The villagers began to sing a remorseful song of parting, whose strains could be heard long after the groups could no longer see each other. It was another bittersweet farewell for Coleman. He had grown to love these uncomplicated people. They were free of hatred and guile, wanting only to survive day-to-day, raising their families, and holding true to their belief in the Great Batru.

As they walked, Coleman carried on a conversation with Ayascho. Now that they were on friendlier terms, he wanted to learn a little about the young man's background. Ayascho told him that he was a young man of one line when his father was killed by the gorga. When his father died, his mother wasted away with grief, dying soon afterward. Ayascho had been on his own ever since.

After Ayascho had finished, it was Coleman's turn to tell his companion about himself. He told the young man that his mother and father were still living, as far as he knew. He had an older brother, four spans older, who had died as a warrior in a terrible war. He had to explain to Ayascho what war was because it was something the young Batru had never heard of nor contemplated before. It was Coleman's brother's example

that led him to become a warrior himself. He had served nearly ten spans and was in many battles before he stopped being a warrior. He told Ayascho, he had been a special kind of
warrior called a Ranger, not that the young man really com-
prehended what that meant.

They continued their friendly chit-chat for many hours.
Coleman noticed the hostility he had always heard in Ayascho's voice was no longer there. *Now, if the young man could only
get past this 'honor' thing, and return to his village, that would be the
icing on the cake*, he thought. However, he knew that was going
to take much more time, and that was something, it appeared,
they both would soon have plenty of after they fell under the
Blessing of the City, the gift of longevity.

Titus continued to drive the party onward, day after day.
They only rested when the thrice complained and became
hard to handle. Lulubelle and Doofus seemed to have more
sense in these matters than did Titus. Coleman could see that
even the soldiers were wearing down; however, they never
complained to their commander, fearing a chastisement from
their strong-willed sestardi.

The party continued to hug the mountains. According to
Myron's map, the next noticeable landmark they could expect to encounter was a mountain of fire; a volcano Coleman
guessed. Although the map was not to scale, he knew it would
take a very long time to reach it, probably twice as long as it

took them to make contact with the other Batru village. Coleman continued to keep track of time on his calendar. They had started two days before *New Span Day*, as Coleman called it. They had reached the other village on the fifty-fifth day of travel.

On the seventy-second day, near dusk, they felt the ground heave and roll; it was another powerful groundshake. It didn't last as long, nor was it as violent as the previous major shaker, but it was unnerving to all just the same. Fortunately, they had left the creepers' domain shortly before their encounter with the Batru villagers, but Titus had to let the party rest the remainder of the day because the two thrice refused to budge. Coleman had learned that although the two thrice were good beasts of burden, strong, powerful, and docile, once they decided to stop, they stopped, that was it. They could be as stubborn as the day was long if it suited them. At moments like that, they would simply plant their front legs, drop their heads low, and dare anyone to move them. A shove with the side of a horn or the dagger-like frill was a painful reminder that, after all, these massive beasts could be dangerous if they chose to be. Fortunately, most of the time, they were as submissive as betzoe puppies.

Rain fell nearly every day, as expected. Clouds bumped up against the mountains and dropped their load of water on the windward side. The p´atezas was drifting lower in the sky at midday, so Coleman could tell they must have crossed the equator at some point in their journey, not that anyone would have noticed it by a temperature change. Humidity still plagued them, but they trudged onward. Several times, they had to cross roaring rivers. Titus wouldn't allow much time to search for safer crossings, so each fording was a harrowing experience for both man and beast.

The fauna and flora changed little. Coleman noticed a few unfamiliar creatures from time-to-time, but Ayascho always told him that he'd seen one like it before. Whether he was correct, mistaken, or just boasting, Coleman couldn't tell, and really didn't care. They had also seen signs of other men, although there was no contact ever made with them.

The mountain range began to bend to the east slightly, and they continued to follow on the lower slopes. On the eighty-fifth day of travel, Gheedan thought he could see smoke rising from the mountain tops in the far distance. It looked like clouds to everyone else, but as the days passed, it became apparent, he was right. According to Myron's map, the mountain of fire stood near a pass in the mountain range. Once through the pass, they would be just over half-way to their destination, Coleman guessed. Titus's men became worried when they caught their first view of the volcano; however, their gait quickened, and even the thrice seemed to be more willing to pick up the pace, at least at first. Eventually, after a couple of more days, they settled back down to their normal slow, steady, and plodding gait.

As the party neared the mountain of fire, it became clear to all that it was in a steady state of eruption. On some days, it appeared relatively calm, spewing only white smoke. At other times, it was in the throes of a violent event. Dark clouds of steam, ash, and smoke filled the sky above the volcano for thousands of feet. The wind blew the ash in a northeasterly direction, away from Coleman's group. Huge boulders were blasted into the air, and then they would fall to the mountain's side and roll down its slope until they couldn't be seen. The little troop of men could hear a rumble deep within the mountain's bowels. The ground shook, and the thrice bellowed, but onward the party nervously trudged.

One evening, the men discussed the dangers of approaching too near the mountain of fire. It was decided that they would make as wide an arc to the west as they could, away from the mountain itself, but not too far from their course home. Titus told Coleman, the mountain had been erupting like it was doing now when they first passed it last span. A couple of his scouts had been overcome by noxious fumes. They grew ill and weakened over time until they crossed-over. He didn't want that to happen again, so he was willing to stay as far away from the mountain as possible, even if it meant adding several days to their journey.

Each day Coleman watched in horror as small pyroclastic flows rolled down the sides of the volcano. He knew that if they were caught in a major event, they would all perish in an instant. There was no outrunning such a calamity, since a flow moved at more than three-hundred miles per hour, carrying rock and hot gases approaching two-thousand degrees Fahrenheit. He decided it would serve no useful purpose to share this knowledge with his fellow travelers. They had to journey near the volcano that guarded the pass through the mountain chain, there was no other way, and besides, Titus was not about to waste time looking for another pathway through the mountains.

It took them nearly five days to make it around the volcano and into Myron's pass. The westerly wind increased and pushed them along even faster. The ground leveled off, but it was covered with many previous lava flows. The area in many places reminded Coleman of walking on broken glass. Man and beast received many a cut to foot and leg before they were through it all. Noticing that Coleman and Ayascho had difficulty traversing the shard-strewn landscape in their bare feet, Titus rummaged through his supplies and found a couple of pairs of sandals. The two were very grateful, and so was he because they had been slowing the party until they donned the footwear.

As the days rolled by, Tondo would occasionally talk with Titus or one of his men about life in the Ancient City. Nearly every time he did, the subject of slavery came up, and Tondo's questions dug deeper into what he considered a vile institution. He was completely ignorant of the practice, and as the men continued their explanations, he became more loathful of it, and his compassion reached out to the suffering slaves.

CHAPTER 2

A SLAVE'S LIFE

She awoke with a start. What was it she had seen in her dream? She struggled to remember. Slowly, the image of a pair of blue eyes, the color of Munnari, came to her. She marveled for she had never seen such a thing; no one she knew ever had. She was fully awake when she heard Ardo's call. "All awake! All arise! Prepare for another day's labor for our master. All awake! All arise!" Ardo moved from shanty to shanty, expecting a response from an occupant of each.

"I'm awake, Ardo," she called as he past the hole of a window in a wall of her dwelling. She stretched, threw off her blanket, and rose to her feet carefully, not wanting to scatter the straw that was her bed. The bucket she had filled with freshwater last night rested on the small table in the corner of the only room in her home. She washed the sleep from her eyes and dried her face and arms on her nightwear, a sack-like gown that barely reached to her knees. It had holes cut into it for her head and arms. She was a tall young woman, taller than all other women on the estate and taller than most men there, as well.

She removed her sleepwear and quickly put on one of her two well-worn tunics. In the dim light of the moons streaming through the window hole, she examined her work togs, checking to see if they needed repairing before heading to the fields. They appeared to be in reasonably good condition. It hadn't been that long ago that she and all the other field slaves wore rags for clothes. It was an appalling situation for her and the others to have such dilapidated clothing that hardly covered their nakedness, but that situation suddenly changed a couple of spans ago. The word from the Big House slaves was that one of the master's guests, a baron of the kingdom, commented on how shabbily dressed the master's slaves appeared, embarrassing the estate's master and his lady. After that incident, cloth was provided to the slaves, and they were expected to sew their own clothes. The material was greeted with mixed emotions because even though suitable clothing was a welcomed relief, it meant additional work. The field slaves already worked from dawn to dusk, leaving little time or light to do more than prepare for the next day, and then get some much-needed sleep before they renewed their never-ending and monotonous routine.

She took a metal comb from a hiding place in the wall of her shanty and quickly ran it through her long, shiny, black hair. She braided her hair into a single plait that ran down the center of her back to her waist. She lifted the comb and stared at it for a moment, recalling a loving memory of days long past. Ardo's distant call snapped her back to reality, and she returned the comb to its hiding place. She put on a pair of worn leather sandals, threw the strap of her small waterskin over her shoulder, and tucked a food pouch into the sash girdling her waist. She returned to her straw bed, quickly looked over her shoulder at the door and window hole, making sure no one was watching. She dug through the straw and pulled out a knife, about two index fingers long, and tucked it into her waist sash. She smoothed the material and made certain the knife's outline wasn't visible. Slaves were not allowed to own or carry weapons, but it was her defense of last resort. If she were caught with it, she knew the punishment would be severe. When she was sure the knife was well-hidden, she dashed off to Mama Dumaz to collect her ration of food for the day.

Mama and Papa Dumaz were elderly slaves who had assumed the duties of cooks for this slave group because they were too old to work the fields anymore. No one knew how old they were, but they had been on the estate for hundreds of spans. They even told stories of life before the current master.

"Hurry, my children, Ardo is waiting," Mama Dumaz warned. A line quickly formed, and each slave traded wooden tokens for a number of large flat-cakes. When she reached the head of the line, she handed Mama Dumaz ten tokens. The old woman was shorter than average, and she looked up at the tall young woman with eyes full of wonder.

"Maaryah," Mama Dumaz began, "you grow taller every day. Will you ever stop?"

Maaryah didn't answer and only lowered her golden-amber eyes in embarrassment. She disliked her unusual height being pointed out. The old woman handed her ten large, thick, flat-cakes, and then Maaryah quickly moved on. She scurried to the tool shed and selected one of the short-handled hoes stored there. She dashed off to the field, and as she did, she ate four flat-cakes and tucked the other six into her food pouch.

Maaryah arrived at the assembly area and found several other field slaves already waiting there. A few more arrived as the eastern horizon began to glow with the coming of day. Ardo waited until the last slave arrived, and then he started making assignments because he was the herder, a title that Maaryah detested for it revealed the master's disdain for his slaves, referring to them as nothing more than lowly beasts of burden.

Ardo was responsible for a herd of slaves, a group of about twenty men, women, and children. It was his job to see that the estate foreman's assignments were completed by dusk. The foreman, Nestor, met with his herders well before dawn and made his assignments. He expected the work to be completed on time, and he did not look kindly upon any failings. A herder was supposed to resolve any and all problems no matter what they might be. The herders were just as terrified of raising Foreman Nestor's ire as were the field slaves. Nestor was a cruel man who seemed to derive pleasure in punishing those whom he deemed to have failed in their assignments. He carried a whip and used it often. Many a slave bore the mark of his malice on their back.

Ardo chose Ponti, a dimwitted young man, to be the lead-worker this day. Ponti was simple-minded, but he was a fast worker, and it would be difficult for all the other slaves to keep pace with him. If anyone fell too far behind the leader, they could expect to hear the warning crack of Ardo's pusher, a whip-like lash all herders were allowed to carry and use to push their herds along. Fortunately, Ardo used his sparingly, only occasionally striking one of his charges, and usually for a good reason.

Ponti was assigned the center row, and the remaining field slaves were relegated to rows either to his left or to his right by Ardo. Maaryah was given the row closest to the main road leading to the manor grounds. By this time, it had become light enough to begin work. Ardo gave the order, Ponti began hoeing weeds in his row, and all the other slaves in the herd began, as well. Maaryah, too, bent over her row, quickly and carefully chopping down weed after weed. She had to be very careful to take down only the unwanted sprouts. If she accidentally damaged a crop plant, punishment would follow. Ardo marched back and forth, checking each row as work progressed, encouraging his herd to work faster and to pay close attention to what they were doing.

Maaryah struggled to keep her thoughts focused on the task at hand. It was boring and mind-numbing work, but she had learned early in life not to let her mind wander. Once, when she was very young, she had accidentally chopped down a precious crop plant. She tried to cover up her mistake by sticking the shoot into the dirt and moving on. The herder discovered what she had done and punished her soundly with his pusher. He beat her and beat her, cursing her with each stroke. Her anguished cries did not deter him. Her mother finally intervened by covering her daughter with her own body, taking many strokes herself. Even though Maaryah was young and healthy, it took many days for her wounds to heal, all the time under her mother's loving treatment. So severe were the herder's strokes, they left scars on Maaryah's lower back. Nev-

ertheless, her painful stripes did not excuse her from her daily
duties. So traumatic had the experience been, from then on,
she always jumped at the sound of a whip's crack.

The reddish p´atezas climbed higher and higher into the
morning sky. Maaryah could tell, it was going to be a comfortable day in the field for the temperature was moderate, and a
gentle Zerio breeze blew from the southwest.

At midmorning, Maaryah noticed two riders moving toward her on the nearby dirt road that led to the manor
grounds. She knew immediately who the riders were: the
steward of the estate, Master Oetan, and his daughter, Mistress Ootyiah. Maaryah tried to make herself inconspicuous,
attempting to hide behind the small-growth crop plants. She
had learned over time that it was best not to catch the lustful
master's eye. She had heard stories of other young slave wom-
en becoming victims of his passion, and it was not that long
ago when he noticed her working in a field. He approached
her on his mount, stopped, and examined her from head to
foot. It had been a terrifying experience for the young woman, and she stood quaking under his wanton gaze. He commanded her to turn in a circle so he could get a good look
at her charms. She wanted to run, but she dared not, for he
would certainly have her caught and punished by his loathsome and cruel foreman, Nestor.

Her ordeal lasted but a moment; however, it felt like forever to her. The master made a couple of unflattering comments concerning her shape and especially her height, and
then he moved on, searching for other young female slaves
that were more to his liking. She spent many a restless night

after that experience worrying the master might make an unwanted visit to her hovel. To her relief, he never did, and she slowly began to relax. Even though rejected, she felt it wise to avoid being noticed by Master Oetan. He could change his mind and his interest on a whim. The two riders passed her, paying no attention to the slaves working in fields on either side of the road. She gave a sigh of relief after they passed.

Maaryah had been born into a slave home. Slaves were not allowed to bond, but the master allowed his slaves to live together if they so desired because their children became the property of the estate; however, these unions were not recognized and could be dissolved at any time and for any reason. As a young child, Maaryah never considered this fact to be a problem because she had never seen nor heard of slave couples on the estate ever being separated.

Every day, Maaryah went to the fields with her mother while her father, a laborer, went to his assignments, usually in a different area of the estate. At the end of the day, the family would reunite, eat flat-cakes at last-meal, and talk. Their lives were simple and hard, but love filled their little shanty.

One day, several spans ago, Maaryah and her mother returned to their home and waited for her father to return; he never did. It wasn't until the end of the next day that she learned her father had been sent away. Neither her mother nor the young Maaryah had been offered a chance to give a heartfelt and loving farewell. He was gone in an instant, never to be seen again.

Maaryah's mother never adjusted to the loss of her loving mate. Her health began to decline over time. She ate very little and grew weaker by the day. Eventually, she was unable to rise from her straw. Maaryah was still only a young child and didn't know what to do other than seek Mama Dumaz's help. The herder was informed of the problem, and then the foreman. Maaryah was not allowed to linger with her ailing mother, and she was sent to the fields, as usual. At the end of the day, she returned to an empty home. Her mother was gone, and Maaryah was left an orphan.

She pulled the stopper from her waterskin and took a drink. She checked the position of the p´atezas in the sky and determined it was near midday. She pulled three flat-cakes from her food pouch with her left hand and began munching on them. She did not stop hoeing, that was not allowed. Ardo's charge was for his herd to hoe the weeds the entire length of the field. It was an all-day job, so there was no time to dally or rest.

At midafternoon, Maaryah ate her three remaining flat-cakes and drank some more water. She could now see the end of her row and figured she would reach it by dusk. She uttered a sigh of relief and continued hoeing, occasionally wiping sweat from her forehead with an arm.

As the p´atezas' disk touched the horizon, Ardo's herd reached the end of their rows. It had been a good day overall; no beatings, no punishments, comfortable weather, and a reasonable work assignment. Maaryah smiled and prepared to be released by Ardo. The herder made one final check of the field, and then he allowed his herd to return to their hovels. Maaryah moved quickly to the tool shed and returned her hoe. She went to her shanty and washed her face, arms, and lower legs. She then fetched a fresh bucket of water from the well and returned to her hovel, placing the bucket on one end of her small table. She took a clay pot and scooped it into the grain sack sitting on the table next to the bucket and waited for Mama or Papa Dumaz to announce last-meal was ready; more flat-cakes.

"All right, children," Papa Dumaz finally called, "bring your grain, come get your tokens and cakes."

Maaryah hurried to the queue and patiently waited for her turn. When she reached the front of the line, she handed Papa Dumaz her clay pot. He quickly examined it, checking for mold or creepers, and announced, "Three cakes and ten tokens," just as he always did when she reached the front of the line. Maaryah nodded her approval, and he poured the grain from her clay pot into a wooden barrel nearby. He handed back her clay pot along with ten wooden tokens that she would exchange for her ten flat-cakes in the morning. She tucked the tokens into the sash around her waist and moved to where Mama Dumaz was handing out the evening cakes.

"Here you are, my dear tall one," Mama Dumaz kindly said. Maaryah responded with an embarrassed grin just as she had in the morning and moved on, returning to her shanty. In the fading light, she ate her cakes and listened to the sounds of quiet conversations coming from the other hovels. A sudden wave of loneliness struck her, but she quickly pushed it away. She didn't want to go through that suffering yet again.

When it was entirely dark, Maaryah took her hidden knife and buried it in the straw of her bed. She removed her work tunic and washed the sweat and grime from her body. She dried herself with a clean rag and put on her sleepwear. She dipped her tunic into the water bucket and gave it a quick cleaning, draping it over an end of her table to dry when she was done. She grabbed the bucket and emptied it in a ditch near her hovel. She went to the nearby well and filled it again before returning.

Maaryah went to the place where she had hidden her metal comb and retrieved it. She undid her braid and ran the comb through her long black hair several times. When she finished, she looked lovingly at the comb. It had been her mother's and was one part of a set she once had. The other part was a matching brush. These were the only items her mother had brought with her when she was taken from the City of Women, her homeland. Her mother was but a young child when an unmet debt forced her family into slavery. Maaryah's mother had hidden the hair grooming set, which was the only way she could have kept it.

When Maaryah was young, she and her mother would brush each other's hair every night. It was her favorite time of day. After her mother crossed-over, someone stole the brush while Maaryah was in the fields. The young Maaryah was heartbroken and cried for days. From then on, she always hid the comb before going to the fields.

She sighed, hid her comb, and crawled into the straw pile in the corner of her shanty—her bed. She covered herself with her lone blanket and tried to fall asleep. Although she was tired from a full day of laboring in the field, sleep escaped her. Anger welled inside her as she considered her life. All she had to look forward to was day after day of the same mundane and meaningless existence that would go on and on for hundreds of spans while under the Blessing of the City; hundreds of spans of loneliness for she refused to seek a mate that could lead to the same suffering that took her mother. Also, she refused to bring children into a life of bondage. "No, never!" she had declared; however, something deep within her soul told her this was not what her life was meant to be. Maybe it was the stories her mother had told her of the City of Women, and the regal and grand appearance of the city's queen that inspired her. Nevertheless, Maaryah knew she was a slave, and there was not a thing she could do to change that unfortunate fact.

When her mother crossed-over, she prayed to the great unnamed god for relief. Day after day and night after night, she made her petition, but her prayers were never answered. She eventually gave up and stopped praying, reaching the assumption that the gods didn't listen to slaves. She was on her own, and she would have to make her own way. Yet, something deep within herself whispered hope and redemption. She was destined to do something marvelous, something grand. With that thought, her anger subsided, and she began to drift into slumber. She hoped her favorite dream would return, the one in which she flew over the trees as freely as the birds do; however, her disturbing dream of Munnari eyes returned.

CHAPTER 3

REFUGE AND PERIL

By the ninety-fifth day of Coleman's journey, his party had passed the volcano, and they had put enough distance between themselves and its dangers to feel safe. They had left the jungle behind and were now on the leeward side of the mountains. Little rain fell on this side, leaving the ground dry and parched. Grasses grew, as well as a few hardy bushes, but not a tree could be seen.

On the one-hundred and first day, they came across a very peculiar looking carcass. It was a small creature, about the size of a large jackrabbit, Coleman speculated, but it was no rabbit. It had needle-like teeth, with two-inch incisors, razor-sharp claws on all four feet, and it was covered from head to tail with quills. Even Ayascho admitted to having never seen such an odd-looking thing. There was evidence that many creatures like this had passed through the area. Also, there were remains of other creatures, as well. All the meat had been stripped away, and only denuded skeletons were left.

Coleman's blood ran cold when he realized what they might be. "I have heard of things similar to this in my homeland," he told the men. "The creatures I am thinking of live in water, though. They are called piranhas. They swarm and eat any living creature that enters their territory. They are small and by themselves are of little threat, but in large numbers, they are very dangerous. We can tell by these bones what these creatures are capable of," he said as he pointed to a nearby skeleton. Titus told Coleman, he and his men had not encountered any living creatures like that on their way in, just a few carcasses like that one but the thought of running into such a pack, or swarm, or whatever, worried them all. Titus didn't have to say a word, as they all picked up the pace, and only the thrice complained.

A few days later, Coleman noticed the party was being followed or stalked by a huge, flightless bird. At first, he thought it was an ostrich-like creature, similar to a ghee—the fur-covered bird he had hunted in the past. However, as it drew closer, it became apparent it was much more dangerous than a ghee. It was two to three feet taller than a man and had an enormous head and a gigantic beak. Coleman had read about such creatures on his homeworld. They were deadly predators during the era following the dinosaurs' extinction. He remembered they were called terror birds. He expected the thing to attack at any minute, but it never did. It would disappear for hours on end, and then show up again, following and watching. The creature seemed to be as wary of the men as they were of it.

At about the time the terror bird was seen again, the men noticed a cloud of dust in the distance, several miles away. As the party crested a small hillock, they rested and watched. Gheedan's sharp eyes could see the cloud was caused by a herd of small creatures. As they watched, it became apparent that this mass consisted of Coleman's so-called land-piranhas. The dust cloud drew closer, and they could feel the ground vibrate. Every so often, they heard a roar as they watched a creature bounding high into the air, dropping back into the dust cloud. The terror bird ran in the opposite direction when it noticed the approaching threat. The men prepared to fend off the creatures, but everyone knew it would be a hopeless fight. They were vulnerable and exposed, with no place to hide nor find cover. They stood in place, waiting for the assault. Fortunately, the dust cloud turned to the north and slowly disappeared over a small hill. The men's hearts stopped racing, and they slowly relaxed. Lulubelle and Doofus nonchalantly chewed their cuds, enjoying the respite from the march, oblivious to the danger.

There was no longer a daily drenching of rain. However, the dry, hot air created many lightning storms that could be seen on the horizon from time-to-time. The boom and rumble of thunder was heard daily. Titus told Coleman about one such storm he and his men had been caught in during their journey to the savage's village. They felt as if they were being attacked by lightning. Spikes of dreadful and blinding electric power struck the ground all around them. Fortunately, the storm passed quickly, and they were spared any injuries. "I certainly don't want to go through that again," Titus admitted. "It was terrifying."

According to Myron's map, the next milestone the party could expect to reach was a flat-topped mountain. Sure enough, it wasn't long before the men could see a lonely mountain peeking above the horizon. As they drew closer, Coleman thought its outline looked familiar. After another day's trek, he could determine what it reminded him of. It looked like Devil's Tower, an eroded laccolith in the Black Hills of northeastern Wyoming on his homeworld. Its nearly vertical, striated slope was an awe-inspiring sight.

It was about this time that the party was beginning to run low on water. Only one small cask remained for man and beast. From a distance, it looked like the area around the flat-topped mountain had ample vegetation and the promise of streams or springs, Coleman guessed. Titus told him, the party had replenished their water casks there on the way in.

From a distance, it was hard to tell how high the monolith stood. The closer they got, the higher it seemed to rise above the plain. When they were about a day's trek away, Coleman estimated it stood at least three-thousand feet above the surrounding plain. Small rolling hills, covered by greenery, surrounded the mountain's base. Just a few green spots could be seen on the mountain itself. It appeared to be mostly solid rock, with only narrow and cramped crevices able to sustain gangly shrubs. A few birds could be seen drifting on the updrafts wafting around the cliffs.

"There must be water there. All we have to do is find it," Coleman told Titus.

"Yes," he replied, "as I said, we found water there before."

By midday, they could see what looked like a waterfall plunging down the mountain's side. The top of the mountain had become shrouded in clouds. Flashes of lightning were seen dancing across the dark, rain-swollen clouds, and the rumble of thunder echoed from the rock walls and rolled across the plain. As the party drew nearer to the mountain's base, a few green shrubs began to poke their heads above the arid soil. It wasn't long before they could clearly make out in-

dividual trees and large bushes. It reminded Coleman of an oasis in the midst of a desert and just as welcoming.

The rumble of thunder seemed to fade, but it remained a constant clamor. The men began to muse to each other how strange that was. Without warning, cresting one of the near-by hills, they could see an ominous dust cloud. It was now apparent to all, the rumble was not coming from the heavens. A mass of snarling, roaring beasts—Coleman's aptly named land-piranhas—was almost upon them.

The men drove the thrice as hard as they could. The brutes bellowed and howled their displeasure, but they moved at a trot with the carts bouncing behind them. As he was jogging along, Coleman quickly estimated the distance they needed to travel to reach the perceived safety of the woods, the speed they were moving, and the closing rate of the herd of gnawing teeth and slashing claws behind them. It was evident, they wouldn't make it, and even if they did, would it matter?

The male thrice gave an unfamiliar howl and stopped. The cart axle had broken; the wheels rolled off, and the bed was dragging on the ground. Doofus could go no further. Pontus, his handler, ran to him and began unhitching the bellowing beast from its anchor. Rao also scurried to assist. The two men struggled to free the beast, but there wasn't enough time. When the snarling mass of teeth and claws was almost upon them, the two men ran for their lives. Doofus was engulfed by a tide of growling, biting varmints of death. The dust cloud washed over them as they brought the thrice down. The poor beast bellowed in agony, twisting its head and body, attempting to throw off the gnawing and ripping pack. Its cries of agony soon ended, and only snarls could be heard.

Coleman quickly ran to Lulubelle's side. "Everyone gather around me! We will make our stand here!" he shouted over the din.

The men formed a tight circle around the thrice and awaited their doom. More and more land-piranhas piled onto the male thrice's carcass, and it was soon stripped to the bone. A few snarling little beasts began to wander toward the huddled

mass of fresh meat. They made their way slowly at first, and then the leaders charged. The soldiers braced themselves for the onslaught. Coleman raised his right index finger above his head and took a deep breath. His finger traced a line of fire ten feet above and twenty feet away from his location, encircling the party in a ring of fire above their heads. It only took him seconds to close the ring, as the other men stared in awe at what they were witnessing. When the circle was closed, Coleman raised both arms above his head, then, with a quick motion, dropped them to his sides. From the bottom of the floating ring of flame, a sheet of fire swiftly dropped to the ground, surrounding the men, thrice, and betzoe in a cylinder of fire. The heat was uncomfortably hot but tolerable. Lulubelle bellowed in fear but did not move. Toto barked his screechy bark and snarled his threatening snarl as a flaming land-piranha charged through the fiery wall. The soldiers quickly dispatched it with their metrens as a few more flaming creatures breached the wall of flame. They were also finished off quickly, and the men readied themselves for more attacks.

Snarls, growls, and yelps of pain could be heard as the men watched the shadowy images of creatures dancing around the flame's perimeter, but no more breached the flaming wall of protection. The roars, howls, and gnars began to abate, and the men slowly relaxed, all but Coleman, that is. Sweat rolled down his contorted face as he struggled to keep the flames alive. Finally, he staggered, and the flaming wall of protection sank into the ground. The men looked around in all directions. They could not see nor hear a threat. Several charred land-piranha corpses lay in a circle around them. In the distance, they could see the bloody bones of the male thrice. A rumble of thunder, real thunder, boomed above their heads, and they looked up. Spikes of lightning arced across the sky and plunged into the ground near them. Ayascho supported the weakened and staggering Coleman. The young man, with the help of a couple of soldiers, tossed him into the remaining cart, and then the party was off, heading for the perceived safety of the trees as quickly as they could move. Spikes of lightning crashed around them as they charged the remaining half-mile to the tree line. Even in their presumed safe haven, lightning crashed into tree and rock nearby. There was no respite for them here. They moved closer to the mountain wall, and the arcs of blinding death continued to assault them. The dark clouds hovered above and began to sink lower. Lightning flashed through them, striking the mountain wall instead of the plain.

Gheedan gave a shout, "Over here, I've found a cave. Hurry! Get inside!"

Everyone moved into the cave through a large opening. Even the thrice and cart made it in. The lightning continued to crash into the mountain's side, chasing away the cave's darkness, but only for an instant. The men relaxed, feeling they had reached a refuge. Just as all were feeling safe, a flash arced into the cave and blasted through Teness in its search for a ground, killing him instantly. The others stood with gaping mouths and stunned by what they had heard, seen, and felt. The smell of burning flesh, mingled with smoke from poor Teness's clothing, drifted through the darkness.

"Look!" cried Titus as he pointed to a large disk-shaped stone next to the cave opening. "Get over there and roll that thing over the cave entrance!"

All of the men, except Coleman, jumped to his command and quickly sealed the chamber. Darkness engulfed them, and only the faintest sounds of the storm outside penetrated the gloom. They could still feel the rumble of thunder as it vibrated over the cave walls and floor, but they began to feel secure in their newly found refuge. Bardas walked over to the cart and began rummaging through it until he found a gravetro oil lamp. It was only a few inches long with an open-topped spout. He located a small gravetro flask and poured oil into the lamp.

He attempted to strike a spark with flint to dried moss in an effort to make a flame. Coleman mumbled, "Here, let me help you with that." He pointed his finger at the flame hole's wick, and puff, the lamp ignited, casting a small glow. Coleman snapped his fingers and leaned back, still reeling from his previous ordeal. He was exhausted, and he had a splitting headache. He closed his eyes and tried to shake the ache from his brain.

Titus stomped over to him and in a gruff voice demanded, "What in the names of the Five Shadows did you do? How did you make that wall of fire? How did you light that lamp? Who are you? Are you a temple priest?" He took a step back when the huge betzoe glared at him, lowered its head-plate threateningly, and growled a warning.

Ayascho quickly came to Coleman's aid, "He is taahso. He has been sent by the powerful god Batru. Tondo is his messenger."

Ayascho dropped to his knees and bowed his head. The soldiers just stared, first looking at Coleman, then to the obeisant Ayascho, and finally to Titus. At this point, Coleman was too weak to care what anyone thought, said, or did. He rubbed his head, gave a weak groan, laid back on the stowed tents, and faded from consciousness.

Coleman awoke with a snort and looked around. The cave ceiling was about twenty feet above him. A small fire had been started in the center of the cavern, and its flickering light cast threatening shadows on the walls. He was still lying in the cart, his back resting on tent skins. He felt stiff and sore. His head throbbed, and he rubbed his eyes. When he sat up, Ayascho rushed to his side.

"Tondo, how are you feeling?" the young Batru asked.

"I feel like I have a hangover. My head is pounding, and I ache all over."

"Ang-hover? What's that?" the young man asked.

"Remember when the villagers eat the mystical fruit and feel sick the next day? That is how I feel."

Ayascho couldn't help himself, piercing the cave's quiet air with a loud laugh. The other men turned from staring into the flames and gawked at Coleman. Toto gave a low bark, jumped up, and leaned his forepaws on the side of the cart, looking down at his master with pure joy. He gave Coleman a big slobbery swipe with his huge tongue and began barking his excitement. The sound hit Coleman in his right ear, sending searing pain into his skull. Coleman grabbed his head and leaned back against the tent skins, groaning in pain.

"Toto, stop!" Ayascho commanded in a gruff whisper. Toto continued barking until Ayascho grabbed him around the neck and wrestled the large beast away from the cart. Coleman sat up again, still rubbing his head and eyes.

"Water! Somebody get me some water," he begged. Titus walked over to Coleman and handed him a waterskin. He drank thirstily.

"The only remaining water barrel was in the other cart. Fortunately, we've found a spring in here, so we have fresh water. How are you feeling?" Titus asked.

"Not so good, but I think I will survive. How long have I been out?"

"Let us see; we got here just before the p´atezas set. I think it's about midmorning now."

Coleman scooted off the cart floor and stood. He felt like the world was spinning, so he grabbed the cart's side to steady himself. "Oy! That took more out of me than I thought it would. I knew I had to do something to save our skins, so I used taah to protect us. Did everyone make it?"

"Yes, sort of. We all made it in here, but a bolt of lightning blasted into the cave and hit Teness. He's gone, crossed-over," the sestardi explained with little emotion. "We found a sealing stone, and we closed the cave entrance. It has to be man-made, but we haven't seen any others, just animal tracks."

"How big is this cave?" Coleman asked as he ran his fingers through his long, sand-colored hair.

"Just what you see. There are no other entrances or passageways." A rumble of thunder echoed through the cave, vibrating the stone around them. "The storm hasn't stopped since we got in here. It's too dangerous to go outside, so we're stuck in here until the storm ends," Titus told him.

Coleman felt a hunger pang. "Do we have any food?"

"Most of the food was in the other cart. There's some dried meat in this one, enough to last us a couple of wernts. We've seen some varmints in here, but I'm not sure you'd want to eat one," Titus told him.

"How did you make a fire?" Coleman asked.

"There are some dead bushes inside the cave opening. We cut them up and used their branches to build a small fire. There's not much wood left, so someone will have to risk going outside to collect more, or we'll be in the dark by the end of another day. I'm hoping the storm will pass by then, but it hasn't let up a bit."

Coleman crossed his right arm over his chest, grabbing his upper left arm. He then began stroking his beard with his left hand. He pondered for a while and then said, "Okay, there is little left for us to do but wait. In the meantime, I think I will shave."

"Zhave? What's that?" Titus wondered.

"I am going to give my face a haircut."

Titus cocked his head quizzically, and a bewildered look fell over him. The Anterrans had never seen Coleman without his beard. They assumed him to be the same as any other furry beast. They figured it was just part of the tall savage. Cutting off the hair on his face had never occurred to them. They intently watched as Coleman found a gravetro pot in the cart, filled it with water from the spring, and placed it on the hot coals of the fire. He then found his sharpening stone nestled with the rest of his gear and began to sharpen his short sword. From time-to-time, he tested the water until it became hot to the touch. He then soaked his beard in hot water and began scraping the hair from his face. Although the sword was sharp, it wasn't nearly as sharp as the obsidian tool he had used in the village. He called for Ayascho's obsidian knife, the one he had given him, and after it was handed over, he continued shaving.

"Oy, that is better, but it is not as good as a razor blade."

The other men watched in wonder as his beard was slowly scraped away. By the time he was finished, he had nicked himself a couple of times. The soldiers kept cocking their heads from side to side. A few even grimaced as they watched Coleman's ordeal; however, no one uttered a word. When he finished, he dipped both hands in the hot water, forming a cup, lifted them, dropped his face into them, and rubbed his face with both hands. He gave a growl of satisfaction and smiled a toothy smile.

"Ha, that feels much better. You cannot imagine how a beard itches when it is hot and sticky. I am glad to be done with it." The other men just looked at one another and shook their heads.

Titus finally broke the silence, "Now, you look like you should. I thought you were some kind of half-man, half-beast. Is that hair on your face gone forever?"

Coleman gave a soft chuckle, "No, it is just like the hair on your head. It will grow a little every day. If I do not shave, I will look like I did before in a detzamar."

"You can't be one of us. No one anywhere grows hair on their face and body like you," Titus grumbled.

"He is not a man like you or me," Ayascho firmly stated, "He is the Messenger sent by the Great Batru."

Titus glared at the young man for a moment, pondering what was just said. Under normal circumstances, he wouldn't even consider this savage's words. But these weren't normal circumstances, and this man, or messenger from the gods, wasn't a normal man. Titus never really believed in the gods, but he never really denied them either. His motto was, 'If the gods leave me alone, I'll leave them alone.' That had been good enough for him through all of his eighty-four spans. Now, he was confronted with the real possibility the gods exist, and he didn't know what to think. He finally concluded, he was no longer an officer, and it wasn't a sestardi's place to think too much. His duty was what guided him, and his duty was to take this Tondo to the king. That thought gave him relief. He didn't have to do anything more complicated than to just follow his orders. He smiled.

"So be it," he said. "What you are is not my problem. I will take you to the king, and then you'll be his problem." Coleman wasn't sure how to take the sestardi's comment, but he was not going to worry about it. They both wanted him to appear before the king, and that was good enough for him.

Over the next few hours, little was said. Everyone sat huddled around the meager fire. Finally, Coleman broke the silence, "Sestardi Titus, I have been thinking about what you told me concerning your age, and for that matter, your men's ages, also. If a person ages as slowly in the Ancient City as you have said, by my calculation, you would still be a boy, and yet you are a full-grown man. How is that possible?"

"I have no idea. Maybe a priest can answer your questions. All I can tell you is, when I reached forty spans, I was a full-grown man. That's when my father made arrangements for me to serve the king as an officer in the city guard."

"Was that the same for the rest of you?" Coleman asked of the other soldiers. They nodded and muttered their agreement, all except Bardas.

Bardas began to speak, as he continued to stare into the flames, "I'm not originally from the Ancient City; I'm from Terratia. It is a large city near Anterra, and it receives a lesser blessing from the gods. I was thirty spans when I reached manhood. That's before I was allowed to join the Anterran king's service."

Titus then spoke, "There is a third city near Anterra. It's called Otterina. The people in Terratia and Otterina have shorter lives, but they still live a long time; maybe six-hundred to eight-hundred spans."

"Would not everyone want to move to Anterra?" Coleman asked.

"Many wish they could, but the king doesn't allow many outlanders to stay more than to meet their business needs. The city guards keep track of visitors, and those who stay too long are escorted out of the city if they have overstayed their welcome. That is one of our duties as guards of the king," Titus instructed.

"I imagine you have your hands full with that assignment."

"The visitors know they have no more than one detz to complete their business. If we have to collect them, we will punish them," Titus explained.

"Punish them?" Coleman queried.

"Generally, no more than one or two broken bones," Titus said with a wry smile.

"That's if they haven't been collected before," Bardas added.

"And what if they had?" Coleman wondered.

"In that case, they are taken to an adjudicator, and he declares the punishment; anything from a sound scourging to death," Titus said.

"Is anyone sent to prison?" Coleman asked, using the godspeak term.

"What's that?" Titus wondered.

"It is a building where people are held against their will, usually for a very long time," Coleman explained.

"There are no such places in the Ancient City. Offenders are bound and kept under guard until punished. Those who violate the law are dealt with quickly at the order of the adjudicators. Scourging is a common punishment for lesser crimes, as is branding. For serious crimes, the punishment is execution."

"Sometimes there's banishment," Bardas added.

"Yes, yes, banishment, but only by the king's decree," Titus clarified.

"What is the method of execution?" Coleman asked.

"Citizens are beheaded; outlanders are stoned to death, and slaves are tormented," Titus instructed.

"Tormented? What is that?" Coleman asked.

"The slave is hung by his wrists from a tall pole and left there until he dies."

"That sounds like crucifixion," Coleman muttered in his native tongue.

"What did you say?" Titus asked.

"What I mean is, it sounds like a horrible way to die." All of the soldiers nodded in agreement. There were a few comments about how torment keeps the slaves in line. Coleman didn't like any of what he was hearing. If Anterra is the cultural center of the world, its punishments are savage and archaic. He wondered what he was getting himself into.

He stood and walked around the cave for a while. His headache was still with him, and his whole body was sore, as well. He'd noticed that all the other men were complaining of headaches, too. He began to wonder if there was something in the air that was causing these symptoms. He took a few moments to examine Toto and then Lulubelle, and they seemed to be quite normal, causing Coleman to chuckle to himself. The thought of a huge dog-like betzoe with a convex headplate and a triceratops-like thrice being normal was amusing to him.

What's normal about any of this? he was wondering to himself.

He could tell by the diminishing glow around the sealing stone, dusk was approaching. They had enough wood to last the night, but after that . . . well, he would just have to wait and see. The storm was still raging, and flashes of lightning could be seen around the edges of the sealing stone from time-to-time. The rumble of thunder still shook the cave often. Coleman walked over to the spring, dipped his cupped hands into the natural basin, and splashed cool water on his face. It felt good, chasing away the throbbing in his head but only for a moment. The ache slowly crawled back into his brain, and he rubbed his head.

"This is really annoying," he grumbled in godspeak.

He had been suffering from a headache since the party's confrontation with the land-piranhas, but for some reason, this ache felt different than a typical headache. He'd experienced taah induced pain before, while he was practicing, but nothing like this. It wasn't subsiding. As a matter of fact, it was growing in intensity. The realization that the others were also suffering worried him. What was causing this? What was happening? He would just as soon leave this place and get back on his way; however, death flashed on the other side of the sealing stone, so he would have to stay here and suffer with his headache.

Coleman awoke with a start. He heard Toto's low-pitched growl of warning. Coleman raised his head and peeked over the cart sideboards. The fire had gone out, and only the glowing red embers remained, producing just enough light for him to see the outlines of the soldiers lying near the fire pit. He listened but could hear nothing but his betzoe's growl and the drip of water into the spring's pool.

"What is it, boy?" he whispered. Toto went silent for a moment, then started growling again. Coleman reached for his sword and slowly slid it from the scabbard. He heard a rustling sound in the near darkness, and his hand tightened on the sword's grip.

"What's the matter with Toto?" came Ayascho's whisper from under the cart.

"He hears something. Be quiet and listen," Coleman warned in a whisper.

The two men didn't move a muscle, their ears straining to catch the slightest sound. A flash of white light pierced the edges of the sealing stone, followed almost immediately by the boom of thunder, and a shaking of the cave. A couple of soldiers rustled, quickly followed by the rhythmic breathing of sleep. Toto's growling stopped, and all they could hear was the drip, drip, drip of water, and the muffled fury of the storm outside.

"My head hurts," Ayascho complained as he shifted under the cart and went back to sleep. Coleman kept watch a little longer, his head throbbing with every beat of his heart. After a long wait, he too leaned back and fell asleep, his unsheathed sword at his side.

Coleman awoke in a stupor. His head swimming as a hammer pounded inside his skull. He could vaguely hear Toto's threatening barks in the distance. He rubbed the sleep from his eyes and sat up. The skimpy light coming through the cracks around the sealing stone indicated there was daylight outside. The fire was out, and only the faintest glow remained of its embers. Coleman thought he saw movement in the darkness. Toto had something cornered in a crevice of the cave wall. He fumbled for his sword, felt its grip, and clutched it in his right hand. He could now see several shadowy figures moving through the cave. At first, he thought they were the soldiers, but he then noticed their motionless bodies lying near the fire ring. Unexpectedly, an ashen face popped into view just inches from his nose. Both he and the face stared at each other in

stunned silence. Coleman could clearly see it was a man's face
with blood-red eyes. He gripped the sword tighter and readied a blow. Just as he started to swing, his arm was grabbed
from behind, and he was wrestled from the cart and slammed
to the cave floor. Three men pinned him to the ground and
held him there. In a flash, Toto charged one of Coleman's assailants, crashing his head-plate into the attacker and knocking him away from his master. A cry of pain and fear echoed
through the cave as a bolt of lightning illuminated the room
with a searing-white flash. Coleman kicked one of his attackers in the face, twisted his right arm free, and swung his sword
as hard as he could. He felt its flat side slam into something
as a scream of pain echoed off the walls. He rolled away and
scrambled to his feet. He focused on the dry wood near the
fire pit, and in an instant, it ignited, radiating light throughout the cavern. Now, he could see many pale-skinned men
shading their eyes from the fire's glare. They stood staring at
Coleman as he waited for another assault. Toto rushed to his
side and growled his fierce warning. The men held no weapons, so Coleman simply waved his sword in front of himself,
its blade reflecting the fire's light. The men looked confused
and nearly blinded by the flames' glow.

Several seconds passed in the deadly standoff. The pale
men parted and a shaman, flanked by two huge lizards, strut-
ted toward Coleman. He looked like a taahso dressed in feathers and furs. His tan skin stood out as he passed through the
pale-skinned men, who obviously quailed in his presence. At
first, Coleman thought the lizards were Komodo dragons, but
after a second look, he thought they resembled huge iguana

lizards from his homeworld. They hissed and stared threateningly at Toto.

"You have invaded my domain, and I will punish you for
your trespass," the man threatened. Coleman looked around
to see if any of the soldiers or Ayascho had awakened. "Don't
look to your friends for help, taahso. I have overthrown their
minds."

In near panic, Coleman asked, "Are they dead?"

"They live, but they will serve me, and so will you, or else.
Submit or die!"

Coleman stood, sword in hand, Toto growling at his side.

His mind raced as he pondered his options. He couldn't tell
what it was, but he had a feeling of peril emanating from his
center, a warning that submitting to this shaman would be di-
sastrous. He began to charge, but he couldn't move. Red filled
his vision, and his head felt like it was about to explode. Anger gripped him, and a wave of energy blasted from his chest,
knocking those in front of him to the ground and pushing
the shaman backward. As the shaman stumbled, the grip on
Coleman's mind was broken. The two lizards rushed forward,
snarling and snapping their tooth-studded jaws. Toto charged,
ramming his head-plate into the lead creature, knocking it
over. The snarling betzoe tore into the giant lizard's underside, biting into its bowels and holding on with his powerful
jaws. Coleman rushed forward, his blade slicing through the
air, cleaving the second lizard's head from its body. This gave
the shaman just enough time to recover. He faced Coleman's
oncoming charge, raising his hands as if to ward off the coming blow. Coleman was stopped in midair and slammed to the
ground. It felt like he had hit an invisible wall. He struggled
to a knee, but he could rise no further as a red fog began to fill
his vision again. He heard Toto give a sharp, painful yelp, but
he couldn't turn his head to see what had happened. He felt
the decapitated body of the other giant lizard-thing bumping
against his legs in its death spasms.

"You will lose! You will die!" the shaman screeched like a
madman.

He's crazy! Coleman realized. He mustered all his inner-power, pulled it to the center of his chest, and focused his
mind on his tormentor. First, the shaman's feathers and furs

ignited, then his hair burst into flames. The red flames spread and fully engulfed the crazed shaman.

The madman screamed in pain and shouted, "You die! You die!"

Coleman felt like his body was in a vice. He could no longer see because red filled his vision. His head reeled in pain, but he would not submit. This was a fight to the death, and he refused to lose.

Suddenly, his vision returned, and the vice relaxed its grip on him. He could see a pale man standing over the immolated corpse of his assailant. The pale man was shading his eyes with one hand, and in the other, he held a large rock. He slammed it into the shaman's skull over and over.

"You monster! Die! Die! Die!" he shouted as each hammer blow fell.

Coleman released his focus and began to relax. He looked at the men around him, scanning from one pale face to the next. There was not a hint of aggression nor malice on any of their faces. The hammer blows stopped, and the man stepped back, dropping the bloody stone to the ground. He looked at Coleman and dropped to his knees. All the other invaders dropped to their knees, as well, reaching out in Coleman's direction. He didn't know what to do next, not until he saw Toto's prone body near the carcass of the other giant lizard. He rushed to the scaly creature, checked to make sure it was dead, and then he rushed to Toto. This didn't look good. Toto was alive, but he had several wicked bites on his legs and body. The poor betzoe couldn't lift his head, although he kept trying when Coleman approached him.

"Easy, boy," Coleman said as he comforted his companion.

One of the pale men, the one who had bludgeoned the shaman with a rock, meekly approached Coleman. "Poison. Your beast is poisoned. It will die soon," the man told him.

"How?" was Coleman's pained question.

"Gangorno's monsters have a poisonous bite."

Toto's breathing was becoming shallower. He could no longer lift his head. Coleman stroked Toto's back and then hugged him. The wounded betzoe's body stiffened; his legs straightened, and he began to convulse. Within seconds, Toto's contractions stopped, and his body went limp. Coleman realized, his trusty companion was gone. He covered his eyes as they filled with tears. He allowed himself only a few moments to grieve.

What of the others? he thought.

He quickly rushed to Ayascho, who was still under the cart. Coleman shook him; he didn't respond. He shook him harder; still no response. One of the pale men dumped a pot of water on the young man, and slowly, he began to revive. Coleman gave a sigh of relief and waited for the young Batru to open his eyes.

After a minute or so, Ayascho was fully awake and aware. He rubbed his head. "I had a mystical dream. A taahso told me, I must serve him, I must be his slave. When I resisted, creatures of shadow tormented me."

"You are all right now. That evil taahso is dead, and you are free. Help me with the others."

The two companions, with the help of the pale-skinned raiders, roused Titus and his men. At first, the soldiers were startled by the unexpected presence of the odd-looking in-truders. They relaxed, somewhat, when Coleman told them what had happened. After all of the party's members had time to recover, Coleman went to the man who had finished off the shaman.

"I am Tondo. What is your name?" Coleman asked.

"I am Yos. I must thank you for freeing us from this mon-ster. He came here and used his evil powers to hold us captive. You are taahso. What will you do to us?"

"I will thank you for helping me. He was a powerful taah-so, and I do not think I could have defeated him without your help," Coleman admitted.

"I'm sorry your beast crossed-over. The taahso's t´onoes were his guards, protecting him all the time. Your beast was very powerful," Yos told him.

The lightning flashed, and the thunder rumbled. Belatedly, the pale men covered their eyes, but they were momentarily blinded even by the tiny bit of bright light that sneaked into the cave.

"We must leave this place. The blazing white light hurts us. Come with me. That must remain here," he said, pointing to Lulubelle.

"I don't think it's a good idea to leave the thrice alone," Ti-tus advised. "Rao, Bardas. You two stay here."

With sadness welling in his heart, Coleman took the time to bury his pet using a shovel from the cart, and then Yos led the others to a dark corner of the cave. A large rock had been pushed away, revealing a small opening. This was where the pale men and the shaman came from. The men squeezed through the opening on their bellies and wiggled down a narrow passageway. Coleman's party had to feel their way due to the total darkness. The pale men seemed to have no problem with the gloom. Within thirty feet, the tunnel expanded, and the men could stand upright. A soft glow of luminescent lichen provided just enough light to help Coleman and the others see as they moved forward.

It wasn't long before they entered a huge cavern. Coleman could see other tunnels leading into the central cavern from many directions. It was like the hub of a wheel, with tunnels connecting to it like the spokes of a wheel. The men stopped at the edge of the cavern and looked around. The ceiling was over fifty feet above them. There were three levels of walkways with doors and windows all around, and all the way to the ceiling. Pale skinned men and women stopped and stared at the unexpected intrusion.

Yos stepped to the center of the cavern, looked toward the ceiling, and shouted, "Freedom! My brothers and sisters, freedom! Gangorno is dead! All hail Tondo, slayer of the evil one!"

Coleman was a bit embarrassed. Yos had a lot to do with this victory. He watched wide-eyed as scores of pale-skinned men, women, and children streamed from the tunnels and mobbed his group. Shouts of joy echoed throughout the cavern. A song of freedom began to reverberate off the rock walls, and as more voices joined in, the volume rose and pained his ears. The crowd lifted their hero high above their heads and marched around with him, singing and shouting in joy. Coleman's other travel mates were also revered in the same manner. The jubilant horde celebrated for the longest time. Titus finally had enough and wiggled loose from his revelers. He landed on his feet and collected his men. When all were gathered, they stood huddled together in the midst of a sea of red-eyed worshipers, pushing away any who tried to grab and hoist them up again. Coleman and Ayascho were released at last, and they darted to Titus's group for protection from the adoring mass.

CHAPTER 4

BATRU'S THUNDER

Bardas and Rao stood near the tunnel's opening, listening to the ruckus echoing into their cave. "I hear the sounds of battle. The sestardi is in trouble," Bardas warned.

"Those red-eyed savages will kill us all!" Rao shouted. He ran to the cart, grabbed two metrens, and rushed back to the tunnel opening, tossing one to Bardas.

"We'll kill any savage who shows his ugly head," Rao threatened, holding the metren's sharp point near the breach.

The two men stood guard, waiting nervously for the expected assault. After some time had passed, they tired of watching and relaxed, but only a little, though. There hadn't been any noise in the tunnel for a long time, and the fire Coleman had started with the remaining wood was growing low, and this worried the two warriors.

"What should we do?" asked Rao.

"We need light, so we must get more wood," Bardas advised.

"Let us cut up the cart; we can use its wood," Rao suggested.

"The sestardi will murder us if we do that. Do you want to carry all that gear on your back?"

"The sestardi is dead. You heard the battle. He's dead, I tell you."

"You don't know that. Remember, he's got Tondo with him."

Rao stood pondering Bardas's words, and then he said, "Alright, we'll wait. But we still gotta get some wood. I got an idea. Help me push this rock in front of the hole."

The two men wrestled a small boulder in front of the tunnel opening, and then Rao slammed the point of his metren into the dirt at the stone's base. It sank deep into the soil, deep enough to make it difficult, if not impossible, to push the stone from inside the tunnel.

"That should do it. They won't get us now," Rao proudly said.

"Good idea, Rao. You're thinking like a sestardi."

"Don't insult me," Rao mused as they both laughed, lightening the tension.

With great effort, the two men rolled the cave's sealing stone back just enough for a man to squeeze through to the outside. The storm had subsided a bit, but the weather still looked threatening. The two men worked with a fury, gathering as much downed wood as they could find near the cave's mouth. After they gathered a sufficient amount, they chopped down several green bushes and dragged everything into the cave, as well. The cave entrance was quickly sealed again, as Lulubelle began munching on the green leaves the men had fetched.

"We will celebrate your victory, Tondo. You will join us, and we will feast," Yos said. It was not a request nor a de-

mand; it was just a matter-of-fact statement. Neither Coleman nor Titus protested. It was clear that their presence was
expected, and for all they knew, the storm was still raging outside, and they were going nowhere. All of the pale-skinned
people were in awe of the outsiders. The children gawked in
wonder at their appearance.

"Yes, we will be happy to join you," Coleman finally said,
watching Titus's reaction. The sestardi's expression didn't
change. Yos began giving orders to all those around him.

A song of praise and happiness started with those nearest them and soon spread to all the others. As the people prepared the festivities, others approached Coleman and his party members, touching them and bowing in deference, thank-
ing them for what they had done. Little tokens of apprecia-
tion began appearing at their feet: a finely crafted metal knife,
a necklace of colorful stones, a gourd of dark powder, and
earrings of shiny metal. Coleman examined each and every
gift, and he wondered where these people had found a metal knife. Titus and his men were particularly interested in the
shiny earrings.

Coleman examined them closely, too, and asked, "Titus,
what do you think these are made of?"

"It looks like zin, a metal of great value," Titus told him.

"Zin, is it? It is called silver in my homeland. It has great
value there, too." Coleman then uncorked the top of the
gourd and poured some of the dark powder into his palm. He
sniffed it. "Hmm, it does not smell like anything. What do you
think it is?" Titus poked at it with his finger and then shrugged
his shoulders. Coleman cocked his head in thought, then ex-

citedly said, "No! This cannot be what I think it is," he said to no one in particular. He looked around for a fire. There were no flames to be seen anywhere; however, he could see several fire pits with glowing embers and food cooking over them. He walked to the nearest one and tossed a small portion of the powder into the embers. A flash of flame jumped from the hot coals with a loud hiss and disappeared in a trail of white smoke. Titus jumped back, shaken by the tiny explosion. The pale men and women near him blinked as their vision returned, and then smiled. They had not been surprised at all. "This is amazing!" Coleman roared. "These people know how to make gunpowder."

"Gon-p´odder? What's gon-p´odder?" Titus asked.

Coleman's mind raced as he contemplated his next words. Titus didn't know what it was. Therefore he surmised, no one in the Ancient City knew about gunpowder, either. What did these people use it for? He wanted to know more before he explained its power to Titus.

"Yos, what is this powder, and why do you have it?"

"We call it Batru's Thunder. It breaks rock and helps us dig."

At the mention of Batru's name, Ayascho joined the conversation. "Do you worship the great god Batru?"

"Yes. Batru led us here and gave us this mountain for our home," Yos told him.

"How long ago was that?" Coleman asked.

"A very long time ago, many generations. Our taahso could tell you; he was the keeper of our story. Gangorno killed him, and then he enslaved us. Now, we have no story."

"That is very sad," Coleman commiserated. He knew just how devastating the loss of a taahso would be to a village. These people had been harmed by a wound that could never be fully healed. "I am sorry for your loss. Is there no one who can take his place?"

"The taahso's son was very young when Taahso was killed. Now, the boy is a young man, but he has no training. Can you help him?"

Titus grabbed Coleman by the arm, "We don't have time for this! Remember that before you make any promises."

"We are not going anywhere until the storm ends. Yos, how long do the storms last outside?"

"I don't know. We seldom go brightside. The p´atezas burns our skin and blinds us. In the past, before Gangorno, we went out at darktime and worshiped the good moon, Munnari."

"Do you not see the blue moon in the eyes of Tondo?" Ayascho asked.

"His eyes do look different. Everything we see is black or white or gray."

Tondo's eyes are the same color as Munnari," Ayascho informed him.

"What do you call yourselves?" Titus asked.

"We are the People of the Mountain, the Cavers. We have lived here for many, many generations. When we need more space, we make new tunnels and homes using Batru's Thunder."

"I will test your young taahso and see if he has the taah. If he does, I will teach him what I can, but he will have to do the rest himself. We cannot stay here very long. We must be on our way soon," Coleman told Yos.

"May Batru grant you his greatest blessing," Yos said, as he bowed low.

Coleman also bowed, and then asked, "Will you teach me how to make Batru's Thunder?"

"Yes, yes! I will ask the thunder-makers to show you how it's done."

"Where is the young taahso? I would like to meet him."

Yos dashed off and soon returned with a young teenage boy.

"This is Hani, son of Taahso. Test him; we must learn if he has taah."

As the Cavers continued to prepare the meal and festivities, Coleman took Hani to a private den and began testing the youth. He used the same method Taahso had used to test him. After only a few minutes, the young man had ignited a small bit of Batru's Thunder.

Coleman smiled. "Hani, you are going to make a fine taahso. You have the inner-power, and you have control already." The boy looked up at Coleman, his face beaming with a broad smile. The two continued their work until they were summoned to the meal.

Everyone enjoyed the feast. The food was tasty and marvelous: meats of various kinds, delectable roots, and mash with a bittersweet flavor. It was all washed down with a slightly sweet juice, which reminded Coleman of diluted lemonade.

"This is a wonderful meal. Thank you, Yos, and thanks to all those who prepared this feast," he told his host. Just then, Titus gave a loud belch. Coleman turned and stared at him incredulously.

"What's the matter with you?" was all that Titus had to say for himself.

Yos clapped his hands together with glee. "We wished to bless you with our best. Thank you. Thank you," Yos kept repeating as he bowed toward Titus. The sestardi looked up, gave a slight nod of his head, and continued gobbling down food.

Coleman, now realizing the Caver custom, swallowed a mouthful of air, and then let out as loud a belch as he could. It wasn't nearly as loud a noise as Titus had made, but Yos smiled in gratitude. Coleman pushed his elbow into Ayascho's side, and he got the hint. He, too, let out a fine belch of his own. Soon, all the soldiers began rumbling their own eructing racket.

"This food is very good. Where does it come from?" Coleman asked.

"Bring the live creatures here for Tondo to see," Yos ordered.

An assortment of vermin, huge creepers, and colorless snakes were dropped in front of the men. Coleman's party looked at the crawling and scrambling mass in shocked horror.

Ayascho took a deep breath and said, "Pass me some of the light meat." He took a slice, looked at it, and then gobbled it down. "What was that?" he asked. Yos picked up one of the huge beetles; its body was at least eight inches long; its six legs were flailing in the air. "That's my favorite," the young man announced. All the others in the party just gaped.

Coleman regained his composure and spoke, "Yes, this has been a fine meal. Titus, what about Rao and Bardas?"

"Ha! Pontus, Gheedan, go relieve the other two."

The two soldiers stood and headed toward the tunnel where they had entered. The Cavers handed each a lump of faintly glowing lichen. It provided just enough light for the men to see a couple of arm lengths ahead in the dark passageway. After a short confrontation, Bardas and Rao let the two into their refuge. It was a comforting reunion for the two guards because they had been more than a little worried about the others' fate, as well as their own. Soon, they joined the festivities, devouring food like the hungry men they were. Pontus and Gheedan hadn't revealed what the food was. They kept it a secret to themselves as a jape on the other two.

After the meal, the Cavers put on a celebration in honor of Tondo and his friends. There was more singing and dancing. Coleman and Ayascho willingly joined the dancing after a bit of coaxing; however, Titus sat stoically, his arms folded over his chest until Coleman physically stood him up. He then reluctantly joined the fun. Now that the sestardi was involved, the other soldiers joined the throng, as well. The festivities lasted for what seemed like a couple of hours to Coleman.

There was no way to tell how late it was, but the excitement of the past day was beginning to weigh on Coleman and the others. Yos noticed Coleman's yawn and invited him to follow as he departed the merriment. They climbed spiral stairs cut from solid rock to the second level. Yos led Coleman to a room with a door covering and a round, open-air window. When they entered, Coleman could see it was someone's living quarters. There was a living room with a cooking area, as well as another smaller room in the back. Coleman was directed to the room in the rear, where he found a large padded platform that looked like a bed chiseled from stone.

"Here, this is for you. Rest yourself until you are ready to teach Hani more," Yos told him. The bed looked too inviting for Coleman to protest. He plopped himself upon the soft skins and quickly fell asleep.

Titus noticed Coleman's departure and assigned two soldiers to follow him. Always the vigilant sestardi, he was not about to lose track of his prime responsibility—bringing Tondo to the king.

Coleman awoke and heard someone snoring in the other room. He found Yos asleep on the stone floor. It was apparent, Yos had given Coleman his bed. He also heard more snoring coming from outside. He stuck his head through the round window hole and saw two soldiers propped against the stone wall; both were sound asleep. Yos rolled over and awoke.

"Hello, my friend. How did you sleep?" Yos asked.

"That is a very comfortable bed. I slept like a baby. Thank you."

"You honor me," Yos told him. "While it is still early, I would like to show you Batru's Heart," he continued.

"Batru's Heart? What is that?"

"Come with me, and I will show you."

The two men quietly stepped past the sleeping soldiers and headed down to the main level. Yos led Coleman through a tunnel on the far side of the main cavern, and then down a set of long and winding stairs. The further they descended, the warmer it became. The luminous lichen on the passage walls, ceiling, and floor provided meager light, but it was enough for Coleman to see his way. The stairs wound down for nearly a half-mile. He carefully followed Yos down, step by step, into the increasing heat, which was becoming uncomfortable, causing perspiration to run in rivulets over their bodies. In the distance, Coleman thought he could see a light deep in the bowels of the adit. As they drew closer to the light, Yos covered his eyes and mentioned how bright it was. When they reached the foot of the stairs, they stopped at a doorway cut into the stone. Before they entered, Yos picked up what appeared to be a pair of glasses sitting on a ledge in the wall. After he put them on, he invited Coleman to take another pair, also sitting on the ledge. Coleman noticed, there were several glasses resting on the stone shelf. They were crudely made, and the lenses were not smooth, but they looked like very dark sunglasses or welder's goggles. He put on a pair and couldn't see anything but a tiny speck of light coming from the doorway. He took them off and followed Yos. When he was completely through the opening, he stopped and gaped in wonder. The huge cavern was full of crystals: some were as big as a man, some as big as tree trunks, some even larger than that. Most were clear; a few were yellow, some red, and some blue;

crystals jutted from hither and yon. The cavern was at least one-hundred feet high, fifty feet wide, and it extended for as far as the eye could see. The crystals collected light from the luminous walls, ceiling, and floor, and seemed to magnify it, making the room brighter than light from the p´atezas. He put on the glasses and immediately took them off again. *The beauty of this place should not be shaded or diminished in any way,* he thought. It was a glorious place, a place of wonder and awe.

A rhythmic pulse of light began, seemingly related to the noise the men were making. The pulses grew in brightness, magnified by the crystals, and then they began to diminish.

"Yos, this is amazing! Thank you for showing it to me."

"Our people come here when they want to be closer to Batru. When we are here, we think and pray. After Gangor-no came, he wouldn't let us visit this place. We had to worship him and only him. People risked death to come here and pray for help. By the  wisdom of the Great Batru, we suffered for a very long time, but our prayers were heard, and he sent you to free us."

The pulses began again and shortly diminished as the men stopped making noise. Coleman didn't know how to respond to Yos's statement. All he had done was defend him-self, and yet he wondered, *Had our party been driven into the cave by an unseen hand?* He thought about how he had killed the two gorgas, and the relief those slayings had brought to the two Batru villages. Was he being directed by a power be-yond his comprehension? The thought unnerved him, but all these coincidences were beginning to be too consequential to ignore.

The two men spent several minutes in Batru's Heart. Yos prayed, and Coleman pondered. Eventually, the heat became too much for Coleman, and he asked to leave. They returned to Yos's home and quietly stepped over the still slumbering soldiers. They talked about life underground for the next hour or so. The soldiers finally stirred and awoke. One peeked through the window and smiled upon seeing Coleman. He smiled back, chuckling to himself. A quizzical look crossed the soldier's face, and then he dropped from view. A short time later, Yos, Coleman, and his two guard escorts went to Hani's home to continue the young man's training.

Titus moved himself and the bulk of his soldiers back to the entry cave. He preferred being near the exit, so he could see when the weather cleared. He also felt uncomfortable, 'sealed in this hole inside the mountain,' as he put it. No mat-ter where Coleman went, two soldiers were always nearby. It didn't bother him, and he generally simply ignored them.

When it came to learning, Hani was like a sponge. Coleman drilled him for hours, and when it became obvious the boy couldn't take anymore, Coleman allowed him to rest and nap. During those times, Coleman met with the thunder-makers for his own schooling.

He learned to mix three different substances to make Batru's Thunder. One was a whitish powder the thunder-makers said they dug from the mountain. Coleman knew that gunpowder included saltpeter—potassium nitrate—and he guessed that was what the white substance was. The Makers, as they called themselves, measured many small scoops of the white substance into one end of a metal drum made of zin—silver—suspended horizontally in the air by ropes attached to each end. Coleman counted as each scoop went into the drum. The drum was about three feet long and about eighteen inches in diameter. Inside the drum were smooth, marble-like stones about an inch in diameter. The Makers then added a few smaller scoops of charcoal they had taken from a large clay pot. For the rest of the day, they turned the drum by hand, mixing and reducing the contents to a fine powder. While the Makers were doing that, Coleman returned to Hani and resumed his training.

After the last meal of the Caver's day, the Makers collected Coleman, and they returned to what he called the *laboratory*. They told him, the first mixing was done. The next step was to add several small scoops of a bright yellow, lumpy powder the Makers said they had also dug from the mountain. Coleman knew right away that it was sulfur. The Makers sealed the drum again and began hand turning it. He was told, this was the final mixing, and it would last for two rests—he understood this to mean two days.

Coleman found it amazing that this primitive culture knew how to make gunpowder. Even more exciting was the knowledge they had of metallurgy. He could see all around the area items made from metal: picks, knives, the goggle frames from the crystal cavern, the silver mixing cylinder. This amazing underworld domain was full of surprises. When he asked how they had gained this knowledge, they told him it was given to their forefathers by the Great Batru and handed down through the generations.

Before he retired, Coleman made Hani perform a few more exercises. He also gave him some homework. Hani was to begin memorizing the clan's history. He was to learn it from those who had heard it repeated by the taahso, Hani's father, before Gangorno came to torment the Cavers' lives.

Coleman then checked on Titus at the entry cave. This provided Titus the opportunity to assign two fresh guards to watch Coleman. The storm was still raging outside. Lightning flashed, and thunder rolled; however, Titus told him it had been relatively quiet all afternoon. They had rolled back the sealing stone, gathered some wood, as well as herbs, roots, and green bushes for the thrice. Things were looking up, he thought, but the weather soon turned threatening, and they immediately scampered back into their shelter and quickly replaced the sealing stone.

After this update, Coleman returned to the Cavers with two fresh soldiers in tow. He hadn't seen Ayascho all day, and he wondered what the young man was up to. As he entered the central cavern, he found him sitting near an ember pit with a young Caver woman.

"So, that's where he's been all this time," Coleman mumbled in godspeak. As he walked past the two, he coyly asked, "Now, what would Nita think of this?" He kept walking; he really wasn't expecting an answer.

As he started climbing the spiral stairs, he heard the Caver girl angrily ask, "Who's Nita?" Ayascho began stumbling over his words. The young woman quickly marched away, leaving him standing alone and bewildered. The soldiers behind Coleman laughed, and he stifled a chuckle himself.

The soldiers posted themselves outside Yos's home, while Coleman and Yos discussed the day's events. They soon turned in for a good night's rest, though it was always night in this place. Coleman longed for the p´atezas and the wide-open spaces. He hoped the storm would soon end, and they could be on their way again. This perpetual darkness had become depressing.

He lay back on Yos's bed pondering in the darkness. He really missed the moons and their wondrous dance through the heavens. The glory of the stars had been so uplifting to look upon after a hard day of hunting in the jungle or travel. Yet, he was amazed by the knowledge the Cavers possessed. These were a people with some astounding discoveries. Too bad they could never leave their mountain caverns. Their physiology had been altered over the generations, and now they were unable and unwilling to leave. Hopefully, they would be able to protect themselves from another intrusion like the wicked and evil Gangorno. The thought of a powerful taahso becoming so corrupt bothered him. The power shamans wielded was be-yond the realm of mortal man, and to turn that power to self-gain was deplorable. He remembered the wicked thoughts that had entered his mind in the past and how he had to break away from their tempting influences. Was the Tempter real? "Can this be true?" he asked aloud in his native tongue.

"Yes, Tondo, can I help you?" Yos asked.

"Oh, sorry, just thinking out loud."

From the other side of the doorway, he heard one of the soldiers say, "Godspeak." Coleman grinned, rolled onto his side, and he soon fell asleep.

The storm seemed to be weakening. Titus passed the word to Coleman that the periods of calm were increasing, and he was planning on departing as soon as he was sure they could travel in relative safety. Coleman continued to train Hani, but he had pretty much reached the limit of his own experience and skills. He made the boy repeat the clan history he had learned a couple of times. He was confident that Hani would get better at it over time. There were still quite a few gaps, but with more time, he felt they would be filled with help from the elder People of the Mountain.

The following morning, the Makers brought Coleman a lizard skin satchel full of Batru's Thunder. He estimated its weight at two pounds. He thanked them and later stowed it in Lulubelle's cart. He now possessed the knowledge and the means to bring this fantastic power to other civilizations. The question he pondered now was, what he should do with this knowledge, if anything? Did he really want to be the one who opens Pandora's Box and loose upon this world the rampant destruction this powder could unleash?

Of course not, he thought, *but how long could such power remain hidden from men seeking to conquer and subjugate others?* For the time being, it would be kept strictly under his control, and he would guard its secret from others.

Early the next day, Titus entered the main cavern for the first time since he had left it three days before. He told Coleman, the sky had cleared, and it was time to leave. Coleman quickly called for Yos and Hani to meet with him. As the word spread that Tondo was about to leave, all of the Caver clan turned out to say farewell. Coleman would not leave until he had given a blessing of good fortune to all who requested one. Titus chafed at the delay, but he knew there was nothing he could do about it.

Finally, Coleman stood before Hani and placed his right palm on the boy's bare chest. "Hani, I give you Batru's blessing. You are now taahso." Coleman expected this to simply be a symbolic display, witnessed by all the clan, a means of empowering the boy in his new calling; however, he felt an energy surge from himself, through his glowing hand, and into the boy's chest, not unlike the power he felt when Taahso had blessed his hunt the first time so long ago or the same type of phenomenon he'd had with Ayascho. The boy's eyes opened wide in shock at the surprising event. Yos and the others nearby felt the energy flow and stepped back in wonder. Coleman smiled, although he too was surprised. "You are now taahso. Your duty is to your people. May you serve them with dignity, honor, and humility," Coleman proclaimed.

No one said another word. Silently, Coleman, Ayascho, Titus, and the soldier escorts departed. The Cavers followed them down the tunnel as far as they could. The party squeezed through the final section of the passageway, and into the entry cave. The sealing stone had been rolled away, and for the first time in several days, Coleman could see the blue sky and the greens of bushes and trees.

How glorious it is! he thought.

He sadly glanced at Toto's grave and then walked through the passageway's breach to the outside world without pausing. The bright light hurt his eyes, and he shaded them with his hand. The others quickly followed, with Pontus leading Lulubelle pulling the cart. She bellowed either her glee or angst; no one could tell for sure, but onward they trudged.

"Sestardi, look at this!" Bardas called after a couple of minutes into the trek. Titus and Coleman rushed to his side. He was holding his metren, examining its metal tip. Coleman could see a small rock clinging to its point. "Look at this," Bardas said as he removed the rock and then stuck it to another part of the metal shaft. Coleman tried it himself a couple of times. Each time, the rock stuck to the metal. Titus tried to place the rock against the wooden portion of the metren, and it dropped to the ground. He picked it up and placed it against the metal shaft, and it stuck again.

"What's this?" Titus asked, and everyone turned to Coleman, expecting an explanation.

"Where did you find this?" Coleman asked.

"I noticed what looked like a lightning strike right there, so I poked the rocks with my metren. That's when this rock stuck to it," Bardas explained.

Coleman examined the charred stone and the smaller rocks that lay on the ground at its base. He reached over his right shoulder and drew forth his short sword, dipping it into the pile of rocks on the ground. When he pulled it back, many small rocks and stone chips were clinging to its blade.

"Interesting," he mused in godspeak as he turned the blade from front to back.

"Tondo, what does it mean? I have never seen rock do that. What evil magic is this?" Bardas questioned in a worried tone.

"This, my friends, is lodestone. I guess the lightning strike magnetized the rock," he explained using godspeak terms.

"Godstone? Mag-an-tized? What are you talking about?" Titus demanded.

"Lode-stone. Mag-ne-ized. Now, you say it."

"Hoy!" Titus quipped with a wave of his arm.

"I might be able to make something important with these stones," Coleman said as he held a lodestone in front of Titus's face.

"Godstone; mag-an-tized; I don't care what you call it, we're not stopping for nothing. Move out!" Titus ordered. The party started moving again, leaving Coleman and Ayascho in their dust.

"Ayascho, help me collect as many of these stones as we can; hurry!" For the next several minutes, they both scrambled, scooping up handfuls of small rocks. They ran to the cart and dumped their loads, then rushed back for more.

After a couple of trips, Ayascho asked, "Tondo, how many of these rocks do you need? I think the beast will start complaining if we don't stop."

"Okay, okay, but this is exciting. When we stop tonight, I am going to make something that will amaze all of you."

"What is it?" Ayascho wondered.

"It will be like magic," Coleman told him with a coy smile. Ayascho had never seen Coleman so excited. The idea of more magic coming from the messenger of the gods excited the young man, too.

It was midmorning when the party left the cave. Individual, puffy, white clouds clung to the mountain's side. As they trudged onto the dusty plain, Coleman looked over his shoulder and could see a brilliant white thunderhead beginning to peak above the mountain's flat summit. He knew the cloud could bring more lightning and thunder by midafternoon. He hoped they would be far enough away by then to be clear of any danger. The more imminent threat was land-piranhas, and possibly terror birds. He instructed the soldiers to watch for danger, although he already knew that's what they were doing anyway.

The party made a quick stop to examine the remains of the male thrice and its cart. The land-piranhas had devoured everything but a few metal items, some wooden planks, and the thrice's bones. The soldiers gathered what they could: an ax head, a shovel, and some weapons. Then the group continued on their way.

Coleman took a deep breath. He felt good. The wide-open spaces were much more to his liking than the dankness and gloom he had just left. He thought about the People of the Mountain. They were very happy with their subterranean life. The fact that they used gunpowder and made metal tools also intrigued him.

Where did such knowledge come from? Where did they come from? They didn't look like Batru. As a matter of fact, they had an appearance that was more in common with Titus and his soldiers. Could they be a clan that separated from the Ancient City people millennia ago? And yet they understood the concept of taah, and they had a taahso. Those two things were solid factors of the Batru life. Possibly, they are a mixed culture, he silently concluded.

He continued deeply in thought, when suddenly, Ayascho, at his side, stopped in mid-stride. Coleman also halted and scanned the horizon in the direction of Ayascho's worried stare. He could faintly see a dust cloud rising in the distance. It wasn't long before everyone was watching the dust cloud's route. It seemed to ebb and flow; it approached and retreated. Coleman thought they were being teased by it. Fear clutched at the men's hearts, and they picked up their pace; however, by late afternoon, the dust cloud had disappeared below the horizon. That gave little relief to the men. The horror of their encounter with the gnawing and biting vermin remained in their thoughts. How much longer would it be before they could feel safe again? No one knew, and that was the hardest thing to bear.

It was almost dark before Titus allowed the party to stop. No one complained about the long march. Everyone wanted to get as far away from the mountain and its menacing thunderhead as they could. They ate a meal of dried meat and hard biscuits, washing them down with water, nothing else. There was no wood for a fire, and they wouldn't have dared light one even if they could. No one wanted to draw attention to their exposed and vulnerable camp. Coleman and Ayascho saw no signs of game, so they didn't even try hunting. This was a barren place, a wasteland. The further they went, the more desolate it became.

After dark, Coleman began his project under the light of the full Munnoga moon. He found a wooden bowl in the soldier's gear and filled it with water. He then carved a piece of wood until it was flat, with a point on one end. As Titus and the others watched, he placed a small godstone rock on the wooden plank and placed them carefully in the wooden bowl. The wooden plank floated and slowly began to turn in the water. The pointed end of the plank stopped in the direction the p´atezas had set. Coleman smiled, turned the stone a quarter rotation, and waited. The plank slowly turned again, this time stopping with its point aimed midway between where the p´atezas set and where it was expected to rise in the morning.

"There we go! That is it," he exclaimed.

"That's what?" Titus wondered as the men crowded around.

"That is north," pointing in the direction the wooden plank was aimed. "South is there, east is there, and west is there," he continued, pointing toward each direction as he called it.

"So what?" Titus wondered.

"Now, we can tell which direction we are going, even on a cloudy day, or at night. That is pretty cool," Coleman exclaimed like an excited schoolboy.

"Goohr? You and your godspeak. I wish you would make sense. This godstone thing is good for nothing. I see no use for it, and it's a waste of our precious supply of water. We already know where the p´atezas rises and sets. The moons tell us the same thing at night. Why do we need this?" he asked incredulously.

Coleman shook his head in disbelief. "Here, let me explain it. I can put three-hundred and sixty marks on this wood, all around the rock. With a good map and this compass, I could tell you the exact direction we need to go to get to the Ancient City or any other place."

"I already know how to get to the city. I don't need no gumpass to show me nothing," Titus huffed.

Coleman looked at Ayascho. The young man seemed disappointed. He was expecting some real magic, but all he could see was a rock sitting on a piece of wood, floating on water.

Coleman shook his head. His comrades didn't understand. How could he explain it to them? "Are there sutro waters near the Ancient City?" he finally asked. "This compass will help the men who travel the sutro´ waters find their destination," Coleman continued. Much to his surprise, Titus and all of his men began laughing as if he had said something extremely humorous. "What is it? What is so funny?"

"Sutro waters? Do you mean the ocean? No one dares go there. The *terrors* kill anyone who does," Rao instructed.

Ayascho's face lit up. "Tondo told us about these creatures."

"What are these terrors, and what makes them so dangerous?" Coleman wondered.

"I've seen them," said Pontus, "They have a big fin on their back, taller than a man. They are as long as ten men are tall, maybe more, and they can swallow ten men at once. That's why no one goes on the ocean."

Coleman couldn't believe what he was hearing. "Pontus, you are pulling my leg."

"What? You want me to pull your leg. Why?"

"Never mind. Have any of the rest of you seen one of these terrors?" Coleman asked. They all nodded, all but Ayascho.

"Yes, Tondo, all have seen them. You, too, will see them when you reach the ocean's shore. I used to watch them feed while standing on the cliffs overlooking the sea. I watched as they attacked other water beasts, and sometimes, they jumped out of the water. It's amazing to see such a huge creature do that." He turned to his troops and asked, "Am I a brave warrior?" To the man, they said yes, some touting dangerous feats they had witnessed him perform. "I would never set one foot in the ocean. I would die before day's end, I'm sure," he concluded.

"I must see this thing," Coleman told them. "So, there are no boats on the ocean?"

"No boats. The fools who have tried were killed by the beasts. They ram the boat, sink it, and then . . . " Titus said before being cut off by an excited Pontus.

"I saw a boat swallowed by one. The entire boat and the six men in it, all gone. Excuse me, sestardi."

"What you are telling me is astonishing. I cannot wait to see this thing for myself."

CHAPTER 5

A WARNING VOICE

Sutro Adept Eezayhod arose early this morning, much earlier than usual. He lay in his bed, staring at the ceiling. Light from the full Munnoga moon shining through the open window cast shadows on the floor and walls. His thoughts turned to his dream, and he pondered in silence for a while. He quickly realized it hadn't been a dream, after all, it was a vision and a call to duty. He glanced over to Attendant T'orbin's bed and saw his loyal assistant still sleeping. The elderly master smiled.

For over six-hundred spans, Eezayhod had served the Temple of the Great Unnamed God. Most of that time, he had served under the Blessing of the City, granting him longevity; however, for the past five spans, he had served in an area far from the Blessing's influence. Usually, younger temple priests were given such assignments, but the Sutro Seer, the senior temple authority, had assigned him to serve, once again, in the area he had served in hundreds of spans earlier. At that time, he was but a lowly tutor, now, he was a sutro adept, a master. Eezayhod, always the obedient servant of his god, did not object. The Sutro Seer acted by the will of the unnamed god, and if Eezayhod were called to serve yet again in this remote place, located far from the temple, he would do so without protest. During his first assignment to the area when he was a young tutor, he served alone. This time, however, the Sutro Seer assigned an attendant priest to assist him. Attendant T´orbin was a young man of only fifty-six. Over the past five spans, Master Eezayhod had taught his helper and pupil, the two becoming good friends in the process.

Eezayhod had often wondered why he, a master priest, had been assigned to a task that was usually given to younger, lower-ranking priests. Now, after his vision, he understood. Representatives from the temple encouraged all who would listen to always nourish the good seeds within themselves. The priests also monitored the progress of the various and scattered cities throughout the known world.

There was a time when all mankind, the survivors of the great calamity of the previous age, assembled near the temple. When peace once again embraced them, Sutrum Seer Myndron sent clans out to repopulate the world. Each clan finding a suitable homeland and starting anew. Slowly, over time, the clan villages became towns, which grew into cities, and cities swelled into kingdoms. There was plenty of land, and the clans were so scattered that conflict became a forgotten concept. Peace once again covered the world. It was one of the priests' duties to monitor these far-flung population centers and report their findings to the Sutro Seer.

Master Eezayhod performed his early morning oblations, offering prayers and meal to the unnamed god. He then sat at the small table he and T´orbin shared and composed a couple of documents, rolling them into scrolls and placing them into a leather tube. He then began preparing first-meal.

Attendant T´orbin awoke with a start. He looked around and blinked in surprise. "Master, you are up early. I'm sorry, let me do that for you."

"Attendant T´orbin," the master began, "you have been my diligent helper these past five spans, and it is now my privilege to serve you." A huge smile covered T´orbin's face as he ran his fingers through his hair. An unasked question filled the attendant's countenance, so the master continued, "Yes, my loyal attendant, I'm recommending the Sutro Seer advance you to tutor. You are ready to assume new and greater responsibilities." It was customary for a master to provide service to his attendant on the last day of the attendant's assignment.

"Master, will you be returning to the temple then?"

"No, my friend, I will not, but you will."

"I don't understand, master. Have you received word from the Sutro Seer?"

"I had a vision last night. I am to deliver a warning to someone."

"I will go with you," T´orbin said.

"No, my son, that will not be necessary."

"Then, I will wait for you here."

"I may not be returning." A look of worry covered T´orbin's face. Eezayhod saw his pupil's concern and said, "The days of my mortal probation may be coming to an end."

Attendant T´orbin couldn't or wouldn't believe what his beloved master had just told him. He sat on his bed, struggling with his emotions. "Master, are you ill? Have you been hiding this from me?"

"I'm very well, attendant. The great god has honored me

with a most important duty. A powerful stranger has entered this land. The cruelty of some people started him down a deadly and sad path. The Tempter has enticed him to nourish evil seeds. I am sent to counsel and encourage him to change his ways before he is fully corrupted. I will attempt to break the Tempter's grip on him and turn him away from the evil path he is on before it is too late."

"But Master, what if this stranger refuses to listen. The Tempter's wiles can be quite seductive," T'orbin warned.

"Yes, I understand that very well. I will not give up. The man's very soul is at stake, and so is the welfare of many others. I will stop trying when I no longer take breath. If he rejects my warning, he will have only himself to blame for his fate," Eezayhod explained.

"Master, you speak as though you know this man will refuse your counsel."

"He is free to choose his own path." T'orbin covered his face with his hands and began sobbing in worry for his beloved mentor. "Weep not for me, attendant. Weep for the untold numbers who could suffer at this stranger's hands if my message is rejected."

Master Eezayhod had just completed preparing the pack animal for his attendant's long journey back to the temple. T'orbin's tears were still flowing, and his head was held low. Eezayhod handed him a leather tube. "Don't lose these documents; I know how forgetful you can be. See that my report is given to the Sutro Seer. The other document is my rec-ommendation for your advancement. It will be a long jour-ney, so don't neglect your studies. You must still pass the Mas-ters' Council. Now, Attendant T'orbin, give me a parting em-brace." The master held his arms wide, preparing to enfold his pupil.

T'orbin wiped the tears from his cheeks and hugged his be-loved mentor. "Thank you, master; I'll never forget you and all you've done for me."

"Don't despair; we will meet again either at the temple or on the other-side. I give you my blessing for a safe return to the city. Now, say farewell and don't look back," Master Eezayhod told the young priest.

"Farewell, master," T'orbin said, his head still held low. He took the pack animal's lead and moved up the trail, heading north.

Eezayhod watched until T'orbin was out of sight. He then put his knapsack on his back, grabbed his sturdy walking stick, and at a quick pace, moved down the trail in the opposite di-rection. He knew it would take several days to reach Purrant Grazius's hamlet.

For the past half-span, Tangundo, Nevesant, and the fol-lowers of Munnevo had ruled over the hapless residents of Grazius's hamlet. Anyone who resisted or showed the slight-

est disrespect was threatened with being fed to the gods of
the mist, and a few examples had been. The inhabitants lived
in abject fear of the outsider's power over them. His close
followers, all outlaws and wicked men, lorded over the people, taking what they pleased and brutalizing anyone who objected. No one had been allowed to leave the village, and a
headcount was taken every morning and evening. Some men
contemplated sneaking away and informing the king's men of
their suffering, but they feared for their loved ones' welfare
when it was discovered they had fled the hamlet.

The small town was isolated and seldom had visitors, so
when the man wearing the cobalt-blue robes of a temple
priest entered the little village, he was immediately noticed.
The residents had seen him before. He'd made regular visits
for the past five spans, offering counsel and bonding rites to
those desiring them. In the past, Master Eezayhod was always
accompanied by his young helper, Attendant T'orbin, but not
today.

One of Tangundo's lackeys intercepted the man dressed in
blue robes, "I remember you, priest. You picked a bad time to
come here," the ruffian growled.

"I have arrived at exactly the right time. Sassin, I can tell
by your dark countenance, you have not taken my last counsel
to heart. The path you're on will lead to death and much sor-
row," Eezayhod warned.

"I have no need to follow you or your nameless god, priest.
I'm following a god I can see and hear. I'm better off now
than I've ever been, and it's only the beginning," Sassin told
him.

"You're following a false god. Now, heed my words, it will end badly for you if you don't change your ways," Master Eezayhod warned.

"I think you should tell that to the master. I'm sure he'll be interested in hearing your warning," Sassin said with a wry smile.

"Take me to him. That's why I've come," Eezayhod declared. The priest was taken to Grazius's home, which was now serving as Tangundo's center of operations. Sassin pounded on the door, and Nevesant let him in. Two other followers of Munnevo were also in the room, acting as Tangundo's bodyguards.

"What is it, Sassin?" Tangundo asked from his chair.

"Master, there's a priest outside. He wants to talk to you. He says I'm following a false god. I know he's wrong, but I think he ought to say it to your face," Sassin said.

Tangundo's brow furrowed, and his expression turned angry. "Tell me, Sassin, what kind of priest is he? What god or gods does he follow?"

"The god of the blue moon, master," Sassin told him.

"Bring him in. I will test his faith and turn him to our side," Tangundo said with a wry smile. Master Eezayhod was brought into Tangundo's presence, and the two silently examined each other. After a long pause, Tangundo began speaking, "I've been told you follow the god of the blue moon." Eezayhod nodded but remained silent. "I am the god of this town, and you will kneel before me," Tangundo demanded.

"You are a false god, seduced by the wiles of the Usurper's vile creations. I am a warning voice from the great god," Master Eezayhod told him.

"You dare bring *me* a warning, priest? *I* will give *you* a warning. Kneel and worship me or die!" Tangundo angrily threatened. Wicked smiles covered the faces of his handful of followers in the room.

"You have been beguiled by the Tempter's deceptions. If you do not change your ways, you will become as corrupt as its masters. Harken unto my words and save yourself," Eezayhod warned.

"Your words ring hollow in my ears, priest. Men, bind the fool!" Tangundo ordered. The three men charged Eezayhod as Tangundo and Nevesant watched. The priest did not move and was quickly surrounded by a golden aura. His three attackers recoiled in pain when they felt the aura's sting.

"I am not yet finished with my message. Now, listen and listen closely, young one," Master Eezayhod said.

Before the priest could continue, the air around Tangundo suddenly turned purple, snapping and crackling with static electricity. He jumped to his feet and rushed toward the priest. Eezayhod raised his hands in front of himself with fingers spread. Tangundo slammed into an invisible wall and was knocked off his feet by the impact. He lay on the floor with the temple representative looking down at him with saddened eyes.

"My son," Master Eezayhod began in a calm voice, "you have embraced ruinous council. The great god has granted you the freedom to choose for yourself good seeds or evil seeds, placed within your soul for a wise purpose. I implore you to always nurture the good seeds, which is the only means to gain happiness and true joy. There is still time for you to change your wicked ways and make amends for the vile things you've already done," Eezayhod counseled.

Tangundo scrambled to his feet, and his purple aura grew heavier and darker. He stepped closer to Eezayhod, and their glowing rays touched, sending a shower of sparks in all directions. "I need no advice from you, old man. You are going to submit to my will. Worship me or die!" Tangundo shouted, his Munnevo-red eyes wild and bulging in anger. The sparks had set the wooden floor ablaze, and the fire began to spread.

"Master, the house is on fire!" Nevesant cried.

"Followers of Munnevo, attack him with your poles," Tangundo ordered.

His two guards picked up their quarterstaffs and began slamming them onto the priest's golden aura. Sassin looked around the burning room, snatched up a small log he found near the fireplace, and started using it as a club, repeatedly crashing it onto the priest's golden aura. The repeated blows of pole and club on his glowing shield drove Master Eezayhod to his knees. Smoke was filling the room, and it became hard to breathe or see. Nevesant, hoping to let the smoke escape before everyone suffocated, rushed to the door, and threw it open. When the door opened, the influx of fresh air stoked the flames, and they erupted with renewed vigor. Nevesant and the three men dashed out of the house to escape the growing inferno and insufferable heat.

Tangundo glared at the kneeling man. "It is the end for you, priest. Worship me or be burned alive."

"I am prepared to cross-over and receive my reward. Are you?" the priest asked as he regained his feet.

"I'll take my reward in this life. I see no need to wait," Tangundo scoffed.

"Your reward will be disappointment, disillusionment, and distress. No one will mourn your crossing," the master prophesied. Tangundo chafed at the priest's words. He could feel the conflagration through his shielding aura, and he chose to retreat from the house. All of his followers and many of the hamlet's subjugated men had surrounded the flame-covered dwelling, watching it burn as Grazius's bondmate howled in despair.

"If the priest tries to get out, force him back inside," Tangundo ordered. "Anyone who defies *my* will can expect the same fate or worse." The flames grew, and the house quickly became fully engulfed. The men watched as a glittering cloud of golden dust rose from the flames and dissipated into the air as it climbed higher and higher.

Attendant T´orbin was walking along the dirt road, leading his pack animal, and voicing aloud verses from the temple's Tome of Life. Master Eezayhod had advised him to prepare for his upcoming Masters' Council. He heard the sound of many approaching hooves. As he watched, thirty or so mounted warriors crested a rise in the road. T´orbin stopped and waited as the column approached. The formation's leader raised his arm, and the column halted. The leader walked his mount up to the priest as a cloud of dust washed over them.

"Attendant T´orbin, where are you off to now, and where is Master Eezayhod?" the commander asked.

"Defetane Hunder, the master has told me to return to the Ancient City. Master Eezayhod has gone to Purrant Grazius's hamlet. I fear for his safety," the young priest explained.

"Why?" the defetane wondered.

"He says a powerful and dangerous stranger is there, and my master has gone to convince him to change his wicked ways," T'orbin explained.

"Is that so? I think I will see what's going on there. I hope your journey to the Ancient City is quick and safe, attendant. All right, men, follow me!" Hunder ordered.

CHAPTER 6

GIFTS AND FAVORS

It was the first day of the detzamar on the Oetan estate, a day that was greeted with relief and fear by the slaves. It was the day they were allowed to collect their ration of meal grain, which was expected to last them for the next forty days. Too often, the master or his underlings skimped on the quality of the grain given to the slaves. Creepers might infest the sacks and sometimes even mold. The slaves had no recourse and no one to voice a complaint to. If they were unfortunate enough to garner an infested or moldy ration, they had to deal with it the best they could.

If that wasn't bad enough, this was also a time the slaves had to personally face the foreman of the estate, Nestor, who oversaw the distribution and determined each slave's measure for the detz. King's Slave Law required that each slave receive sufficient food to meet their needs, but the quality of the food was never addressed. Rather than risk running afoul of the law, masters and foremen made certain their slaves received a sufficient amount. Quality was in the eye of the beholder and left much to the discretion of those in control.

On this day, the slaves were allowed to end their labors well before dark. They returned to their hovels, fetched their empty grain sacks, and queued up in front of the granary. Foreman Nestor was always in a sour mood on these days. He deemed the shortened workday a personal affront, and he despised 'this wasted time,' as he put it.

Maaryah patiently waited in the queue as she crept closer to the granary doorway, wondering with trepidation how the feared estate foreman would greet her. Nestor was a short man, short and stocky, his arms and legs muscular and powerful. He seemed to detest anyone taller than himself, and he especially despised taller slaves. The fact that Maaryah was tall, without a doubt the tallest woman on the estate, worried her, so she hunched over, trying to diminish her height. She feared the foreman's ire would burst its bounds, and he would strike out at her with his loathsome whip, the one he always carried with him, coiled, and hanging menacingly at his right hip.

Slowly, ever so slowly, it seemed, the line crept forward. She was now close enough to peer into the granary's shadows, and she watched as empty sacks were exchanged for full ones. Finally, Maaryah stepped into the gloom of the building. She approached Foreman Nestor and presented her empty sack without saying a word. He looked up into her face, and she noticed an unexpected expression in his eyes and on his countenance. She had grown accustomed to his angry and hateful stare, but this look frightened her even more—a look of lust. It made her skin crawl.

A wicked smile crossed his lips, and he said, "Ha, Maaryah, I've reserved the master's best for ya." He pointed to a stack of grain sacks to his left. "Ya can take one of thems. Ya'll also notice they're bigger than these ones," he said as his eyes turned to the pile of grain sacks the other slaves were drawing from.

A shudder ran down her spine. The powerful estate foreman was plying her with an unwanted favor: an abundance
of untainted grain. If she accepted his offer, she would be
expected to return his gift with an offering of her own—her
body. The thought sickened her, and she turned, grabbing
a sack from the stack all the other slaves had been drawing
from. Without uttering a word, she quickly stepped forward,
attempting to leave the granary before the foreman could react. She was stopped when Nestor grabbed her upper left
arm in his powerful grip and yanked her close to himself. His
fingers dug into her flesh, and it hurt, but she didn't utter a
sound. He pulled her down until their eyes were level with one
another.

"How dare ya reject my gift. I will let ya think on it for a
detz, but if ya do it again, there'll be cons'quences." He raised
his coiled whip in front of her face, and then he shoved her
away. Maaryah dashed out of the granary, not slowing until
she got to her hovel. She hid in its shadows, breathing heavily
as tears welled in her eyes. After she regained her composure,
she opened her sack of grain and poured a portion onto her
small table. She began looking through it for creepers.

Usually, the days crawled by for Maaryah, but not this detzamar; they seemed to rush by faster and faster. She watched
as her grain supply decreased wernt-by-wernt, and her fear
increased day-by-day. She had never felt so trapped; she had

nowhere to turn; there was no escape for a slave. She even considered running away, but just as quickly, she rejected the thought. Should she be caught, and assuredly she would be, an adjudicator could sentence her to be hung from a pole, tormented until death took her, a slave's most dreaded end. Her only possible escape was the sea cliffs and the cruel, sharp rocks far below. She cried herself to sleep every night.

The first day of the detz had arrived, and Maaryah found herself waiting in the granary queue once again. Maybe Foreman Nestor had forgotten about their last meeting, she hoped. Maybe his interest had moved to another unfortunate victim. Maybe she would have to defend her virtue. She absentmindedly patted the knife hidden in the sash around her waist.

Before she knew it, she was at the granary doorway. She stepped inside and looked into the foreman's hateful eyes. She quickly lowered her gaze in submission.

"Oy, tall one, have ya reconsidered my offer? It still stands, and so does my promise. What's it to be?" he growled.

She handed him her empty sack, paused for a moment, and looked at the stack of untainted grain. She quickly grabbed a sack from the tainted stack and attempted to dash away. Nestor grabbed her by the arm again and yanked her down. His glaring dark-brown eyes were hovering menacingly in front of her fear-filled golden-amber eyes.

"I warned ya there'd be cons'quences. His right hand clutched his coiled whip and held it in front of her face. She uttered a cry of fear. He swung the coiled whip back then bashed its hard leather handle onto Maaryah's head, stunning her. He pushed her away, and she fell to the granary floor. He stood over her and dropped the whip's length over her body. She whimpered in fear as he drew it up into a coil again. "I'm not finished with ya yet. Reject my gifts, will ya? Ya'll be sorry for it. By the time I'm finished with ya, ya'll be more than happy to accept my offering. Now, get out!"

Maaryah stumbled out of the granary, clutching her sack of grain in her right hand and holding her head with her left. She examined her hand and saw blood. Stumbling into her hovel, Maaryah dropped the sack of grain onto her table and then fell upon her straw bed, sobbing. Foreman Nestor was a cruel man, and she knew he pleasured in giving others pain. She had seen and heard of other unfortunate slaves who had drawn his angst. He'd made their lives a living sleep-terror. Now, it appeared, she would face her own. She thought of the sea cliffs and wondered if it was time to end her miserable existence.

As she was falling into the depths of despair, a feeling of calm embraced her. The thought that this suffering was not all her life was meant to be returned. Something greater, something marvelous, was in her future. The image of a pair of blue eyes she'd seen in her dreams came to her.

How is that possible? she wondered, for she had never met anyone with blue eyes. *That was . . . unnatural,* and the vision startled her, increasing her dread.

Maaryah slowly calmed herself, rolled onto her back, and wiped the tears from her cheeks. She lay there for a while, regaining her composure. It wasn't long before she arose, opened her sack of grain, and poured a portion of it onto her small table. She began picking through it, looking for creepers.

CHAPTER 7

BATRU'S EYE

Titus roused the party long before daylight, and they were on the move just as the first glint of dawn began to lighten the eastern sky. As the firmament began to brighten, the men witnessed an unexpected phenomenon; bands of color stretched horizontally across the eastern sky. To Coleman, it looked like a rainbow that had been laid on its side and stretched. The parallel opaque bands of color were more brilliant and vibrant than any rainbow he had ever seen. The col-

ors reached high above the horizon and lingered there until just before the p´atezas' disk broke the skyline. As the star's bright light increased, the colored bands diminished and faded, finally disappearing altogether. It was the most glorious sunrise or p´atezas rise Coleman had ever seen.

The men continued their relentless march to the Ancient City. Many times, dust clouds could be seen in the distance, but they never drew near. Dust devils kicked up from time-to-time, adding to the surreal landscape. The flat-topped mountain had disappeared from view days before, and their next landmark, according to Myron's map, was a huge hole in the ground. Because the map was not to scale, Coleman had no idea how big this hole was, nor could he guess what it might be or what created it. He wondered if it might be like the Grand Canyon from his homeworld.

They had already traveled nearly three-quarters of the distance they needed to go. One-hundred and thirty-three days had passed since they began their journey. They no longer saw dust clouds in the distance. For the last two days, they had been followed by a terror bird. Coleman didn't think it was the same one they'd seen earlier, but it was hard to tell for sure. The creature never got closer than several hundred yards, so it was difficult to see any of the huge bird's markings. This one appeared to be just as curious about his group as the first one had been. It just followed along behind them, matching their pace. It would disappear for hours, and then someone would notice it had returned. Was it sizing them up for an attack? That was the question on everyone's mind.

Their provisions were getting low. Most of the dried meat

had been eaten. The Cavers had given them some things, but all feared what they might be. They had decided, the Caver food would be saved as a last resort.

On the one-hundred and thirty-sixth day, Coleman and Ayascho prepared for a dangerous hunt, initiated by desperation. They hid in a narrow wadi. They waited quietly for the terror bird. After a few minutes, they could hear its footsteps, and they prepared their attack. When they heard the beast's steps pass by them, they jumped from their hiding place and attacked; Coleman using his bow and Ayascho his atlatl—the levered spear. Both missiles struck the beast's body. The creature gave a loud squawk of horror and pain. It turned on its assailants, preparing to attack. Another arrow was launched and penetrated its neck. The giant bird sounded a pained screech, sprinted away from its attackers, and soon collapsed. Ayascho finished it off with his metal Cavers' knife. Coleman gave a loud whistle, and the rest of the party hurried back to them.

"We will have fresh meat tonight," he told the smiling men.

"Good job, you two. I think we'll just stop here. It's time everyone had a rest, anyway," Titus told them. Coleman thought it unusually generous of the sestardi to grant them such a respite, but it was very much welcomed. He was a tough commander, but he knew how and when to push his men, and he also knew when to rest them.

It was only midafternoon, and the men took full advantage of the extra rest. A couple of soldiers gathered dry scrub brush for firewood while Ayascho and Coleman butchered the giant bird. Bardas and Pontus were considered the best cooks, so they had the honor of preparing and roasting it. While they slowly turned it over a roasting spit, everyone else rested wherever they could find shade. Lulubelle wandered around, digging for roots with her horned beak.

By dusk, the roasting bird was done, and the men feasted. After everyone had eaten their fill, there was still quite a bit of meat left over. The two chefs cut the remainder into strips and let them slowly dry near the fire. It would be enough to feed the party for many days. The hope of not having to delve into the Caver stash for a while longer brought smiles to all their faces.

After dark, Coleman lay on his back, looking up into the astonishing beauty of the night sky. None of the moons had risen, and Coleman could see the complete canvas of stars. It's magnificent! he thought. They seemed to be beyond number. It was like looking into a Milky Way that covered the entire night sky. Suddenly, a beam of light streaked across his view. Several more soon followed. It was an exciting display—a meteor shower. He had seen meteors shooting through the night sky before, but never as often as this night. Some of the others soon began commenting on the phenomenon. As he listened to them talk, he learned that events like this occurred regularly. The one they were watching tonight was one of the more spectacular showers. It returned at nearly the same time each span; Not unlike my homeworld, Coleman thought. A little pang of homesickness struck him, but his loneliness was diminishing. This was his home now, but he was still having difficulty adjusting to that fact from time-to-time.

The trek continued for the next couple of days without incident. Gheedan pointed out a ridgeline rising above the flat plain in the far distance. He had the sharpest eyes, and it was another day before it became clear to Coleman what he was seeing. Sure enough, Gheedan was right. There was nothing on Myron's map indicating a ridgeline in the middle of this barren plain, but of course, that wasn't surprising.

Near midafternoon, Coleman noticed a large cobalt-blue rock shoot from beneath the right wheel of Lulubelle's cart.

The soil of the plain was clay, and rocks were only found in the wadis. Coleman picked it up and hefted it. Ayascho joined him as he examined the surprisingly heavy stone. It looked like a glob of melted blue metal to Coleman.

"This must be a meteorite," he told Ayascho.

"What's a meet-ro-mide?"

"Me-te-or-ite. Remember the shower of falling stars we watched the other night? This is what some are made of. Most burn up in the air, but this one fell all the way to the ground. I have never seen a blue one before. Let me check something," Coleman continued.

"Do you mean this fell from the sky the other night?"

"I do not think so. This was under the soil; a cartwheel uncovered it, so I think it has been here for a very long time." He reached into the cart and pulled out a godstone and placed it on the meteorite. It stuck. "This is iron; I mean gravetum."

Titus walked over to the two men and examined Coleman's find. "I see you've found another worthless toy. Is this good for anything?" he asked.

"It's gravetum. Someone could make a cooking pot out of this. If it's good quality iron, it could be used to make a sword," Coleman told him.

"A sword from this?" Titus was skeptical.

"Maybe, I do not know for sure. I think I will keep it. It may be useful."

Over the next several hours, the men found a few more blue meteorites, and Coleman collected them all, storing them in the cart.

The following day, they reached the ridge-line. Coleman, Titus, and Ayascho climbed the steep cliff, and from the ridge top, they looked into a gaping crater at least a thousand feet deep and more than a mile across. The soil inside the crater was cobalt-blue in color, just like the meteorites.

"Batru's eye," Ayascho muttered reverently.

"What is this place?" Titus wondered.

"This, my friends, is a meteor crater. A falling star did this," Coleman told them. The other two didn't say a word but only gaped at the view before them. "Those meteorite pieces we have been finding are what is left of the giant stone that made this," Coleman guessed.

"When we passed this place before, I thought it was only a ridgeline. I should have taken a closer look," Titus admitted.

"Are you sure this wasn't made the other night?" asked Ayascho.

"This crater was made a long, long time ago. If it had happened the other night, we would have known it. I doubt we would have survived the impact." Coleman waved to the soldiers at the foot of the ridge and motioned for them to join his small group. As each soldier arrived, he stood in wonder and awe at what he witnessed.

"It's like the gods scooped out a handful of dirt," said one.

"Why is it blue?" asked another. Everyone turned to Coleman, expecting an answer.

He simply shrugged his shoulders and said, "It must have come from the blue moon," but that was only a guess.

After about twenty minutes, Titus ordered everyone down and back to the thrice. Each man took one long, final look, and did as the sestardi ordered.

CHAPTER 8

WEAKNESSES OF THE LAW

Several days had passed since Maaryah's last confrontation with Foreman Nestor. So far, she hadn't experienced any repercussions for her rejection of his self-serving gift. Nevertheless, worry-filled her days, and apprehension filled her nights. She found it hard to sleep, and she awoke at the slightest sound. By the end of each labor-filled day, she was exhausted.

This day's assignment was particularly difficult. It had been a hot day, and the field Maaryah's herd had been assigned contained longer than usual rows. Every slave in her herd struggled to finish their assignment before dusk. The crack of Ardo's pusher was heard more than once. As darkness fell, the herd was dismissed, and a drained Maaryah returned to her hovel. She quickly washed the grime from her body, dipped her clay pot into her grain sack, and filled it. She dashed off to collect her evening flat-cakes and her ten tokens.

She returned to her hovel and sat at the table, eating her dreary meal. She felt her weariness and inhaled deeply. She couldn't even finish all of her flat-cakes. She stood, undid the sash around her waist, and buried her knife in the straw of her bed. She removed her work tunic, washed her body, and put on her sleepwear. She rinsed her work tunic in the bucket and hung it over the end of her table as she did every night. She climbed into her straw bed without undoing her braid and was about to fall asleep when she remembered she hadn't drawn a fresh bucket of water for the morning. Wearily, she crawled out of bed, took the bucket by the handle, and left her hovel. She walked to the ditch, emptied the bucket, and headed for the well.

Before she got there, she noticed a dark figure moving haltingly in the shadows. She stopped and waited, trying to determine who it might be. Suddenly, terror struck her as she realized it was Foreman Nestor. She turned and tried to dash back to her shanty. He intercepted her, grabbing her forearm and spinning her around. He pulled her against his body and rubbed his cheek against hers.

"Let me go!" she cried.

The strong man pulled her tighter against his body. "Come, now, Maaryah, ya can be my friend for a night, can't ya? I'll reward yer friendship," he told her, his words slurred, and his breath smelling of wine.

"Leave me alone!" Maaryah shouted.

"Don't resist me, ya ungrateful wench," he growled. "I'll make ya more worthy than ya are now. Stop fight'n me!"

"You can't do this," Maaryah screeched. "It's against Slave Law."

"What ya know about Slave Law? Who told ya?" Nestor grumbled, still holding her tightly.

"I've heard others talk about it in the fields. Let me go!" she demanded.

"Forget Slave Law; it never had no meaning to me, no way.

Now, give me a snug," he rubbed his cheek against hers again, and she recoiled, causing him to lose his balance. His grip loosened, and she broke away from him. She swung her wooden bucket as hard as she could, hitting him across the shins.

He howled in pain and fell to his knees. "Ya spawn of the Five Shadows! Ya'll regret that, but first I'm gonna finish what I started." He jumped up and tackled Maaryah before she could react. He pinned her to the ground and clawed at her sleepwear, attempting to tear it from her body.

She pounded her fists into his shoulders and back, but it only made him laugh. "If you do this, I'll tell everyone what you've done and then kill myself. Explain that to the master," she threatened.

Nestor stopped and went to his knees. "Ya haven't the will," he growled.

"I'd rather cross-over than live with the memory of your filthy act. I'm sure the master will want to know why a young slave killed herself. He'll ask questions. He'll learn the truth. He'll demand his loss be covered. Can you pay for a slave?" Maaryah's fear had transformed into anger, and her golden-amber eyes bore into the foreman's. Nestor thought for a moment and ran his fingers through his hair. Maaryah sat up; her defiant and angry eyes fixed on her assailant's face. Rage filled Nestor's soul as he examined the slave's truculent stance. He drew back his right fist and punched her as hard as he could in the forehead, knocking her unconscious. He stood, uttered a curse, and staggered into the darkness.

Maaryah awoke with Munnoga's bright rays shining in her eyes. She looked around and realized it was still night. She sat up and felt the ache in her head. She struggled to her feet, re-trieved her bucket, and went to the well. She filled the bucket with fresh, cool water, and splashed some onto her face. She noticed a tear in the neck of her sleepwear and sighed. She would have to find time to repair it. She went back to her hov-el and crawled into bed, fearing her waking sleep-terror had just begun.

Maaryah awoke hearing Ardo's distant call. She rubbed the sleep from her eyes and felt the pain of her forehead. She touched a fleshy bump, and the pain increased. Ardo's call was closer, and she could hear his footsteps.

"I'm awake," Maaryah muttered as he approached.

Rather than passing by, as usual, he stopped at her window hole. "Maaryah, Foreman Nestor wants you at the Separation House. Quickly, my girl, don't delay."

Maaryah was up in a flash. She had no time to spare if she were to make it there by dawn. This was the first time she had been assigned to the Separation House. The slaves called it the house of horrors because those working there were bru-talized more often than anywhere else on the estate. Foreman Nestor made it his center of operations, and he patrolled the floor often, punishing those he deemed to be slackers. Besides that, as the harvest neared conclusion, the demand on the separators increased, and their days became longer. Lamps were lit at dusk, and the slaves' toil continued well into the night. Maaryah didn't need to worry about that just yet; it was still early in the season; however, she had to learn a new skill, and if she didn't learn it fast enough, she would be punished. Undoubtedly, it was for this purpose the foreman reassigned her to the Separation House. She wondered how long this additional suffering was to last. She hated her miserable life even more.

Maaryah arrived just as the other slaves were filing into the huge wooden building, so she moved to the end of the line and advanced with the others. She had no idea where to go nor what to do once she got inside. She tapped the shoulder of the woman in front of her and asked, "I've never been here before. What do I do?"

The woman turned around and looked up at her, surprised at first by her height. "Find an empty workstation and watch the others. You'll see what you have to do. Be sure to summon a runner before you're out of seeded lint or before your bins fill because if the lint fouls the rollers . . . well, the foreman won't be pleased." The woman turned around and entered the building, quickly moving to a workstation. Maaryah entered, paused, and looked around. Work had already begun in the dim light of dawn. Men and women were operating cranks with their right hands and feeding puffy white lint containing seeds through two rollers. The seeds fell into a bin in front of the rollers, and the seedless lint dropped to a bin on the opposite side. Children dashed from place to place. It's a hive of furious action, Maaryah thought. As she searched for a vacant station, she felt a hard rap across the back of her head. She clutched her scalp in pain and turned to see Foreman Nestor standing behind her, holding his coiled whip.

"Move it, you worthless vestang!" he growled. He gave her a hard shove, and she stumbled forward, nearly falling over a seated separator furiously cranking and feeding lint between the rollers. Maaryah quickly found a station and began cranking and feeding. She quickly realized it wasn't as easy as it appeared. The lint stuck to the rollers, and the seeds failed to fall free. She felt another hard rap across the back of her head, and she uttered a sharp cry of pain. "Clean those rollers and crank faster or you'll feel my whip on your back," Nestor bellowed.

He turned away and patrolled the floor, shouting angry epithets as he did, demanding more effort from the separators and the runners. He returned to Maaryah's station. By this time, she had cleared the rollers and was cranking and feeding. Nestor glowered at her as he passed, and just as he did, the rollers became fouled again. He hit her across the back of the head once more with the hard leather handle of his whip. He grabbed her upper arm and jerked her to her feet.

"I'm gonna enjoy beating some usefulness into ya!" He swung his coiled whip and hit her on the side of her left thigh and buttocks. She yelped in pain, and her amber eyes flared in anger. "When I'm done, ya'll be happy to give me what I want, willingly."

Nestor was about to hit her again when he heard Sire Oetan's call, "Nestor, there you are."

The estate master approached, and as he did, Nestor pushed Maaryah down. "Get back to work. If ya foul the rollers again, ya'll be sorry!" He turned, faced the estate master, and asked, "Sire Oetan, what ya want?"

"I've just received a message from Megatus Idop. The king has called for a show of force by the Pannera to chase away some brigands who've dared to cross the Magheedo River. The prince will be with us. I'll be leaving at midday. I have some tasks I want you to oversee while I'm away."

"How long will ya be gone, sire?" Nestor asked.

"That's hard to say; could be a couple of detzas, I think. Now, come with me, and I'll show you what I want done," the master said as he marched out. Nestor looked down at Maaryah, who was still clearing the rollers of her machine. He kicked her hard and then followed the estate master.

At the end of the day, Maaryah returned to her hovel. The first thing she did was to pull up the bottom of her tunic and examine the new wounds the foreman had inflicted on her. Welts were on her left thigh and higher. She also had a nasty bruise where he had kicked her. She sighed and continued her evening routine; however, this night, she wore her waist sash around her sleepwear, her knife hidden in its folds, just in case.

Several days had passed since her assignment to the Separation House. She had seen Foreman Nestor only from afar; he appeared to be focused on the new tasks the master had given him. She'd become better at being a separator. She learned the number of seeds in the lint meant an adjustment needed to be made concerning the speed that the rollers were moving. Lint still fouled the rollers from time-to-time, but she was getting better at it. At least it was a change of pace from her mundane and repetitive field duties she had been performing for span after span. She realized that even this new assignment would become a mind-numbing bore once it was mastered, but for the time being, she enjoyed its simple challenge.

A few more days passed, and Maaryah felt her life was tolerable once again. She guessed it wouldn't last because Foreman Nestor was still here, and she was sure he would never forget her rejection, nor would he let it go. As she focused on her duties, she heard Nestor's gruff voice nearby. His heavy footsteps marched past her. He began cursing the separators and runners, as usual. Maaryah lost her focus, and the rollers fouled. She frantically tried to clear the mess before the foreman noticed her plight. He finished his diatribe and stomped past her. She sighed in relief, but just as she thought all was well, she was yanked from her stool by her long braid and drug across the floor. She clutched at the foreman's hand gripping her braid and held on, kicking and twisting as he dragged her out of the building and onto the dirt. She rose to her knees and was about to stand when his right fist slammed into the side of her head, stunning her and dropping her face-first into the dust. She lay in the dirt, her mind in a dark fog.

Nestor's angry voice was in her ear, "Ya ready to bend to my will?" All he desired now was to break his victim's will.

"Never!" she heard herself whisper. An instant later, she heard the crack of his whip, and then searing pain flashed across her back. It was as though someone had laid red-hot embers onto her flesh. Maaryah's agonizing scream split the quiet of the morning air.

Nestor drew close and spoke into her ear again, "This is only the beginning. When the First comes around again, ya better take my gift, or ya'll get more stripes across yer back. Now, get up and get back to work. Be quick about it!" Maaryah slowly rose to her knees, her back in burning misery, her mind reeling. She touched the rear of her left shoulder with her right hand and then examined her palm; it was bloody. She staggered to her feet and stumbled into the Separation House. She returned to her machine and sat. The back of her tunic was split and had turned crimson red from the blood oozing from her agonizing wound.

Maaryah continued working until the end of the day. She returned to her hovel, taking painful, halting steps. When she finally got there, she collapsed onto her bed of straw and began weeping. She didn't even rise to get her evening flat-cakes and ten tokens. She continued to lay there in the dark.

"Maaryah, are you awake," Mama Dumaz called.

Maaryah was still lying on her stomach, her face in the straw. She replied with a muffled voice, "Hoy."

Mama Dumaz entered and sat on the straw next to her. "Come, child, remove this bloody thing, and let me treat your wound." Maaryah carefully removed her tunic and laid face down on the straw again. In the dim light from the moons

streaming through window and door, Mama Dumaz examined the nasty bloody welt across Maaryah's back; it went
from her left shoulder to her right hip. The elderly woman
dabbed away the dried blood with a wet towel and gently ap-
plied ointment to the wound, causing Maaryah to flinch in
pain from time-to-time. "I've brought your flat-cakes and tokens. You must eat if you're to heal, my girl," Mama Dumaz
counseled.

"I want to die," was all Maaryah could say.

"Now, now, child, stop thinking like that. You have a long
life before you."

"A long life of suffering and misery," was Maaryah's muffled reply.

"A slave's life is a hard and cruel one, but you'll find a measure of happiness in time. Papa Dumaz and I have. Why not
you?"

"I just want to die."

"I understand, Maaryah. That's your pain speaking. I'll return in the morning and check on you."

Mama Dumaz stood and walked to the doorway. Before
she passed through it, she heard a muffled, "Thank you,"
from Maaryah. Mama Dumaz smiled and left. Maaryah lay
on her straw bed, her back burning in agony, a blistering desire growing within her center to avenge herself upon that
loathsome and cruel foreman.

CHAPTER 9

CURSE THE RED MOON

Nevesant mounted a draft animal and trotted out of the hamlet. He had taken the animal from a farmer who used it to plow his fields. The boy knew the harvest was in, and the farmer wouldn't need the beast until the weather turned warm again, after the approaching cold and wet season. The owner was outraged but dared not object because the boy was protected by the ruffians who had invaded the hamlet.

Nevesant guided his mount to the top of a hill overlooking the small town far below in the valley. On the other side of the hill's slope was a small copse of trees. Nevesant dismounted, tied his mount's reins to a tree branch, and walked back to the hill's crest. He moved to the other side of the slope and began practicing with his sling. His skill was improving, and he felt it was only a matter of time before he became as proficient with it as his mentor and master, Tangundo.

As he practiced, he contemplated his good fortune in be-friending the tall beast-man who was like a god to him. He thought about the fate of the three men who had invaded their camp long before. Tangundo had forced them into the mist, and they never returned, unlike his master who had gained a special relationship with the fearsome gods within. Neve-sant thought about Buffo's demise, as well. All these deaths were of little consequence to the young man. The three villagers, Gund, Fino, and Turvy, despised the orphan boy and had aways treated him cruelly. Buffo was an outlaw and a murderer. *All of these men got what they deserved,* Nevesant thought, and their deaths hadn't bothered him in the least; however, the priest's death in the flames of Grazius's home was a different matter. Master Eezayhod had always been kind to the boy and shared his food while offering him loving advice whenever he visited the hamlet. Nevesant had even considered becoming a priest himself. Although he had warm feelings for the friendly and kind priest, his feelings for the god he represented were cold as the snow on the distant mountains. How could this unnamed god allow his loving mother to die in childbirth? How could this cruel god permit his father to be crushed to death by a runaway cart? No, he couldn't don the blue robes of that god's priests. He now followed a god he could see and commune with. And just as important, his belly had been full ever since his master took over this hamlet; the hamlet whose residents couldn't have cared less had he starved to death. As he continued his sling practice, he grew angrier at those who had rejected and abused him. He pretended to be slinging rocks at their heads, and his accuracy improved.

Nevesant turned his face skyward and noted the position of the p´atezas. "Ha, midday; time to eat," he said aloud. He walked to his mount, untied its reins, climbed atop, and made his way to the top of the hill. When he reached the crest, he noticed in the distance a column of mounted men approaching the hamlet. He immediately knew who they were. At their current speed, it would take less than half a segment for them to reach the village. He dug his heels into his mount's sides and galloped off the hill in a mad dash.

"Master, king's men are coming!" Nevesant repeatedly shouted as his mount galloped into the hamlet. The followers of Munnevo quickly gathered near their master's newly acquired residence and operations base as Nevesant rode up to them. "Soldiers on mounts are coming! They'll be here soon!" he shouted.

Tangundo rushed from the house, "You say, soldiers are coming?"

"Yes, master," Nevesant said breathlessly.

"How many?"

"At least thirty, maybe more. They're on the north road."

Tangundo ran the fingers of his right hand through his hair. He then tightened the knot holding his kerchief in place and then began speaking, "Men, we must leave. Fetch mounts, anything you can ride. Be quick about it!" he ordered.

"Master, you won't fight them?" one of his followers asked.

"Too many. We must flee, but we'll be back. Now, hurry!" Tangundo shouted. He mounted the animal he'd appropriated wernts earlier and galloped out of the hamlet, his followers in tow.

Less than half a segment later, Hunder and his detachment rode into the small town. A disheveled and pathetic looking Grazius ran up to Hunder. "Defetane," he shouted as he began catching his breath, "brigands took over the village. If you hurry, you can catch them. They went south. Their leader is a sorcerer. He took my sword of authority."

"A sorcerer? What has he done?" Hunder asked.

"He surrounds himself in purple fire, and he knocks men

down with a wave of his hand. He killed the priest, Eezayhod. Burned him up in my home, he did. He's fed some of our people to the gods of the mist. Also, there are three village men missing, long time lost. He probably had something to do with that, too," Grazius wailed, his voice betraying his fear and anguish.

Hunder's expression turned sour, and his eyebrows furrowed. He sat in silence, pondering before he spoke. After a short delay, he asked, "How many are with this sorcerer?"

"Fourteen outlaws and that orphan boy Nevesant. I knew he'd be no good," Grazius spat.

"The priest was killed?" Hunder asked. Grazius nodded. "All right, I'll put an end to this marauder's dark magic. Men, follow me!" Hunder and his men rode out at a cantor.

Tangundo led his men on the south trail for a segment. Their mounts were sweaty and frothing at the bit, at least those few mounts with bridles and bits. Tangundo dismounted and looked around. "We'll continue on foot. Leave the animals here." He marched off into the trees.

A short time later, Hunder and his men reached the abandoned mounts. "Pindee, Fundeg, collect these animals and take them back to the village. See that they're returned to their owners. The rest of you follow me!"

Hunder ordered his best tracker to lead the way and follow the outlaws' trail. It led the king's men to the foot of a cliff, its crest looming high above them. The detachment dismounted and stood staring up at it. "They went up there," the tracker said, pointing.

"Hoy, let's get to it," Hunder ordered. His men began climbing.

Without warning, a dozen or more small boulders rained down from above. A large rock bounced off the cliff face and hit a king's man on the shoulder, causing him to lose his grip. He slid down the rough stone, only stopping when his feet hit the flat ground at the cliff's base. He sat on the dirt, rubbing his painful wound. Another volley of rocks rained down from above. Hunder's men began retreating, making their way back to level ground.

"Defetane, what are we to do? They'll pick us off one-by-one if we try to scale that wall," one of the king's men wailed.

"You're right, seshtane. We'll have to move around them; take 'em from the rear. Have the men mount up. There's got to be another way to get to those vestangs," Hunder growled. The injured man was helped to his feet, and then the detachment was off, looking for a way to safely scale the obstacle.

"Master, they're leaving," one of Tangundo's followers observed as he peered over the cliff's edge.

"Yes, Andent, they are, but they'll be back."

"What are we to do, master?" a worried Nevesant cried.

"First, we hide and prepare. When we're ready, then we'll take them down. Men, follow me, into the trees, as far as we can go. Don't dally! Get going!" Tangundo shouted as he trotted off, plowing through the brush and trees, his outlaw band following close behind.

It took Hunder and his detachment half a day to reach the top of the cliff they had tried to scale previously. By then, their quarry was long gone. Hunder sat on his mount and looked around. "Verdeto, see if you can pick up their trail," he commanded.

Verdeto, the tracker, dismounted and began walking around the area. After a few moments, he knelt down, examined the ground, and called, "This way!" He took his mount by the reins and headed into the thick woods.

At dusk, Hunder's detachment reached a wide, swift-running river, further across than a man could toss a stone. "They entered the water here. No telling where they ended up; this side or over there," the tracker said, pointing to the opposite shoreline.

"Alright, men, we'll camp here for the night. We'll resume the chase in the morning," Hunder announced. The men dismounted and prepared camp.

On the opposite side of the river, Nevesant, in hiding, observed the king's men making camp and resting their mounts. After dusk had turned to darkness, Nevesant slinked away and rejoined his master and the others.

"What are they doing?" Tangundo asked.

"Making camp, master."

"Good. We'll move up a creek until we reach the biting fish, then we'll continue on dry land. We must confuse their tracker or at least slow our pursuers and put distance between them and us," Tangundo told his followers. They began moving up a creek that flowed into the river, taking advantage of the light of the three moons.

At midmorning, one of Tangundo's men gave a sharp cry of pain and scurried out of the water. "I just got bit!" he shouted. All the others quickly exited the creek before they, too, became victims. Their master refused to let his exhausted and hungry men rest. He drove them onward all day and didn't stop until dark, as heavy clouds blocked the moons' glows. Everyone was drained and quickly fell asleep. Just as they fell into a restful nod, the clouds tore open and drenched the land. Tangundo's men cursed their misfortune and sought shelter wherever they could find it. They spent the rest of the night huddled together under a large tree whose spreading branches caught much of the clouds' pelting rain; however, huge drops of water falling from branch and leaf continued to bombard the men all night. Everyone but Tangundo looked miserable. The master was the only one smiling.

"Defetane," Verdeto began, "I've lost their trail. The rain has washed it away, and the creek has risen. There's no likelihood we'll catch them now."

Hunder gave a growl of frustration and disappointment. "Curse the red moon! Alright, we'll return to the village. I'm going to make it our base of operations. We'll get those vestangs, yet. That sorcerer will pay for what he's done."

CHAPTER 10

CONTENDING WITH THE GODS

Several days after the blue crater's ridge dropped from view, Gheedan began pointing and shouting. "The Mountains of Magheedo! I see them! We're nearly home!"

Through a dusty haze, Coleman could vaguely see a bump on the horizon. He had learned to trust Gheedan's keen eyesight. The party's pace quickened. Even Lulubelle was moving faster than usual.

After several more days, they came upon green bushes and some green grass. Birds were seen overhead, swirling, and flitting on the air currents. Also, large rodents were seen popping their heads above their burrows. Their color and markings reminded Coleman of giant meerkats, with bodies nearly a yard long. The critters chirped warnings to their group and continued spying on the intruders. Gheedan walked over to Coleman and pointed. About a half-mile away was a small herd of gazelle-like creatures grazing on the green grass.

"I think we eat well tonight. Am I right, Tondo?" he gleefully asked as he patted Coleman's bow peeking above the hunter's left shoulder.

"Yes, Gheedan, I think you are right. Ayascho, look over there!" The young man followed Coleman's pointing hand. Another herd of large deer or elk-like creatures could be seen grazing sublimely. That night, the men rested on green grass with full stomachs.

The next day, the party bumped into the Magheedo Mountains, a range of rolling hills with peaks no higher than about two-thousand five-hundred feet. They were rugged and covered in lush vegetation. Coleman felt a cool, damp breeze coming from the southwest. The soldiers told him, a marsh and the ocean were in that direction. It was a welcomed respite from the dry, hot air they had been suffering under for such a long time.

The party needed to reach the Magheedo Pass, but Titus's dead-reckoning was off. They had ventured too far southwest, so they had to head northeast for a couple of days, paralleling the mountains. Coleman reminded their leader, as often as he dared, that his gumpass, as it was called by the others, could have avoided the extra travel. Titus didn't want to hear it. He was embarrassed by his mistake, and worse than that, he had to endure scoffing and angry remarks from his men. Coleman dropped it after he thought he'd teased Titus enough.

On the third day of their detour, they reached the pass. It took another three days to arrive at the Magheedo Plain, an expanse of cultivated fields, sprouting what looked like wheat, oats, and other cereal grains. Coleman was impressed by the green, neatly manicured fields. He could see irrigation ditches carved into the rich, dark soil.

"These fields feed the citizens of all three great cities. They have always provided food enough for the people as well as beast and slave," Titus told him.

The fact that Titus made a distinction between people and

slaves was not lost on Coleman. Titus had said it as though slaves weren't people, only chattel, lower than domesticated animals. Coleman didn't like his attitude, but it was no different than the rest of his men. Coleman had never experienced a society fully accepting of slavery, and he braced himself for what he might have to witness.

The little caravan wended its way through the bountiful land on a dirt road. Coleman was told that there were two main dirt roads on the Magheedo Plain: the one they were now on, called the North Road, and another called the East Road, which paralleled the east sea and eventually squeezed between the eastern end of the Magheedo Mountains and the ocean. There were no roads in the west because of the Great Magheedo Marsh, a huge, impassable wetland south and west of the mountains, full of weak-ground. Coleman came to understand that term to mean quicksand.

Although Myron's map didn't show it, the next landmark they were to encounter was the Magheedo River. Coleman was told, it was a small river in comparison to most of the others they had encountered and crossed while in the Wilderness. Titus said it would take another four days to reach it. Coleman was looking forward to washing off the dust and grime he had collected over many days. They had found a spring when they entered the Magheedo Pass, but certainly too small to take a dip in. He wanted something deep and wide enough that would allow him to swim for a while. Even a good soaking would be a welcomed delight. Since water had been scarce while crossing the dry wasteland, he had let his beard grow again. Shaving with a jagged obsidian knife without water was a torture he refused to endure. The stubble collected dust and dirt and made him itch. He craved some relief.

The temperature was much cooler on the plain. At night, Coleman felt chilled for the first time for as long as he could remember. The sultry air of the jungle, the dry air of the Cavers' cavern, and the arid heat of the wasteland were much the same to him. He started using the wrap Taahso had made long before. The soldiers were envious. It was beautiful, soft, and warm, making the nights much more comfortable.

At midday on their fourth day on the Magheedo Plain, shouts and the clanging of metal could be heard far in the distance. The soldiers craned their necks to see where the sound was coming from. Titus stopped the party and climbed atop Lulubelle's back, standing on his toes, trying to peer over obstacles in the direction of the noise.

"Sestardi, it sounds like battle," Bardas shouted up to him.

"Yes, Bardas, yes, it does. I'll bet my salt a patrol is fighting brigands." He jumped down from Lulubelle's back and began issuing orders. "Men, secure your weapons. Pontus, Tondo, Ayascho, you three stay with the thrice and follow after us."

"I can help. I will go with you," Coleman told him.

"No! You will stay with the thrice. I'm not going to risk losing you this close to the city. Hurry men! With me!"

Coleman stood, watching the fully armed soldiers charge

down the road. He was surprised and disappointed. "What is this all about?" he finally asked Pontus.

"Brigands. They are outlaws from the mountains. They raid the farms and caravans on the roads. This is the season they come down from their hiding places and plunder. The king sends the guards to chase them away. Most of the time, they just run. Once in awhile, they'll fight. It all depends on how desperate they are and their numbers."

"I still think I can help," Coleman clamored.

"If you go, the sestardi will spend his time watching over you, protecting you from being killed. That would risk his life. We'll just do what he said. Let's go!" Pontus gave the thrice a tug on her ear, and off they went at as fast a pace as Lulu-belle would allow. The sound of battle was still ringing in the air, and Coleman wanted to get into it before it ended. His Ranger training harped at his subconscious. He was trained to head to the sound of battle, and that is where he wanted to be.

Soon, Coleman's pace quickened to a trot, with Ayascho at his side. The distance between the two men and Pontus was increasing with every step. Pontus began yelling, "Get back here, Tondo! You'll get us both in trouble!" Coleman ignored him and picked up the pace. Pontus began shouting odd words. Coleman guessed they were profanities, but it wasn't long before Pontus could no longer be heard.

After a five-minute jog, they reached the banks of a swiftly running stream. Coleman thought it more like a creek, but he guessed it must be the Magheedo River. On the far side, only about sixty to seventy-five feet away, he saw a group of soldiers gathered around a prone body. There were several other dead or dying men scattered around the opposite shoreline. Most of the soldiers were sobbing, unashamed by their display. One was on his knees, pounding his fists into the muddy dirt. Coleman started crossing the swiftly running but shallow river, with water reaching to his chest at its deepest point. Three of the soldiers noticed him and drew their swords, preparing to attack. Coleman and Ayascho stopped while still in mid-stream and began backing away. To Coleman, the soldiers looked desperate—no, they looked crazed. He held up both hands, his left still holding his bow, and said, "I am not a brigand. I am with Titus. Is he here?"

"Who is Titus?" one of the soldiers shouted.

"You will die for what you've done!" another screamed as he began advancing toward the two intruders with his sword drawn.

"Titus? Titus! He's the sestardi the king sent into the Wilderness. If you're with Titus, where is he?" another yelled as the sword-brandishing soldier stepped into the water.

"I'm here!" Titus shouted as he pushed through reeds and bushes, followed by his men. "He is with me. Don't hurt him!" he shouted in desperation. The soldier stopped his advance and stood knee-deep in the water, still brandishing his sword menacingly.

"What has happened here?" Titus asked.

"The prince is dead. He was knocked into the water and has drowned!" a soldier cried and began weeping uncontrollably.

"How long was he in the water?" Coleman shouted.

"We don't know. We found him floating face down and pulled him out. He has crossed-over," the soldier sobbed.

"Let me look at him. I might be able to help," Coleman yelled.

"He no longer breathes, and he's turned blue. He has crossed-over, I tell you, and rests with the gods now," another shouted back.

"If he is already dead, then it will not matter if I take a look at him, will it?"

"Let him examine the prince," Titus yelled to the soldiers standing around the prince's body. "He has great powers."

"Alright, but if you defile his body, I'll kill you," someone threatened.

Coleman stepped quickly past the soldier standing in the river, watching the man's eyes, unsure if he would strike or not. When Coleman reached the prince, he dropped his bow, lowered to his knees, and examined the young man. "Help me get this off," he commanded, pointing to the prince's armored chest cover. No one moved. "Do not just stand there; move it!" A soldier in ornate armor gave Coleman a stare of indignation. Obviously, he was the commander, but two others did as he had ordered. The prince was indeed blue. Maybe it was too late, but Coleman would do what he could. He had always been grateful for the first aid training he'd received while he was in the military. He had also taken a few advanced First Aid courses on his own. He knew a Ranger's life was a dangerous one, and he perceived, someday, his additional training would come in handy, but never in his wildest dreams could he have imagined it would be under such bizarre circumstances.

He knelt next to the prince and placed his palms in the middle of the man's chest. He pressed down firmly and then quickly relaxed, repeating the motion nearly twice per second. He silently counted until he reached thirty. He then tilted the man's head back, pinched the prince's nose, covered the prince's mouth with his, expelling his breath into the young man's lungs. He repeated it two times. There was no response from the prince. Coleman then began pressing down on the prince's chest again, performing CPR for another count of thirty. Suddenly, Coleman sat up, raised his fist, and slammed it down on the prince's sternum, performing a precordial thump. He knew it wasn't a recommended procedure under most circumstances, but at this point, what did he have to lose? However, the prince's guards reacted in horror.

"Kill him!" the commander shouted.

Titus and Ayascho placed their bodies between the advancing soldiers and Coleman's back. "Let him do his magic!" Titus pleaded. The commander raised his arm, and his men stopped their advance.

Coleman continued performing CPR and breathing into the prince's lungs. As he continued, he couldn't restrain himself from shouting his distress and worry over the prince's lack of response. "Come on, prince, breathe! You can do it! Wake up, take a breath!" he shouted in godspeak. Coleman looked heavenward and shouted, "Come on, prince, you can do it! Take a breath!" To the shocked and fearful witnesses, it appeared he was contending with the gods for the prince's spirit using the speech of deity. Coleman took another deep breath, expelling air into the prince's lungs again, and then he continued performing chest compressions, all the while commanding in godspeak for the young man to breathe. In a little over a minute, the prince began convulsing. Coleman turned him on his side, and he vomited water. He could feel the young man's pulse, and his chest began to rise and sink as he took breath once again. The prince coughed and sputtered for a long time, but he had regained his color.

"I told you he has magic," Titus stated proudly. All the others were amazed. The prince was a dead man, and yet this strange-looking, tall and hairy savage had brought him back from the other-side.

Coleman noticed blood on his hands, so he examined the prince more closely. He had a severe wound on the back of his head. It looked like blunt force trauma, probably from being hammered by a mace or a club.

"I am sure he has a concussion," Coleman told the commander. "Cover him with a blanket, if you have one, and raise his feet slightly above his head. We do not want him to go into shock."

"I don't understand those words. What are you saying?" asked the commander.

"Godspeak," Ayascho and Titus chimed in unison.

"He has a bad head injury. That is what we need to worry about now. Get some blankets," Coleman dictated. The commander nodded his head, and a soldier dashed off, returning a few minutes later with a couple of blankets. Coleman carefully covered the prince with one, then rolled the other and placed it under his feet.

"He is not out of danger yet," he told the commander. "I do not want him moved. Build a fire to keep him warm. I will stay with him until his condition improves."

A fire was quickly started, and Coleman examined each fallen man, some in armor, others wearing only tattered clothes. Every one had been hacked or clubbed to death. "There is nothing that can be done for any of the others," he announced. He then made himself a comfortable place for his vigil. The commander joined him. It was obvious, he was going to remain with the prince, as well.

Pontus and Lulubelle soon crossed the river and stopped nearby. Coleman mentioned he felt chilled, so Ayascho retrieved his wrap from the cart and gave it to him.

"I am Megatus Idop, commander of the Pannera. Who are you?" the commander asked.

"I am called Tondo. What is a Pannera?"

"The Pannera is the three-hundred guards who protect the city. The king sent us to put down the brigands. They've been causing trouble lately. Tondo? The Tondo? Ha, I remember now. You are the one the priests asked the king to bring here."

"Yes, that is what I have been told. What do the priests want with me?"

Megatus Idop laughed, "Who knows why the priests do what they do? It's a mystery to us all, but after watching you bring the prince back from the other-side, I can see why they want you. Are you a priest, too?"

"No, not in the least," Coleman chuckled. "Is megatus your rank?"

"Yes. I am the leader of all these men. The king relies on

me to protect him, his family, and to keep the city safe from the likes of these brigands," Idop explained, pointing to a dead man in tattered clothes lying nearby.

"What happened here? How was the prince injured?" Coleman asked.

"My second in command, Megato Oetan, who leads the Prince's Contingent, protected him while I maneuvered a detachment to trap and destroy the brigand gang. The soldiers told me they were surprised by a large band of the cutthroats. Oetan is missing. I fear he was killed, and his body washed downriver. I have ordered a search. Most of these dead are the prince's guards. Only eight remain alive." Idop looked closer into Coleman's face, then continued, "Your eyes are the color of the blue moon. I have never seen such a thing before. What is that on your face?"

Coleman picked up a dry branch, stirred the fire with it, and then tossed it into the flames. "Hair grows on my face. And no, I am not a beast."

"What is that?" Idop asked, pointing to Coleman's bow.

"It is called a bow. I use it for hunting and protection."

"You must show me what it does."

"I will when it is safe to leave the prince." Just then, the prince coughed and groaned. He bent his knees and then straightened them again.

"Your Highness, can you hear me?" Idop asked. There was no response. The prince seemed to relax, and his rhythmic breathing indicated he had fallen back to sleep.

Coleman touched the prince's forehead and then his cheeks. "He is cold. He is losing body heat. We must keep him warm, or we may lose him." Coleman draped his wrap over the prince. The Megatus made a hand gesture to his soldiers. One dashed off and returned with another blanket and handed it to Coleman. "Thank you," he said. "It is colder here than any of the other places I have been. I appreciate the blanket."

"The Zerio wind brings cooling breezes from the ocean," Idop told him.

"How far are we from the Ancient City?"

"About seven marches," Idop answered. He could see that Coleman didn't understand. "A march is the distance the Pannera can travel in a day on foot, so we are seven day's travel away. A man in a hurry could do it in four or five days. A man riding a fast samaran can do it in two or three days, but he may kill his mount in the process."

"What is a samaran?" Coleman asked.

Idop ordered a soldier to fetch one. A few minutes later, the man returned leading an odd-looking, four-legged creature. At first, Coleman thought it was a furry horse, but as it came closer, he thought it looked more like a camel without a hump. He finally decided it looked like a llama more than anything else, a very large llama, with a head resembling a horse.

"We use samarans as pack animals and mounts. They can also draw carts. They don't seem to mind pulling carts or carrying packs, but it takes a very skilled samaran master to train one as a riding mount," Idop told him.

Coleman walked over to the samaran and touched its soft fur. It was as big as a horse and seemingly just as powerful. It had a long tail of straight hair and hooves like a horse.

"We also use its hair to make clothes. We shear them just as the warm season begins. Their fur is then sold and made into clothes, blankets, and other things. The blanket you're using is made from their hair." Coleman shifted the blanket over his shoulders. The samaran spooked, reared its head back, and spit a glob of sticky saliva through its nostrils onto Coleman's face. "Ha, they also spit," Idop laughed.

"Ah, that's nasty. Yuck!" Coleman sputtered in godspeak. He could hear laughter coming from the soldiers. He went to the river and washed his face. He returned to the samaran and looked it in the eyes. "Now, there will be no more of that," he scolded. "Does it have any other bad habits?"

"They'll step on your feet if they don't like you," one of the soldiers shouted. Coleman quickly took a step back. The soldiers laughed again.

He decided he'd made enough of a fool of himself and returned to the fire. "It looks like a fine animal. Maybe I will get one for myself one day."

"My brother raises samarans and knows all about them. If you want, I'll introduce you to him, if he's there when we reach the city," Idop added.

"It would be an honor to meet your brother."

Coleman and Idop continued their chit-chat until dusk. Titus's band of soldiers established their camp near the river, set up their tents, and made a cooking fire. Idop's men did the same. Later, a hot meal of meat and vegetables was served. Idop's men also provided Coleman's party with fresh bread, baked in metal pots on the cooking fires. This was the first time Coleman had tasted bread since he'd arrived on this new world. He savored every bite, although he detected a slight bitterness. He noticed Ayascho staring at the portion he'd been served.

"Take a bite, Ayascho, you will like it," Coleman advised. Ayascho finally took a small nibble and made a face. "What, you do not like it?" Coleman asked.

"It's strange. No, I don't like it."

"Too bitter?" Coleman asked.

"No, it's not bitter. It just feels . . . it feels different in my mouth," Ayascho told him.

"Oy, if you do not want it, give it to me."

Ayascho tossed the remainder to Coleman and took a bite of meat. "Ha, much better," he said.

The prince stirred, then tried to sit up. Coleman quickly moved to his side and gently pushed his chest down. "Just lay back. You are badly injured," Coleman told him.

"Water! Give me water," the prince pleaded. Idop quickly answered the prince's cry with a waterskin, pouring cool water into the young man's mouth. He drank for a long time, then sputtered and coughed.

"Easy, prince, not so fast," Coleman advised.

The prince pushed the waterskin away, closed his eyes, and

fell into a troubled slumber. He seemed to toss and turn all night. Coleman and Idop took turns watching him, but neither got much sleep. Every time the prince rustled, both men would check on him. The rest of the Prince's Contingent were much the same. They kept their distance, but all were very concerned about his welfare. They kept looking to Coleman for comforting reassurance, but he could give none.

Although the prince had been pulled back from death's door, he still had serious problems. Coleman worried that there was the possibility his royal patient could develop pneumonia. Also, the prince's head wound was quite severe. He undoubtedly had a concussion and a fractured skull. If all that wasn't dire enough, the head injury included a gaping two-inch laceration that had bled a lot, which was good, naturally cleansing the deep cut. Coleman felt he should suture the wound as soon as he could, but he didn't know what to use. He would have to address that issue in the light of the morning.

Both Coleman and Idop arose early the next day and examined the prince, who was breathing heavily. "His head wound is still open. I need to suture it closed. I must use a needle and some very thin but strong string," Coleman told Idop.

"Zoo-t´er?" Idop asked.

"I will sew it up," Coleman explained.

"Men! Does anyone have a needle and string?" the megatus called to the soldiers nearby.

One warrior rummaged through his pack, and then he dashed to his commander. "Here, sire, take mine."

Idop handed them to Coleman. He examined the bone needle, and it looked good enough, even though it was larger than he would have preferred; however, the string wouldn't do at all. It was too thick and loosely twined, which could lead to infection. He thought for a while, as he rolled the needle between his finger and thumb. He then looked in the direction of a samaran and came up with an idea.

"Samarans have long tails, right?" he asked Idop.

"Yes. Why do you ask?"

"I will need several long hairs from a samaran's tail. I also need to boil some water."

The megatus issued orders, and the soldiers quickly complied. While the water heated, Coleman washed his hands as well as he could. He first rubbed them with wet sand and removed as much dirt and grit from under his fingernails as he could. He then shaved the hair around the prince's wound using an arrowhead, and then he cleaned the wound with warm water. He threaded the needle with a samaran hair and dipped them into the boiling water. A few of the observers said he was performing a priestly ritual. He simply ignored them. After all his preparations were done, he began suturing the wound. All the others watched him intently. He told them about germs and the importance of sterilizing things, but it was obvious they didn't comprehend a thing he was saying.

After a few minutes, he was finished, and Idop examined his work. "Yes, I've seen this done with other great wounds.

Most of the time, it didn't make any difference. The cut would turn into a mass of green scourge, and the man would eventually cross-over."

"I have done all I can to avoid that. We will have to wait and see," Coleman announced to everyone. He then used the heated water to shave, much to the astonishment of Idop and his men.

They spent the day watching over the prince, as he drifted in and out of consciousness. By the morning of the next day, the laceration looked much better. It was surprising to Coleman that the prince's wound was healing so quickly. The prince hadn't come down with a fever, either, and that was another good indication he was healing. On the third day, the prince regained consciousness, drank some water, and ate a few bites of food. He carried on a coherent conversation with Idop for a couple of minutes before falling back to sleep.

"I think it's time we take him back to the palace," Idop said. "Tondo, do you agree?"

"He certainly cannot walk or ride, but a cart will do. We will need to cushion the bed of the cart with green branches. I do not want him to be bumped and shaken too much," Coleman advised.

For the next hour or so, they prepared. Lulubelle and her cart were drafted by the megatus. Coleman made sure his possessions and collections remained, but everything else was dumped on the ground. Titus and his men dared not object. After noticing their dismay, Coleman persuaded Idop to loan them a couple of pack samarans.

By midmorning, they were on the road and marching to the Ancient City. Coleman had learned from Titus that they were now under the Blessing of the City, the gift of longevity. That started when they had stepped foot onto the Magheedo Plain. Coleman didn't feel any different, but according to Titus, they were aging much slower now.

"The full effect of the Blessing only comes to those living nearest the Ancient City," Titus reminded him. That was all good and well, Coleman thought, but his biggest concern at present was getting the prince there alive.

By the end of the second day of travel, they had reached the Teg-ar-mos Wall. It was a stone barrier more than thirty feet high and ten feet thick. Coleman could see watchtowers fifty feet high at regular intervals in both directions for as far as he could see. He was told, the wall ran from the east side of the peninsula to the west side. King Teg-ar-mos had it constructed over one-hundred spans ago as the first line of defense for the Ancient City.

The Prince's Contingent passed through massive wooden

gates that were nearly as high as the two towers flanking them, and the party established their camp on the south side of the wall. Later that day, a caravan also passed through the gates and set up camp not too far away. It consisted of three thrice-drawn wagons. The caravan master invited the soldiers to join them after the p´atezas set and partake in entertainment and singing. Coleman, Idop, Titus, and two guards from the Prince's Contingent remained with the prince. The other soldiers and Ayascho joined the festivities. From a distance, Coleman thought it looked and sounded like a gypsy camp.

It wasn't long before Ayascho returned looking dejected. "Money; they say I must have money. I told them I didn't know what that was. They asked me if I had anything to trade. I told them I wanted to keep the things I have. They made me leave, and the soldiers laughed. Tondo, what is money?" Ayascho asked.

Coleman and the others explained commerce to the young Batru. It was really his first brush with it since Myron's visit to his village. He soon gained a basic understanding of what it was all about, but he had no idea what things were worth, and for that matter, neither did Coleman. However, during the explanation led by Idop, Coleman learned that the realm had three basic coins: regums, bhats, and arjents. Regums were made of zanth, which he knew was gold, and much larger than a silver dollar from his homeland. It was the coin Myron had shown him at the Batru village. Only the very rich used them and sparingly. Bhats were common coins used by the gentry and were made of zin, which he had learned was silver. They were nearly an inch in diameter. Idop told him that one-hundred bhats equaled a regum. Arjents were common coins used by the lower classes and were made of something called eez. Idop showed him one.

It was smaller than a bhat and appeared to be copper. He learned that one-hundred arjents equaled one bhat.

Coleman also learned that barter was a common practice in the realm. Farmers traded their wares for other goods and services. Animals were also bartered in the same manner. Idop told him that sometimes slaves were bartered, but that was unusual because of the high prices placed on slaves. Coleman shuddered at the thought of entering a culture in which people were treated as property. He took a deep breath and exhaled sadly.

Over the next several days, the prince's condition improved markedly. The laceration was nearly healed, much faster than anticipated. There was no infection, nor pneumonia. Idop mentioned several times what a great healer Tondo was. The prince was now conscious most of the day, but his head ached, and his vision was blurred. He tried to stand but said he felt dizzy, so he was encouraged to remain prone.

In all this time, Coleman's furry wrap had kept the prince warm and comfortable. Suspicion crept into Tondo's thoughts. "Is it possible Taahso's cloak could have anything to do with his fast recovery?" he wondered aloud in godspeak.

"Tondo, what did you say? I heard you say something about Taahso," Ayascho said as they walked along the road adjacent to the prince's cart.

"I was just wondering if Taahso's . . . " he suddenly

stopped in mid-sentence, and then decided not to continue his thought.

"You're wondering if Taahso's cover has something to do with the man's healing, aren't you? I have been thinking the same thing," Ayascho admitted.

"We really cannot be sure, so it would be wise if we keep this to ourselves," Coleman advised.

"Okay, Tondo," Ayascho told him.

Coleman was amazed that Ayascho had used the godspeak word okay. No one else ever had, mainly because it was a word only Tondo could pronounce properly. He used the term often, usually in an absentminded manner. Ayascho had heard it hundreds of times by now. "I think you are beginning to sound like me; okay," he said to the young man with a smile.

"Okay, Tondo, if you say so."

A couple of days before they were to arrive at the Ancient City, Lulubelle became belligerent, bellowing her angst. She refused to be harnessed to the cart and started rooting around the area. "I was afraid of this," Pontus told everyone. "The thrice's time has come. It must lay its eggs before going on. One of the caravan males must have caught her the other night," he snickered.

They let Lulubelle alone for the rest of the morning. She found a secluded spot near a small stream and dug a nest using her beak and forefeet. She laid twelve gray, oblong eggs. Each was about eight inches long and had a leathery shell. She then covered the nest with dirt and meandered back to camp.

"The thrice is ready now," Pontus said. "We can move on."

Coleman was intrigued. "Megatus Idop, do you or any of your men have a large box I could use? I will need to fill it with dirt."

"What are you planning to do with it?" Idop asked.

"I am going to collect those thrice eggs and bring them with us. Your brother raises samarans. I think I will raise thrice."

Idop had the soldiers remove a medium-sized trunk from one of the pack animals. Idop removed his personal items and placed them in a leather bag. Shortly thereafter, with the help of Ayascho and a few soldiers, the trunk, now full of dirt and eggs, was placed in the cart next to the rest of Coleman's gear. The prince objected because it cramped him even more, but Coleman ignored his complaints. He smiled to himself, "If the prince is complaining, that is a good sign," he mumbled in godspeak.

About midmorning of the next day, as the Prince's Contingent continued toward the city, a large group of men riding regal samarans approached them. Coleman could tell by the banners they carried and their ornate ware; this was royalty. A burly man approached Idop. He wore finely crafted metal armor, inlaid with gold. His head was protected by a shiny helmet with a gold top spike dripping with red streamers and emblazoned with a golden crest. Coleman knew in an instant; this was the king.

"Where is my son?" he demanded of Idop, who bowed his head low and then pointed to the cart. The king jumped from his mount and rushed to the prince. "My son, my son, speak to me," the king pleaded.

"Father! Have we arrived?" the prince asked groggily.

"I couldn't wait to see you, so I rode out this morning to find you. I had to see for myself that you still lived. The report from the messenger Megatus Idop sent said you had been severely wounded by brigands. How are you?"

"I feel dizzy, and things still look blurry, but I'm getting stronger every day. Megatus Idop and Tondo have been taking good care of me."

Idop approached the king and bowed again. "Your Highness, forgive me," he begged.

"We will see if you are worthy of forgiveness. For now, I will spend time with my son. Leave us!" the king angrily ordered.

Idop retreated and told everyone to move away from the cart, giving the king and the prince their privacy. For nearly an hour, the two men conversed. Coleman was afraid the king would tire his son, but when he voiced his concerns to Idop, he was warned to keep quiet, so he did. Finally, the king gave the prince a hug, marched to his samaran, and mounted. He then reigned the beast over to Idop and stopped, staring down at him. "Where is Megato Oetan?" the king asked gruffly.

"He was killed by brigands, Your Highness," Idop told him.

"Just as well," the king growled. "I am greatly disappointed in you, megatus. This was meant to be a training exercise for my son, and through your incompetence, it became a disaster. You and the Prince's Contingent will report to me the morning after you arrive in the city," he ordered. The king turned his attention to the tall outlander standing near Idop. He gave Coleman a long, hard look, then he kicked his heels into his samaran's sides and galloped off in the direction of the city, his entourage in tow.

Coleman didn't like what he had just heard. Idop was in big trouble, but Coleman wasn't about to make things worse by asking him a bunch of probing questions. A pall of despair fell upon the entire contingent. Even Titus and his men seemed depressed, and yet, they were not accountable for the prince's condition in any way.

CHAPTER 11

STANDING BEFORE THE KING

At midmorning of the day following the king's visit, Titus's party could see the city wall in the distance. It was much higher than the Teg-ar-mos Wall, nearly twice as high, with a few tall sandstone-like buildings rising up from behind it. The wall stretched around the city for miles. The sand-colored stone blocks were large and well-formed. They had been fit together with great craftsmanship. Coleman's gaze was so fixed on the magnificent bulwark; he was oblivious to anything else. Ayascho poked him in the ribs and pointed to a ghastly scene on the side of the road only a few yards away. A dead man was hanging by his wrists from the top of a thirty-foot-high pole, and there was a severed head mounted on a pike near the pole's base. Scavenger birds were picking at the flesh and eyes of the man on the pole. The severed head was also partially devoured, a carrion bird standing atop it. Ayascho dashed to the opposite side of the road and retched.

"What is this?" Coleman asked Titus.

"This is the punishment for helping an escaped slave. The head is from a citizen traitor. The man on the pole is an escaped slave. That is the punishment I told you about: torment."

Coleman had seen some awful sights during his many combat deployments, but this scene rated as one of the most despicable things he'd ever seen. It was barbaric beyond measure. He thought he had steeled himself for something like this, but the actual horror was more shocking than he expected.

Scores of people congregated near the huge open gates leading into the city. As Coleman's group approached, a path was cleared as people stepped aside to let the military unit pass. Men, women, and children dressed in robes of differing colors stared as the soldiers marched past them. A few onlookers pointed fingers at the tall, hairy man near the cart. Coleman quickly realized they were pointing at him.

When he passed through the gates, he gazed upon a display of commerce he had not seen before on his new world. Two main lanes wended their way into the bowels of the city, one to his left and another to his right, each flanked by booths and stalls full of foods and wares. Odd-looking animals in wooden cages chirped and growled as potential buyers examined them. Two-story and three-story sandstone-like buildings rose above the clamor of the marketplace. The hustle and bustle of shouted bartering assailed his ears.

Coleman's moment of awe was quickly interrupted by the approach of an official-looking party of men dressed in red robes, walking in front of a regal-looking carriage pulled by two magnificent samarans. The men and carriage stopped, and one of the robed men approached.

"Megatus Idop, I relieve you of your charge. I now assume responsibility for the prince," he said in a commanding voice.

"I am relieved," Idop uttered quietly.

"Remember, you and the Prince's Contingent have been

summoned by the king. You will report to the palace in the morning."

"Yes, of course, Counselor Mordez," Idop said dejectedly.

The robed man turned to Titus. "Sestardi Titus, it is good to see you again. We thought you had perished in the Wilderness. The king wishes your presence in the morning, as well. Bring the Tondo and his slave with you," he said as he took the measure of Coleman with his eyes. The red-robed man then strode to the cart and spoke quietly with the prince for a while. He then assisted the royal into the carriage, and it disappeared down one of the city streets with the other red-robed men trotting behind it.

Idop, Titus, and the soldiers marched to a large stone building abutting the inner wall. It had the appearance of a barracks. Coleman and Ayascho silently followed. They entered the large bay room containing about fifty bunks. Idop assigned Coleman and Ayascho a small room adjacent to the main bay. The men began unloading Lulubelle's cart and storing their gear in the billet. When the cart was empty, Pontus took her to the stables. By Coleman's count, it had taken them one-hundred and ninety-six days, nearly half a span, to travel from Ayascho's village to the Ancient City.

Coleman and Ayascho joined the soldiers' mess at dusk. Large pots of beans and meat were cooking in the two walk-in fireplaces at either end of the building. On side-tables were placed several small loaves of bread and flasks of oil. The men sat at long tables with benches while they ate their meals. The conversation was much like all the meals Coleman had shared with other soldiers: stories of women, stories of drinking, more stories of women, and much bluster, sprinkled liberally with unfamiliar words that Coleman assumed were profanities. Ayascho acted awkward and self-conscious. He was not accustomed to such crudeness, and it assaulted his innocence.

Many of the men began touting their many conflicts, usually versus brigands, obviously in an effort to impress the odd-looking newcomers. Not surprising to Coleman, he was asked to relate some of his battles, as they chuckled at their perceived insult to the hairy Wilderness savage. Much to their surprise, Coleman spun a mighty tale of a mission he was involved in during the Venezuelan Campaign. It had been a close quarter's battle with pistol, grenade, and military tomahawk. He related his story in terms these men could understand; firearms became swords; bayonets became daggers; grenades became exploding rocks. Most of the soldiers followed his narrative with bated breath. The more seasoned veterans were not so easily convinced about the veracity of what he was telling them. One of them finally asked, "Exploding rocks? So, after this great battle of yours in that distant place, how long did it take you and your men to walk out of that wilderness?"

"We did not walk out. We flew out on giant gravetum birds," Coleman told them with a huge, hairy grin. There was a moment of silence, and then the entire room erupted in roaring laughter.

"Gravetum birds? Exploding rocks! You got us good, Tondo. But that was a great story, anyway," they kept repeating.

Soon after Coleman completed his tale, two duty guardsmen entered the barracks and escorted Pontus, Rao, and two men from the Prince's Contingent to the king's palace. Later that night, Coleman and Ayascho returned to their room. Ayascho made his bed on the hard dirt floor because the rope and straw bunk was too uncomfortable for his liking. Just as Coleman was drifting off to sleep, he heard the young man say, "Tondo, I believe you flew out of that wilderness. Someday, you must tell me how."

Early the next morning, Coleman awoke, shaved, and put on the fine clothes Atura had made for him so long ago. He pulled his long hair into a ponytail and tied it with a strip of leather. He awakened Ayascho, and they went to the mess hall for a bite of food. A few soldiers were already milling around, and they gaped in wonder at the now clean-shaven savage. Some of the guards were the cooks for the day, and they needed an early start. Coleman found two wooden bowls and scooped servings of pottage for Ayascho and himself. There were no utensils, so they used their fingers. The pottage was a thick broth, laced with vegetables, beans, and a smattering of meat. It was very tasty, Coleman thought. Other soldiers were beginning to join them. The day guards quickly left for their posts, and the night guards arrived shortly after Coleman and Ayascho finished eating, all marveling at Coleman's now hairless face.

Megatus Idop soon arrived and escorted Coleman and Ayascho back to their room. "We will be leaving for the palace soon. You will be allowed to bring one short sword or one dagger with you into the Throne Room. You will address the king as *Your Highness*. While you are there, do not speak unless spoken to. Is that understood?" Idop asked.

"Yes, it sounds simple enough," Coleman replied. Ayascho nodded. Coleman placed his sword in his back harness, as usual. Ayascho wore his Caver's knife at his waist.

"Good. You should know, last night, the king's counselors questioned some of the sestardi's men. They also interrogated a couple of my men from the Prince's Contingent. If the king asks you any questions, always answer truthfully, and make your response as short as possible." Coleman could tell Idop was nervous.

"What is the king going to do?" Coleman asked.

"I don't know. He will surely reward you for restoring his son's life. As for me . . . oy, that's another story. More than one-hundred and ten spans have I faithfully served the House of Teg-ar-mos, and now it comes to this." He was a man in despair but not for his life; it was his honor that was at stake. Coleman could relate, having suffered a similar fate some years ago on a different world.

"I will put in a good word for you if I can," Coleman promised.

"Megatus, the time has come," Sestardi Titus said from the open doorway.

The troop formed up outside of the barracks. Idop's men formed one column, and the sestardi's men formed another. They marched in unison down the city roads with Coleman and Ayascho following close behind. It took them over a quarter-hour to reach the palace. Coleman was beginning to realize just how large the Ancient City really was.

The troop marched up the few palace stairs and reported to two men in red robes standing in front of two huge wooden doors. The robed men eyed each soldier and allowed them to pass through the doorway. When Coleman and Ayascho reached them, one of the red-robed men spanned his arms, blocking their path. They were closely examined for additional weapons. When the robed man was satisfied they had only what could be seen, they too, were allowed to pass.

They entered a large room with benches against the walls. Several people were already there, waiting for their turn to proceed. All eyes turned to Coleman's group, and he could hear whispered comments. His party continued on. They marched down a wide hallway to another waiting room, and there they stopped, staring at another pair of huge wooden doors. All of the soldiers stood at attention, not uttering a word, waiting for the king's summons.

About ten minutes passed before the doors swung open, although it seemed much longer to Coleman. The men marched into the Throne Room and stopped thirty feet from the throne. The palace was constructed of the same stone that the city walls were made from; probably sandstone or something like it, Coleman guessed. The room was over one-hundred feet long and about fifty feet wide. He looked up at a ceiling thirty feet above, supported by rows of bare columns. Colorful scenes depicting battles and hunts of strange-looking animals were painted on the walls. The king sat on a lavish and ornate throne resting on a platform, which was eight to ten feet above the floor. A stairway covered by a scarlet runner trimmed with gold bands ascended to the foot of the throne. Ten guards holding metrens stood at attention near the stairs. King Teg-ar-mos sat upon the throne dressed in an exquisite royal-purple robe, trimmed with gold. He wore a golden crown and glared at the soldiers from his perch.

In a loud voice for all to hear, the king proclaimed, "Oetan is dead, and just as well! He failed in his duties, and the prince was nearly killed. Therefore, We declare Oetan disgraced; his holdings are forfeit. He is stripped of title and stewardship. Let the scribes record it; let the heralds proclaim it."

The king nodded, and in a commanding voice that echoed through the room, a counselor shouted, "Megatus Idop, present yourself before the king!"

From a dark, shadowy place at the right side of the stairs, an odd-looking man stirred. "In the balance weighed; now, a price to be paid," the little man uttered in a whiny voice. Idop marched forward with all the self-confidence he could muster. He stopped five feet from the stairs, bowed his head, and waited.

"You are stripped of your title!" the king growled in an angry tone. Idop looked up in shock, and then he slowly sunk to his knees and bowed his head low. "The prince lives, and so shall you," the king grumbled in a deep and menacing voice. "However, your lapse of good judgment nearly cost Our son his life. We have taken into account the service you have rendered to this Throne over many spans. Therefore, We have decided simply to dismiss you from the Pannera and take one knuckle." Idop did not move. He remained kneeling, looking at the floor. "You may speak," the king told him

Idop looked up and sadly stated, "Take my life, Your Highness. It is no longer of value to me." He was almost begging.

"We have another assignment for you. We will get to that matter later," the king told him. "Braydo, proceed with the punishment."

From behind the stairs, a mountain of a man emerged. He stood more than six and a half feet tall and had a very muscular build. He was dressed in a white tunic, secured at the waist by a wide, black leather belt. He wore dark hide arm guards that covered the back of his hands and extended more than halfway up his muscular forearms. He pulled a large, shiny dagger from a scabbard at his waist while making an arm gesture. Two guards lifted a heavy wooden square table and placed it in front of the kneeling Idop. "Stand, Idop, and receive your punishment," Braydo ordered.

"Stretch forth a finger; then let it linger," the obnoxious little man squealed.

Idop stood, placed his left hand on the table, and spread his fingers wide. Braydo quickly dropped the knife downward in a well-practiced motion, severing the first knuckle of Idop's little finger. He was staring into Braydo's eyes the entire time and flinched only slightly.

"Sliced in twain; and now, the pain," the little man squeaked.

Braydo picked up the severed joint, leaned forward, and stuffed it down the neck of Idop's tunic. He peered into Idop's eyes as an evil and wicked grin crossed his lips. Coleman had seen men like Braydo before. They could be found in every race and culture he'd ever met. They were the ones who pleasured in dispensing pain and suffering. A burning anger radiated from Coleman's center. Ayascho shuffled a few steps away from Coleman's side and nervously stared at him.

Braydo wiped the blood from his blade on Idop's tunic, and then he stepped back, returning the knife to its scabbard. After another arm gesture, the table was removed. Idop stood motionless; however, the pain of his ordeal was clearly etched on his face. Blood dripped from the wound and pooled at his feet. "You may return to your place," the king finally said. "The men from the Prince's Contingent, come forward." The eight survivors of the brigand's attack approached the throne and kneeled in unison just short of Idop's pool of blood.

"Here comes the eight; what is their fate?" the little man continued with his annoying rhymes.

"You have failed in your duties. You allowed the prince to be attacked and severely wounded. We will not tolerate such gross incompetence. You are removed from the Prince's Contingent and reassigned to the Royal Stables. You will take the place of the cleaning slaves until We think you have paid for your failings. In addition, you will each receive ten stripes. Guards, take these men to their punishment."

"Under the scourge; their failings to purge."

That little toady is beginning to get on my nerves, Coleman silently groused.

The king sat back on the throne and paused in thought for a few seconds. "Ha, Sestardi Titus, come forth with your men." The detachment marched forward, formed a line, and kneeled in unison.

"On your knees; did you please?" the little man continued his annoying prose.

"Very impressive, sestardi. How many did We send into the Wilderness?"

"A detachment of eleven men and one sestardi, Your Highness," Titus responded.

"Where are the others?" the king asked.

"They crossed-over in the Wilderness. We faced many perils, Your Highness."

"We imagine you did, sestardi. Is this the Tondo We commanded you to bring to Us?" the king asked as he pointed to Coleman with his scepter.

"Yes, Your Highness, he is."

"Ha, you have fulfilled your assignment. We congratulate you and your men for a job well done. We promote you to sestardus and assign you and your men to the Prince's Contingent. We expect you to be more reliable than the others."

"Yes, Your Highness," Titus gratefully replied.

"You and your men will also receive double salaries for one span. We reward those who please Us. And, as you have seen, We punish those who fail in their duties."

"Yes, Your Highness. We will serve you with honor."

"Your men are dismissed. We want you to remain."

"A higher employ; they will now enjoy," the rhymer continued.

The men marched out of the Throne Room, their heads held high. Titus moved to Idop's side, avoiding the blood still slowly dripping from Idop's wound.

"Ha, We have been waiting to meet the Tondo ever since the priests told Us about you, although We had doubts We ever would. Step forward, man from the Wilderness."

"A tall savage; a long passage," the rhymer tuned.

What an annoying little man, Coleman thought. He moved to a place just short of Idop's original blood pool and bowed.

"You will kneel before the king!" shouted Braydo. Two guards rushed at Coleman, grabbing him from behind and attempting to force him to the floor. He had never kneeled to anyone, and he wasn't about to start now. Anger filled his soul as he struggled with the guards. Suddenly, a wave of energy blasted from the center of his chest, pushing the guards back and knocking them to the floor. A visible wave dissipated as it continued through the air. It seemed to move in slow motion, and when it reached the king, it gently ruffled his hair. Braydo charged Coleman and swung his right arm at him. Coleman partially blocked the blow, but the stiff hide from the giant man's arm guard struck his head with a glancing jolt. For an instant, Coleman saw stars, but his Ranger-trained reflexes allowed him to instinctively recover quickly enough to take advantage of the big man's mistake. The strike had left Braydo off-balance, allowing Coleman to throw his hip and leg into the big man's forward motion. He flipped Braydo in mid-air and dropped him onto his back like a rock to the hard, stone floor. Coleman dropped a knee into the prone man's solar plexus, knocking the air out of him and rendering him helpless. He quickly reached over his shoulder and unsheathed his sword, placing it at Braydo's neck, causing a trickle of blood to ooze over the blade. The other guards were stunned by how quickly all this transpired; however, they soon reacted, and they charged Coleman with their metrens raised, preparing to strike killing blows.

The king stood and shouted, "Stop!"

Immediately, the guards halted. The king looked down at the tall savage. Coleman feared he had really blown his chance to impress the king, but he was not about to kneel. Braydo lay on the floor, his arms and legs flailing as he tried to regain his breath. Coleman lifted his blade to see it had left a red line of blood across the big man's neck.

"You won't send him to the other-side? Why not?" the king finally asked.

"I see no need to kill this man, Your Highness." Coleman wiped the blood from his blade on Braydo's tunic just as the big man had done to Idop. Coleman stood, sheathed his sword over his shoulder, and bowed.

"He certainly desires to kill you now. What will you do if he tries?" the king wondered.

Coleman ended his bow and looked up. "I will stop him with as much force as is necessary, no more, no less."

The king walked down the royal stairs and stood in front of Coleman while standing on the last step. "You act like royalty. Are you?"

"No, Your Highness."

The king's dark-brown eyes bore into Coleman's soul. He thought he could actually feel the king's probing stare. The

king walked around Coleman as he examined him from head
to foot. "We detect in you something We seldom see in others. You are an independent spirit, beholding to no one. You
choose your own path and refuse to be dictated to. You are
an ultimate free spirit, very unusual. Are you a danger to Our
kingdom?"

"I have no desire to be a danger to anyone, but I will defend myself," was Coleman's earnest reply.

"Will you defend Our kingdom?" the king asked.

"Okay, why not?" Coleman responded flippantly and with
a shrug of his shoulders.

"The Sutro Seer told Us you were a peculiar one, and now
that We have taken your measure, We agree." The king moved
closer to the outlander and placed his right hand on Coleman's
left shoulder. In a loud voice for all to hear, the king proclaimed,
"For returning the prince from the other-side, We grant the
Tondo citizenship, and advance him to the rank of tetzae. He
will be known throughout the realm as Sire Tondo. He kneels to
no one; a bow will suffice. Let the scribes record it; let the heralds proclaim it." Coleman bowed a respectful bow, and the king
nodded his head in recognition. The king then looked in Ayascho's direction. "You, come here," the king commanded. Ayascho looked left and then right. "Yes, you," the king said. The
young Batru hunter quickly stepped to Coleman's right side and
dropped to his knees. Coleman frowned. "You may stand, my
boy," the king told him. The king then examined Ayascho with
the same scrutiny he had Coleman. "We have heard about the
savages of the Wilderness, but this is the first one We have ever
seen. Is he your slave?" the king asked Coleman.

"I am not a slave!" Ayascho shouted in anger. The guards stiffened and readied their metrens. The king calmed them with a wave of his hand.

"We detect in you a mystery. You love the Tondo, yet you hate him. Very curious." The king then faced Coleman. "We've been told you have done some amazing things. You commanded the gods to return Our son after he had crossed-over, and by your command, he was. We've also been told you have power over fire. Show Us."

Coleman paused, then looked around and noticed a scribe sitting at his table. "Excuse me, Your Highness." He walked over to the scribe's table. "Do you have a blank sheet?" he asked the man in the red robe. He was handed a large sheet of the material the scribe was writing on. It looked and felt like paper, but it was light tan in color with many chip-like imperfections. He tore it in half and began folding it into a paper airplane. The scribe stared in puzzlement as it took shape. When he was done, he returned to the king.

"Watch this," he told the king with a wink and a smile. He tossed the paper airplane, and it glided through the air. When it was about fifteen feet away, he pointed and snapped his fingers. The airplane burst into flame, disappearing in a cloud of smoke.

"The king's desire; a master of fire!" the toady rhymer uttered in amazement.

"Then it is true; you can command fire! And what was that thing you made that rode on the air?"

"It is called paper airplane," Coleman told him, using words from his native tongue.

"Is that godspeak?"

"It has been called that, Your Highness."

"Say more godspeak for Us."

Coleman took a deep breath and collected his thoughts before responding, "Four score and seven years ago our fathers brought forth on this continent, a new nation, conceived in Liberty, and dedicated to the proposition that all men are created equal."

The king leaned back and scratched his head. "We have never heard such words before if they can truly be called words. You must tell Us what it means; however, that must wait until later. Now, We have other things to do."

The king returned to his perch. By this time, Braydo had regained his breath, so Coleman offered him an arm to help him off the floor. Braydo slapped it away, stood up, and limped to his station behind the throne's stairs.

In a loud voice, the king proclaimed, "Sire Tondo has performed a great service for the kingdom. He contended with the gods, and he brought the prince back from the other-side. We will honor him with a feast this evening." The king stood and continued, "Sire Tondo is given stewardship over the estate once held by the disgraced Oetan. Let the scribes record it; let the heralds proclaim it."

"He cannot wait; for his grand estate," the rhymer intoned.

"Idop!" the king bellowed.

Idop rushed to Coleman's left side and kneeled before the king. "Yes, Your Highness."

"You may stand. Your long service to this Throne has not been forgotten. We assign you to the position of king's counselor. You are to advise the Tondo in his affairs and report to this Court regularly concerning his welfare."

"Thank you, Your Highness. You are most generous."

"At first, disgraced; again, emplaced," the rhymer spouted.

"Sestardus Titus," the king called.

Titus quickly went to Idop's side and kneeled. "Yes, Your Highness."

"You may stand. We have been told the Tondo favors the thrice you used during your journey. We present it to him as a gift. See that it is done."

"Yes, Your Highness. By your command."

"Given a thrice; without a price," the bothersome little lackey pronounced.

"Our business is concluded. All of you are dismissed," the king declared.

"Out the door with you four; out the door with you four," the rhymer sang in his scratchy voice. The four men marched through the door and into the waiting chamber. Idop grabbed his still bleeding finger and held it tight, an expression of pain etching his face.

"Let me see it," Coleman said to him. He examined the wound. "It needs to be treated before it becomes infected." Coleman rubbed his palms together until they glowed red, and then he enclosed Idop's fingers with both hands.

An expression of shock crossed Idop's face. "The pain is gone!" he shouted. "Is there no end to your powers?"

"You still need to get this cleaned and bandaged," Coleman instructed. "Who was that annoying little man sitting in the shadows?"

"That's the Rhyming Baron," Idop told him. "He's a cousin of the king and was made a king's counselor."

"What else does he do?"

"That's what he does. He humors the king, so he keeps him in the Throne Room."

"I'd like to bounce a rock off his head," Ayascho grumbled. A guard turned to Ayascho and approached him, an angry glare covering his face.

Idop quickly intervened. "He's an outlander. I will instruct him," Idop told the guard.

"I would have this savage punished for his insolence, but since you, megatus, defend him, I will forget what I heard this time. I know you will keep your word and teach this idiot. I do not suffer fools on my watch," the guard warned.

"Thank you, sestardi," Idop told the man. Then he turned to Ayascho, "The Rhymer is royalty. You cannot threaten a rezus, even in jest," Idop warned as he grabbed Ayascho and pushed him down the hallway. All four men quickly exited the palace under the watchful and stern glares of the guards.

CHAPTER 12

ANOTHER APPALLING REALITY

The men strolled back to the barracks, each silently reviewing in their minds what had happened during their exchanges with the king. When they arrived at the barracks, they found many of the Pannera in formation witnessing the punishment given to the dismissed members of the Prince's Contingent. The last of the eight was tied to a post and was being scourged. A non-officer called each stroke as it fell, "Eight . . . Nine . . . Ten!"

The soldiers were then dismissed to their duty stations. Whether they were on duty or not, all disappeared quickly. The scourged and bloody man was cut loose, and a couple of his friends helped him into the barracks. The mess hall had been turned into a makeshift aid station, with the eight men sprawled face down on tables; friends were attending to their wounds. Coleman felt these men had been treated unjustly. It was obvious they had put up a good fight. More than half of their number had been killed, including their leader. He decided to do what he could. He walked from man to man, placing a hand on each one's shoulder as he passed. A look of astonishment crossed each man's face as Coleman touched him, but not a word was uttered. After he had touched the last one, he walked to his room and collapsed on the bed, exhausted.

Ayascho entered a few minutes later with a bowl of leftover pottage and a small loaf of bitter bread. Coleman took them, dipped the bread into the pottage, and began eating.

"Oy! It gets better the longer it cooks," he said.

Idop soon entered and sat on the bunk across from Coleman. His injured finger was wrapped in a soiled cloth. Coleman cringed but said nothing. "Tondo, if we take the thrice, it will require ten days to reach the estate," he advised.

"Tell me about that place," Coleman said.

"It's one of the finest holdings on the peninsula. It has a grand house and many outbuildings. Oetan raised divitz there. He was quite wealthy."

"What is div-eetz?"

"It's a plant that grows a fluffy white fiber we use to make cloth."

"It sounds like the same plant that grows in my homeland. There, it is called cotton. So, Oetan made a lot of money growing divitz? Hmm . . . by the way, what gives the king the right to take away a man's property?"

"He's the king. All land in the kingdom belongs to him. He can do what he wants with it."

"He owns everything? That is ridiculous. Has anyone ever stood up to him, told him no, you cannot do that?"

"Let me think," Idop rubbed his head. "I recall an incident some fifty spans ago. One of the rich landholders offended the king—I don't remember how—so the king reclaimed half of the offender's holding. The man objected, and he started meeting with other landholders bent on sedition. He caused quite a stir, at least until word reached the king. It wasn't long after that when the Pannera fell upon him, and he was taken to the city. He was never seen nor heard from again. His holding was divided and given to the king's friends and family."

"The king acts like a Nazi," Coleman bluntly stated.

"I don't know what that word means, but you shouldn't repeat it. The king has ears everywhere."

"Were you involved?" Coleman asked.

"No, I was megato in command of the young prince's contingent at the time."

Coleman only shook his head; then he sat pondering the implications. The king was right about one thing: he was an individual spirit. Living under the dictatorial rule of a monarch was not to his liking one bit. He wondered if he should simply pack up his belongings and head back to the Batru village. He knew he would find freedom there. But he still had many questions, and the Ancient City probably held the answers.

He finished his pottage and bread; then, he set the empty bowl on the floor. "When do I see the priests? They are the ones who summoned me here."

"They know you've arrived, so you'll see them in a time of their choosing and not before. They are a mysterious bunch, and powerful, too. You will simply have to wait."

"Okay. I must attend the king's feast tonight, and you two are my guests. We will leave for the estate tomorrow morning."

Coleman and his companions reported to the palace at the appointed time. It was dusk when they were ushered into the Dining Hall. Coleman was dressed in his best clothes. Ayascho was still wearing the soiled and worn leathers he'd been wearing throughout the journey. It didn't seem to bother him, though. Idop had exchanged his Pannera tunic for a red robe, which indicated he was now a king's counselor. They were guided to their seats by men with the mark of slavery tattooed on their foreheads. Coleman noticed, only men had been invited to the event. Four long tables, positioned in the form of an unjoined open square, occupied the room. The king sat at the head table, and men in elegant tunics and red robes sat at either side of the king and at the other tables. The prince was sitting at his father's left. Three vacant places were to the left of the prince. Coleman was invited to take his place adjacent to the young royal, Idop next, and then Ayascho.

They were served meat, bread, and vegetables, which Coleman had never seen before. Metal steins full of frothy liquid were also served. Coleman gingerly sniffed the brew, and the odor burned his nostrils. He took a small taste. It was dreadfully bitter. He thought it might be beer, but it had an awful taste. The others, including Ayascho, quaffed it down and seemed to enjoy it. Coleman took another taste. He almost retched. It burned his tongue and left a severe bitter taste in his mouth. He signaled for one of the slaves to bring him water.

"What is this stuff?" he whispered to Idop.

"Tondo, the king has brought out the best for you. Drink up," Idop said as he raised his stein.

"I cannot drink this. It tastes awful."

Idop looked surprised. He grabbed Coleman's stein and took a drink. "This is the best. Look, even Ayascho likes it." Ayascho started drinking a second stein full.

"Ayascho, slow down. This is like the mystical fruit. If you do not, you will regret it in the morning," Coleman warned in a loud whisper. Ayascho paused momentarily, then took another quaff.

Throughout the meal, two nearly naked and sweaty men wrestled in the space in the middle of the tables open square. Occasionally, one or both wrestlers would ram into a table, upsetting steins and scattering plates. Not exactly the dinner entertainment Coleman would have chosen, but be that as it may, all the other men enjoyed it, interrupting their conversations to shout an encouraging word to their favorite.

Finally, one of the wrestlers put his opponent in a vicious arm lock and dislocated the man's limb. The match was over, the victor declared, and a coin purse was tossed to the winner by the king. A few other coin pouches were exchanged as bets were paid off.

As soon as the wrestlers departed, a rousing cheer echoed through the chamber as a troupe of scantily clad women paraded into the room and cavorted around the tables in a provocative dance of sensual gyrations. The men cheered and hooted, some making crude remarks. Coleman sat motionless as the women swooned and dipped, twisted and bent. Each woman carried a slave mark on her forehead. Some of the dancers seemed to revel in the men's lewd attentions, while others, the younger ones, were wide-eyed with fear. He eventually pulled his eyes away from the arousing spectacle and glanced at Ayascho. The young Batru was staring at the dancers through bleary eyes. Before the dance was over, he passed out, his head and chest lying on the table. Two slaves carried him out and deposited him in a side room.

The women continued their gyrations, and when a dancer got too close to a table, an inebriated celebrant would reach out and attempt to grab the girl. One of the men was successful and pulled a woman into his clutches as she shrieked in mock terror, a smile on her face all the time. The man rubbed his cheek against hers, and she giggled. Tondo noticed the man slip what looked like a coin into her hand. She smiled, and he said, "Later," then released her. There was no doubt in Tondo's mind what had just transpired. He then noticed a much younger girl in the clutches of another man. It was obvious she didn't like being manhandled by the brute, and after a short struggle, she escaped his clutches and rejoined the troupe as the spurned man's comrades mockingly laughed.

The women completed their dance and sashayed out of the room to the cheers and whistles of the rowdy men. Tondo followed them with his eyes and watched as the slave master took the coin from the older woman and grabbed the girl who had resisted the lecherous celebrant's advances, forcing her into an alcove. Coleman could hear her cries as she was repeatedly slapped. He rose, ready to intervene, but he was stopped by Idop grabbing his arm. Tondo looked at him angrily. Idop leaned his head in the direction of the king. The king was standing, and almost immediately, the hall fell silent. Tondo took his seat and watched as the slave master came out of the alcove, tightly gripping the girl's upper arm, nearly dragging her along as he moved away. It was another shocking display to Tondo. The impact of the young woman's suffering fell over him like a dark shroud.

Tondo was snapped out of his introspection as the king began to speak. "I have invited you here to honor the Tondo," the king announced in a loud voice that echoed through the hall, no longer using the royal We he had used in the Throne Room. "I remind you, he was fetched from the Wilderness at my command. The timing could not have been more fortuitous. The prince was set upon and grievously wounded in our recent expedition against the brigands. All feared he had crossed-over. Then came the Tondo. He wrestled with the gods and demanded they return my son's spirit. The deities listened to him, and my son lives." He pointed to the prince with an upturned palm, and the hall erupted in applause, everyone standing. A few men even jumped onto the meal boards. The prince repeatedly nodded his head in recognition to each table, appearing a bit embarrassed.

"The Tondo has great powers and is no one to trifle with. He is under my protection and is now tetzae. The priests will want to meet with him when they are ready, so keep that in mind when you deal with him. Let us now honor him with the Victor's Shout!"

The king pulled his sword from its scabbard and held it

high above his head. Everyone in the hall, except Coleman, stood and did the same with either sword or dagger. A low, guttural growl came from each man that increased in volume until the entire hall seemed to quake from the noise. When the volume was hardly bearable, and following the king's lead, a shout exploded from each man's throat as they slammed their weapon, point first, into a table plank. Everyone took their seats, a wall of blades vibrating in front of them.

"The Tondo, show my guests the fire magic you showed me this morning," the king said.

A slave brought a piece of paper to Coleman and placed it on the table in front of him. He took a deep breath and folded it into another paper airplane. When that was done, he stood, tossed it into the air, and watched it loop. When it had reached the apex of its flight, it exploded in a ball of fire and disappeared in a puff of smoke that gently floated to the ceiling. Coleman snapped his fingers and sat. It was so quiet in the room he could hear men breathing.

After a few moments, the king stood again. "The Tondo is the fire-master. He is under my protection. Remember that," the king's voice boomed through the hall. "Now, let us return to the celebration." He waved his arm and sat.

Two more nearly naked and muscular men strode into the room. Coleman could see that these two were slaves, unlike the wrestlers. They each carried a wickedly jagged gravetum dagger nearly a foot long. They marched to the king's table and raised their daggers in the air. One had a nasty scar on his right cheek, and the other had two cauliflower ears and a bulbous nose. Obviously, it had been broken many times.

"Your Highness, we are prepared to die for you," they said in unison.

"To the death!" the king said in a loud voice.

"To the death!" the combatants repeated together. The hall erupted in bedlam as the onlookers made wagers and shouted encouragements to their favorite.

Idop leaned over to Coleman and advised, "I'll take the one with the scar on his cheek. I bet ten bhat."

"I will have nothing to do with this!" Coleman shouted over the rising din. He stood and headed to the room where Ayascho had been deposited. He found him asleep on the floor, an empty bed next to him. Just as he was about to rouse his comrade, the prince stepped into the room.

"Tondo, I must speak with you, but not here," he said, looking over his shoulder.

"What can I do for you, prince? Are you feeling all right?"

"My wounds are almost healed, and I feel stronger; however, there is a nagging vision in my dreams that you must help me with. It poisons my soul. I will visit you at your estate."

"I will do all I can to help you," Coleman assured him.

"Thank you, Tondo. I've wagered fifteen bhat on Scar Face. Who did you bet on?"

Coleman gave the prince an icy glare and then lifted Ayascho. "If the king asks about me, tell him I had to take my sick friend back to the barracks."

"He's busy watching the fight. He bet fifty bhat on Ugly. I think he'll lose," the prince stated confidently.

"Come on, boy, we've got a long way to go," Coleman said, hefting Ayascho, the boy's feet dragging on the floor.

"Where're the girls? Where'd they go?" Ayascho asked in a slurred voice.

The two stumbled towards the barracks. Along the way, Coleman dunked Ayascho's head in a samaran trough, but to no avail. Ayascho was too far gone. When they stumbled into their room, Coleman dropped the young man on his bunk and watched as he immediately began to snore.

"You are such a sorry sight," he grumbled.

Coleman went outside, climbed the wall's inner stairway, and stood atop the parapet. He gazed into the night sky. A crescent Munnoga, the silvery-white moon, was beginning to creep above the western horizon. Munnari and Munnevo, the blue and red moons, were directly overhead, side-by-side crescent moons. He stood watching them, amazed as always by what he saw. The stars sparkled, and occasionally, a meteor streaked across his view. He took a deep breath and tried to purge his mind of the image of two men fighting to the death for the pleasure of others. It was another appalling reality of his new life. He looked at the blue moon and shouted his outrage in godspeak, "Why am I here? What do you want of me?"

Coleman arose early in the morning and went into the mess hall to eat some pottage. He had a short conversation with a couple of the men who had been scourged, and they thanked him for whatever it was he had done for them. Their comrades had covered their wounds liberally with a greasy ointment that was always used on scourged men's wounds, and it had the smell of menthol. He was told that most of the time, the men fully recovered, although they would always carry welts as a reminder of their ordeal.

Idop and Titus soon joined him. Titus said the thrice and cart were waiting in front of the barracks; all they needed to do was load his belongings, and then, they could leave for the estate. With the help of a couple of the recently promoted Sestardus Titus's men, Coleman's possessions were loaded into the cart. He went to the sleeping Ayascho. The young man was still lying on his bed and hadn't moved since he'd been dumped there the night before.

"All right, Sunshine, up and at it!" Coleman's booming voice bounced off the stone walls of the small room. Ayascho moved a little. Coleman grabbed his shoulder and shook him. Ayascho swatted at Coleman's arm and squinted at him through eye slits. "I have no sympathy for you. You made quite a spectacle of yourself last night, and now, you are going to suffer for it."

Ayascho groaned and rubbed his head. "I don't feel so good. I think I'm going to . . . " He leaned over the edge of the bed and vomited onto the dirt floor.

"Now, you can clean up that mess, too," Coleman commanded. He couldn't tolerate the smell, so he went outside for some fresh air. Two counselors met him near the doorway. They bowed to him, and he returned their bows.

"This is for you, sire," one of them said as he handed the outlander a leather tube. "This document gives you stewardship over the former Oetan Estate. It is now officially renamed

The Tondo Estate. Can you read?" the counselor asked.

"I can read godspeak, but not this," he answered, a little embarrassed.

The counselor gave him a bewildered look, then said, "You can be assured everything is in proper order." The other counselor handed him another leather tube, then both counselors bowed, and having completed their assignment, turned and walked away without so much as a fare-thee-well.

Coleman opened the second cylinder and let the rolled parchment slide into his hand. "What is this?" he asked Idop.

The new king's counselor unrolled the scroll and scanned it. After a few long moments, he looked up and said, "I think it's a document of citizenship and rank. The king has granted you the rank of tetzae."

"What does that mean?" Coleman asked.

"There are six ranks in the kingdom. The lowest class is slave, and it really isn't a rank at all because a slave is not a citizen and doesn't hold a rank. Outlanders are not citizens either, but they are considered to be of a higher order than slaves. They are subject to and protected by King's Law, whereas slaves are governed by Slave Law. The first true citizen rank is freed-man. Freed-men were once slaves who have been granted their freedom. They are considered citizens of the lowest order. After freed-man comes commoner. A commoner is a citizen. These men can hold property, and they can be advanced to the next two ranks, tetzae and tetzus, by decree of the king. There are a few hundred tetzae in the kingdom. Tetzae men are mainly landholders, but the king occasionally grants the title to someone who does not hold land—

one who has performed an extraordinary service for the kingdom. The title of tetzae is passed from father to child."

"Can women hold land?" Coleman asked.

Idop laughed. "No, they can carry the tetzae rank, but they are not allowed to be landholders. Only men are capable of such an important duty."

Coleman frowned, then asked, "What happens to a landholder's woman and family if he dies?"

"Usually, the king rules that the man's holdings are passed to his oldest living son. If he doesn't have a son, the holdings are passed to his closest male relative; for example, his brother."

"What happens to the man's woman in that case?" Coleman wondered.

"If the brother accepts the holding, he also assumes responsibility for the care of the woman and daughters."

"And if the man does not have a living male relative?" Coleman knew he was stretching the point.

"I don't think that's ever happened, but if it did, it would be up to the king to make the final ruling."

Coleman didn't like what he was hearing. The women in this culture were considered second-class citizens, only slightly elevated from slavery. "Okay; now, tell me about the tetzus rank."

"The rank of tetzus is a special rank the king grants only to landholders who have greatly pleased him by extraordinary service. Currently, there are only four in the entire kingdom. This rank is never passed on to the next generation, their children becoming tetzae at birth. Also, the tetzus lords of the kingdom are zumars. They can be called upon by a unanimous consensus of the kingdom's adjudicators. They then form the Zuma and choose a new king if the previous king crosses-over. They are expected to follow the advice given to them by the keepers of heraldry. They may also rule on the king's worthiness to rein, if necessary."

"These tetzus seem quite powerful. They could choose one of their own to be the new king," Coleman guessed.

"The king must be royalty, a rezus. The lords are not rezus and cannot rule. Therefore, they are expected to choose fairly, based on the rules of heraldry," Idop explained.

"What rank comes after tetzus?" Coleman asked.

"The royals, the rezus rank. Rezus are close relatives of the king. They can be no more than thrice removed from the king's direct bloodline. The prince, of course, is rezus. There are about two-score rezus men in the kingdom."

"Let me see: freed-man, commoner, tetzae, tetzus, and rezus, that's five. You said there were six ranks. What is the sixth?"

"That's the king's and queen's rank. And there is only one king. The queen crossed-over some thirty spans ago."

"Okay, I should have known. The king is in a class of his own; that figures," Coleman's tone was dripping with sarcasm.

"The rezus also have ranks. The king is the highest, of course. The prince, who is the oldest son, is next; this also includes all princesses, the daughters of the king and queen, and there are none at this time. After that are the dukes, they are the king's and prince's younger brothers. This kingdom has no dukes. After the dukes come the barons, they are close relatives of the king. Don't ask me to explain the line of succession; it's too complicated for me to understand. But I can tell you this: only men can rule."

"Why am I not surprised by that?" Coleman said wryly. He scanned one of the scrolls. "Why are these documents, and also the one that summoned me here, written on this material and not paper?" Coleman asked.

"Paper is something new. It has been in use for only fifty spans, and the Court does not trust its longevity. We have used parchment for hundreds of spans; its strengths and weaknesses are well known. All important official documents are written on parchment," Idop instructed.

Just then, Ayascho stumbled out of the barracks. "Did you clean up your mess?" Coleman asked in an annoyed voice.

"Yes, Tondo. I'm so sick I don't think I can walk."

"You worthless creeper. Get in the cart, and you better not get sick on any of my things," Coleman sternly warned.

Titus approached him and extended his arm. Coleman was expecting to shake hands, but Titus grabbed his forearm, so after a momentary pause, Coleman grasped his, as well.

"I want to thank you for all you have done for me and my men, Tondo. Thank you for saving our lives. We're in your debt. I hope to see you again soon."

"And I, you," Coleman replied with a smile.

Coleman took Lulubelle by the ear, the way he had seen Pontus do, and led her through the city gates. He paused, looking perplexed. Turning to Idop, he asked, "Which way do we go?"

"That way," Idop was pointing towards the east. They left the road and went cross-country. The cart bounced over the rough terrain while Ayascho groaned and moaned inside it.

CHAPTER 13

GUESTS OF THE ESTATE

Coleman set a leisurely pace while he and Idop chatted. Idop told him that Oetan has a bondmate—a wife—and a young daughter. Since the estate was somewhat isolated, they probably hadn't received word of his death yet. The heralds usually started making their announcements in the northern regions, at the many towns and villages on the Magheedo Plain, and then they worked their way south. It could take up to forty days to cover the entire kingdom. Since Idop expected they would reach the estate before the heralds did, it would be up to them to share the tragic news of Oetan's death and disgrace, as well as his bondmate's and daughter's displacement. To make matters worse, Lady Oetan was no longer considered of tetzae rank, either. Because Oetan was held in contempt by the king, having had his holdings and title stripped, his bondmate, who gained the title via their bond, suffered the same fate. Oetan's daughter, on the other hand, still retained her tetzae rank by birth.

Idop continued to explain how Lady Oetan had hosted some of the grandest and most exciting social galas in the entire kingdom. They were held on a regular basis, once every three spans at the Oetan city house located in the upscale district of the Ancient City. The festivities would last for several days. Some thought she was maneuvering to get her bondmate promoted to tetzus rank, a lord of the kingdom, and until the other day, her efforts appeared to be succeeding.

Idop went on to explain, "Oetan was my close friend. We advanced through the ranks in the Pannera together. I have known his bondmate even longer, for over one-hundred spans, even before Oetan and she were bonded. There was a time when I favored her, but she had eyes for Oetan and his title. Unfortunately, we are both demoted and simple commoners once again."

"But you are the king's counselor," Coleman reminded him.

"Yes, but my primary duty is to keep watch on you for the king. Do you understand that?"

"Yeah, that is very clear to me. How do you plan to carry out your duties?" Coleman asked.

"I have been giving it some thought. I think I will send a written report to the palace every detzamar for a king's counselor to review. I just hope there's a scholar at the estate who can assist me with the scribing."

Coleman chuckled. "Okay, but I pity the poor counselor who has to read it. I bet ten bhat he will die of boredom." Both men laughed as they continued through fields of hay, passing a scattering of farmhouses and outbuildings along the way.

After seven days of travel through field, meadow, and orchards of olive-like trees growing on the Lord Penno Estate, they reached a forest of tall trees, large bushes, and wild game. Idop told Coleman, this woodland marked the boundary of his estate. They still had another three days of travel before they reached the manor grounds, though.

While Idop and Ayascho set up camp, Coleman hunted. An hour later, he returned, holding the carcass of a large bird the size of a turkey. As he walked, he plucked it. When he reached their camp, he tossed the bird to Ayascho and then washed in a nearby pool fed by a spring. He returned to the camp and started a conversation with Idop, who was sitting on a log looking forlorn.

"You said my estate begins here. So, how much land do I own?" he asked.

"You own nothing, just like Oetan. The king owns all land. He has given you stewardship, so be grateful. This is one of the largest estates in the kingdom. The entire southeast peninsula is yours to oversee," Idop explained.

"If you and Oetan advanced through the ranks together, how did Oetan get such a large estate?"

"He was the megato of the Prince's Contingent for many spans. He impressed the young prince, so the king rewarded his service with a stewardship. The previous estate holder and his entire family had crossed-over after suffering a deadly illness."

"Did the king reward you for your service? After all, you were the megatus and Oetan's superior."

"Oetan was born tetzae. I was born a commoner. The king granted me tetzae rank only fifty spans ago. Now, I'm a commoner once again," Idop grumbled as he hung his head in shame.

"Okay. Just how big is this estate, anyway? I wish I could see a map."

Idop scratched out a map in the dirt at their feet with a stick. It looked like a hand with three fingers extended. "Anterra, the Ancient City, is here, near the middle of the central peninsula. Down here, in the southeast corner of the Anterra peninsula, is a smaller peninsula. That is your estate. On the large western peninsula is Terratia, and on the large eastern peninsula is Otterina. They are Anterra's sister cities."

"Okay, that helps. Now, I have an idea of where we are. Are there any other large cities nearby?"

"There are cities far to the east, and caravans come from there selling goods, especially salt from the City of Women. There's also a myth about a lost city in the middle of the ocean where the people have black skin, but I think it's only a story."

"Tell me about the City of Women?" Tondo asked.

"I can only tell you it is where our salt comes from. I've been told the city is run by women. Sounds ridiculous to me."

Coleman responded with a frown and said, "When we get to the estate, you will have to draw a map of the world for me. By the way, what is this world called?"

"This world's name?" Idop asked with a confused expression. Coleman nodded. "This is the Kingdom of Teg-ar-mos."

"No, I mean the whole world's name," Coleman clarified as he spread his arms wide. Idop cocked his head and looked even more perplexed. "So, it has no name?" Coleman wondered.

"I told you already; this is the Kingdom of Teg-ar-mos."

Coleman quickly realized Idop's world was limited to the kingdom. He had the same myopic view as Titus. "Can you tell me about the world beyond the kingdom's boundaries? What does it look like? How many continents are there?" he asked, using a godspeak term.

"I don't know what you're talking about. What I've told you is all I know. I have never gone further than the Mountains of Magheedo. I'm sure a caravan master can tell you more."

"As the leader of the Pannera, didn't you worry about an invasion from the east?"

"No, never. There is no history of trouble coming from the east or the north. My biggest concern was that one of the sister cities would go to war with us. That has happened from time-to-time in the past."

"Why? Power? Riches? The Blessing of the City?" Coleman wondered.

"Land. The Magheedo Plain is where most of the food is grown. The cities have fought over who has the bigger share, especially in times of drought. But King Teg-ar-mos has maintained the peace for over twenty spans. He says war is too expensive, and Anterra already has the largest share of the Plain."

"What do the other cities think of that?"

"As long as the farmers can grow enough food to feed their kingdoms, we will have peace."

"What about the Blessing of the City? Are the other cities jealous that Anterrans live longer than others?"

"If the king's house falls, the Blessing will be lost to all,"

Idop said in a practiced voice. Coleman looked into Idop's face and felt a warning of deception coming from his center. He pondered Idop's statement. He was still a loyal servant of the king, even though he had been treated harshly. His duty as the leader of the Pannera would have put him in a position to know more about the city's defenses and strategies than almost anyone else. Coleman quickly surmised, if a monarch wanted to deter an attack, such a story might do the trick or at least start a debate, which could possibly allow a spy enough time to get the word to his king.

While they had been talking, Ayascho was roasting the bird over the fire, and Lulubelle dug for fresh, juicy roots. Idop had pilfered a few ripe vegetables growing on the Penno Estate before reaching the woodland, which were cooking in a gravetro pot hung from a tripod made of green tree limbs. As Coleman and Idop continued talking, Ayascho busied himself with the cooking duties. When the red p´atezas disk touched the horizon, he announced last-meal was ready. As was his custom when assigned as the cook, he cut a piece of meat off the roasting bird and raised it above his head with both hands, offered a silent prayer, and then he cast the offering into the fire.

Idop watched intently then asked, "Will he do that every time he cooks a meal?"

"Oh, yes. Ayascho honors his god and thanks him for what he blesses him with," Coleman explained.

"Seems like a waste of good meat if you ask me," Idop admitted.

"The great Batru is closer than you think," Ayascho told him. "You have seen the power of his messenger. If you want blessings, you must give thanks to the one who sends them." Ayascho cut a piece of meat for himself and began eating. The other two did the same.

"So, I take it you do not follow the teachings of the gods," Coleman said as he took a bite of meat.

"My mother taught me to worship the unnamed god, but I find it hard to believe in a god with no name. The priests say the name is too sacred to repeat," Idop said.

"I know the name of my god; he is Batru. Me and my people are his children. He has given us the Law and his name, and we are blessed when we obey him," Ayascho told them.

"That is true. I have lived with his people, and the Law brings order to their lives. Unfortunately, if the Law is followed blindly, without compassion, it can lead to suffering," Coleman opined.

"That is the fault of the People, not Batru. At first, I hated you for the changes you brought to my village. Now, I have learned the wisdom you shared with us was from the Great One," Ayascho admitted. Coleman was taken aback by the young man's concession.

"I thought you two were the best of friends," Idop said. Coleman and Ayascho looked at each other with startled expressions.

"Have we become friends?" Coleman cautiously asked.

Ayascho hesitated for an instant, then said, "Yes, I think we have." The men continued their meal in thoughtful silence.

The three arose early the next morning as the reddish-orange glow of dawn was just beginning to warm the eastern horizon. They ate a breakfast of leftover bird and vegetables. Lulubelle started her day by digging for more roots and became annoyed when Coleman grabbed her ear and led her to the cart; however, she submitted to his will and was soon harnessed. As a reward, he fed her the remaining raw vegetables Idop had picked the day before. That seemed to improve her mood.

Coleman took the time to examine the thrice eggs he had stored in the wooden trunk. He touched the dirt to see if it felt too warm. It seemed okay to him, but what did he know? He thought about turning the eggs, but an inner feeling encouraged him to leave them as they were. It seemed the natural thing to do.

Idop and Ayascho broke camp while Coleman was busy with Lulubelle and the cart. They were on their way just as a red p´atezas cleared the horizon on its daily stroll through the heavens.

By midafternoon, they had cleared the woods and reached a field of yellow flowers. The flowers covered the ground for as far as the eye could see. A handful of men and women were tending the plants. As he watched the workers, he heard the snap of a whip.

"What is this?" Coleman asked as they moved along a clear lane between fields of the flowering plants.

"This is divitz, don't you recognize it? I thought you said

divitz grows in your homeland," said Idop.

"Yes, it does, but I am not a cotton farmer. I have never seen it with yellow flowers. I thought it just grew white puffs."

"The yellow flowers wither, leaving a pod. When the pod ripens, it opens, and the white divitz appears. Oetan told me all about growing divitz; more than I ever wanted to know," Idop admitted.

"What is it good for?" asked Ayascho.

"You can make clothes out of it. Idop's robes are made from it," Coleman told him. Ayascho looked from yellow flower to red robe and back again, then shook his head in disbelief.

They continued for a couple of more days, passing many more fields. Some had been recently planted; others remained fallow. As far as Coleman could tell, it seemed to be a well-run operation. They passed a vineyard, and Coleman snacked on a bunch of ripe grapes. They were sweet and tangy, although seedy. Idop told him that Oetan made the best wine he'd ever tasted. The vineyard was small and only produced enough for Oetan's personal use.

"If Oetan was the leader of the Prince's Contingent, when did he find time to manage all this?" Coleman wondered.

"He was only called upon to perform his duties when the prince chose to go on audit, usually after the harvests. The contingent would protect him as he examined what was garnered for tax purposes. Oetan would leave his estate's affairs in the hands of his foreman, Nestor. He told me, Nestor did an outstanding job of managing the estate in his absence."

By midafternoon on the tenth day of travel, as they crest-

ed a low knoll, Coleman got his first view of the estate man-
or house, standing a couple of miles away. It was too far distant to make out much detail, but he was very impressed by
what he saw. In a grove of tall trees planted near the buildings
to provide shade and protection from the wind, stood a large,
two-story, light tan building with a red-tiled roof. It reminded him of a Mediterranean villa. Around the large manor sat
many smaller outbuildings and a large barn. He feasted his
eyes on the beauty of his new abode.

"Is that the sutro waters?" Ayascho asked excitedly.

"Yes, my Wilderness companion, that is the ocean," Idop
told him.

Coleman had been so thrilled about the estate he hadn't
noticed the lucid blue waters beyond. He took a deep breath

and was transfixed by the amazing sight before him. The villa sat on a bluff, overlooking an ocean of sparkling blue. The
beauty of the water reminded him of the Caribbean Sea.
Coleman waited several minutes as he scanned the glorious
scene. This was all his. He felt giddy, and a huge smile filled
his face.

It took more than an hour before they reached the estate
buildings. As they approached, Coleman noticed odd-looking
chickens feeding near the barn. He took a second look; they
weren't chickens, after all. They were the size of large roost-
ers, but they looked more like two-legged lizards or tiny dinosaurs adorned in feathers. Some were reddish-brown, some
were green, and a few were white. He then noticed a samaran
tie bar and a water trough conveniently placed for visitors to
secure and water their animals. Coleman unhitched Lulubelle
and led her to water, all the time staring at the chicken-like
creatures as they scratched and pecked the ground for food.

Lulubelle drank her fill and stepped back. A young man
with the mark of a slave on his forehead came to Coleman's
side and nervously offered to take charge of the huge beast.
Coleman thanked him, and the man took Lulubelle's halter
with some trepidation. It was obvious he didn't have any experience with thrice, but after a little coaxing from Coleman,
Lulubelle was led to the nearby barn. Idop fetched one of the
cases from the cart that contained the official documents and
tucked it in his waist belt.

Coleman noticed a smaller but rather stately looking building about a hundred feet from the manor house. "What is
that?" he asked, pointing at it.

"That's the guesthouse. Visitors to the estate stay there until their business is completed," Idop told him. He then took a deep breath and headed for the manor house.

The three men walked into a fancy, walled courtyard near the main entrance of the villa. In the center of the courtyard sat a large sundial, or more correctly, a p'atezas dial, made of shiny brass-like metal, similar in color to his sword. Its face was at least three feet in diameter and divided by long lines etched into the metal; the spaces between the long lines were marked by several shorter lines. There was also writing on the dial, but it was unreadable by Coleman. The p'atezas dial rested in the center of a twenty-foot diameter mosaic of multicolored stones in a geometric design. The design included various shades of reds, yellows, blues, greens, and white. Flowering plants climbed trellises on the high inner walls of the courtyard.

Idop allowed his companions only a short delay to admire the courtyard's beauty before he led them to the front doors of the manor house. The doors were at the top of a short set of wide stone stairs, and when the men reached the top step landing, the doors opened. A stout slave dressed in a clean and tidy white tunic greeted them. A puzzled look crossed his face, but it quickly passed.

"Megatus Idop, it is good to see you again. May I inform the lady of your arrival?" he asked.

"It's good to see you too, Doros. Please tell Lady Oetan she has important visitors," Idop instructed.

They were ushered into a spacious waiting room. Very large, open-air windows in two walls of the room allowed in plenty of

light and a gentle breeze. Sturdy benches of tan-colored wood
rested near the walls. Idop stepped to the center of the room
while Coleman and Ayascho remained near the entryway. A
middle-aged slave woman soon entered carrying a tray with
two pitchers and three ceramic cups. She was dressed in a plain
white dress that went from neck to floor and had short sleeves.

"Megatus, do you prefer wine or water?" she asked.

"Teema, you are looking more beautiful than ever. You
know I can't pass up the finest wine in all the kingdom," Idop
said as he picked up one of the cups. Teema blushed and
poured wine into it. She then glided over to Coleman and
Ayascho, carefully balancing the tray. She stopped in front of
Coleman, looked up into his whiskered face, and stifled a surprised cry. She worriedly glanced at Ayascho and then back
to Coleman. "These are my friends, Teema. They won't hurt
you," Idop assured her.

"Yes, megatus. Would you . . . you cavaliers prefer wine or
water?"

"Wine!" Ayascho almost shouted.

"Thank you, Teema," Coleman began, "both of us will
have water." Ayascho frowned and accepted his cup. Teema
left the room and returned a short time later with a tray of
white, damp, and rolled towels. The visitors rubbed the grit
and grime from their faces, arms, and hands. Coleman felt delighted as he cleaned sweat and dirt from his whiskered face.
His delight turned to embarrassment when he noticed the
crud on his towel. Teema collected the now filthy brown towels and hustled out of the room.

A few minutes later, a matronly middle-aged woman wearing a flowing pink gown of ankle-length came into the room. Her arms were bare, and the bodice of her dress began just below her neck. She had tied a white sash around her waist. Her medium-brown hair was tied in a long braid that went half-way down her back. Following her into the room came a stunningly beautiful young woman. She was dressed in a light-blue gown, similar in design to the other woman's dress, and she also had tied a white sash around her waist. Her hair was very light-brown and draped in a ponytail over her left shoulder. When the young woman saw Idop, her light-brown eyes lit up, and when she smiled, it nearly made Coleman melt. He stood like a smitten schoolboy, gawking at her loveliness.

"Megatus Idop, it is a pleasure to see you again," the older woman said as she extended both hands.

Idop held her hands at arm's length and said, "Lady Oetan, the pleasure is all mine. You are more beautiful every time I see you. And your daughter; how charming you are, my dear." Lady Oetan smiled, and her daughter giggled at Idop's pleasantries.

Lady Oetan examined Idop from head to toe. "You're wearing the robes of a king's counselor." She then noticed the soiled bandage on his left hand, "And you are injured." A concerned look suddenly crossed her face. "What has happened? Where is Oetan? You must tell me!" she almost begged.

"Lady Oetan, the Prince's Contingent was ambushed by brigands, and the prince was severely wounded. Megato Oetan has crossed-over." Lady Oetan gave a gasp of despair.

"Papa . . . Papa is dead!" the young woman cried. She covered her face with her hands and began sobbing uncontrollably. Lady Oetan took her daughter into her arms and tried to comfort the weeping girl. Coleman was surprised by how well the older woman was bearing the tragic news. Sadness welled in his throat for the weeping younger woman. Idop said nothing more and let the two women grieve.

After several minutes, Lady Oetan guided the young woman to a bench, and she sat, still weeping loudly. Lady Oetan then returned to Idop and looked him in the eyes. "I have known you a very long time, Idop. I can tell when you are keeping something from me. What is it?" she asked in a commanding voice.

"The king feels Oetan and I failed in our duties. He has stripped us of our rank as tetzae, and he took a knuckle from me," Idop told her, raising his bandaged left hand as a witness. A gasp escaped Lady Oetan's lips, and she quickly covered her mouth. "He has removed me from the Pannera. I am no longer the kingdom's megatus. But it is even worse than that, my lady."

"Hoy, go on," she shuddered.

"He has held Oetan in disgrace and stripped him of all his holdings, as well. I am sorry to bring you such tragic news.

"What are we to do, Mama?" the young woman pleaded through her tears.

"I don't know, child; I must think."

Idop pulled the official cylinder from his waist belt, opened it, and handed the scroll to Lady Oetan without saying a word. She reluctantly took the document and read it slowly. When she finished reading it from top to bottom, she examined the official seal stamped into red wax. She dropped the document on the floor and nearly collapsed. Idop caught her and gently guided her to a bench.

She covered her face with her hands momentarily, then she took a deep breath and stood. "The Tondo? Is that an outlander title?" she asked.

"No, my lady. It's the new steward's name. He is here, with me," the counselor said, pointing with an upraised palm in Coleman's direction.

The young woman gasped and stared at the two wild-looking men near the entryway. "Mama, are they savages?" the young one asked.

"Quiet, my dear," Lady Oetan commanded. She walked to Coleman and Ayascho and examined them. "Oetan told me there were savages in the Wilderness. I thought they were just stories and myths. You must be Sire Tondo," she said, looking up into Coleman's blue eyes.

"Yes, Lady Oetan, and this is my friend Ayascho. We come from the Wilderness, but we are not savages."

Lady Oetan took another look at the two roughly dressed and odd-looking men; then, she noticed the stubble on Coleman's face. She returned to Idop. "This must be some kind of dreadful drollery the king has inflicted on us. I can't believe he would displace us and give our holdings to these, these . . . " she stopped before completing her statement.

"Sire Tondo provided a great service to the kingdom by bringing the prince back from the other-side. I was there. I saw him grapple with the gods. He breathed life back into the dead prince, and by command, returned our liege's spirit to the realm of the living." Upon hearing this, Lady Oetan bowed her head and strained under an invisible weight that seemed to crash upon her shoulders.

"Mama, where will we live? Can we move to the city house?" the young woman asked.

"No, child, everything is gone. We have nothing; absolutely nothing. Idop, have you brought me the body of my bondmate?"

"No, my lady. The ambush took place in the river, and his body was washed away. I had men search for him, but he was never found." The young woman's sobs grew louder.

"Teema, towels for my daughter and me," Lady Oetan commanded. The house slave quickly fetched towels and handed one to each woman. Lady Oetan regained her regal composure and walked back to Coleman. "May we at least keep our clothing?" she asked as she scanned him and Ayascho again. "Surely, they will be of no use to you."

"Lady Oetan, I did not know your husband, but I believe he acted with honor and bravery while defending the prince. I feel the king has treated him, and by extension, you and your daughter, with injustice. I cannot change the king's decree, but there is one thing I can do. For as long as you wish, you and your daughter will be guests of the estate. This house is your home, and I will not take it from you, especially after passing along such dreadful news. The guesthouse will be sufficient for my needs," he told her. She stared into his blue eyes as the heavy weight of apprehension was lifted from her shoulders. Coleman could see her regal front beginning to collapse; then she began to sob. Her daughter rushed to her side. The two women embraced and continued weeping together. "Idop, we should leave Lady Oetan and her daughter to grieve," Coleman advised. "If there is anything I can do for you, please do not hesitate to ask."

"You have done more than I would have dared ask already. May the gods bless you for your kindness," she said.

The three men quickly left the manor house. Coleman paused at the p´atezas dial, looked it over, and then left the courtyard following behind the other two men. He could still hear weeping coming from the house, and it broke his heart. He was grateful to have the opportunity to ease their grief and worry somewhat. Without his help, they would have been left with few options. He knew from what Idop had told him along the way Lady Oetan had many friends in the kingdom. Maybe she and her daughter could have sought help from them; however, without title or funds, she would have been in dire straits indeed. The king's callousness angered him. How could he be so cruel to these unfortunate women, especially after their great loss? Had he no compassion?

The men walked to the guesthouse, and Idop entered, followed by Coleman and Ayascho. The counselor opened the window shutters, allowing light and a breeze to enter the stuffy room through the open-air windows. The main living area was about twenty feet square and furnished with good quality, utilitarian wooden furniture. Colorful tapestries hung from the walls depicting hunt scenes. Coleman and Ayascho explored the remaining rooms while Idop sat. The two found a large bedroom and a second smaller bedroom. There was a small cooking area tucked away at the rear of the house. When they finished exploring, they returned to Idop.

"This is a very nice place. I can get used to it," Coleman said with a smile.

"It is much bigger than any family lodge in my village. Do all your people have such big places to live in?" Ayascho asked.

Idop chuckled. "Oy, no. Only the very rich can afford such dwellings."

"*Rich?* What does rich mean?" Ayascho wondered. Idop and Coleman explained the concept to him, but neither believed he fully understood the idea when they had finished.

"I think you will understand better the longer you live with these people," Coleman finally advised. Idop nodded his agreement.

The counselor took the other two men on a tour of the nearby buildings. Besides the manor house and the guesthouse, there was a large brick barn with a blacksmith shop attached to the northeast side, a small cabin made of wood used by Nestor the foreman, and tucked behind a knoll, not viewable from the main buildings, were many slave quarters. It reminded Coleman of a low-level row house with several single-family rooms attached to each other. Each room had a stone fireplace and a dirt floor. Simple benches and tables were the only furniture. Each room had a single, small, open-air window to let in a little light, bathing the room in perpetual gloom.

CHAPTER 14

THE GUESTHOUSE SLAVE

"**D**oros!" Lady Oetan called.

"Yes, my lady," the male house slave replied as he stepped through the doorway.

"I want Foreman Nestor fetched. I must see to the needs of the men in the guesthouse," she told him.

"As you wish, my lady."

Maaryah was busy at her machine in the Separation House, her back still burning from the wound caused by Foreman Nestor's cruel whip. It was taking a long time to heal because she could not rest from her duties, causing it to break open often and bleed. It continued to pain her with a burning sting that had lingered and would not diminish.

While she was focused on her tasks, she felt someone near her. The foreman's voice was in her ear, "The First is quickly coming. Are ya ready to accept my gift?"

Maaryah replied without interrupting her work, "Never." Nestor drew back his coiled whip and was about to slam it into Maaryah's head.

"Foreman Nestor!" a young male voice called.

Nestor stood up and glared at the approaching young man. It was Eos, the manor house errand slave boy. "What ya want?" Nester growled.

"Lady Oetan wants to meet with you as soon as you can join her," Eos told him.

Nestor cuffed the boy on the side of the head. "Ya'll address me properly, ya lil' frizzard stink!"

"Yes, Foreman Nestor. Sorry, Foreman Nestor," Eos said while rubbing the sting from his head.

"What does the lady want?" the foreman gruffly demanded.

"I don't know, Foreman Nestor. It may have to do with the three visitors who just arrived."

"Visitors? Alright, I'll meet with her now." Nestor leaned down again and spoke into Maaryah's ear, "I'll be back, and ya'd better give me a different answer then." He turned and tromped out.

"Foreman Nestor," Lady Oetan began, "I've just been informed, the estate has a new steward. His name is Sire Tondo. He and his slave are from the Wilderness. They look like savages. Megatus Idop is with them. They have taken up residence in the guesthouse. I want you to find a woman to serve as the guesthouse slave."

"New estate steward? What's happened?" Nestor wondered. He began worrying about his contract and what this change would mean to him personally, although he kept these thoughts to himself.

"Master Oetan has been killed by brigands," she told him. "I don't want to answer any more questions. Have the new woman report to Teema in the morning." Lady Oetan turned and left the room.

Nestor had many questions, but he would follow Lady

Oetan's orders until he had a better understanding of exactly what was going on and who was really in charge. Before he
left the manor house, he had a short conversation with the
two slaves serving there, and he gleaned what little information they could provide concerning the change in stewardship.

Why would the new master choose to live in the guesthouse? This
question and many others rolled around the foreman's mind
as he rode back to the Separation House.

As he approached, a wicked and perverse thought slith-
ered into his cruel mind, and his face lit with a nefarious
smile. He stomped into the Separation House and marched
to Maaryah's workstation. He grabbed her by the upper left
arm and jerked her to her feet. "Ya'll be pleased to know, I'm
changing yer assignment." Maaryah looked into his mirth
filled face with trepidation. "Ha, that's true. I'm making ya
the guesthouse slave. Ya'll be serving the new estate master, a
tall savage they tell me. I've been told, Megatus Idop is with
him, and there's also a savage slave from the Wilderness, too.
I'm sure ya can provide them with all the comfort they'll desire. Ya'll be their pleasure-girl." He laughed as he examined
Maaryah's terror-stricken expression.

She knew of Master Oetan's lustful reputation, and she assumed all masters were the same. She had heard that this Idop
commanded the dreaded Pannera, the city guards who hunted
down runaway slaves and hung them from poles upon an adjudicator's order. The thought of being in the presence of savages was horrifying. Were they as bloodthirsty as she'd heard?

"Now, ya see where yer stubbornness has put ya. I'm sure
ya'll be receptive to my gifts by the time they're done with

ya. I can wait; I don't mind used merchandise." His evil grin made her sick, and her expression must have shown it. He pushed her down hard and stomped into the middle of the large room, shouting curses and threats at all the slaves.

By the time Idop finished the tour of the manor grounds, it was late afternoon, and the shadows were growing long. When they returned to the guesthouse, they found three large pitchers of water and three washbasins waiting for their use. Fresh towels were laid on the table. The men washed the dust and dirt from their faces and arms, and again, Coleman was embarrassed by how soiled the towels were. Teema arrived shortly after they had refreshed themselves and collected the things they had used. Idop told her to have Doros prepare the bathhouse.

An hour later, as the p´atezas was setting, the three men strolled to a small building behind the manor house. Inside was a tiled room and a pool of warmed water. The three disrobed and soaked for more than an hour. Ayascho was a bit skeptical of the whole idea at first, but he followed the lead of the other two and seemed to enjoy it thoroughly. Teema brought the men cups of cool wine. Idop sipped, and Ayascho guzzled. Coleman warily sniffed his cup, and the odor burned his nostrils. He touched the tip of his tongue to the liquid and recoiled as it burned.

"Teema!" he shouted. "Bring me water and lots of it." Teema quickly responded, and Coleman gulped down the entire cup. "More!" he yelled. She handed him the large clay pitcher she was holding. He grabbed it and drank directly from it.

"Tondo, what's the matter?" Idop asked with a curious gaze.

"I cannot tolerate this wine. It burns and tastes horrible. It is the most bitter-tasting stuff I have ever tried."

"Bring Tondo some juice of the grape," Idop commanded Teema.

"Yes, megatus, but it will take some time. I will have to send someone to the wine house."

"Very well," he told her, and then he addressed Coleman. "I remember, you couldn't drink the king's brew, either. That's very strange. I have never seen such a bad reaction to the best blend one can find. Even the worst of drink wouldn't burn, at least not until it was swallowed."

By the time they had finished bathing, dusk had passed into night. They returned to the guesthouse and sat chatting for a while in the dim light offered by the moons' glow streaming through the room's windows and open door. It wasn't long before Doros entered with a tray of food. Teema followed him with pitchers of wine and water.

"Megatus, the juice of the grape will be here soon. I told the boy to run," she said.

"That will do, Teema. By the way, I am no longer the king's megatus. You may refer to me as *counselor* from now on."

"Yes, sire."

"Also, I'm a simple commoner now," he told her in dismay. She bowed and exited the room with Doros following.

The tray was full of meat, cooked vegetables, bread, and

oil. The men used their fingers and ate mostly in silence, dipping pieces of bread into the oil. The soothing bath had relaxed them, making them lethargic and sleepy. After a while, they noticed a young man running toward the manor house carrying a waterskin. Shortly after that, Teema entered with a pitcher of grape juice. Idop took a taste, and so did Ayascho.

"Tastes fine to me," Idop said. "A little too sweet for my preferences, though."

"It's okay," Ayascho agreed.

Coleman sniffed his cup and then took a tentative taste. "Hmm, it seems okay to me. So, what could make it so different? Of course," Coleman exclaimed in godspeak, "the fermentation process!"

"What did you say?" Ayascho wondered.

"If you let grapes, or grain for that matter, sit for a while, their sugars turn to alcohol. It could be this form of alcohol, or possibly something to do with the fermentation process— maybe the yeast—that causes me to have such a bad reaction." He glanced at the bitter bread he'd been eating. Ayascho and Idop just stared at him. Neither had a clue about what he was talking about, the mix of godspeak terms leaving them befuddled. "Thank you, Teema. This will do just fine."

"Lady Oetan has instructed Foreman Nestor to assign one of the others to serve you. She will be coming from the Separation House, so she won't be here until the morning. She hasn't had any training yet, but I will teach her all I can. Please, don't blame me if she fails in her duties, sire," Teema pleaded.

Coleman could tell by her worried expression and tone that

she was terrified that the new girl wouldn't measure up. "Why are you so concerned about this woman?" he wondered.

"If she does something that offends you, master, Foreman Nestor will punish us both," she admitted.

Coleman was taken aback. She had called him *master*. That would never do. He had been raised under the principles of freedom, and that each individual was granted certain unalienable rights by their Creator. He had even placed his own life in jeopardy to grant and secure these freedoms for others. And now he, Master Tondo, stood between this woman and her pursuit of happiness. The realization sent a chill down his spine, and it sickened him. For now, he would only address her immediate concerns, but this was an intolerable situation for him to bear.

"What the new woman does will be sufficient, Teema. There will be no punishments as long as I have anything to say about it," Coleman said in a calm voice.

"Thank you, Master Tondo, you are most kind," she said as she bowed, and then she returned to the manor house. Coleman closed his eyes and pondered. He hadn't given the whole situation much thought since he'd arrived at the Ancient City. He looked upon the slaves as servants, but the realization that he was now the holder of unfortunate thralls—an unwilling slave master—and steward of a slave estate, came like a bolt from the blue. What was he to do? That question was easy to answer. How he would do it was another matter entirely.

"In the morning, I want to tour the entire estate and learn what is going on. I need to meet the people who run the day-to-day affairs. I particularly want to meet this Nestor fellow. It appears he is someone I need to understand."

"It will take more than a day to tour the entire estate. As I told you, this is one of the largest in the kingdom. It will take many days to see it all," Idop informed him.

Darkness had fully fallen, and the men went to bed. Although there were oil lamps they could have lit if they chose, the three men were tired and in need of rest. Coleman lay on his bed in the larger bedroom listening to the steady, heavy breathing of Ayascho, who was asleep on the floor. Coleman heard footsteps pass by the open window of his room. Curious to find out who it was, he got out of bed and saw a dark figure enter Nestor's cabin.

When does the man rest? Coleman wondered in silence.

It wasn't long before he could see the dim light of a lamp shining through the cabin's window. Teema rushed to the cabin with a tray of food and drink. She was almost running. The man's gruff voice greeted her, and she dashed back to the manor house. She quickly returned with a washbasin and towels. He heard a slap, and then Teema stumbled back to the manor house sobbing.

This Nestor is a real piece of work, Coleman thought to himself.

He clenched his fists and took a step toward the cabin; however, he stopped short. He wanted to march over to Nestor and give the foreman a taste of his own medicine, but he calmed himself as he pondered the aftereffects. If he acted on his emotions, there would be consequences, very serious consequences. He felt trapped. He took a deep breath and calmed himself. He returned to his bed and let his troubled thoughts drift for a while before falling asleep.

Idop and Ayascho were already up and moving about when Coleman awoke with a start. He sat up and rubbed his eyes. "The sundial!" he exclaimed in godspeak.

"What did you say, Tondo?" asked Idop from the living area.

"I must go to the courtyard," Coleman told him. "My subconscious often conjures up thoughts in the early morning. There is something wrong with the sundial," he excitedly noted, using a jumble of godspeak words.

"What?" Ayascho asked.

"It is like having a dream but different. My mind is telling me there is something unusual about the p´atezas dial. I must see what it is," he told the other two in an excited voice.

He quickly dressed and bolted to the courtyard. When the other two caught up to him, he was counting the main lines on the p´atezas dial's face.

"There are only fourteen major lines here," he told them when they reached his side.

"Yes, that's right. So, what's the problem?" Idop asked. Ayascho had no idea what they were talking about.

"If I were to complete the circle, I figure there would be twenty-two lines. I was expecting twenty-four. I mean, in my homeland, there are twenty-four lines. Maybe you measure time differently?" he wondered.

"I've never seen anyone get so excited over a p´atezas dial.

Are you all right?" Idop voiced with concern.

"Tell me, what are the major lines called?" Coleman asked.

"They are segments, and the smaller lines are called terms."

Coleman stood, thinking for a moment. There were fourteen major lines, or segments, on the dial, and each segment was divided by ten smaller lines called terms. How could he get a reference for time between his homeworld and this one? What could be used as a common reference point?

"Ah, yes," he finally said aloud to himself in godspeak. "My resting pulse rate is sixty beats a minute. So, if I count the number of beats it takes for the p´atezas' shadow to cross the smaller lines, I will be able to determine the relationship between Earth time and the kingdom's time."

He was satisfied with his simple but elegant solution. Unfortunately, the p´atezas had not yet crept above the courtyard wall. He would simply have to wait. In the meantime, he dashed off to the bathhouse, disrobed, and jumped into the lukewarm water.

Doros quickly entered and wondered in a worried tone, "Forgive me, master, I didn't know you would want to use the bath so early. May I have the water heated for you?"

"That will not be necessary, Doros; however, my friends and I will be touring the estate today. Please see that samarans are prepared for us to ride."

"Yes, Master Tondo, I will see to it," Doros answered and was surprised when his master's expression turned dour.

Coleman returned to the guesthouse and ate a breakfast of bread and fruit. Through the window, he could see three samarans being led to the tie bar near the courtyard.

"Before we start the tour, I want to meet with Nestor," Coleman told Idop.

"He's already in the fields. I heard him leave before light," Idop told him.

"Okay, I will catch him later."

Coleman went to the p´atezas dial and noticed that light was now shining down on it. The hand—or, so he called it because he couldn't recall what it was properly named— was casting its shadow on the dial's face. He waited until the shadow reached one of the interval lines, and then he began counting his pulse. It took three-hundred and seventy beats for the shadow to cross to the next interval line.

"Hmm, maybe my heart rate is a little elevated," he said aloud to himself. He continued counting. By the time the shadow reached the next minor line, the count had reached seven-hundred and thirty beats. "That is about six minutes per term line," he said in godspeak. "If I extrapolate that, it means each segment line is roughly one hour. By my reckoning, there could be twenty-two major divisions on this p´atezas dial, meaning there are twenty-two hours in a day." He chuckled to himself. "Is there no end to the surprises I find here?" he continued in godspeak.

He hadn't noticed that Idop and Ayascho had joined him. They stood transfixed as he mumbled his indecipherable jargon. "I've never seen anyone so fascinated with a p´atezas dial before. Tondo, you amaze me. And, sometimes, you worry me," Idop confessed.

"This p´atezas dial tells me there are twenty-two hours in a day. That helps to explain why I never seem to get a full night's sleep."

"What?" asked Ayascho in confusion.

"Orwers?" asked Idop. "Do you mean segments?"

"Hours, segments . . . at least now, I understand. There are twenty-two segments in a day," Coleman proudly announced.

"*I* could have told you that," Idop bluntly stated.

"Tell me what you're talking about," Ayascho demanded. Coleman and Idop went into a lengthy dissertation on time for the young man's benefit, but when they were finished, he was more confused than when they had started.

As the men walked to the samarans to begin their tour of the estate, Coleman noticed Doros, Teema, and another woman hanging olive drab drapery around the manor house doorway and window frames.

"What are they doing?" Coleman asked, pointing to the main villa.

"Lady Oetan is beginning her mourning seclusion. She and her daughter will remain inside and take no visitors until forty days have passed," Idop explained.

Coleman now realized that olive drab was the color of mourning in this culture. "Did you ever tell me what the daughter's name is?" he asked.

"Her name is Ootyiah."

"You said Oetan had a young daughter. I thought she was a child," Coleman admitted.

"She is hardly more than that. I believe she turns forty soon. I'm sure she and Lady Oetan had already begun planning her tandeban. That would have been when she was presented to Anterra's gentry. If Oetan hadn't been disgraced, she might have bonded with a royal."

"But she is still tetzae by birth, right?" Coleman asked.

"She is, but no self-respecting suitor from the gentry will want her now. She and her mother are without means, and she no longer has a dowry. It belongs to you, along with all other estate possessions. She is displaced and destitute." Coleman frowned.

Idop hopped onto his steed and watched with amusement as Coleman and Ayascho struggled. Coleman had some experience with horses during his Ranger training. It wasn't uncommon for him to be involved in a military operation that required the use of horses either as mounts or pack animals. But a samaran was something else entirely. The saddle was somewhat familiar, but it didn't have stirrups. He had difficulty with his samaran holding still while he tried to mount. Ayascho wasn't doing any better. He and his samaran were going around and around in circles.

After getting a good chuckle while watching the other two struggle, Idop dismounted. "Now, watch me," he said. He took a step back and then launched himself into the air, throwing his right leg over the saddle. "Now, you try it. Remember, you must mount from the samaran's left side."

Well, at least that is familiar, Coleman thought. He steadied his mount and jumped aboard just as Idop had done. He almost fell off the opposite side but managed to grab the saddle. It took Ayascho a couple of tries before he was finally on.

The three then rode west into a field of yellow flowers. As they rode, Idop instructed the other two on the finer points of riding a samaran. Coleman learned that the mounts had five gaits: walk, trot, canter, gallop, and amble. Everyone preferred the amble gait because it was a comfortable, non-jarring pace for both rider and mount. The samarans seemed to be able to maintain the amble gait all day without tiring.

As they rode amongst the flowering plants, Coleman found slave row-houses scattered throughout the fields. They soon came upon a large wooden building resembling a warehouse, and Idop told him it was the collection and separation building called the *Separation House*. "This is where the picked divitz is taken to be prepared for sale. Men, women, and children work from dawn to dusk, separating the divitz seeds from the lint or fibers by hand."

"If I only knew how to make a cotton gin," Coleman mused in godspeak to no one in particular. The other men just stared back at him, perplexed.

They continued their grand tour all morning. "How many slaves work this estate?" Coleman finally asked.

"Oetan once told me he had over two-hundred. But that was a long time ago. I guess it would take at least that many to run this estate. That's a good question for Nestor. I'm sure he can tell you exactly how many there are."

"Who feeds these people?" Coleman asked.

"People; do you mean slaves?" Coleman nodded. "*You do,* my friend. It's the law. The estate master must provide enough food for each slave. It doesn't have to be tasty, but it has to be sufficient to sustain life."

"Who determines what is sufficient?"

"The king!" Coleman and Idop said in unison.

By midday, they had swung north and were inspecting the operation there. It looked to be more of the same as far as Coleman could tell. They noticed a slave boy riding a samaran approaching.

"Master Tondo, Teema has sent me with food and drink."

"How thoughtful of her. I was beginning to get hungry. What is your name, son?" Coleman asked.

"I am Eos, master."

"Well, Eos, thank you for finding us. I wager it was not easy."

"No, master, I've been searching for the longest time." He dismounted and handed Coleman a leather pouch filled with meats, nuts, and fruit wrapped in linen packages. He returned to his mount and removed two skins from the saddle hooks. "This one has water, and this one has wine, master," Eos told him.

"You did well. You can return now. And give Teema my thanks." The men took a short break and ate their fill under the shade of a small tree. "How old do you think Eos is? I wish I had thought to ask him," Coleman mentioned to Idop.

"He probably doesn't know, but I'd say he is twenty, maybe twenty-five spans," Idop guessed.

"Where I am from, I would guess he was fourteen or fifteen years . . . I mean, spans."

"Ayascho. Those lines on your face, do they have a special meaning?" Idop asked.

"They count my age and experience."

"I count five lines. So, does that mean you're only five spans old?"

"It has been five rains since my first hunt. I think that means five spans."

"Ha, how old are you?" Idop questioned.

"I don't know. It's not important. What matters is how long I've hunted."

After their meal, the three men continued the tour. They swung east, and by midafternoon, they reached a field white with divitz. Several men and women of all ages were picking the crop. As they approached, the trio could hear cries of pain as the sound of punches or kicks were delivered. They headed to the sound and found a prone man, curled into a fetal position while a stocky man with sandaled feet repeatedly kicked him.

"What is going on here?" Coleman demanded as he reined his samaran near the two.

"I'm teaching this lazy dung creeper a lesson. He claims to be sick, but I can tell when someone is fake'n," the assailant told him, as he gave the prone man another kick.

"Stop that!" Coleman ordered, and then he dismounted. "Enough!" Coleman continued as the assailant cocked his leg for another assault.

"Who in the names of the Five Shadows are ya, anyways?" the attacker demanded.

"Nestor, he is Sire Tondo, and by royal decree, the new steward of this estate," Idop informed him.

"Megatus Idop, I thought you was a king's counselor. Why the red robe?" Idop didn't answer. Realizing Idop wasn't going to respond, Nestor continued, "New steward, eh? Lady Oetan sent word for me to find a guesthouse slave for the new master." Nestor scanned Coleman's frame. "I chose a tall one for ya; one the three of ya will appreciate sharing if ya get my meaning, sire."

Coleman didn't like what he was hearing. "So, you are Foreman Nestor," Coleman said in a stern voice. "I have heard about your abilities, and now, I have witnessed your cruelty." The foreman stared with anger at Coleman, his eyes scanning the tall man from head to foot. Coleman could tell the foreman was intimidated by his height; Nestor was more than six inches shorter than the new estate holder. *He's a bully,* was Coleman's first impression of Nestor. He was a burly man with powerful looking arms. He wore leather trousers and a leather tunic gathered at the waist by a wide brown belt. A coiled whip hung from that belt.

"Sire, I can't allow these dung creepers to fake illness. All work would stop if I did."

Coleman reached down and helped the man to his feet. He appeared to be middle-aged. His skin tone was flushed, so Coleman felt his forehead. "This man has a fever," Coleman stated in anger. He went to his mount and retrieved a waterskin. "Here, drink this." The man drank as though he were parched. "You are finished for the day. Now, go to your home and rest."

"Thank you, master. I will work twice as hard tomorrow," the slave said. He then departed, walking briskly through the field of white.

Coleman then turned to the overseer and said, "Nestor, walk with me for a while." Coleman strode away from the others. He was about to give the foreman a dressing-down, but he didn't want their conversation to be overheard. He had no desire to undermine the foreman's authority, but such cruelty and bad judgment were to end immediately. "Nestor, I have heard many good things concerning the way you manage this estate. I want you to remain as foreman, but you cannot abuse these people. I will not allow it."

"These people?" Nestor began with a laugh, "They's only slaves, sire, and I must be tough with 'em, or they'll get lazy. If one can get away with it, theys all they'll try. Work will stop, and the crop will be lost. Surely, ya understand that," Nestor instructed.

"If you are truly as good a manager as I have been told, you will find a way that does not involve kicking and beating people, especially one who is obviously ill."

"People? Ya ain't never had no slaves before, have ya sire?" Coleman shook his head. "Oy, he ain't that sick. I can't allow 'em to slack a bit. That's the way it's done. That's what theys expect, and that's what keeps 'em work'n hard."

"Nestor, this is not a debate. I have told you what I want done, and I expect you to carry out my orders. Have I been clear enough?" Coleman said in a perturbed tone.

"Yes, sire, I will do as ya says." The two returned to the others, and Coleman mounted his samaran.

"Nestor, this is a fine operation you have here. Keep up the good work," he said in a loud voice for all to hear.

"Thank ya, sire," Nestor replied as he bowed. The trio ambled off toward the east under the foreman's angry glare.

Coleman's party ambled their mounts until they noticed the ocean just visible through the puffs of white. The p´atezas was low and to their front when they reached the bluff overlooking the ocean. The beach was about fifty feet below. *The air smells fresh and salty, just like at home,* Coleman thought. The waves crashed against offshore rocks, sending sprays of water high into the air with a roar. A cool southerly breeze brushed against their faces.

"Look, over there!" Ayascho shouted excitedly while pointing. "There's something big in the water." Idop and Coleman looked in the direction the younger man was pointing. Coleman's gaze caught the flash of movement in the ocean. A huge dorsal fin was cutting a wake. He guessed it was at least a hundred yards from the beach. It was hard to estimate size from that distance, but the creature appeared to be huge. The fin passed through an area where no light from the p´atezas was reflected, and the trio could see a huge shadow just below the surface.

"Tondo, is that the . . . the great sea creature you told us about?" Ayascho asked in wonder.

"It could be a whale, but I am not sure," Coleman responded.

"There are many beasts in the sea, but one never forgets its true horror. That, my friends, is the *terror* of the ocean. It devours anything or anyone who enters its realm," Idop warned.

"What's it called?" Ayascho asked.

"It is only known as 'the terror,' and that is sufficient." The men watched in awe as the fin and shadow patrolled the ocean swells. After a short time, the fin submerged, and the shadow disappeared into the depths.

"I thought you said the story about A-hob wasn't true. But it's true, it's true!" Ayascho was almost dizzy with excitement. Coleman was beginning to wonder himself. Whatever it was, it was as big as a whale.

The men led their mounts westward along the bluff, keeping a safe distance from its edge as they moved west. It wasn't long before they arrived back at the manor grounds. They could hear the rhythmic pounding of metal against metal coming from the far side of the barn. Coleman dismounted, handed the reins to the samaran caretaker, and strolled to the sound. His two companions followed him. When he rounded the corner of the barn, he could see a stout man pounding glowing red metal with a large hammer. He wore a leather apron, and sweat was pouring off his face. Right away, Coleman noticed, this man was not a slave; he didn't carry a mark on his forehead. There was also a younger man with a slave's tattoo sitting near a flaming forge, pumping bellows.

"Hoy!" Coleman shouted above the hammering.

The stout man continued pounding for a few more strokes. "Can't stop. Gotta strike while the gravetum's hot," he answered. He then examined the metal bar he was holding with tongs. He tossed it into the forge. "Haro, heat it up again." The younger man started pumping the bellows furiously. "You must be Sire Tondo," the man said with a bow. "How may I be of service?"

"Yes, I am Tondo. What is your name?"

"I am Pendor, the gravetum worker and blacksmith. I can fix or make almost anything you need, so long as it's gravetum."

"I am glad to meet you, Pendor. I imagine you are a very important man around here."

"Yes, sire, I am. All you need do is ask Foreman Nestor; he'd agree," Pendor said without a hint of conceit.

"You may carry on. I am sorry to interrupt your work." Pendor grabbed the heated metal bar with his tongs and began hammering away at the glowing metal.

Coleman and his friends retreated to the bathhouse and refreshed. He and Ayascho were very sore. Neither was accustomed to riding and to do so for an entire day left both with regrets; however, the warm waters of the bath soothed their pains. Doros collected their soiled clothing and left clean white robes for their use. They discussed the day's events and shared what each considered their favorite highlight. Pitchers of wine and grape juice arrived, and they quenched their thirsts. Coleman reminded Ayascho to sip, not guzzle. The young man was slowly beginning to control his passion for strong drink. Of course, Coleman drank only juice.

The men lounged in the warm water for over a segment, and then they dressed in the robes Doros had left for them. They returned to the guesthouse. Coleman entered first and found a woman standing at the table, placing a tray of meat and vegetables at its center. Her back was to the door, and she didn't notice him enter. She was clad in the same type of utilitarian white dress that Teema wore. She was much taller than Teema, taller than most men Coleman had seen. A braid of lustrous black hair hung down the center of her back that reached below her waist. He could only see her back and profile, but she appeared to be a very lovely young woman.

"Good timing, I am starved!" Coleman said with gusto. The woman jumped at the sound of his booming voice and knocked over the water pitcher. Water gushed across the table and started dripping onto the floor. She became flustered and didn't know what to do next. At first, she turned toward him and gave a quick bow, and then she lifted the overturned pitcher. She grabbed a towel from the bench and began sopping up the water. In her rush, she knocked over the pitcher of wine, and it crashed to the floor, sending wine and shards of pottery to the far corners of the room. The three men stopped in place and gaped as the disaster unfolded. She sank to a bench and began sobbing uncontrollably, her hands covering her face.

At that moment, Teema entered, deftly dodging past the men as she rushed to the other woman. "What have you done?" Teema demanded in an angry tone.

"He scared me, and I knocked over the water pitcher. And then I knocked over the wine," the poor young woman admitted.

"Oy, for the love of the gods, Maaryah, how could you be so clumsy? Master Tondo, I will see that this mess is cleaned up immediately. Maaryah, fetch more towels, and make it quick." The young woman dashed out of the guesthouse and ran to the back of the manor house. While she was gone, Teema mopped up as much of the wine and water as she could, all the time apologizing profusely.

"Calm yourself, Teema. It was my fault. I should not have startled her," Coleman confessed.

"I will see that the girl is punished, but please, don't tell Foreman Nestor," she pleaded.

"There is to be no punishment. This is only an accident, and it was my fault." Teema stood and faced Coleman. It was then he noticed a nasty looking purple and red bruise on her cheek. "What is this?" he asked as he lightly touched her wound. She flinched.

"I was slow in bringing Foreman Nestor his wash water last night."

"He hit you for that? There must be more to this, so tell me what it is."

"I can never please him when he's in a foul mood, master," she said.

Coleman cringed again at his unwanted title. "Yes, go on," he encouraged.

"If I bring him water to wash with first, he hits me for not bringing food first. If I bring food first, he hits me for not bringing water first. It all depends on his mood, master."

"That will end. I have already talked with Foreman Nestor, and I told him there will be no more of that. If he strikes you again, you are to report it to me. Do you understand?"

"Yes, master." She looked at him in wonder. Maaryah's footsteps could be heard, and she soon dashed into the room, her arms full of towels. "Quickly, child, clear the table, and I will sop up the spill," Teema ordered.

Coleman was amazed by how quickly the two women worked. It took only a few minutes for them to clean up the mess. They hustled out of the room and returned a few minutes later with fresh pitchers of wine and water. They placed them on the table, stepped back, and waited for the men to seat themselves. It was Teema's duty to anticipate their needs, and she closely watched them with a trained eye. Maaryah stood looking down, her chin touching her chest. Coleman moved to her and gently lifted her chin with a finger. She jumped at his touch. He looked into her eyes and saw fear and despair. She was a lovely young woman with high cheekbones and almond-shaped, golden-amber eyes. She shivered when she noticed his blue eyes, and for a long moment, she couldn't stop staring at the unexpected and chilling sight. She recalled the recurring dream she'd been having and shuddered in fear. She soon caught herself and dropped her gaze in submission.

"I am sorry I scared you. I will be more careful in the future," he promised.

"Please, master, don't send me to Foreman Nestor; please, please," she begged as she absentmindedly touched her left shoulder with her right hand. "It will never happen again," she pleaded.

"I have no intention of sending you to anyone. It was my fault. The only damage is a clay pitcher and some wine. Hardly worth punishing someone for. Now, you and Teema may go." Maaryah looked at Teema. The older woman gave a nod, and the two started to leave the room. In her hustle and bustle, Maaryah's work gown had slipped over her left shoulder a bit, and when she turned to leave, Coleman noticed a nasty, fresh looking welt there, just visible above the neckline of her utilitarian tunic. The memory of the abuse the poor slave girl from the dancing troupe received for spurning the boorish reveler jumped into his mind. "Wait!" he ordered. "Maaryah, what happened to your back?"

Maaryah turned around, wearing a startled expression, and bowed her head. "Foreman Nestor used his whip on me a short time ago, master," she admitted in a timid voice as she touched her left shoulder with her right hand again.

"Come here and let me take a look at it," Coleman coaxed.

The young woman looked at Teema with pleading eyes, but the older woman just looked down. Maaryah walked to her master, submitting to his command. She untied her gown's front laces, turned her back to him, and unexpectedly, slipped both arms out of her tunic through its neck, exposing most of her back and clutching the loose material to her chest. Coleman hadn't expected her to bare her entire back to him, but what he saw chased away his titillating astonishment. A horrible looking welt ran diagonally across her back from left shoulder to the right side of her waist. He could see it was a recent wound, for it was still healing. Several smaller, older welts were also visible on her lower back. Maaryah began to tremble and weep.

"Does it still hurt?" he asked.

"Yes, master, very much so," she replied in a quavering voice. Without saying a word, he lightly touched her naked left shoulder. When she felt his hand on her bare flesh, she flinched in fright and gave a startled cry of anguish. Unexpectedly, the burning pain she had tried to ignore for wernts diminished and then disappeared. She looked over her shoulder and saw Coleman's smile. He gave her a wink and lifted his hand from her shoulder.

"That will do, Maaryah," he told her in a gentle voice, still surprised she had bared her back in such a way. She quickly put her arms through the neck of her gown, tied its laces, and faced him. "Why did he do this to you?" Coleman asked in a concerned tone.

"I was slow in learning my new duties at the Separation House, master," she replied, her voice shaking, her head turned, and her chin touching her right shoulder. Coleman could tell by her demeanor she wasn't telling him everything.

"What else?" he asked in a stern voice.

"Please, master, don't make me tell you. I'm . . . I'm ashamed."

"I need to know what my foreman is up to. I want you to tell me why he did this to you." Coleman would not relent. Anger was beginning to well at his center, for he had a dire suspicion of what she was about to tell him. As his anger grew, the others in the room could feel it like the heat radiating from an oven, and they shifted uncomfortably in their places.

Maaryah's eyes were staring at the floor as she spoke, "I . . . I wouldn't surrender to his lust," she admitted as tears rolled down her cheeks. Coleman gazed into Teema's face and saw a look of anger and frustration, etched there by past experience.

"You have done nothing to be ashamed of. I'll put an end to such abuse. Both of you may go." The women exited, and the men ate.

Coleman didn't say a word, and while eating, pondered his next step. As far as he could tell, Nestor knew how to keep this estate running efficiently. Coleman, himself, had no idea about how to run a divitz plantation or any other major farming enterprise. Although he had spent many summers of his youth on his grandfather's farm, he considered himself little more than a farmhand. If he let Nestor go, who would see to the harvest? What else needed to be done, and what preparations needed to be made? How do you sell divitz? How would he care for all those in his charge without the foreman's help? He didn't know a lot of things, but what worried him the most was the things he didn't know he didn't know. What made the situation even worse: he didn't even know how to read or write in this strange language.

"Is there anyone besides Nestor who can handle such a large operation as this one?" Coleman finally asked Idop.

"Probably not; Nestor's the best. Everyone I know attests to that. All the remaining strong foremen are working other estates," Idop advised. "What difference does it make if he beats a slave from time-to-time? He gets the work done. Isn't that good enough?"

"How would you like to be beaten at the whim of an overseer? How would you like it if you were told how you were to live your life each day? How would you like it if . . . " Coleman stopped. How much different was Idop from a slave in this kingdom? He had even sacrificed a knuckle to the dictates of a king.

"Slaves are slaves. They are here to serve us, the freeborn. That's the order of things; it's the great chain of being, and your silly fretting over a few beatings is ridiculous," Idop spouted in an angry tone.

Coleman took a deep breath and calmed himself. Idop had lived with slavery all his long life, and he wasn't about to change his thinking quickly. As Coleman saw it, there were two tasks before him: convincing these people that slavery was a condition, not a race. And he had to convince the slaves that freedom had its own costs.

"Have the slaves any rights?" Coleman asked Idop.

"Under Slave Law, they have the Right of Person. That means they can't be killed without the order of an adjudicator. Also, women can't be accosted, at least involuntarily."

"Accosted?" Coleman wondered.

"Forced coupling," Idop simply stated.

"Then how is it that my foreman can beat a woman for not submitting to his wanton cravings?" Idop didn't answer. After some thought, Coleman guessed that once spurned by a slave girl, anything she did from then on wouldn't meet expectations, allowing the foreman to punish her as he pleased. "My homeland once allowed slavery. It became an illness that tore the kingdom apart. I am sure the same thing will eventually happen here. People desire to be masters of their own destinies, and eventually, they will have it. You may own a slave, but at night, he will dream of freedom."

"They are not people; they're slaves. The marked are born to serve the freeborn. That's just the way it is and always will be. Anyway, what do you know about the dreams of slaves?" Idop scowled.

Ayascho decided to enter the discussion. "Slaves are not born with those marks, are they? How does a mark change what's in a person's heart? The great god has given his children freedom so we can make our own choices. In that way, we either learn to follow Batru or Uragah, to nurture the good seeds or the evil seeds, growing in knowledge and wisdom by the choices we make. If slaves aren't allowed to freely choose, how can they grow? Slavery is evil because it thwarts the great god's plan." Idop was silent. Coleman simply nodded.

After dinner, Ayascho, still dressed in a white robe, went outside and sat under the large oak-like tree at the front of the guesthouse, watching the small feathered creatures as they pecked and scratched the ground. Idop, having changed into the red robes of a king's counselor, walked down to the ocean and strolled along the beach. Coleman remained in the guesthouse. He changed into the only other set of clothing he had; the fine leathers Atura had made for him so long ago. He sat at the table and contemplated his options as darkness began filling the guesthouse. Idop and Ayascho both returned at the same time, said a few words in passing, and went to their separate rooms for a good night's rest. Sometime later, Coleman heard Nestor ride up on his samaran, and he heard the foreman's heavy footsteps as he returned to his cabin.

"He may have many bad traits, but laziness is not one of them," Coleman thought. The man worked from before first light until well after the p´atezas had set, even longer than the slaves did.

The foreman went into his cabin and lit an oil lamp. Coleman quickly followed and was standing outside in the shadows when Teema arrived with a tray of food and drink. Nestor berated the woman for not bringing wash water and drew his arm back to slap her. She cringed as she prepared to receive the blow. He suddenly stopped as Coleman entered the dimly lit room.

"Get water for me to wash with, and towels," Nestor commanded the woman. He looked at Coleman. "Yes, sire, what can I do for ya? May I offer ya some wine?"

"No, thank you," Coleman replied as he pulled up a bench and sat across the table from Nestor. "Go ahead, sit, eat. You have had a long day." Nestor didn't hesitate, sat, and began eating. He ate as if he were famished.

Teema soon returned with water and fresh towels, and then she quickly exited. Nestor washed his hands, arms, and face; then, he continued eating. He guzzled his wine, and it poured out of the corners of his mouth.

He eats like a pig, Coleman thought to himself. "Tell me about your day. I want to learn about your duties," Coleman finally said.

"First thing in the morning, long before dawn, I gave the herders their assignments, then I made the rounds. Ya have to be sure the lazy dung creepers are up and working. Ya can never trust 'em to do anything on their own. If ya ain't watching, they ain't doing. That's my motto." Nestor grabbed a whole loaf of bread and bit into it as large crumbs fell to the table. He took another swig of wine and belched. "That is good; the best. Ya sure ya don't want some, sire."

"No, thank you. I have already eaten. So, were all the lazy creepers up and working?"

"Yes, sire! Theys know better than to try to fool me. I see to it that theys all know their duties, and theys doin' 'em. I just gotta kick 'em in the arse once in a while."

"Kick any arse today?" Coleman asked calmly.

"Only that lazy Tiro, but ya let him go. Bad mistake, sire. He got away with it today. I'll bet a regum he and two others will be sick tomorrow. Just ya wait and see."

"That is a bet I am willing to make," Coleman bluntly stated.

Nestor choked on his food, then took a gulp of wine. "That's just a fig'r a speech, sire. I don't got no regums, no ways."

"What's a herder?" Coleman asked.

"They's slaves whose job it is to see their herd—the other slaves—gets the work done. If theys don't, well theys gotta answer to me," Nestor explained.

"Tell me what you did in the afternoon," Coleman urged.

"I spent all afternoon and evening in the Separation House. The last fields of divitz is just start'n to pod, and the pickers are get'n ahead of them separators. I'm gonna have to add more on the hand cranks."

"This is a big operation. Do you have any other foremen to help you?"

"By the gods, no! Any foreman worth his share don't need no help. I tell the herders what's to be done, and theys see to it. I gotta keen eye, and if something ain't right, I catch it right away. I can be anywheres I need to be, and I can do anything that needs do'in," Nestor bragged.

"What is your pay?"

"Megato Oetan pays me one in every hundred. Considering this is the biggest operation on the Anterran Peninsula, that's fair. Why do ya ask, sire? Are ya planning to change my contract?"

"I have no plans to do that. You will be paid the agreed amount through the harvest. By the way, one in every hundred what?"

Nestor laughed. "Ya never done divitz before have ya, sire?" Coleman shook his head. "I get one bale per hundred. Foremen on smaller estates get one in a hundred and twenty, maybe less. But this is a big estate, and I'm worth every bale. Just ask anyone."

Coleman could see, the man had no doubt of his worth, that was clear. "How many slaves are working the estate?" he wondered.

"Two-hundred and fifty; man, woman, and child, sire."

"Do you know Maaryah?" Coleman asked.

"Yes, sire, I knows 'em all. She's young, robust, and tall. That's why I picked her for ya. She'll keep yer feet warm on a cold night," Nestor said, displaying a wicked smile.

Coleman gave his foreman an angry glare before continuing. "Did you whip her?"

"She was working as a separator 'til this morning. Lady Oetan wanted a new girl for the guesthouse; for ya and the others. Anyways, she was lazy and slow-witted, so I helped her learn a bit faster. She was begin'n to get the hang of it. Now, I gotta train someone new. Bad timing, just plain bad timing, I says."

"I heard you made improper advances toward her."

"Improper advances? What in the names of the Five Shadows does that mean?"

"Did you try to violate her Right of Person?" Coleman asked, his blue eyes boring into his foreman.

Nestor looked confused and cocked his head as if he didn't understand. After a short pause, he took a deep breath and began speaking with certainty, "Half'a these fools lie, and the other half don't tell the truth. Don't believe noth'n theys says and only half of what ya sees. Ya'll be the wiser for it, sire."

There may be some truth in what he said, but Coleman didn't trust the man, and he hadn't answered the question. He was a vile, earthy man who saw the world in his own twisted way. Right now, Coleman needed him, so he would do nothing. It was a bitter pill to swallow, but swallow it he must.

Coleman had Nestor review all he had done that day, asking pertinent questions along the way. He could tell, Nestor didn't like having to report to him, or anyone for that matter.

"I thank you for taking the time to tell me what happened today. I will expect a report every night."

"Every night, sire?"

"Yes, *every* night. Oh, and remember, no beatings without my permission; that includes Teema."

"Yes, sire. It's gonna make it hard to get all the work done, don't ya know?"

"I am sure you will find a way. After all, you can be anywhere you need to be, and you can do anything that needs doing, right?"

"Yes, sire," Nestor replied meekly. Coleman stood and left the cabin. Nestor pondered his options. *I oughta let the estate fall apart. That'll show the fool,* he thought. However, he quickly realized his payout and reputation would suffer. He would have to succeed, somehow, for the remainder of the harvest season, no matter what. He could then revisit his options. In anger, Nestor threw his clay cup, and it hit the cabin wall, shattering, the sound of shards bouncing across the dimly lit floor.

"Teema, more wine!" he bellowed.

Coleman heard the cup shatter, and he chuckled. He walked down to the beach and strolled across its glistening sands. Only a gibbous Munnoga floated in the night sky, and it cast a silvery light over the waves and sand. The scene brought memories of a world far away. For just a moment, he pretended he was home, walking a Pacific Ocean beach in the San Francisco Bay Area. It was there he had lived a much easier life, a life he understood well. His thoughts quickly returned to the here and now. He would just as soon turn this whole operation over to Lady Oetan and leave. But leave to where? He had no idea. He had yet to meet with the priests, and maybe they could help him understand his visions, his new powers, and, most importantly, his purpose here. Yet, they seemed to be in no hurry to meet with him, the one they had the king fetch. He resigned himself to play the waiting game. In the meantime, he would try to bring some peace and less suffering to those under his stewardship.

As he was walking along the beach, his sandaled foot struck a rock or shell—something hard anyway—poking out of the sand. He bent down and tried to lift it. The object resisted his attempts, so he dropped to one knee and dug it out of the damp sand. He examined it, but he really couldn't tell what it was in the dim light. It was surprisingly heavy. He decided to take it back to the guesthouse and get a better look at it in the morning light.

"I had better get to bed," he said to himself. "Every night is a short night," he mused as he thought about the p´atezas dial's revelation. When he got back to the guesthouse, he placed the object he'd found on the table and turned in for the night.

He awoke with the red glow of the p´atezas shining in his eyes. He peeked over the edge of the bed and saw that Ayascho was not on the floor. He rubbed his eyes and felt pain in his legs. He arose and limped bow-legged into the living room. Ayascho was sitting on a bench examining the object Coleman had left on the table the night before.

"I hurt. I can't walk right," Ayascho said. "What's this?" he asked as he examined the object.

"I found it on the beach last night. Let me look at it." The object was longer than his hand with fingers extended. It weighed more than a pound and was colored in several shades of gray. It was roughly the shape of a triangle with a dip in the broad end, opposite the point. Its edges were striated. Coleman kept turning it over and over in his hands and then held it in his palms.

"This looks like a shark's tooth, from one heck of a monster shark," he said aloud using godspeak. Ayascho just looked at the object. He had learned to wait for Coleman to explain himself if he chose to. "I know what this is. It is the tooth of a megalodon or something like it!" Coleman exclaimed.

"What's a meg-harh-don?" Ayascho questioned.

"We saw one from the bluff, remember. Now, I know why no one goes on the ocean. This is just one tooth, and the monster has more than a hundred teeth like this. It could bite you in half and not even know it," Coleman teased as he lunged toward Ayascho while holding the tooth like a dagger. Ayascho jumped back and fell to the floor. Coleman chuckled and helped him up. It was then he noticed the fresh meat, fruits, and a bowl of what appeared to be odd colored eggs on the table, so he decided to pause for breakfast.

"Oy, one thing is for sure, no one is going surfing today or any other day. A great white is bad enough, but this thing is a real monster. No wonder they call it the *terror*."

Coleman tore an end piece off a loaf of bread, dipped it into the oil bowl, then munched it down, and tried to ignore the bread's mild bitterness. He picked up one of the eggs and examined it. It was about the size of a chicken egg, only more elongated. The shell was dark gray in color and hard. He cracked the shell and discovered the egg had been hard-boiled, so he peeled the thick shell away. The egg itself was olive drab in color. Coleman sniffed it. *Smells like a chicken egg*, he thought to himself. He took a knife and cut it in half. It had a rust-colored yoke. He took a small, tentative bite and smiled.

"Ayascho, have you tried one of these?" he asked.

"No. I didn't know you could eat them. What are they?"

"These are eggs. Remember the thrice's eggs? These are like those, only smaller, and they taste great. Try one," Coleman encouraged. Ayascho took one from the bowl, peeled away its shell, and started eating. He also smiled.

Idop walked into the room, "It's about time you woke up. I thought you were going to sleep the day away," he said in mock annoyance.

Coleman picked up an egg, "These eggs are great! Where do they come from?"

"They're frizzard eggs; nothing special," Idop told him.

"What is a frizzard?"

Idop walked to the front door and signaled for Tondo to join him. When Coleman did, he pointed to the chicken-like dinosaurs scratching and pecking the ground in the yard. "Sire Tondo, those are frizzards. If you don't even know that, you're in a lot more trouble than I thought."

Coleman, feeling foolish, simply nodded in agreement and went back to the table to finish his meal.

Idop stood in the doorway, silently watching the frizzards feed. An impish grin slowly crept across his face. He turned toward the other two and spoke, "Ayascho," he called, "Tondo told me, you're the fastest runner in your village. Is that true?" Ayascho nodded. "I bet you can't catch a frizzard." Ayascho didn't answer and just sat looking at the counselor. "Only the fastest runners can catch a frizzard. I doubt you can."

Coleman could see by Idop's expression he was up to something, so he thought he'd play along. "I think you are wrong, counselor. Ayascho can do it faster than it takes to count to fifty."

"No one has ever caught a frizzard that fast. They're too shifty. I bet he couldn't catch one at all," Idop challenged.

"Ayascho, prove him wrong. Show him how fast you really are," Tondo encouraged. Ayascho just sat, looking at the counselor.

"He won't try. He doesn't want to embarrass himself. After all, he's just a man from the Wilderness," Idop spewed.

"Ayascho, are you going to stand for that? Defend your Batru brothers' honor. Show this Anterran who is the fastest," Coleman goaded. He didn't know where this was going, but the idea of watching Ayascho chasing a frizzard around the barnyard had to be entertaining. The thought brought forth memories of his youth when he tried to catch chickens on his grandfather's farm. At the very least, he was sure he'd get a good laugh out of it.

Ayascho finished the bunch of grapes he was eating, rose from the table, and strode to the doorway. Idop stepped aside, and Ayascho looked out into the barnyard. "Which one?" he asked.

"The green one," Idop said, pointing to a green frizzard about ten strides away.

Ayascho was off in a flash. Coleman dashed to the door and started counting. Both he and Idop were wildly laughing as they watched Ayascho scrambling after the green frizzard as it dodged and squawked its fear. Just as Ayascho was about to grab it, the frizzard turned back and ran toward the guest-house.

"Twenty . . . twenty-one . . . twenty-two! Hurry, Ayascho!" Coleman shouted through his laughter.

Ayascho was about to grab the frizzard again, but it turned quickly and avoided him. A huge cloud of dust was being kicked up by Ayascho and the frizzard as they dashed back and forth. The frizzard was squawking in terror the whole time.

"Forty-one . . . forty-two . . . forty-three! Hurry, Ayascho! Time is almost up!" Coleman shouted.

Coleman and Idop could see the desperation on Ayascho's face as he dashed back across the front of the guesthouse once again. The frizzard made another quick turn, but Ayascho was ready this time, and he grabbed it with both hands, pulling it to his chest. He stood breathing heavily, a huge smile covering his face. The frizzard continued squawking its fear with its tongue hanging out of its mouth.

"I knew you could do it!" Coleman shouted.

"I'd have never believed it if I hadn't seen it with my own eyes," Idop declared.

"What do I do with it now?" Ayascho wondered.

"Look at the poor thing," Idop said, "its tongue is hanging out. You've overheated it."

"Could it die?" Ayascho asked with concern.

"Ha! Yes. You need to cool it down," Idop told him with a grin.

"How do I do that?"

"Dip it in the water trough, over there," Idop advised while pointing. Ayascho moved toward the trough as he stroked the frizzard's head, attempting to calm the poor frantic creature. Idop leaned toward Coleman and whispered, "Watch what happens when that frizzard gets wet."

When Ayascho reached the water trough, he slowly lowered the frizzard into the water, making sure its head remained above the surface. He glanced back at Idop and Coleman, giving them a toothy smile. Unexpectedly, the creature's terror-filled squawk changed to surprise, and then it began to wriggle, squirm, and kick; its sharp beak pinched Ayascho's hand, and its taloned feet clawed at his wrists. He yelped in pain and dropped the frizzard into the water trough. The creature struggled, its scrawny wings flapping wildly. Using its beak, the frizzard climbed onto the trough's edge. As its taloned feet gripped the wood, its body shook, and water flew in all directions. It then spread its wings wide, lowered its head, and sounded an alarming low guttural growl. It jumped to the ground and attacked Ayascho, pecking his sandaled feet and pinching his toes. Ayascho gave a cry of pain and took off at a run, the frizzard nipping at his heels.

Coleman and Idop were howling in laughter as Ayascho dashed past them, heading toward the barn, zigzagging and crying out in pain as the frizzard continued pinching and pecking his heels. He cut back and ran toward the two men. He ran in a tight circle, which confused the frizzard long enough for him to dash into the guesthouse and slam the door. The frizzard ran to the door and hit it feet first. It bounced back, its wings flapping as it continued its angry growl. It noticed

Coleman and Idop nearby, lowered its head, and charged them. The two men dashed off in opposite directions; Idop heading for the barn and Coleman rushing toward the manor house. The frizzard went after Coleman and quickly caught up to him, nipping at his heels. Coleman ran in circles and then dashed for the barn, following Idop.

The counselor quickly climbed the loft ladder and watched as Coleman charged into the barn, jumped to the third rung of the ladder, and scampered onto the loft. Both men peered over the loft's edge, eyeing the angry frizzard as it patrolled back and forth, waiting for the men to come down, all the while growling its anger. It took some time, but it finally tired of waiting and left the barn.

Coleman looked at Idop and laughed, "And I thought you didn't have a sense of humor."

Coleman and Ayascho were much too sore from the previous day's samaran riding to do any riding this day, so Coleman planned to take a more detailed tour of the estate buildings. As they were leaving the guesthouse, he noticed Maaryah standing alone, near the cliffs. He hadn't seen her all morning, but he guessed she was the one who had brought them their morning food and drinks. As he thought about her, he realized he hadn't seen her since last-meal yesterday evening when she and Teema had served them. He was about to go to her to make sure she was all right, but he changed his mind

when he saw Teema rushing toward her. He turned and followed Ayascho into the barn.

Teema scurried to Maaryah and grabbed her upper right
arm. "What are you doing here, child? There's work to be
done." Maaryah wiped away tears streaking her cheeks. "Why
the tears, girl?" Teema asked while still holding Maaryah's
upper arm. Maaryah only stared down at a terror patrolling
the waters below, and she said nothing. "Where were you last
night? Your bed hasn't been slept in." Maaryah didn't answer
and began wiping away more tears. Teema was becoming
frustrated, and she shook Maaryah by the arm. "Answer me,
girl, this instant!" Teema barked.

"I went back to my home."

"Your home! That's far away. I told you, you're to sleep in
my room at the manor house now. Why did you go back?"

"I'm afraid," Maaryah whined.

"Afraid? Afraid of what?" Teema wondered.

"I won't go in the guesthouse at night. I won't!" she shouted above the noise of the pounding surf.

"You left the master and his companions to fend for themselves all evening? I should beat you myself. It's your duty to
see to their needs," Teema scolded and emphasized her angst
by shaking Maaryah again.

"I won't!" Maaryah shouted as she leaned forward.

Teema's grip tightened on the young woman's upper arm,
and she pulled Maaryah back from the brink. "My child, what
are you doing?" Teema shrieked, her voice expressing her
fright.

"Let me go! Let me end my suffering!" Maaryah cried.

Teema pulled the young woman away from the cliff's edge and turned her so they faced each other, gripping her by the upper arms. "What's all this? What suffering? What has the master done?" Teema asked.

"He's done nothing, yet, but my life is horrible. I can't stand it no more. Papa was taken, Mama died, and now this," Maaryah began weeping openly, covering her face with her hands.

"Stop your blubbering! Tell me what you're afraid of."

Maaryah took a deep breath and attempted to regain her composure. "Foreman Nestor chose me to serve the new master and his companions because I wouldn't give myself to him. It's his punishment. He says I'll be their pleasure-girl. I'll kill myself first."

"Silly girl, you belong to the master; accept it. Stop this foolishness right now!" Teema demanded.

"I won't go to the guesthouse at night; I won't!" Maaryah shouted.

"You have duties there, so you must. I expect you to stay there until the master dismisses you," Teema sternly told her.

"Teema, I'm afraid. I'm afraid of what he might do. Don't you understand?"

"Only too well, child; however, I think our new master is not like Master Oetan. He could have tossed Lady Oetan and Mistress Ootyiah out into the cold without so much as a cloak, but he didn't. He's allowing them to remain here as his guests. He even chose to live in the guesthouse rather than force them out of the Big House. He protected me from Foreman Nestor last night. And he told me to tell him if the foreman hits me again. Now, I expect you to perform *your* duties and enough of this foolishness. You are not to hide in your shanty ever again. Do you understand?"

"I won't be anyone's pleasure-girl," Maaryah stated bluntly.

"I doubt you will be. I believe this master is kind. He's a blessing sent by the gods," Teema told her.

"And if he isn't?" Maaryah worriedly pleaded.

Teema took a deep breath and sadly replied, "The cliffs and terrors will always be here."

As Coleman and Ayascho made their tour of the manor grounds, they noticed all the buildings were made from sand-colored brick. The bricks were roughly uniform in size, very hard, and resistant to weathering. It appeared to Coleman, they had been kiln-baked. Tall brick columns with long wooden beam spans supported the roofs, such as in the barn. Nowhere could Coleman find an arch, and he smiled at this realization.

After a couple of segments exploring, they had finished. On the way back to the guesthouse, they made a detour and limped to the bluff overlooking the ocean. Idop joined them there. They saw the beach had disappeared, and the sea level had climbed nearly half-way up the cliff. A terror's huge fin could be seen not far away.

"What's going on here?" Ayascho wondered. "Why is the water so high?"

"It must be approaching high tide," Idop assumed. If Idop

was correct, it would mean a high tide of more than twenty feet.

"Now, that is what I call a high tide, a very high one," Coleman noted.

"I've seen it higher. When there's a sutrum high tide, the water will rise to just below where we are standing," Idop told him.

Coleman stood pondering the phenomenon for a while. "I guess the positions of the three moons have a lot to do with that," he finally concluded.

"Do you mean the moons make the water go up and down like this? How is that possible?" Ayascho wondered.

"Oh yes, the moons probably cause a lot of things. I would bet, they may even cause many of the groundshakes we've been through," Coleman told him.

"Why do you say that?" Idop wondered.

"Gravity," Coleman simply replied in godspeak. He noticed his companions' puzzled expressions. "Gravity is what holds us to the ground. All large bodies have it; this world as well as the moons. It pulls at everything," Coleman explained. His friends' expressions didn't change, so he decided to end his explanation before he added more to their confusion.

The men then moved to the guesthouse and were greeted by a tremulous Maaryah, placing a tray of food on the table. Coleman had lost track of time and was surprised to learn it was already midday. As the three men were eating, Maaryah nervously stood nearby, shifting from one foot to the other, wishing she could hide somewhere.

After a short time, Teema and Doros entered with bundles

of clothing. "Lady Oetan would like you to have these things. They were Master Oetan's clothes," Doros told Coleman.

He examined the items. There were tunics and a few toga-like robes. All were finely crafted and included various patterns. Coleman took a tunic and went into his bedroom to change. When he returned, Idop and Ayascho started laughing. The tunic he wore was much too small for him. He had accidentally ripped open one of the sleeves because of the girth of his upper arm. The material was stretched across his chest, and the tunic was so short, it looked like he was wearing a miniskirt. It was obvious, Oetan was a much smaller man than he.

"Thank Lady Oetan for these things, but obviously, I cannot wear them. Ayascho and Idop, see if any fit you."

The other two men were closer to Oetan's size, and the clothes fit well enough. Coleman still had only two changes of leathers.

Teema began speaking, "Master, I'm sure Maaryah can make appropriate clothing for you." She turned, facing the guesthouse slave, and continued, "It's one of her duties."

Maaryah was shocked by Teema's revelation. She swallowed hard and said, "Master Tondo, I'll do my best.

"Thank you, Maaryah. The clothes I have are showing wear, and they are of a style the folks around here are not accustomed to."

After Teema and Doros left, Ayascho began scratching and soon removed his tunic, standing in the center of the room in his village loincloth. "I don't like this thing. It makes me itch," he said, pointing to the tunic on the floor.

"I am sorry, my friend, but you will have to get used to it. These are the things people wear here," Coleman advised. He noticed Maaryah was staring at the floor, causing him to smile at her embarrassment. Reluctantly, Ayascho put the tunic on again, but he continued scratching for the remainder of the day.

In the afternoon, Coleman called for ink, quill, and paper. For the next hour or so, he drew plans, crumpling and tossing out several drafts. His biggest problem was figuring out how to use a quill properly, dropping globs of ink on his work from time-to-time. Finally, he was satisfied with what he had accomplished.

"What's that?" Ayascho asked as he and Idop hovered over the drawing.

"The samaran saddles are missing something very important," Coleman informed him. "This, my friend, is a stirrup. Instead of having your feet dangle along the samaran's sides, you put them in stirrups attached to the saddle. The rider will be more comfortable and more stable."

"I'll have to see it to believe it," Idop said. "I've never had a problem riding. I don't see why it has any value."

"Oh, believe me, you will see the difference immediately. Trust me on this," Coleman told him.

When he had completed the plans, he presented them to Pendor. After several questions from the blacksmith, he was told it would take a day or two to complete three pairs. Coleman told him that would be acceptable. He decided not to say anything to Seemo, the samaran handler until he had the finished product, but he knew Seemo was going to have to alter the saddles to accommodate the new addition.

The three men relaxed for the remainder of the day. For Coleman and Ayascho, it was a welcomed respite from all their travel and activity over the past five detzamars. Both men felt their weariness and napped all afternoon. Idop grew restless and left the others to their ease. He made his way along the cliffs and threw rocks into the ocean below. He didn't like this idleness, but he understood the ordeal the other two had been through. He wondered if he could have made such a dangerous trek. Maaryah remained in the guesthouse as instructed by Teema, waiting to serve the men, struggling to sew her master's new clothes, and grateful that he and the savage were napping.

The next several days came and went with little fanfare. Coleman toured his estate riding a samaran every morning. Both he and Ayascho were becoming accustomed to their new mounts, their soreness diminishing day-by-day. Pendor had finished the three sets of stirrups, and Coleman helped Seemo prepare a saddle for use by one set. The samaran handler well-understood saddles and was very helpful in making the modifications. The next day, Coleman rode all morning on his modified saddle with stirrups, and then had Seemo examine both his samaran and the saddle for any unwanted side effects.

Both seemed just fine, so he had two more saddles converted to the new design. The counselor still had his doubts, but when Coleman stood in his stirrups and fired an arrow from his bow, his opinion quickly changed. Due to his military background, Idop immediately realized the implication this meant for riders in combat. A mounted unit of warriors so equipped and armed with bows could be devastating to an unprepared foe.

Idop practically begged Coleman to help him make a bow for himself. Ayascho wanted one, also. It had taken Coleman what he referred to as weeks of trial and error to construct his bow, and the materials he'd used in the Wilderness were not available to him now. After some thought, he decided to experiment with a metal bow. He drew up plans and showed them to Pendor, the blacksmith. After Coleman explained the bow's purpose, giving him a demonstration with his wooden composite bow, Pendor told him, he would need to use sutro gravetum ore. Pendor didn't have any, and it was very hard to come by. The little he had seen always arrived by caravan, and was very expensive. Coleman thought for a few moments, then he went into the barn and returned with two five-pound chunks of blue meteorite.

"Will this work?" he asked.

Pendor examined the heavy stones closely, wiped the sweat from his brow with his forearm, and said, "Sire, I'll give it a try. I'll know by midday tomorrow if it's any good."

As it turned out, the meteorite chunks produced the best sutro gravetum Pendor had ever worked with. It was difficult to heat properly and form, but he was able to create two cobalt-blue bows. After some testing, Coleman determined that

although inferior to his composite bow, they were quite ade-
quate. From that day forth, the men practiced archery for at
least one segment every morning.

Maaryah kept her promise and started presenting Coleman
with new clothing. The utilitarian dress for men of the gentry was the tunic. He wasn't fond of them. He preferred trousers and instructed Maaryah to start making them for him.
Her first attempt at making the unfamiliar garment didn't
turn out so well, but she quickly adjusted her technique, and
in short-order, she began producing comfortable and durable
trousers made from heavy cotton twill similar to denim. The
only complaint Coleman had was that they came in a dingy
white color only and soiled quickly.

The three men settled into a daily routine: in the morning, they would explore the estate. During one of these excur-
sions, they found a brick kiln. It looked like a large operation,
but no one was present when his party found it, and it looked
to have been unused for quite some time. During his nightly briefings with Nestor, he learned that it was fired up and
used only when needed. They also found a large lake, fed by a
stream that disappeared into the forested area on the boundary of the estate. An outlet stream meandered its way to the
ocean many miles away.

Their afternoons were free, so Coleman began pleading
with Idop to teach him to read and write, but Idop resisted. He told Coleman, he wasn't a scholar and had little pa-
tience for teaching anyone anything. After Coleman's continued pleas, he relented. Their first few sessions were an exercise in frustration for both. It wasn't so much that Idop was, in

fact, a bad teacher—actually he was horrid—but the biggest problem, Idop wasn't very literate himself. The only written records they had to work with were the official documents of summons, rank, and stewardship of the estate. Idop stumbled over words like a young schoolboy, and he grew increasingly frustrated when he couldn't read a word. This happened many times, over and over. Coleman had wanted Ayascho to learn to read and write, too, but after their frustrating struggle of the first couple of days, he was no longer expected to join them. A few days after that, with great disappointment, Coleman gave up on the whole effort.

"Is there anyone in the city who can teach me?" Coleman asked.

"I don't know about teaching, but you can hire readers to read and write documents for you. I used a reader when I commanded the Pannera."

"I really need to learn this for myself," Coleman told him.

During his explorations, Coleman found a bundle of wicker-like splints stored in an out of the way place in the barn, near where the trunk containing the thrice eggs was stored. Seemo told him, the material was used for making baskets. There were a couple of older slaves who were quite adept at basket weaving, but Nestor had sent them into the fields until the harvest was over. Coleman took some of the material with him to the guesthouse. At night, he would sit in front of the fireplace and weave, just the way Tzeechoe had taught him. He called it his *therapy*. He missed his friend. He even missed Atura, and he wondered how they were doing.

CHAPTER 16

RETRIBUTION

Defetane Hunder and his men had made Grazius's hamlet their base of operations ever since the wicked sorcerer, Tangundo, eluded them. The village residents took the men in and were gratified to have the king's guards there to protect them. Hunder and his men had done a few searches for the band of outlaws before the weather turned for the worse, but after the cold and wet season had arrived in force, Hunder decided to keep his men in the hamlet, choosing not to risk their health and well-being. He sent two of his men back to the city, first, to inform his commander of the situation and to make his liege, King Ben-do-teg, aware of the threat. Also, his men were to return with a wagon load of supplies. It was Hunder's plan to remain stationed at Grazius's hamlet, and after the seasons changed for the better, he'd continue his search for the malefactors. This land was his area of responsibility, and he would not allow such evil and wickedness, the worst he had ever seen, to go unpunished. When the season had turned to mild days and warmer nights again, Hunder and his men sallied forth in search of the reprobates in earnest.

After Tangundo and his band had evaded the king's men, they made their way to the outlaws' old hideout deep in the woods. They lived off the land as they had done before, but no one was satisfied with returning to that hard life. By threats and promises, Tangundo kept his little gang together. They were anything but pleased with their change of fate, but each follower of Munnevo knew the only thing they could do was wait and hope that Tangundo would lead them forth and reclaim what the king's men had taken from them. Their master's promises gave them hope, and they endured in their struggle to survive.

During the times when he and his men had plenty to eat and could relax from hunting and trapping, Tangundo taught his followers how to make and use slings. Tangundo, himself, had become quite proficient with the weapon. Nevesant had also become skilled with the rock-flinger. The other men were having varying degrees of success learning how to use the weapon; it wasn't a skill easily mastered, and it took time and much practice. It seemed to everyone, time was not an issue, and Tangundo saw that his men practiced regularly or suffer for their lethargy.

Tangundo made several attempts to create another weapon from his homeland. A weapon that could shoot wooden shafts great distances, he told his men. Unfortunately, his attempts had always ended in failure. The weapon easily broke, becoming useless and requiring the master to try building a newer and stronger version. He finally ended his attempts in frustration when he realized his followers were losing confidence in their master's abilities. He returned to his rock-flinger and drilled his followers even harder.

A half-span had passed while Tangundo and his marauders remained in hiding. The followers of Munnevo were beginning to complain more often about their circumstances. The short time they had spent as rulers of Grazius's hamlet had left them aching for more of the good life.

"Master, how long are we to remain here in the woodland? Don't you think those king's men woulda gone back to their castle by now?" Sassin wondered.

"Miss your easy meals, Sassin?" Tangundo retorted.

"Yes, master, that and more. You promised we'd rule over others. All we rule over now are trees and rocks," Sassin grumbled.

"Hold your tongue, Sassin, or you'll regret your insolence!" Tangundo threatened. He looked around and saw the other men staring at him, anger and frustration etched on their p´atezas darkened skins. Even Nevesant, his most loyal follower, appeared irked. "What is it, Nevesant? Speak your mind."

"Master, we've been here at the hideout a long time. We haven't seen one sign that the king's men are still looking for us. I think we should go back to the village and see what's there," the young man suggested.

Tangundo thought for a moment before responding. "Do all of you feel the same?" Every one of his followers responded in the affirmative with nods or grunts. "Are you ready for what's coming? We're going to have to face those king's men eventually. Can you handle that?"

"We got you, master," Nevesant offered.

"True, but I can't do it by myself. The lot of you will need to pull your own weight. You think you're ready to commit to such an effort?" Tangundo challenged.

The men looked at each other before responding, all but Nevesant, who stood nodding his head. Finally, Sassin spoke, "Master, we're tired of this place. You gave us a taste of the good life. Now, we want more. As for me, if we retake the town, I'll follow you anywheres. If we don't, I'd sooner be dead."

"Brave words, Sassin, but they're just words. Do you really think you'll feel the same while staring at a king man's blade?" Tangundo wondered. He pulled the sword of authority from his belt and held its point in front of Sassin's face. His follower didn't cower, his angry glare staring into his master's Munnevo-red eyes. Tangundo held the sword for a long time, but Sassin didn't flinch. Tangundo's veiled expression lightened, and he lowered his blade. "Very good. I can tell you're ready. In the morning, we'll begin our return to Grazius's.

The cold season had passed, and Defetane Hunder, leading his men, were back patrolling the land around Grazius's hamlet. The weather had turned for the better, and his for-

ays were now being made more often. He had yet to find any
trace of the evil sorcerer who had murdered the temple priest,
Eezayhod. Hunder swore, he would not return to the castle
until he had captured or killed the wicked one.

"Grazius," Hunder called from atop his mount.

The hamlet leader scurried to the officer and bowed. "Yes,
my liege?"

"Me and my men are going on patrol again. We won't be
back for a wernt or more. You are to defend your village with
the sword I've given you," Hunder ordered.

"Yes, my liege," Grazius weakly replied as he lifted a soldier's short sword.

"If that murderer returns, use it this time. Is that understood?"

"Yes, my liege," Grazius responded a little more forceful-
ly this time, although it was clear his conviction to his duty
was feeble. Hunder gave him a scowl, dug his heels into his
mount's sides, and it took off at a trot, the rest of the detachment following in a double column formation.

Tangundo stopped, and his men gathered around him. He
looked high and low, scanning the area carefully. "What is it,
master?" Nevesant wondered.

"I feel a warning rising, here," he said as he tapped his
chest. "Nevesant, I want you to go ahead and see what it is.
Now, mind me, be careful, and go as stealthily as you can."

Nevesant nodded, a worried expression on his face. The young man quickly disappeared into the trees.

A segment later, he returned. "Master, king's men. They're camped not far from here. I think it's the same ones from Grazius's. What can we do?"

Tangundo looked around and noticed the nervous expressions on his followers' faces. "Now, where is your resolve, Sassin? What about the rest of you? Are you ready for this challenge, or should we go back to the cave and hide a little longer?" Tangundo challenged. His men looked into each other's faces and began responding with pathetic and weak vows of support. Tangundo's Munnevo-red eyes flashed with anger, and his purple aura ignited, chasing away those nearest him.

Nevesant stood his ground, just outside the burning rays. "Master, I won't forsake you. I know we can defeat them. We can use our rock-flingers."

"Alright, Nevesant, the two of us will take them on. At least one follower of Munnevo is a man," Tangundo spat. The others hung their heads in shame, grumbling their resentment.

Finally, Sassin spoke, "I'll go with you. I ain't no coward," he pulled out his sling and held it high. The other men, having been shamed by Nevesant's and Sassin's vows of support for their master, straightened their backs, and stepped forward, as well.

"Good. Now, I'll make a plan. Nevesant, tell me all you've seen."

For the remainder of the day, Tangundo strategized. He realized he didn't have the manpower, weapons, nor the resolve of his followers to attack the king's men directly. He had to use wile and guile if he were to prevail. As his men prepared last-meal, Tangundo and Nevesant explored the area and found a nearby gully with steep sides that would serve his plan well. While everyone ate, Tangundo shared his scheme. They were to initiate it first thing in the morning.

Tangundo and his followers were up and about before light. Nevesant and Tuffen were assigned the dangerous mission of drawing the king's men into the gully Tangundo had chosen for his ambush. Nevesant and Tuffen stealthily moved closer to the king's men's camp, watching and waiting. Hunder's men were just waking when the two outlaws arrived.

"Do we wait or what?" Tuffen nervously asked the younger man.

"I think we should do it now. Their mounts ain't ready. That'll give us a chance to get away before they get started. We'll leave a trail for them to follow," Nevesant whispered. Tuffen looked scared, but he nodded his head. Both men jumped up and stepped from their hiding places, their arms swinging their rock-flingers above their heads. Two large stones flew into a small gathering of king's men as they prepared first-meal. Tuffen's stone missed, but Nevesant's rock hit a king's man in the back of the head, knocking him senseless. The two assailants turned and dashed into the bushes.

"Go get 'em, men!" Hunder yelled to the soldiers who had been targeted. "The rest of you mount up. We'll chase 'em down."

Nevesant and Tuffen charged through the heavy weald, purposely breaking small branches as they passed. The soldiers on foot were no match for the fleet-footed Nevesant, but Tuffen was falling behind. It wasn't long before the outlaw was caught and dispatched by a soldier's sword. Nevesant heard Tuffen's dying screams, and in near panic, he quickened his pace.

After a quarter-segment, Nevesant reached the gully he and his master had found the day before. The young man charged into it, splashing up the small rivulet that ran through the gully's steep sides. As he dashed forward, he scanned to his right and to his left, looking for his comrades. He could see no one. Fear gripped him as he sprinted forward. He could hear mounted soldiers gaining on him, their curses and threats loud in his ears.

Nevesant rounded a bend in the gully and saw his master sitting on a boulder a stone's throw in front of him, a kerchief veiling his face. Tangundo showed no sign of worry. The young man rushed past him, turned, and waited. It wasn't long before Hunder and several of his men rounded the bend and halted their mounts.

"That's close enough!" Tangundo shouted.

"Are you the sorcerer who killed the priest?" Hunder shouted back.

"Yes, I am. I'll give you the same choice I gave him. Kneel before me or die," Tangundo warned.

Several more mounted king's men joined their commander, and others on foot could be seen moving up the gully.

Tangundo moved a little closer to Hunder and then

stopped. "Alright, king's man, what's it to be? Surrender or die."

Hunder drew his sword from its scabbard and pointed it at the sorcerer. "Kill him!" he ordered.

Tangundo armed his rock-flinger and twirled it above his head. Nevesant did the same. The followers of Munnevo rose from their hiding places and began slinging stones at the king's men below them in the gully. Tangundo released his stone, and it hit Hunder on the nose guard of his helm, knocking him off his mount. Several other king's men were also hit by the slingers' stones. Hunder staggered to his feet and was hit again by another stone flung by Tangundo. The king's men protected their heads with their arms and attempted to retreat. Another volley of rocks dismounted a few more king's men and took down two mounts. Tangundo ignited his purple aura and rushed toward Hunder. The defetane staggered and prepared to receive the assault. Tangundo's sword flashed, and Hunder's sword hand fell to the ground still clutching his sword. Tangundo grabbed the king's men's commander and set him ablaze in purple fire. Hunder's cries of agony took the fight out of his men as they watched their commander succumb to the sorcerer's purple blazing assault. A handful of king's men turned and ran in the opposite direction, but they were intercepted, and their escape blocked by Tangundo's men.

The battle ended as quickly as it began. Hunder's smoking and lifeless body lay at the sorcerer's feet. Several king's men lay unmoving, and a few others struggled to regain their senses. The guards near Tangundo crawled away from his awful purple glow, whimpering in fear. Tangundo glowered at his enemies, his red eyes burning into their souls. The surviving king's men bowed their heads in submission, hoping the crazed sorcerer would spare their lives.

"If you want to live, you will kneel before me and swear your allegiance. If you don't, I will send you into the perpetual mist. Which is it to be?" Tangundo shouted. The prone king's man closest to him rose to his knees and bowed his head. It didn't take long for the others to do the same. The threat of being forced into the deadly mist was incentive enough to submit to the sorcerer's demand. Every king's man knew cruel gods lurked within the mist. Could this sorcerer be one of those gods? Could he be their emissary?

Sassin had retrieved a sword from an unconscious and dying soldier, and he was standing over a kneeling king's man. "Master, this is these men's seshtane," he growled.

"Seshtane?" Tangundo wondered.

"A non-officer rank. He's the second in command. What ya want me to do with him?"

"Kill him!" Tangundo immediately ordered. Sassin swung his sword, hacking the seshtane across the back of his neck, killing the helpless prisoner instantly. "You're now the seshtane," Tangundo told Sassin.

For the next half-segment or so, Tangundo's men rounded up the survivors of the ambush. Over twenty king's men had joined the followers of Munnevo. Two or three king's men had escaped on mounts. The remaining king's men lay dead or dying, and the dying were mercilessly dispatched by the followers of Munnevo upon Tangundo's order. Tangundo organized his gang, mounted his men on captured samarans, and headed for Grazius's hamlet. Sassin led the way with Hunder's head impaled on the new seshtane's sword.

With bloodlust filling their dark hearts, Tangundo and his men stormed into Grazius's hamlet as men, women, children, and frizzards scattered. The invaders began looting and burning. Nevesant took particular delight in tormenting those who had abused him in the past. As retribution burned within his hateful soul, and with his hands now bloodied, he no longer governed his hate and anger. The young man delighted in executing a hamlet man who had treated him particularly cruelly in the past.

Tangundo didn't dally at Grazius's hamlet. He quickly advanced on other hamlets and towns, using terror as his tool. Tangundo's violent return was meant to send a clear message to all that the emissary of the gods of the mist was not to be resisted. He conscripted young men into his band, slaughtered older men as an example of his ruthlessness, and turned a blind eye to his men's abuses of the women they subjugated. From time-to-time, he sent a few victims into the death-dealing mist. As his numbers increased, more and more small communities fell to his men's swords and his burning aura. In only a few detzamars, Tangundo's gang of outlaws had grown into a small army of hundreds.

Another citizen of the kingdom had just finished his testimony before King Ben-do-teg. A band of outlaws, brigands, or cutthroats had invaded the land. His kingdom was under attack, and another town had fallen to this ruthless invading force.

"This is intolerable! It's time I use overwhelming force against this threat," the king shouted. "Summon my champion. Assemble all of my guards. I will lead them personally."

CHAPTER 17

MEETING THE WUR-GORS

The season was changing, and there was a chill in the air on some nights at the Tondo Estate. Nestor told him, it wouldn't be long before the last of the divitz would be in and ready for sale. He was told, it looked like a very good span, and he could expect to make some good coin, more than Oetan had from the last harvest. Nestor made sure Coleman knew just how indispensable his management of operations had been. Coleman simply nodded his head and smiled. The man was speaking the truth, although Coleman didn't like him, and he never felt comfortable around his hard-nosed estate foreman.

One afternoon, Nestor rode in from the fields very early. It was only midafternoon. This was unusual because Nestor never returned to his cabin until well after dark. Trailing behind him was a young man, his hands bound at the wrists and a leather cord around his neck, the other end secured to Nestor's saddle.

"Sire Tondo, we's got a big problem that needs ya to make a rule'n," Nestor bellowed, a wry smile crossing his lips. "This dung creeper was caught steal'n." Nestor dismounted, untied the cord from his saddle, pulled the young man along as if he were a dog on a leash, and handed the leather cord to Coleman.

"What's ya gonna do, sire? I told ya, if you lets 'em get away with one thing, they's only gonna get worse. Now, they has."

Coleman examined the man from head to toe. He looked to be about sixteen or seventeen, but in this place, looks were deceiving. He was dressed in the tunic of a field hand. It was tattered and badly soiled. His feet were bare. The slave's head was bowed, and his eyes were looking at the ground. "What is your name, young man?" Coleman finally asked.

"His name is Deemeos, sire," Nestor said.

Coleman turned to his foreman and, in a stern voice, grumbled, "Let him answer for himself. Deemeos, is that right?" The slave nodded his head slightly while staring at the ground.

"When the master asks ya a question, frizzard stink, ya better answer!" Nestor barked.

"Nestor, your samaran looks thirsty. Take him to the water trough and wait there," Coleman commanded in an irritated tone. Nestor angrily did as he was told. The water trough was about fifty feet away, which took the foreman out of the conversation completely. Coleman removed the cord from around the young man's neck and untied his hands. "Now," he began, "what is this all about?" Deemeos didn't say a word and continued staring at the ground. "Stealing is a very serious transgression. Did you steal?" The slave remained silent. Coleman lifted the young man's chin with a finger and looked into his dark-brown eyes. He saw fear and anger staring back at him. It was unsettling. "Did you steal?" Coleman asked again.

"Master, we's hungry," the young man finally told him nervously.

"What did you steal?"

"Meal from the granary, master."

"Why? Are you not given enough for your needs?"

"No, master; I mean, yes, master?"

"Oy, which is it?"

"We is hungry, master. We ain't had enough food for the three of us."

"You have a family? A bondmate? A child?" Coleman asked, a bit surprised because of the young man's youthful appearance.

The slave looked into Coleman's face and cocked his head as if he couldn't believe what he had just heard. "No bondmate; slaves ain't allowed. No child, either. I got my ma and pa; they's old."

"So, you stole food from the granary for your mother and father? Are you not given enough food?" Coleman had learned, the slaves were given a portion of grain once each detzamar, on the first day of the detz. They were expected to make their portion last through the next forty days.

"Foreman Nestor cut our measure. He said my ma and pa ain't working hard 'nuff. He said, 'half-measure for half-work.'"

"So, he reduced your food portion by half, is that right?"

"Yes, master. We's hungry. We tried to make it last, but we ran out three days ago. By my reckon'n, we got 'nother five days before we get a new portion. I'm afeared my ma and pa ain't gonna make it that long. Theys get'n weak. I'm afeared they gonna die." Deemeos was almost in tears.

Coleman signaled for Nestor to rejoin the conversation.

"Deemeos tells me you reduced their food ration. Is that true?"

"Yes, sire. His ma and pa are picking only half the divitz they should in a day. Half a portion for half a day's work, I says."

"How old are they?" Coleman asked.

"Don't rightly know, sire," Nestor admitted.

"They ain't my real ma and pa, master. They took me in when my real pa was killed, cutting down trees for Master Oetan. My real ma crossed-over sometime before that. Don't know why. Pa never talked about her; said it hurt too much."

"You were left on your own. Didn't Master Oetan care what happened to you?"

"I was too young to be much use in the fields, or anywheres. Ma and Pa took me in 'cause they thought maybe I could help 'em cause they's old. And now, I do."

This is intolerable, Coleman thought. His anger was stirring, and the other two men shifted uncomfortably and shuffled a step or two away from him. "I can't believe this is happening. What am I doing in the middle of all this insanity?" Coleman grumbled aloud in godspeak.

"Sire, I don't understand," Nestor beseeched.

"What? Oh, yes. What is the punishment for stealing?"

"That depends on what was stole. He took a sack a grain. Usually, that would be a finger or two."

"Is that your recommendation?" Coleman asked his foreman as he stared into Deemeos's eyes. The young man shuddered.

"No, sire. He's a strapping and strong young'n. Don't need

to permanently damage the goods, I says. A good beating would teach 'em. I can do it right here and now," Nestor advised with glee in his voice as he lifted the coiled whip from his belt. The young slave whimpered at the sight of it.

"Deemeos tells me they are out of food. They have been out of food for three days, and they still have five days to go before the First. Do you really think an old man and an old woman can survive without food for that many days?" Coleman was now glaring at his foreman.

"It's their fault, sire. They didn't use their ration right. If they can't manage their food, don't blame me."

"Hoy, I am! I understand, Slave's Law requires all slaves receive sufficient food, right? You trying to get me in trouble with the king?" Coleman was nearly shouting. "Besides that, I could lose these slaves to starvation. How are you going to repay me for that loss, Nestor? How many regums do you have?"

"I ain't got none, sire. I can't pay for no slaves," his eyes wide with shock and surprise by Coleman's twist.

"You told me you get one bale in every one-hundred. How many bales will that be, Nestor?"

"Don't know, sire. Won't know 'til the harvest is done."

"How much are you going to make on your share?" Coleman asked with a steely stare.

"Depends on the price, sire, but it ain't enough for no slaves."

"Keep that in mind for the sale. If I lose any slaves because you starved them to death, it will come out of your contract. Is that clear?"

"Yes, sire, but my contract wouldn't pay for one."

"Maybe you could take their place then?" Nestor's head snapped back in shock. "Now, what are you going to do about my starving slaves?" Coleman demanded.

"I'm gonna make sure they's fed, sire."

"Good, and you better hope none drop dead before the First because I will blame you for their deaths. Now, go and deliver more food to them immediately!"

"Yes, sire, as ya says." Nestor mounted his samaran and trotted off under Coleman's icy glare.

He turned to Deemeos. "Why are you still here?" The young man raised his head and looked into Coleman's blue eyes. He was confused, and then he glanced to his right and then to his left. "Now, get going! And I had better never see you again like this. Is that understood?"

"Yes, master. Thank you, master." Deemeos took off at a full run, quickly disappearing into a nearby field.

Ayascho had been watching the spectacle from his favorite resting place under the large tree that shaded the guesthouse. He walked to Coleman's side and asked, "What was that all about?"

"I was just putting the fear of Staff Sergeant Coleman into Nestor," he replied using godspeak terms.

"What does that mean?"

Coleman didn't respond. He only smiled, made a sharp military-style left face, and marched to the guesthouse, leaving Ayascho scratching his head. Coleman noticed Maaryah standing near the corner of the building, watching him with a smile covering her face. It was the first time he had seen her smile. *She looks radiant,* he thought.

Idop, too, had been watching and listening from an open window of the guesthouse. "So, you let that chetzy get away with it. I bet he goes back to the others and boasts about how he fooled his stupid master," Idop scolded.

"The boy and his family are starving, and you expect me to have half his hand cut off or have him whipped nearly to death? He should not have been put in a situation like that. Nestor showed bad judgment again. I will not tolerate that kind of stupidity when lives are at stake, even if they are *only* slaves."

"You'd think they were your children," Idop shot back.

"Well, they are, at least until they can fend for themselves," Coleman retorted as he walked to his favorite chair, sat, picked up an unfinished wicker basket, and started weaving.

Idop watched him for a few moments, all the time wondering what Coleman meant by his last remark. *He is an amazing man, Idop finally concluded, but could he be a threat to the kingdom? Only time will tell.*

Coleman went to the bathhouse before dinner, and he relaxed in the warm water. After dinner, he took a stroll along the beach as dusk fell. He noticed the water beginning to rise, so he quickly scrambled up the cliff trail and returned to the guesthouse. By then, it was dark. Maaryah had stoked the fire in the guesthouse fireplace and was waiting for him when he returned.

"Where is Ayascho and Counselor Idop?" he asked.

"They've gone to their beds, master," was her reply.

"I wish you would not call me master," he countered.

"What would you have me call you, master?"

"My name is Tondo. Call me Tondo."

"Oy, no, master, I couldn't do that. It wouldn't be right, and Foreman Nestor would learn of it and be angry," she explained with worry in her voice.

"Why?" he questioned.

"Master, slaves are not allowed to talk like that to their masters. If Foreman Nestor found out, he would punish me."

"Well, I certainly do not want that," Coleman said in an exasperated tone. "Tell you what; call me sire. Would that be permitted?"

"As you say, mast . . . I mean, sire." Coleman sat in his favorite chair and started weaving his basket. "Will that be all, sire?" Maaryah asked.

Coleman had been pondering his experience with Deemeos and Nestor all afternoon and evening. He realized he didn't really know much about the people under his stewardship. He had decided to change all that, so why not start right here and now?

"Maaryah, come here and sit down. I do not know anything about you. Tell me about yourself." The young woman did as he commanded and sat on a bench near the fire. She sat in silence, the flickering flames reflecting off her face and jet-black hair. "Ha?" Coleman finally said after an awkward silence.

"I don't know what to say, mast . . . I mean, sire."

"Let us begin at the beginning. How old are you?"

"I don't know for sure, sire. My mother told me, I was born two days after Master Oetan's daughter was." Coleman thought and decided she looked to be about the same age as Lady Oetan's daughter. That would make her about forty spans. Coleman was amazed. She appeared to be twenty, if that.

"Are your father and mother living on the estate?" he asked.

"No, sire. Master Oetan sent my father away when I was very young."

"That is so sad. You must miss him," Coleman commiserated.

"I really don't remember much about him; I was only a little girl. I remember I was sad. My mama missed him something terrible. She said he was the love of her life. After he was taken, she got sick. I think she just gave up. She crossed-over when I was just old enough to take care of myself," she explained with rising emotion.

"Did someone take you in and help you grow up?" Coleman asked.

"No, sire. Others may take in a boy, but never a girl."

"How old do you think you were when your mother died?"

"I don't rightly know, sire. I may have been twelve spans."

Coleman thought for a moment. With the slow rate of aging here, a child of that age would be like an eight to ten-year-old. It was amazing she survived on her own. He took a moment and examined her beauty. "You are very pretty. You must have been a beautiful child."

"Oy, no, sire. The other children called me bad names and

made fun of me. I was too tall and too skinny, and they all said
I was ugly."

"So, you are the ugly duckling who grew into a beautiful
swan," Coleman muttered using godspeak terms.

"Sire, I don't understand."

"Oh, it is a story from my homeland about someone whom
everyone thought was an ugly child, but the child grew into
the most beautiful person of all. Just like you have," Coleman
was smiling.

"Oy, no, mast . . . sire. I'm much too tall, and Teema says
I'm awkward and fumbling."

She is indeed tall, Coleman thought; *probably around five feet ten
inches. She's taller than any other woman I've seen so far on this world,
and she's taller than most men, including Ayascho and Idop.* "Well, I
think you look beautiful," Coleman declared. For an instant,
their eyes locked, and then, she quickly dropped her gaze as
her expression changed to worry. He could see he had made
her uncomfortable, so he decided to change the topic. "What
are your dreams, Maaryah?" he asked.

"Dreams? I sometimes dream I'm a bird, sire," she admitted. That wasn't what he meant. He wondered if she had any
aspirations or desires, but he quickly realized it was a silly
question. She had no freedom, no hope of a life any different than today's. "Yes, go on. You dream you are a bird; then
what?"

"I fly over the fields and past the trees. I even soar above
the ocean. It's so exciting and wonderful. Then I wake up,
and the dream is gone, but I feel happy, sire."

A dream of freedom and escape from her dreary existence, Coleman thought. "Maaryah, would you like to ask me any questions?" he offered. Coleman could see she was carefully pondering her next words.

After a short delay, she cautiously asked, "Why are you so kind to me? Why are you so kind to everyone? I saw what you did today with Deemeos. I couldn't believe what I was seeing. I expected something awful was gonna happen, and then Deemeos is running home, happy and unhurt. If it was anyone but you, it would have been terrible, sire."

"Maaryah, I believe everyone, both men and women, should be treated with respect, no matter what their place in life is. They are deserving of my respect unless they do something to lose that respect. Do you understand?"

"I think so, sire. Why do you feel that way?"

"My mother and father taught me," he quickly answered.

"They must be very nice. Where are they?"

Coleman smiled. Maaryah had forgotten to include *sire* or *master*. He thought they were beginning to have a normal and pleasant conversation; the way equals do. "They live a long way away. So far away, I will probably never see them again."

"That is very sad. I miss my mother," Maaryah sympathized as she stifled a yawn.

"It is late," he said. "I am sorry to keep you up so long. I have enjoyed our time together this evening. I hope we can do it again soon."

She stood, and when she did, Coleman jumped to his feet, as well; however, he could see Maaryah's surprise as worry again filled her face. She bowed and quickly left the guesthouse, nearly at a run. Coleman returned her bow, but she had already darted from the room. He thought of her confession about Nestor's unwanted advances, and he quickly realized her fears. He sat and stared into the flames, his mind conjuring up past memories of home and family.

He awoke to the sound of singing coming from the guesthouse living room. He looked over the edge of his bed and saw Ayascho was already gone, as usual. Almost every morning, the other two men were up and about much before he awoke. They seemed to be quite happy with six to seven segments of sleep a night. Coleman, on the other hand, required seven to eight, and he always seemed to go to bed well after they did.

While he slept, the other two would go to the bathhouse and soak for a while. Ayascho had really taken a liking to a morning bath. Coleman preferred to take his bath in the late afternoon, washing off all the dust and grime he collected during the day. Sometimes, the other men would join him, but usually not. The others also liked to go to bed just after dark. Coleman preferred to stay up for at least a segment or more and ponder various aspects of his new life.

He began to focus on the sound of singing in the other room. He got out of bed, put on clean white trousers and a white cotton short-sleeved shirt, and walked into the main room. He found Maaryah placing food on the table and singing as pleasantly as a bird.

"That is a lovely song," he said. Maaryah flinched and went silent, knocking over a cup with her hand. She righted it, then turned to Coleman and gave him a curt bow. "I startled you again. I am sorry, Maaryah." He approached her and watched as her golden-amber eyes widened in fear. She quickly lowered her gaze when he stopped in front of her. He took her hands in his and noticed she was trembling. "Maaryah, relax and look at me," he gently commanded. She reluctantly lifted her gaze and looked into his face. "I am not like Nestor. You have nothing to fear from me."

She saw kindness and compassion in his expression. This time, she couldn't lower her gaze and continued looking into his kind Munnari-blue eyes. The vision from her dreams came to mind, the image of a pair of blue eyes. Something in her center confirmed the truthfulness of his words. Her fear of the new estate master fled like smoke in a breeze.

He released her hands and continued, "Your voice is lovely. Please, keep singing. What is the song about?"

"It's a song my mother used to sing to me. It's about the unnamed god and how he loves little children, mas . . . sire."

"Who are his children?" he asked. Just then, Idop and Ayascho returned, wearing their bathrobes and turning the quiet morning into loud, jarring chaos.

"Hoy, food! I'm starved," Idop blared. He quickly sat on the bench and started eating. Ayascho also sat, lifted a bunch of grapes in both hands, and raised them above his head. With his head bowed, he silently offered a prayer. No one said a word until this ritual was completed.

Coleman then said to Maaryah, "There is one of his children now." He was smiling and pointing toward Ayascho. She returned his smile with one of her own. "You should hear Maaryah sing. She has the voice of an angel," he said to his companions.

"Ain-zahr? What's that?" Idop asked as he let out a loud belch.

"Something you are not," Coleman quipped as he sat next to Idop. "Please, Maaryah, continue singing." Reluctantly, she continued her song. Her tone was magical, and the men sat in silence, listening to her pleasing strains. When she finished, Coleman and Ayascho applauded. "Wonderful, wonderful. Do you know any other songs?"

"Only a few others, sire."

"I hope you will share them with us someday. I do not think I have ever seen you so happy. You look even more beautiful this morning." Maaryah gave a curt bow and looked embarrassed. "Last night, I bet you dreamed of being a bird, and you soared over the ocean. Am I right?" Coleman asked.

"Yes, sire, I did." Coleman gave Idop a nudge in the ribs with his elbow.

"How did you . . . " Idop began just as Coleman's elbow struck home.

"And you said I did not know the dreams of slaves," Coleman blustered as he gave Maaryah a wink. He grabbed some cheese and began eating. "Maaryah, have you eaten yet? Sit down, join us," Coleman offered.

"Oy, no, sire, I can't do that," she pleaded.

"Okay, okay, I would not want to cause the kingdom to come undone." He turned his head and grinned at Idop. He could tell, the counselor was not amused, but was it because of the offer he made the slave, or was it his comment about the kingdom. He finally concluded, it must be both. "Maaryah, you can go. And thank you." She bowed, exited the room, and headed toward the manor house, marveling at the new master's politeness. "I have decided that I am going to meet every worker on the estate," Coleman declared to the other two.

"Wur-gor? What's that?" Idop wondered as he munched some bread.

"I do not like these people being called slaves. They are not animals, they are people, and I want to get to know them better."

"They're slaves, not people! By the face of the unnamed god, why would you want to meet them?" Idop challenged.

"Well, after the episode with Deemeos yesterday, I have concluded that I need to know more about each person who works for me. Did you know he was orphaned when he was just a little boy?"

"So what? That happens to slaves all the time, and to freeborns, also," Idop hissed.

"Maaryah has been an orphan since she was very young, too. I find that enlightening."

"If you say so. I'm not looking forward to this. How long is it going to take, anyway?" Idop quizzed.

"Until it is done. You do not have to join me if you do not want to," Coleman told the counselor. He watched as Idop thought about escaping this perceived ordeal.

Idop then said, "I will go with you. Anyway, I don't have anything better to do. I'm under orders from the king to watch over you. It would be bad for me if some slave put a knife between your ribs, and I wasn't there."

"My, my, Counselor Idop, I did not know you cared for me so much," Coleman chuckled. The comment caught Ayascho as he took a mouthful of wine. He nearly spit it all over the table and began coughing. Coleman's chuckle turned into roaring laughter as Ayascho joined in. Idop, too, began to laugh.

It was still early when the three men rode off on their samarans. They noticed Doros, Teema, and Maaryah removing the mourning drapery from the manor house door and windows. "I see their mourning period is over," Idop explained.

"Has it been forty days already? Oy, how time flies when you are having fun," Coleman mused. He was looking forward to meeting the young Mistress Oetan again. Ayascho examined Coleman's face closely, and then he smiled. "What are you looking at?" Coleman barked.

"You want to see the pretty young woman again, don't you? I can tell," he laughed.

"Ah!" Coleman exclaimed as he dug his heels into his samaran's sides. The beast gave an anguished bellow and took off at a gallop. Coleman had to grab the saddle quickly. Otherwise, he would have tumbled right off the back of his mount.

It wasn't long before they came upon a work party of seven men, all slaves. It was obvious a wagon wheel had come loose and rolled off, dumping its load. They were standing around looking perplexed as the two large draft samarans hitched to the wagon bleated and fussed.

"What's going on here?" Idop demanded.

"Counselor, the wheel came off the wagon, and the logs rolled down the bank," one of the men answered.

"Don't just stand there! Go down and fetch the wheel so you can fix it!" Idop ordered like the megatus he once was. All seven men jumped to the command and scampered down the embankment. They soon returned, huffing and puffing, rolling the wheel up the moderate grade. "Now, let's see what we can do about this," Idop uttered.

Coleman intently watched as Idop directed the men. *He is concise, clear in his orders, and demanding of his troops. The mark of an excellent commander,* Coleman thought.

It wasn't long before the wagon was repaired and ready to go. Now, all they had to do was get the logs loaded again. Idop ordered the slaves into action. Coleman dismounted and followed them down the embankment.

"Where are you going?" Idop growled.

"The same place you and Ayascho are. Let us get to it," Coleman shouted back. The two quickly followed him down the grade. The logs were about eight feet long and six to eight inches in diameter. Coleman hefted the end of one. "I guess these are at least two-hundred pounds each," he muttered using a godspeak term.

"They look to be about two stones," Idop said.

"I don't understand. What are the two of you saying?" Ayascho wondered.

"It means they are very heavy. We will need three men on

each one. Now, be careful. We do not want anyone getting hurt."

Coleman directed three men as they lifted the topmost log. They slowly made their way up the slope and dropped it on the wagon's bed with a loud thump. The startled draft sama-rans let loose with mournful cries, but they didn't move. While the first three men were doing that, Idop organized another three men into action. Coleman directed Ayascho and the last worker to another log. He then ordered Idop to help them. The three men struggled up the slope, following in the foot-steps of the others. They dropped their load in the wagon, as well, and turned to see Coleman carrying a log on his shoul-der, the veins in his neck were bulging under the strain. The other nine men just stood and gawked at the spectacle.

When Coleman reached the wagon, he dropped his load on top of the other logs. "You know, I could have used a little help. You guys looked like a bunch of lazy jaybirds sitting on a fence watching the world passing by," he grumbled using a godspeak term.

"Tondo, how did you get so strong?" Ayascho asked in amazement.

"I used to workout every day when I was a warrior."

"Worg-ott? What does that mean?" Idop wanted to know.

"I exercised. I would lift heavy things over and over. It made me stronger. You know, that felt pretty good. I think I will talk with Pendor and have him make some weights. Then I can show you what I mean, and you can get stronger, too." Ayascho liked the idea, but Idop, true to his nature, was skep-tical.

After a few more trips, the men had all the logs back on the wagon. By then, it was midday, and Teema's errand boy, Eos, had found them. He delivered a midday meal. There was at least three times as much food as usual. Before they left the estate grounds, Coleman had mentioned to Maaryah about his plan to talk with the other workers and get to know them. She must have passed this information on to Teema, and anticipating his every need, Teema prepared extra food. She knew even before he did, he would invite the workers to partake with him. He passed the neatly wrapped linen packages around until all the men had one, and he marveled at their excited countenances. Then he, too, took one and began eating the fruits, nuts, and cheeses provided. Idop and Ayascho drank wine, while Coleman and the workers drank water. One of the workers offered Coleman a flat-cake. He took it and ate. It reminded him of a whole-wheat pancake, but it had a slightly bitter aftertaste.

While the men ate, Coleman asked them questions: what their names were; what did they do; did they have family living on the estate? The workers were skeptical and suspicious at first, but they soon warmed to their kind and friendly new master. Ayascho also joined in the conversation. He didn't consider these men slaves. They were just other men to him. Idop, on the other hand, didn't like such fraternizing with these lowly creatures. It wasn't something even a disgraced commoner like himself would do, and certainly, not one of tetzae rank should even consider. He sat in silence and fumed.

Coleman fed the two draft samarans apple-like fruit Teema had included with the meal. At least they looked like apples, but they had the flavor of pears. The beasts gobbled down the treats and nudged Coleman with their noses for more. He gave each another, and then he mounted his samaran, said farewell to the workers, and headed back to the manor grounds.

When he got back to the guesthouse, he drew up plans for barbells and dumbbells. He knew this would be a rather large order because he would need several of each with different weights.

When he explained his request to Pendor, the blacksmith stood shaking his head. *Master Tondo was certainly an odd one,* he thought. "You come up with the strangest requests," Pendor told him. "Sire, when will you pay me for the stee-rups and bows?" he asked.

Coleman looked surprised. He'd thought Pendor's services simply came with the estate. He apologized profusely for his tardiness and gave the blacksmith ten bhat from the estate's petty cash fund. He then promised to pay him two bhat for each finished dumbbell and barbell. He wanted ten barbells and ten pairs of dumbbells with differing weights. It was obvious, Pendor was delighted with the master's offering, a signal to Coleman that he had probably promised too much.

When he returned to the guesthouse, he found Idop and Doros waiting for him. "Sire, Lady Oetan requests the pleasure of yours and Counselor Idop's attendance at last-meal tonight," the house servant pronounced in a regal and stately manner.

Coleman couldn't help but notice Idop's broad smile when he heard the invitation. "Tell Lady Oetan I always take my meals with my good friend, Ayascho," Coleman replied.

Doros looked puzzled. "Sire, are you saying you want your slave to dine with the ladies?"

"Ayascho is not my slave; he's freeborn and my friend. Go now, Doros, tell the lady what I said."

"Yes, sire, as you wish." He trundled back to the manor house. Idop's smile turned into a frown, and there was a furrow between his raised eyebrows. Coleman could see, Idop was more than a little disappointed, but he said nothing. A few minutes later, Doros returned. "Lady Oetan says, you may bring your *friend* with you. May I tell the lady you and your guests will be attending?"

Coleman glanced at Idop. The man looked desperate. While still watching the counselor, Coleman responded, "Yes, you may tell Lady Oetan, it will be our pleasure to take dinner with her this evening."

"I will fetch you when last-meal is served, sire," Doros told him.

"Very well," Coleman simply replied. Idop nodded a 'thank you' and disappeared into his room. Doros returned to the manor house. Coleman stepped outside and went to the napping Ayascho, who was sitting on the ground with his back against the trunk of his favorite tree. "Wake up, Ayascho. We are going out for dinner."

Coleman went to the bathhouse early. After he finished his bath, he tied his long sandy hair in a ponytail that trailed

down the back of his neck. He put on a fine new toga-like robe
that Maaryah had sewn for him. It was brown with white trim
around the edges. Coleman could see, the guesthouse slave had
put a lot of effort into it. He felt a little self-conscious and wondered what to expect at dinner that evening. This was the first
real social event he'd been invited to since he arrived in the
kingdom. He certainly didn't consider the king's feast, held in
his honor, to be a proper social gathering. It was far worse than
any bachelor party he'd ever attended. But, now, a real lady
had invited him, and he truly wanted to impress her, and especially her daughter. She considered him a savage, and he certainly wanted to change that unfortunate first impression.

Ayascho stepped into the main room of the guesthouse.
He was also wearing a toga-like robe. His was tan in color.
It was from Oetan's collection that the lady had given to the
new estate master. Coleman hoped she wouldn't be offended because a savage was wearing it. He sighed, feeling a little
ashamed of himself for such a thought.

"Is this the way you're supposed to wear this thing?" Ayascho asked.

"You look fine to me," Coleman said. "How about me?"
Ayascho just shrugged. Idop stepped from his room. He
looked very handsome in his red counselor's robe. "You clean
up pretty good, counselor," Coleman teased.

"What's that supposed to mean?" Idop shot back.

"I guess it lost something in the translation. It means you
are looking good."

"Thank you, I think," Idop quipped. Ayascho began
scratching.

CHAPTER 18

DINNER WITH THE LADIES

W hen the shadows grew long, Doros strolled to the guesthouse and ushered the three men to the manor house. "Please wait here," Doros said, "The lady of the house will be with you shortly." The portly Doros trundled across the room and through a doorway covered by a curtain.

The room they were in appeared to be a parlor where guests were greeted. It was the room they were in when the tragic news of Oetan's death was announced. The ceiling was high, at least twelve feet above them. Ornate molding decorated it. The walls were covered with tapestries depicting trees, bushes, and flowers. It presented a more genteel atmosphere than the hunt scenes displayed on the tapestries of the guesthouse. Tables, benches, and chairs were scattered around the walls, leaving the center of the room clear. A large rug covered most of the tiled floor. Intricate geometric patterns of varying shades of green were woven into it. Lit oil lamps rested on several of the tables and provided a soft, golden glow in the diminishing light of day.

Idop went to a table where three pitchers, washbasins, and a stack of towels had been placed. He poured water into a bowl and quickly washed his hands, arms, and face. Coleman, following Idop's lead, did the same, as did Ayascho. A smile lit

Idop's face when Lady Oetan made her appearance.

"Welcome, welcome," she began in a melodic voice. "I am so pleased you could come." It sounded like a well-rehearsed greeting. Coleman recalled what Idop had told him about the festive events she was hostess to in the past at the city house. She wore a floor-length dress of olive drab, the color representing mourning. It had a modest neckline, and her arms were bare from the shoulders down. A plain light gray shawl was draped over her left shoulder. It crossed her back and reappeared on her right side under her arm. It was gathered in her left hand at the waist, leaving her right arm exposed and free. Her medium-brown hair was tied in a braid that was gathered and secured to the back of her head. He guessed she was a little under five feet six inches tall. She was a lovely woman of middle-age. Coleman could see no gray in her hair, but he guessed she had to be over one-hundred and fifty spans old.

"Sire Tondo, it is a pleasure to see you again." She was now standing in front of him. She bowed, and he returned one of his own. She raised her right arm and waited for him to take it.

"Greetings, my lady," he said awkwardly, "Let me again express my condolences for your loss."

Lady Oetan looked down for a moment, then said, "Thank you, Sire Tondo. You are so kind." He released her hand, and she turned her attention to Idop.

"Ha, Counselor Idop, I am so pleased you are here." She did not bow, but he grasped both of her hands in his and smiled. "Counselor Idop and I have known each other for a very long time," she said to Coleman. Her attention then fell upon Ayascho. "Please, introduce me to your . . . your *friend*," she asked.

"This is Ayascho. He and I have traveled a very long distance to get here," Coleman told her.

"You will have to tell us about your journey during the meal. It must have been exciting."

"Much too exciting," Ayascho finally chimed in. Lady Oetan smiled a pleasant smile, but Coleman could detect a hint of anger in her eyes.

"You must excuse my daughter's tardiness. She always fusses over her hair whenever we have guests," Lady Oetan told them.

"Now, Mother, you've exposed my secret," came her daughter's voice as she entered the parlor. Coleman almost gasped. He thought she was the most gorgeous woman he had ever seen on two worlds. Her very light-brown hair hung in ringlets over her shoulders. She was wearing an azure-blue, full-length gown. Its sleeves just covered her elbows. The exposed right sleeve was split down the center and drawn together with widely spaced white ties, exposing the skin of her upper arm in a peek-a-boo effect. The neckline was modest but dipped a little lower than her mother's did. She also wore a shawl, white in color, draped over her left shoulder, and encircling her body, but the free end also went over her left shoulder, freeing both hands. The shawl had an azure-blue border pattern on both ends.

She quickly glided to Coleman, extended both hands toward him, and smiled such a demure smile that Coleman thought he'd melt. She did not bow. Without thinking, he gently took hold of her hands, and the two stood looking into each other's faces, neither saying a word.

After an awkward few moments, she broke the silence. "Sire Tondo, I'm sorry we were not properly introduced on your first visit, but as you can understand, it was a very trying moment for my mother and me." Coleman didn't say a word, but he continued to stare into her eyes. "Master Tondo, are you all right?" she asked, her lovely countenance turning into a concerned expression.

"Excuse me, Miss Oetan, I lost myself in your loveliness," Coleman finally said with as much charm as he could muster. He felt pretty proud of himself for recovering with such flair.

She smiled, then asked, "Meezz? Is that a salutation from your homeland?"

Coleman thought for a second. "Salutation? Salutation? Oh, yes, it is. I am sorry. I am still learning your speech," Coleman stuttered. "Yes, Miss is a salutation of respect from where I am from."

"You mean your people have a different tongue than worldspeak? I have never heard of such a thing," the young woman confessed.

"Master Tondo, you may address my daughter as Mistress Oetan," the young woman's mother advised.

"Oy, Mother, such formality is unnecessary. Please, Sire Tondo, you may call me Ootyiah. I would like that much more than Mistress Oetan. Will you say a few words in your different speech?"

Coleman smiled broadly and began speaking in his native

tongue, "You are the most beautiful woman I have ever met."

"Mother, can you believe that? It makes absolutely no sense to me. What did you say?"

Coleman subconsciously cleared his throat, "I said you are pretty."

"Master Tondo, you have a tongue of zanth," she replied with mock humility.

"What do you call this language?" she asked.

"It's called godspeak," Ayascho interrupted.

"I am sorry, where are my manners? This is my friend Ayascho," Coleman said.

"I'm very glad to make your acquaintance, Ayascho. You're the first savage I have ever met," the young lady said without a hint of guile. Ayascho frowned but said nothing.

"Lady Oetan, I hope you are feeling better," Idop interjected.

"It has been difficult. It was such a shock. But let us not dwell on such matters. This should be a happy occasion," the lady advised with a forced smile.

After all the introductions and pleasantries were exchanged, Lady Oetan invited the men into the dining room. It was another high-ceilinged space; the ceiling covered by ornate molding. Floor standing candelabra-like oil lamps were placed in each corner, and there were two smaller ones on the table in the center of the room, bathing the dining area in a warm glow. Tapestries with floral designs covered the walls. Coleman was directed to a seat at the head of the table. Lady Oetan sat at the opposite end. Idop took a side seat, next to the lady, and her daughter sat opposite Idop. Ayascho awkwardly moved to a seat next to Coleman on the same side of the table as Idop.

The place settings included what looked like a large, plain white ceramic earthenware plate, nearly twelve inches in diameter. Next to it was a ceramic finger bowl, a shiny brass-like dinner knife, and what appeared to Coleman to be a single chopstick made of brass-colored metal with a pointed end. A small towel was placed near the finger bowl. A white ceramic cup sat near the finger bowl. Each place setting was the same.

As soon as everyone was seated, Teema and Maaryah entered with pitchers of wine, grape juice, and water, filling the party's cups. They quickly went to the serving area and returned carrying platters of food, including dark and light cooked meat slices, vegetables, fruits, and nuts. Coleman was presented with a tray first. He wasn't sure what to do, so he deferred to their hostess.

"Please, Lady Oetan, you go first," he said.

"Sire Tondo, as master of the estate, you have the honor of being served first," she advised. He shrugged and took a slice of meat with his fingers. Mistress Oetan giggled. He felt embarrassed. Teema then took the tray to Idop, and he skewered a slice of meat with his chopstick and placed it on his plate. Teema offered the tray to Ayascho, and with flare, he gently stabbed a slice of meat with his chopstick and dropped it onto his plate with a plop. He looked at Coleman with a toothy smile. The other trays of food were offered in the same manner. When his plate was full, Ayascho raised it above his head and offered a silent prayer. The others stopped and watched.

"What's he doing?" Lady Oetan quietly asked.

"He's offering thanks to his god," Idop whispered.

"Ha," Lady Oetan said in a subdued voice.

After a few moments, Ayascho was done and set his plate down. The others began eating in quiet. Coleman and Ayascho closely watched the others and followed their examples in executing proper etiquette. They used the chopstick like a fork to hold an item that needed to be cut with the dinner knife. They would then eat using their fingers. Coleman asked Maaryah to bring him another chopstick, and then he began eating, using two chopsticks and not his fingers.

Mistress Oetan watched and then asked for a second chopstick for herself. She struggled with them for a while and then resorted to using her fingers. "You do that so easily," she finally said. "Don't you like using your fingers?"

"My people prefer to use utensils to eat with. We sometimes use our fingers but usually only for things we call finger food," he told the gathering.

Ayascho also asked for another chopstick, and Coleman watched as he fumbled with them.

"No, like this," Coleman said as he held up his hand and moved his set like pincers. Mistress Oetan tried again and soon succeeded. Ayascho was managing much better, too.

"Seems like a wasted effort," said Idop. "A good knife and a couple of fingers are all you really need."

"I think I will invite all of you to the guesthouse for dinner one day and show you how to eat with a fork. But first, I must ask Pendor to make some," Coleman told the group. They looked at him in bewildered silence.

After a few seconds, Lady Oetan began speaking to the estate master, "Please, tell us about your travels. None of us have ever been beyond the Magheedo Mountains. Tell us what lies on the other side."

For the next segment or so, Coleman related the highlights of their journey from Ayascho's village to the Ancient City. Ayascho jumped in from time-to-time, but he preferred to sit back and listen to Coleman's storytelling. Teema and Maaryah stood a respectful distance from the table in case they were needed. They, too, listened with rapt attention as Coleman's recollections unfolded. He could see Doros's feet below a doorway curtain.

When he completed the adventure tale, Mistress Oetan applauded enthusiastically. "That must have been so much fun!" she exclaimed.

Coleman and Ayascho looked at each other in amazement. "It was dangerous and grueling," Coleman finally said. "Death stalked us at every turn. A man died, not to mention a thrice. It was anything but fun."

"How big did you say that gor-gorn beast was?" Idop asked skeptically.

"It's called a gorga. It's half as big as a thrice," Ayascho told him.

"And you killed one with a stone knife and the second one with wooden missiles? That's too incredible to believe," Idop accused.

"I helped with the second one," Ayascho proudly said as he pulled the gorga fang strap from under his robe. He held it up for all to see.

"It's huge! It looks like a wicked dagger," Mistress Oetan

gasped.

"Go ahead, Tondo, show them your awards," Ayascho urged. Coleman reluctantly pulled at the leather strap around his neck and displayed his two giant gorga fang trophies.

Mistress Oetan clapped her hands in glee, "It's true! It's all true!" she almost shouted. "You are so brave. I wish I were a man, so I could do such great things," she clamored.

"To be quite honest about it, Mistress Oetan, I was more than a little scared. When you are staring down a charging beast like a gorga, you would have to be insane not to be terrified. But when you are in that kind of a situation, there is nothing left for you to do except face your fate. Is that not right, Ayascho?" He simply nodded his head up and down in agreement.

"That was such a thrilling tale, I'm nearly out of breath listening to all your adventures," Lady Oetan said in a charming tone. "You are both brave and cunning. Wouldn't you say, Counselor Idop?"

"Yes, my lady. They are extraordinary men to survive such an ordeal. Sestardus Titus and his men hold Tondo in high regard. Titus told me he saved their lives more than once," Idop told her. "That was a fascinating account. I felt I was with you and Ayascho." Idop turned and addressed the beautiful Ootyiah. "There is something I've wanted to hear ever since we arrived at the estate. Mistress Oetan, may I persuade you to play the vant and sing for us?"

"Ha, my dear, please do. You have such a lovely voice. I don't think Sire Tondo and Ayascho have ever heard a vant before; have you?" Lady Oetan asked.

"I am afraid you have me there. I have no idea what a vant

is," Coleman admitted as Ayascho simply shook his head.

"All right, Mother and Counselor Idop, as you wish," the young woman acquiesced. "Doros, fetch my vant."

"Yes, my lady. I will have it here in an instant," came his quick reply through the doorway curtain. Coleman could hear the man's footsteps as he climbed stairs and strolled across the floor above them. A few moments later, he entered the dining room carrying a harp-like instrument. It was smaller than a harp, and its base sat upon a special stool designed for it. The vant's frame was made of wood, and it had about twenty strings.

Doros placed a chair near the vant. Mistress Oetan stepped to it and sat. She brushed her hair back and began to strum the instrument softly. Her playing was magical. The melodic tones reached into Coleman's soul and gave him peace. She continued playing for several minutes, and when she stopped, her mother and Idop began applauding. Coleman and Ayascho quickly joined them.

"That was lovely, my dear. Please sing for us," Lady Oetan asked.

The young woman started playing the vant again, and after a short introduction, she began singing. Her voice was clear and strong. Coleman paid no attention to her words; he simply reveled in the sweet serenade. After five minutes, she stopped singing, and with a few concluding plucks on the vant, the room fell silent. At first, no one did anything. It was as if the listeners had been put into a delightful trance. Lady Oetan soon began to applaud, and the others quickly joined in, including Teema, Maaryah, and Doros.

"That was lovely, Ootyiah. You have mastered both the vant and your voice. I'm so proud of you," Lady Oetan beamed.

"You sing and play the vant like an angel. That was simply marvelous. How long have you been playing the vant?" Coleman asked.

"Only about twenty-five spans," she replied. "What's ainzahr?"

"Angel. It is a messenger from the gods," Coleman told her.

"You're a messenger from the gods. Can you do that?" Ayascho challenged.

"I will talk to you later. I would love to hear you sing a duet," Coleman continued.

"What's a doo-wet´?" the young woman asked.

"Duet; it is when two people sing together." He looked at Maaryah and saw the terror on her face. She quickly looked down. "Maybe we should do that another day," he said, realizing he'd somehow blundered.

"That would be fun," Mistress Oetan enthusiastically replied. "Do you sing, Sire Tondo?"

"Thrice run away when I sing," he jokingly replied.

"Hoy, who else are you thinking of?"

"I am not sure. It was just a thought," he said in a trailing voice. Ayascho yawned.

"It is getting late, isn't it? This has been such an enjoyable evening. I hope we can do it again, soon," Lady Oetan said as she stood.

"Thank you, my lady. I can't remember when I have had such a delightful time. Ootyiah, your music was just wonderful," Idop beamed.

"It was the crème de la crème," Coleman uttered with embellishment. "That means it was the best of the best." He took her hand and gave the back of it a kiss. She gave Coleman a warm smile and giggled. For an instant, he forgot where he was. After a few long seconds, he released her hand and went to Lady Oetan. He gave her a curt bow, "Thank you, my lady; this has been such a pleasure. I hope to return the favor."

"You are very gracious, Sire Tondo. I've enjoyed your company, immeasurably. I wish to thank you again for all you have done for us," the lady said as she bowed.

"Thank you, my lady," Idop interjected as he took both of her hands. Coleman turned and exited the room. Ayascho quickly bowed and followed Tondo with Mistress Oetan right behind him. Idop placed Lady Oetan's arm through his, and they both walked across the room and through the doorway.

The men soon left the manor house while the women watched them from the top of the manor house stairs. Mistress Oetan gave a final wave as they departed the courtyard. The light of all three moons made it easy to traverse the short walk from the manor house to the guesthouse. Coleman detoured and headed for Nestor's cabin, tucked neatly behind the guesthouse. He received Nestor's report and left. He heard another cup shatter against the wall of Nestor's cabin, and he chuckled. By the time he got back to the guesthouse, Ayascho and Idop had gone to bed. He sat in his favorite chair and started weaving his basket in the light from a small lamp.

"Will there be anything else, sire?" he heard Maaryah ask from the shadows.

"Oh, Maaryah? I did not see you there. I am sorry I frightened you at Lady Oetan's dinner party," he told her. "But you do have a wonderful singing voice. I would love to hear you and Mistress Oetan sing together someday."

"Oy! No, sire, that would be all wrong. Mistress Oetan would be offended," Maaryah pleaded.

"That is too bad. Maybe, someday, all that will change. I will not force you to do anything you do not want to do, Maaryah," he told her.

"Thank you, sire; you are very kind. Is there anything else?"

"No, you may go. I hope you dream of flying over the fields and ocean tonight." She smiled, bowed, and left. Coleman's thoughts turned to the beautiful Mistress Oetan. "Ootyiah; what a lovely name. What a beauty she is," he said quietly to himself. Unexpectedly, he felt his euphoria invaded.

You own them, just like you own the slaves. They must submit to your every whim. Take what you want. They dare not object.

These uncomfortable thoughts darkened his mood and assaulted his reason. He literally shook his head to chase them away.

"I will not succumb to such abhorrent thinking," he uttered faintly. He forced his mind into another place. He thought of family vacations with his parents and older brother. He thought of summers spent on his grandfather's farm when he was a boy, all the time while weaving a basket. Soon, his mind was at ease, and he had forgotten the wayward thoughts that had invaded his peace.

In the morning, the three men ate first-meal and then made their rounds of the estate. Coleman stopped and spoke with everyone he saw. There were many quizzical faces, and no little worry when the new master of the estate approached them. By the time their conversations were over, both had a clearer impression of the other. Generally, the slaves or wur-gors as Coleman and Ayascho began calling them, were less fearful of their friendly master and the savage. The word had already gotten around that since his arrival, he refused to allow Foreman Nestor to beat any slaves, and as far as they could tell, no slave had suffered such a fate. They even learned, Foreman Nestor had relented in his punishment for Deemeos and his ma and pa. They had expected to find Deemeos with half a hand or a scarred back, but much to their surprise, Nestor delivered a full sack of untainted grain to their hovel that very same day. This new master was a curious one, and all felt better for their futures after talking with him and tracking his actions.

In the afternoon, Coleman talked with Seemo, the samaran handler, and learned he had been born on the estate and had cared for the samarans for the last thirty spans. He also spent time with Pendor, the blacksmith, who was a commoner, and his helper, Haro. Coleman learned, Haro actually belonged to the estate and not Pendor. The blacksmith offered reduced rates for his services since he didn't have the additional expense of hiring a helper. Haro was also learning the trade and had been assisting Pendor for more than twenty spans, so Coleman concluded that he probably had learned quite a bit about metalwork himself in all that time.

From the blacksmith's shop, Coleman dropped in at the manor house, entering through the kitchen door at the rear of the building. Both Teema and Maaryah were surprised by the unexpected appearance of their master coming through the back door. When Doros heard a male voice in the kitchen, he rushed in to see what was going on. The four sat around the wooden work table and chatted for almost a segment. Coleman already knew Maaryah's story, so he focused mostly on Teema and Doros.

Teema had been in the service of the estate for more than one-hundred and fifty spans. She had been born on the estate, and her mother and father still worked the fields. She had been Mistress Oetan's nanny, which was a common custom of the gentry.

Doros had been a slave from birth, also. His mother served in the king's palace. He didn't know who his father was. He learned his trade in the palace and was quite accomplished in his duties of service to the royals. Some fifteen spans ago, he was given to Master Oetan as a reward for Oetan's service to the king. He had worked on the estate ever since.

When Coleman left the kitchen, he headed for the cliffs overlooking the ocean. The tide was in, and the beach had disappeared. He watched as a terror glided through the water less than a hundred feet from shore. Coleman could see why no one ever sailed the seas on this world. He wondered if there was anything he could do to change that. He quickly realized he wasn't a sailor, had no nautical experience of any kind, and then pushed the thought to the back of his mind. Conquering the ocean would have to be left to some other intrepid adventurer.

CHAPTER 19

AN ESTATE ROMANCE

As the shadows grew long, Coleman headed back to the guesthouse and changed into his bathrobe, as was his regular routine. When he entered the bathhouse, he stopped short. Mistress Oetan was relaxing in the water on the opposite side of the pool.

"Master Tondo," she called, "please, join me. Doros has made the water temperature just right."

Coleman diverted his eyes and fumbled his words, "Uh . . . uh . . . I am so sorry for intruding. I did not think anyone would be in here."

"That's not a problem. I sometimes like to bathe before dinner. It's so relaxing," she cooed.

"Excuse me, I will leave and come back later after you have finished," Coleman told her, his eyes still looking away from her.

"Master Tondo, are you embarrassed? Don't your outlander people bathe together," she innocently asked.

"Ah . . . umm . . . generally, no," he mumbled.

"Oy, I am very sorry. Here, let me leave. I have finished, anyway." She started to rise from the water. Coleman quickly turned his back and stared at the entryway. He could see Teema appear from a side alcove, carrying a white robe. When he dared to turn and look again, Mistress Oetan was covered by the robe. With Teema's assistance, she slipped on her sandals and quickly scooted past him.

"I'll be sure to take my bath earlier in the afternoon from now on," she announced as she passed. Her smile was just as lovely as ever. Teema also shuffled past him and disappeared through the doorway. As soon as the women were gone, Coleman stepped out of his robe and dove into the pool. He remained underwater until his lungs hurt. He slowly returned to the surface and let the air expel from his lungs in a long, loud hiss. He sat on the underwater bench staring at the tiled ceiling.

During dinner at the guesthouse, Coleman began the conversation by asking, "Idop, is it normal for men and women to bathe together in this culture?"

"Ha, most people don't have bathhouses or slaves to prepare the water, so when one gets a chance to bathe, you just do, no matter who's there," Idop told him through bites of food. "Why do you ask?"

"I went to the bathhouse this afternoon like I always do, and I found Mistress Oetan in there taking a bath, naked as the day she was born."

"Did you join her?" Idop asked.

"No. I am not used to sharing my bath with a woman; at least one I do not know very well," he said with a coy smile.

"So, your people don't share baths, do they?"

"No, not really, at least not public baths. We do swim together, but we wear bathing suits. I was really surprised to find her there, and then to be invited to join her was even more surprising."

"Swim? Suits in the bath? You do have some strange customs, my friend. So, now, what are you going to do about your afternoon bath?" Idop wondered.

"She told me, in the future, she will take hers earlier in the afternoon."

"Did she say how early?" Ayascho asked with a broad smile.

"Do not even think about it," Coleman shot back as he bounced a bread roll off Ayascho's forehead.

Later that evening, after his meeting with Nestor, Coleman walked to the cliffs. The water had receded, and a sliver of beach could be seen. The white sands were glistening in the light of the blue and red moons. He stood, staring at the horizon, wondering what lay on the other side. After a few minutes, he heard footsteps approaching. He didn't turn to look, suspecting it was Ayascho or Idop.

"It's a beautiful evening," Mistress Oetan's demure voice declared as she slipped her arm through his. Coleman turned his head and looked down into her light-brown eyes.

"This is such an amazing place—the beauty of the ocean below us; the blue and red moons above. Would you like to go for a stroll on the beach?" he asked. She squeezed his arm gently and nodded her head.

The two carefully made their way down to the beach. They walked along the soft, damp sand, holding their sandals in their hands. *I haven't been this close to another woman in years or spans*, he thought. This young woman had captured his attention and his heart, as well.

She talked about life on the estate and how lonely it was at times. There were no others except her mother and father, and he was gone quite often in the service of the king.

"Were there no other children on the estate?" Coleman asked.

"Only slaves, and Mama wouldn't hear of her daughter playing with the likes of a slave girl. 'It's just not proper, my dear,' she told me."

"I can see why you would be lonely."

"I loved it when we went to the city house. There were so many people there, and I would talk to everyone I could. It was so much fun, especially the social gatherings. I would watch from the balcony and pretend I was talking with a prince. That was when I was only twenty or thirty," she said. Coleman chuckled. "What's so funny," she asked.

"In my homeland, a girl of twenty or thirty is a full-grown woman, not a star-struck teenager," he told her using god-speak terms. "How old do you think I am?

"I guess you haven't reached one-hundred yet."

"I am about thirty-three. I am younger than you."

"Mama said, outlanders age faster. But you still look very young and strong. Teema learned what you did when the wagon wheel came off and dropped all the logs. You're as strong as three men."

"Word gets around the estate pretty fast, I see," he said.

"Sometimes, the slaves know things long before we do, it seems," she admitted a little perturbed.

"Look!" Coleman exclaimed. "Do you see it?"

"See what?" she asked. He pointed, and they both watched as a huge dorsal fin cut through the water no more than fifty feet offshore.

"Hoy! I see it! I get shivers all over when I see one so close," she admitted.

"I will protect you, Mistress Oetan," Coleman declared as he shook the stick he'd been carrying, waving it around like a sword.

She laughed and said, "Please, call me Ootyiah, won't you? We don't have to be so formal." He dropped the stick and faced her.

"Okay, Ootyiah, but your mother told me to call you Mistress Oetan. What are we going to do about that?"

"I think Mama will just have to get used to it," she said as she gazed searchingly into his blue eyes.

"Ah, how does a man show his affection toward a woman here?" he asked, a bit ashamed of his ignorance.

"We snug," she told him.

"What is that?" he asked.

"Here, let me show you." She stood on her tip-toes, and he bowed down. She placed her cheek next to his and pressed into his gently. She quickly recoiled and giggled.

"What is the matter?" he asked, a bit surprised.

"Your cheek is scratchy; it tickles," she admitted as she rubbed her cheek.

"I will remember to shave closer next time. Let me show you how a man shows affection for a woman in my homeland." He then gave her a gentle kiss on the lips and watched her reaction. At first, she was taken aback, her eyes opening wide in surprise. But as he held his lips to hers, he pulled her body closer to his, and her eyes closed, and so did his. She responded by pressing her lips tightly against his. They remained in an embrace for some time, neither knew how long. He slowly pulled his head back, and her lips followed his for a moment.

"That was exciting. What do you call it?" she asked.

"It is a kiss. Now, you say it." He knew she would have trouble with the word.

"Ghizz? Is that right? Ghizz?"

"Not bad for a first try. And not bad for a first kiss, either."

"Let's do it again. That was fun," she breathed with excitement. He kissed her again, and this time, she pulled herself tightly against his body. After a long, warm embrace, he pulled away.

"Wow! You should be careful. Another kiss like that and I will have to jump into the ocean to cool down. You would not want me to be eaten by a terror, would you?"

Ootyiah laughed, and then she spied someone watching them from the top of the cliff. "I think that's Mama. I thought she had gone to bed already. I better go back to the house."

"I will go with you. I do not want you to get into trouble on my account. We will face her together."

The two walked up the steep and winding path and entered the manor house through the front entrance. "Mother, are you there?" Ootyiah asked in a cautious tone.

"Lady Oetan has just gone to bed, Mistress Ootyiah," Doros told her.

"Oy, I'm sure she will have a few words for me in the morning. Thank you, Sire Tondo, for such a nice evening. I hope we can do it again soon," she said with a coy smile.

"Pleasant dreams, my lady," Coleman said as he bowed and

turned around. Doros escorted him to the door. He took a deep breath as he made his way through the courtyard. He felt like he was gliding on air. He had a smile from ear to ear, and after he left the courtyard, he twirled on his heels and skipped a few steps. It had been a long time since he had felt this happy.

When he entered the guesthouse, he found Maaryah waiting for him. "What can I do for you, sire?" she asked.

"That will be all, Maaryah," he told her as he plopped down into his chair and started weaving his basket. He began humming a lively, happy tune from his homeland. Maaryah paused in the doorway, glanced over her shoulder, then continued on her way.

Coleman awoke early the next day while it was still dark. He could see the faint glow of dawn in the eastern sky through a window. Ayascho was still asleep on the floor, so he carefully stepped over him, quietly dressed, and walked into the main room. Maaryah had already placed three washbowls, three pitchers of water, and a stack of small towels on the table between the bedroom doorways. He washed his face and shaved in the lukewarm water using an arrowhead as a razor. He felt his face, making sure there was no stubble remaining. "I will have to make sure I shave after my bath today," he said quietly to himself in godspeak.

"What did you say?" Ayascho muttered as he stumbled into the room, wiping the sleep from his eyes.

"Oh, nothing important," came Coleman's reply.

"So, where do we go this morning? Are we going to meet more wur-gors?" Ayascho asked. Coleman had noticed, Ayascho was really a gregarious individual, and he liked being with other people. He had a pleasant outlook on life and treated everyone as his equal. How different he was now than during their earlier encounters. *He actually has an amiable personality,* Coleman thought. Their relationship had grown from antagonists to allies and from allies to close friends, tempered by their shared experiences and deadly encounters. Coleman knew they would defend one another to the death, if necessary. He smiled at Ayascho.

"What is it?" the young man questioned with a quizzical look. "You cut yourself again. You're bleeding." Coleman wiped his face with a towel and noticed blood. He dabbed the wound for the next several minutes until it stopped bleeding. "I'm glad I don't have to do that every day," Ayascho admitted.

"Yes, my friend, it is an annoyance." Idop entered the room and washed his face. Ayascho did the same.

"Where do we go today?" Idop asked.

"I think we will go to the Separation House and see what goes on there," he told them.

Just then, Teema and Maaryah entered the guesthouse carrying food and drink. They placed the chargers on the table. Teema bowed to the men, and then, she exited the house. Maaryah bowed and waited in an out-of-the-way corner, ready to respond to any request the men might make.

"Good morning, Maaryah, you are looking particularly

charming today," Coleman said in a canorous tone. Maaryah smiled and bowed but said nothing.

"I noticed you didn't return to the house after your meeting with Nestor last night. Where'd you go?" Idop nonchalantly asked.

"Oh, I went to the cliffs and looked at the stars for a while. Why?"

"Mistress Oetan came by and wanted to know where you were. Did she ever find you?" Idop wondered.

"Yes, she did."

"And then what?" Idop questioned.

"We went for a stroll on the beach, and we had a pleasant conversation; not that it is any of your business, counselor," Coleman told him with feigned displeasure.

"So, you went for a walk, *unchaperoned*, with the most beautiful young woman in the kingdom, and all you did was talk?" Idop exclaimed in disbelief.

"Oy, not exactly."

"Come on, tell us. What did you do?"

"You are awful nosey today, Counselor Idop. Do you plan to include this in your report to the king?"

"Tondo, you've got to tell us what happened. I have to know!" Ayascho excitedly blurted.

"Okay, I will tell you. I kissed her," he said teasingly.

"What does that mean?" Idop carped.

"That is for me to know and for you to find out."

"Please, Tondo, tell us. I can't wait to learn what that means." Ayascho was nearly bursting with excitement.

"I never kiss and tell. I am sorry, but it is a very old custom of my homeland, and I would be breaking my code of honor if I did." Ayascho slumped down on the bench. Idop threw a towel at Coleman, then returned to his meal. No one noticed Maaryah brushing away a small tear running down her cheek.

Seemo had four samarans waiting outside the barn as the men approached; one of the mounts more regal-looking than any of the others.

"Why four?" Coleman asked.

"Master, Mistress Oetan wishes to go riding with you this morning," Seemo answered. Ayascho and Idop looked at Coleman with knowing smiles.

"What?" Coleman challenged.

Just then, Ootyiah stepped out of the barn. She wore a light-green dress of mid-calf length, with long sleeves that went to her wrists. Underneath her dress, the men could see she wore dark-green, tight-fitting pants that covered her ankles. Her feet sported brown sandals with straps that went above her ankles and beneath the pants. Her hair was pulled back and tied in a single braid that went halfway down her back. Ayascho stared at her beauty; Coleman did too.

"Mistress Oetan," Idop finally said as he bowed, "what can we do for you?"

"Do you cavaliers mind if I join you?" she asked.

"This is unusual. Why would you want to join us on a boring jaunt around the estate?" Idop questioned.

"Oy, to be honest, counselor, I had a terrible row with mother this morning. I need to get away for a bit. I hope you cavaliers don't mind."

"What was your quarrel about?" Coleman asked with concern.

"I'm sure you can guess," she replied with a knowing smile.

Idop and Ayascho turned and faced Coleman, neither saying a word, waiting for his response; none was forthcoming. Ootyiah deftly mounted her magnificent samaran and tightly gripped the reins.

"I think it would be best if you remained here," Coleman finally said. "Let us not make things worse than they already are."

"I'm going for a ride, and if you men won't go with me, I'll go by myself," she declared in a defiant tone.

"That's not wise, my lady. There could be brigands or disgruntled slaves lurking in the fields," Idop warned.

"I can take care of myself, counselor!" she grumbled as she dug her heels into the samaran's sides. The beast brayed with a forlorn clamor that surprised the men. She was off in a bolt. The men quickly mounted and followed her at a gallop. After a few hundred yards, she reduced her samaran's pace to an amble. The men caught up, and they rode four abreast.

Coleman could see, the young woman was fuming, so he decided not to say anything until she had a chance to calm down. After a few minutes had passed, he spoke, "We plan to visit the Separation House today."

"Good!" she huffed and pulled her reins to the right, bumping Ayascho's mount and forcing it to a sudden stop. He was thrown against the animal's neck and had to grab it to keep from falling. Coleman thought she was acting like a spoiled teenager, but he followed her and said nothing more.

They soon arrived at the Separation House. Coleman thought it looked like a beehive of activity with Nestor barking orders like an angry drill sergeant. He eyed the party warily as they rode up.

"Yes, sire, what can I do for ya?" he asked as he bowed.

"I have come to meet the workers. Do not let me disturb your efforts. You may continue."

"Wur-gors, who's that?" the foreman asked.

"The slaves," Idop interjected.

"By your leave, sire," Nestor bowed again and started barking orders as he rushed from one place to another.

Definitely an A-type personality, Coleman thought to himself.

The men and Ootyiah entered what looked like a large warehouse. There were scores of people inside; most were briskly turning hand cranks on devices that looked like old-style washing machine ringers. Coleman watched as the workers, called separators, were cranking with their right hands and feeding divitz lint through the rollers with their left hands. In this way, the seeds were separated from the fiber. The seeds fell into a box in front of the rollers, and the divitz fiber passed through and dropped into a box on the other side. When the fiber box was filled, another worker, called a runner, would empty it, and take the fibers to the cleaning and baling area. Men and women were separators; children were runners and hustled back and forth, filling lint boxes when close to empty and emptying full fiber boxes and seed boxes.

Coleman was received in the same manner as all the other places he'd visited, mostly with trepidation. He talked with each and every person, certainly not as long as he would have liked because he didn't want to cause too much of a disruption to the smooth-running operation.

It was early afternoon before Coleman's party left the Separation House. Eos, Teema's errand boy, was waiting for them at their samarans with their midday meals. They collected the food bundles and found a secluded and shady area nearby to eat their meal. Coleman felt a twinge of guilt as he realized the wur-gors received no breaks. They worked from early light until darkness fell, sometimes even later, he learned. A disturbing thought crept into his mind. He shook his head at the realization.

"Tondo, what's the matter? I can tell when something is bothering you," Ayascho said.

"I am running a sweatshop," he told him using the godspeak term. "I am treating these people like slaves. I cannot allow this to continue," he admitted in a troubled voice.

"Oy, they are slaves, not wur-gors, and so what? They know no better and never will," Idop countered with callousness.

"Papa always said the slaves were born to serve us, the freeborn. He told me, it is the great chain of being, the natural order of things," Ootyiah said, clearly displaying her naïveté concerning the slave's plight.

Coleman leaned his back against the tree that shaded them, deep in thought, and he began rubbing his brow. Idop and Ootyiah carried on a friendly conversation, reminiscing about times past. Ayascho sat quietly, watching and listening as the two carried on their conversation, trying not to stare at the beautiful young woman.

After fifteen minutes or so, Coleman stood. "It is time to return," he stated.

The group mounted their steeds and headed back to the barn. When they arrived, they noticed Lady Oetan waiting at the courtyard entrance. She turned and disappeared behind the courtyard wall.

"Your mother does not look happy," Coleman warned.

"Don't worry, Sire Tondo, I will talk with her, and things will be all right. Thank you for such an enlightening morning. I have never visited the Separation House. There is so much happening in there. Nestor is an excellent foreman," she said.

They turned their samarans over to Seemo and went their separate ways. Ayascho napped under his tree. Idop went to the guesthouse and prepared his report for the king. Ootyiah returned to the manor house, but before she did, she let Coleman know she would be taking her bath shortly. He wasn't sure if her announcement was a warning or an invitation. He decided to go to the barn and give the samarans a good brushing, but before he did, he searched for Lulubelle the thrice. He found her peacefully munching on some hay in the corral behind the barn. He gave her a good ear rub and fed her some fruit left over from his midday meal. He then returned to the barn and began brushing samarans.

By the time Coleman had finished brushing the mounts, it was late in the afternoon, so he changed out of his day clothes, donned a robe, and headed for the bathhouse. He slyly peeked in and found it deserted. He disrobed and stepped into the warm water. He had brought a shaped obsidian stone with him and began scraping away the stubble on his face that had grown since the morning. He rubbed his hand over his cheeks and neck, making sure his skin was not scratchy. He didn't want his whiskers to tickle a certain young lady if the opportunity arose again.

Just as he was sure they wouldn't, he heard footsteps. He looked up and saw Lady Oetan glaring at him from across the pool. The two stared at each other in silence for what seemed an interminable period. Coleman could see she was struggling to contain her anger, then she bowed.

"Sire Tondo," she began, "I watched you and my daughter from the cliffs last night. I demand to know what you were doing."

"We were talking," he explained.

"It looked as if you were doing more than that," she scolded. "It looked like an embrace to me."

"Yes, that is true. We did embrace, and I kissed her." Lady Oetan gasped and quickly covered her mouth with her hand. "A kiss is like a snug. It is harmless," he explained, attempting to ease her distress.

"A snug is not harmless! Did you dishonor my daughter?" she finally blurted.

"Lady Oetan, I assure you I have the deepest respect for your daughter, and I would never dishonor her in any way."

"You were alone with her all morning. What were you two doing all that time?"

"We were not alone. Counselor Idop and Ayascho were with us the entire time, my lady."

"Praise the gods!" she loudly sighed. "At least the counselor is a proper chaperone. What are your intentions with my daughter? I demand to know."

"My intentions are strictly honorable. Please believe me," he begged. He could tell her anger had subsided a bit. Unexpectedly, her strong front collapsed, and she began to weep. "What is it, my lady? I give you my word that I have done nothing to deserve your worry or your unease. I must admit, I am attracted to your daughter, but I would never do anything that would jeopardize your trust."

"Do you really understand what honor is? You're an outlander, after all."

"Honor is not something exclusively held or understood by the citizens of this kingdom. It is universal, and I always try to act with honor in all I do. Have I done anything to give you a different impression?"

"No, sire, you have not, at least until now. You have treated us better than any citizen of the kingdom ever would. I just worry about Ootyiah. She has been so rebellious recently. She sometimes refuses to listen to me. She has become headstrong and willful, and it worries me, especially now that her father has crossed-over."

"You have nothing to fear from me, Lady Oetan. I will always treat your daughter with my deepest respect."

"Yes, yes, I believe you now. I've been so worried. She is all I have left in the world, and should anything bring her harm, I would . . . I would . . .." She couldn't complete her thought and covered her face with her hands, sobbing. She quickly regained her composure and bowed. "I will leave you now. You have given me your word, and you have my trust." She turned and left the room. Coleman exhaled heavily and rubbed his forehead. He took a deep breath and then sank slowly into the water, disappearing from view.

That evening, after Nestor arrived, Coleman went to his cabin to receive his daily briefing. When Nestor finished the report, Coleman surprised him with another dictate. He ordered his foreman to give all the wur-gors a one segment rest at midday.

He thought Nestor would cry upon hearing the order. "Production will suffer!" the foreman barked. But he relented under the outlander's cold glare. As Coleman left the foreman's cabin, he heard another clay cup shatter against the wall. "Teema, more wine, and lots of it!" Nestor bellowed.

Coleman laughed to himself and made a mental note to have the estate potter make more clay cups. The foreman had been going through a lot of them lately.

He walked to the cliffs and waited hopefully. If Ootyiah showed, there would be no stroll along the beach this night. The tide was in, and the beach was gone. It wasn't long before he heard her soft footsteps. He turned, smiled, and welcomed the lovely young woman.

"I was hoping you would join me tonight," he said as he reached out and took her by the hands.

She drew near to him and whispered, "I've been looking forward to being with you, alone, all day." She stood on her toes and stretched her face towards his. He gave her a snug on the cheek. This time, she didn't recoil.

"I shaved especially close for you this afternoon," as he rubbed his cheek. She laughed and then kissed him on the lips.

After several seconds, she lowered herself and gazed into his blue eyes. "I think I like ghizz more than snug," she told him.

"Me, too," he said. "Your mother paid me a visit this afternoon while I was in the bathhouse."

"So, that's where she went. I wondered what she was doing. What did she say?"

"She loves you very much. She wanted to know what my intentions with her daughter are."

Ootyiah drew closer to him and asked, "What did you tell her?"

"I told her my intentions are strictly honorable. She said she trusts me, but I am not so sure she really does. How did she put it? Oh yes, 'You're an outlander, after all.'"

"I'm glad you're an outlander. You are very different from anyone I've ever met. And all the adventures you've had . . . " her voice trailed off.

"You do not know the half of it," he chuckled.

"What does that mean?" she asked.

"It means I have not told you everything about me and how I got here."

"Please, you must tell me. I want to know everything about you."

"In time, my princess, in time. I do not want to rush things."

"Counselor Idop told me you have many magical powers, like the priests. How did you get them?"

"I really do not know. They began when I arrived in Aya-scho's land. I may have powers I have not yet discovered," he admitted. She stretched up and gave him another snug. He returned it with a kiss. They walked along the cliffs, arm in arm. "I went to the barn after our ride today and brushed all the samarans. The one Seemo says is yours is a beautiful animal. It must be special," he said as they walked.

"You brushed the samarans?' she asked with a sour expression.

"Yes, why not? I enjoy brushing the animals. I even gave Lulubelle, the thrice, a good ear rub. Is that so unusual?"

"Yes, yes, it is. The master of the estate doing things only slaves should do. Is Seemo not performing his duties properly?" she asked with concern.

"Ha, he is doing a fine job. It is obvious the creatures are well cared for. They love him, and he loves them. He even tried to stop me, but I would not quit. I enjoyed doing it."

"Oy, I guess that would be all right, but don't tell me you cleaned their stalls," she said with a concerned look.

"No, not today. Seemo had cleaned them in the morning."

"Good. It wouldn't be proper for the master to do such . . . such lowly slave's work," she warned.

"I spent many warm seasons on my grandfather's farm when I was a boy, and one of my duties was cleaning the stalls and shoveling manure."

"Gan-farder?" she said in a quizzical tone.

"Grand-father, my father's father."

"Didn't he have any slaves to do that kind of awful labor?"

"Oh no, slavery was abolished in my homeland a long time ago."

"So, freeborns have to do that kind of awful work themselves? How disgusting!" she spouted.

"There is a lot to be said about shoveling manure, my dear. It taught me that honest work is never too lowly. Once you have shoveled manure, you can do just about anything. It is all up from there," he jokingly chimed.

"That sounds horrid. Let's not talk about cleaning stalls anymore. I don't like it. You asked about my samaran. What do you want to know about it?"

"It is a beautiful animal. Where did it come from?"

"My father traded one of our best slaves for it in celebration of my twelfth span. That was the only time Papa ever sent away a slave for anything, but he did it for me," she beamed.

Coleman was disgusted with the whole concept of trading people like they were property. Ootyiah didn't know any better, so he kept his thoughts to himself. Suddenly, he realized, *If Master Oetan had traded and sent away only one slave, that slave had to be Maaryah's father. This poor naïve girl, she has no clue of the suffering her father's gift had caused.*

They turned around and slowly walked back the way they had come. They continued talking about Ootyiah's early years and what life was like growing up on a divitz estate. Munnari and Munnevo rose above the trees, bathing the landscape in their glow. He gave her a goodnight kiss at the courtyard entrance, and they parted. As he returned to the guesthouse, he kept mulling over in his mind the connection between Ootyiah and Maaryah.

For the next several days, Coleman continued making his rounds through the estate with Ayascho, Idop, and Ootyiah in tow. He and Ootyiah continued their evening rendezvous near the cliffs, but he would never let their strolls go beyond sight of the manor house.

Ootyiah talked about the gala events her mother hosted at the city house. She still had plans for her tandeban—her presentation to the gentry. Coleman could tell, she really didn't fully understand the consequences of the king's ruling that disgraced her father's name and stripped her family of all their holdings. Life had gone on just as before, and her mother was shielding her from the awful reality of their plight. Coleman was glad he could help them, but eventually, she would have to face her family's disgrace and deal with it. She still held her title, but that was all. She and her mother were dependent upon him for everything else: their food, their lodging, and the very clothes on their backs. Nevertheless, he would continue to honor his promise and allow them to remain as guests of the estate until something could be worked out for their benefit. After all, he had all the time in the world now that he lived under the Blessing of the City.

However, one thing continued to bother him. It was Ooty-iah's utter disregard and dismissal of the slaves' plight. Try as he may, she never grasped the concept that slaves were people and were no different than freeborns. To her understanding, slaves were different and would always be different.

"My dear," he told her, "All men are created equal and en-dowed by their Creator with certain unchanging rights." She couldn't accept that concept because she didn't see slaves as people. He did see a glimmer of hope when they discussed Teema. She had been her nanny when the girl was very young. Ootyiah had grown to love and appreciate the house slave. Coleman hoped he could get her to extend those feelings to other slaves, as well.

After a wernt, a ten-day period, Pendor had completed sev-eral sets of barbells and dumbbells; the weights were perma-nently attached to the bars. He began a regular, early morn-ing routine with Ayascho and Idop. They established a make-shift gym in the barn. By the morning of the third day, Idop and Ayascho were so sore they could hardly move without groaning. Coleman, too, could feel the soreness in his muscles, but it didn't deter him, even when the others protested. After a couple of wernts or so, the soreness began to subside. At the beginning of a new detzamar, Coleman changed the routine, and the others began to complain all over again.

"No pain, no gain," he kept telling them in godspeak. He repeated it so often, they too began to say it every morning as they started their routines. It became a chant that all three would start yelling when things got particularly difficult.

"I think my arms are getting bigger," Ayascho beamed after the second ten-day period.

Coleman grinned and just repeated, "No pain, no gain." Then the three started chanting it over and over.

One evening, after their stroll, Coleman escorted Ootyiah back to the manor house. Usually, he dropped her off at the courtyard entrance, but it was a cool night, so she invited him into the house to warm himself by the fire.

"Teema, bring us some warm drinks," Ootyiah commanded. The two stood with their backs to the fire, enjoying the warmth. She turned and faced him, and then she gave him a long snug on his cheek. He kissed her on the lips and pulled her closer to himself.

Teema returned with a tray of drinks, and surprisingly, she screamed and dropped the tray onto the floor. The ceramic cups shattered, scattering shards and liquid in all directions. Ootyiah jumped in fright and uttered a sharp shriek of shock.

Lady Oetan was immediately in the room. "What has happened? Teema, why did you scream?"

"Lady Oetan . . . Master Tondo . . . Mistress Ootyiah,"

Teema stuttered, unable to collect her thoughts.

Lady Oetan looked at Coleman with an icy stare. "Hoy, Teema, I'm waiting," she said in an angry tone. Coleman could tell Teema was terrified. She kept looking at him and then at Lady Oetan and back again, not knowing what to do or say next. Obviously, he could tell, she feared that one or the other's wrath would fall upon her.

"Please, Teema, tell us what frightened you," Coleman coaxed.

"I . . . I came into the room to serve you your warm drinks, and . . . and . . . " She stopped and looked down.

"Oy, Teema, don't stop there. Go on!" Lady Oetan chided.

"I thought Master Tondo was biting Mistress Ootyiah's face." Teema was completely undone. She began wringing her hands in fear of what her master might do next.

"Teema, relax. Mistress Ootyiah and I were only kissing," Coleman told her; however, he was looking at Lady Oetan. "Let me show you." He took Ootyiah's hand and kissed the back of it. "That is a kiss. I just kissed her on the lips. It is like a snug. Is that so bad?" he asked.

"Outrageous!" Lady Oetan carped. "There will be no more snugs or ghizz tonight. Teema, you may go. You can clean this mess after I have finished talking with Sire Tondo. Ootyiah, my dear, you may leave, as well."

"Oy, Mother, stop acting like I'm only a thirty-spanner. I'm old enough to do as I wish, and anyway, Sire Tondo has been a perfect cavalier," Ootyiah told her.

"I'm not so sure he has, and I need to establish some clear expectations. Now, please go." Ootyiah gave her mother a look of disgust, kissed Coleman on the cheek, and left the room. He could hear her angry footsteps pounding up the stairs. "So, Sire Tondo, here we are again. I think your understanding of honor and mine are not the same. What have you got to say for yourself?"

Coleman felt like an idle schoolboy who had just been caught passing multi-sensory data in class. He didn't know what to say and simply stood in thought for a few seconds. Lady Oetan stood straight as a board. He thought he could hear her foot tapping the floor beneath her gown. He finally began speaking, "Ah, yes, here we are again. What would you have me say?" he asked.

"What are your intentions? Do you plan to court my daughter in a proper fashion?"

"I am not sure what that means."

"You have been going on late-night strolls alone with her. I don't know how such things are conducted in your outlander kingdom, but here, that is simply unacceptable. I can see that Ootyiah is drawn to you, so I have allowed her some independence; however, that is at an end," she informed him as she examined the mess around her feet. "Again, I ask, do you plan to court my daughter in a proper fashion?"

"I do not understand what a *proper fashion* means," he admitted.

"The proper way for you to get to know my daughter is to spend time in conversation with her, and with a proper chaperone, I might add. No more snugging and ghizz. Such intimacy is shameful and improper. I'm sure I can make arrangements with Counselor Idop."

The thought of Idop following Ootyiah and himself around was not appealing. "That will not be necessary, my lady."

"Then, I will instruct Ootyiah there will be no more nightly strolls near the cliffs or anywhere else with you. Do you understand?"

Coleman nodded and meekly replied, "Yes, ma'am."

"Good. Teema, you may return and clean up this mess." Teema immediately came into the room and began cleaning.

Coleman bowed to Lady Oetan and walked out of the room with as much bravado as he could muster after such a humiliating experience. Lady Oetan had put an end to his nightly rendezvous with Ootyiah, but as he thought about it, he didn't think it was such a bad thing, after all. He needed a little time and some space, anyway. He certainly wasn't ready to commit to a permanent relationship with anyone. There were still too many unanswered questions about his role in this world, questions that continued to plague him.

He went to the guesthouse, plopped himself down in his chair, and began weaving a new basket. Ten completed baskets surrounded his chair. Producing baskets wasn't his goal, therapy, however, was.

After he finally retired for the night, he found it difficult to sleep. His thoughts had become dark and sinister. *How dare Lady Oetan talk to you that way, especially after all you've done for her? She owes you, and you can collect anytime you want. Beyond that, you're master of the estate, and no one would dare challenge your authority or your actions. You're the king's friend, remember?*

In his dreams, he wrestled with a shadowy figure that turned out to be an image of himself. He awoke in a cold sweat and was in a foul mood for the next several days. When Ayascho brought it to his attention, he admitted his dreams had become perverse. Ayascho reminded him of the power of the Tempter and how a person's dreams were often a way the Tempter enticed people to go down evil paths. After previous similar experiences, Coleman was beginning to think the Tempter was more than just a myth. Ayascho's words gave him some solace, and he found it easier to chase the wicked thoughts from his mind, but only after he made a secret promise to himself.

CHAPTER 20

MARKED FOR LIFE

It wasn't much after his humiliating encounter with Lady Oetan that Coleman finished meeting the remaining wurgors on his estate. Everyone he talked to told him how much they appreciated the midday break he had instituted. Nestor even admitted that production hadn't declined; it had actually improved.

"Treating people decently pays off," he told his foreman.

"Thems ain't people, theys slaves, but I wouldn't 'ave believed it if I didn't see it with mine own eyes," Nestor said. "But ya still canst trust 'em. Theys still gotta be watched all the time. I caught a dung creeper napping on the job the other day. Gave him a good kick in the arse, I did."

"I guess I can't expect too much progress all at once," Coleman grumbled in godspeak.

"Beg'n yer pardon, sire?" Nestor wondered.

"Keep up the good work, Nestor, but do not damage any of my *property*. Do you understand?"

"Yes, sire, as ya says."

One early afternoon, as the three men returned from their rounds, they heard an alarming shriek coming from the manor house. They quickly galloped to the courtyard and bounded off their mounts, Coleman leading the way as the men burst through the main door. They found Maaryah kneeling on the floor with Mistress Oetan standing over her, raising above her head something that looked like a riding crop. She swung it down just as Coleman reached her, blocking the blow with his hand. It hit his open palm with a loud smack, giving him such a jolt of searing pain that he instinctively grabbed the weapon, jerking it from Ootyiah's hand, tearing at her flesh. She screamed in pain and anger.

"Look what you've done!" she yelled as she showed him the red mark on her palm. He looked at his right hand and saw it was bleeding. He didn't say a word and showed her his wound as blood began to flow.

"Oy, that wouldn't have happened if you hadn't stopped me."

Lady Oetan was now in the room. "What happened, my dear? I heard an awful commotion."

"This clumsy oaf spilled a pitcher of wine all over my favorite gown. I know she did it on purpose. I was about to chasten her when Sire Tondo stopped me." He opened his bleeding palm and showed it to the girl's mother.

Lady Oetan gasped. "I'm sure Ootyiah didn't mean to cause you any harm, sire. It was an accident," the lady said in a very yielding manner. It was obvious to Coleman she feared what he might say or do next.

"I know she did not mean to injure me. She intended to do this to her," he said as he pointed his closed and bleeding hand toward Maaryah.

"Look what she's done. Just look at me," Ootyiah growled as she brushed the folds of her gown. The front of Ootyiah's beautiful blue dress was covered with red wine. "She needs to be punished. If you won't let me do it, send her to Nestor."

Coleman couldn't help but notice Maaryah shudder. "I have already told Nestor no one is to be beaten without my permission."

"Then, what are you going to do about this? Are you going to have her punished or not?" Ootyiah asked indignantly. Maaryah, still on her knees, looked up at Coleman. Fear was on her face, but anger was in her eyes.

"How many stripes should she be given, my dear?" Coleman asked as he opened his hand again and let blood fill his cupped palm. It soon began dripping onto the carpet.

"Teema, get a towel for Sire Tondo, and then do something about the blood on the floor," Lady Oetan called, trying to relieve the tension of the moment. "Please, let me treat your hand," she continued. Coleman stared at Ootyiah with icy blue eyes.

Finally, the young woman said, "I'll let you determine how many, but she needs to suffer at least a score. Just look at me, I'm a mess, and my beautiful gown is ruined."

"A score! Look at what only one has done." He held out his bleeding hand in front of Ootyiah's face. He then continued,

"You can't be serious. Such punishment is cruel and unusual. Therefore, my decision is no stripes. Maaryah, you are to try to clean the wine stains from Mistress Oetan's gown. If the stains do not come out, you must make her a new one."

"Yes, sire," Maaryah meekly replied.

"A gown made by that *worthless* slave? I wouldn't wear it even if she could!" Ootyiah barked.

"Then, it will be your choice," Coleman growled. Teema gave Coleman a towel, and he wrapped his hand, putting pressure on the wound with his fingers. Ootyiah gave a huff and stormed out of the room, stomping up the stairs. Coleman shook his painful hand and exited the house without saying another word; Idop and Ayascho following. He held the whip in his left hand, taking it with him. He wondered if Ootyiah would ever speak to him again. But after some thought, he decided he didn't really care one way or the other. If Idop was right, and she was the most beautiful woman in the kingdom, her beauty was only skin deep. He felt sad at this realization and for his loss. He had seen more in the young woman than was really there. He had been truly happy for a brief period, but now, he felt lonely again.

When he got to the guesthouse, he sat in his chair and picked up his unfinished basket. Sadly, he quickly realized his right hand was too badly injured, and the searing pain made it too difficult to concentrate on the task. There would be no therapy for him until his hand healed.

"Why don't you do that magic on yourself that you do for others?" Idop asked.

"It does not work on me. I can only help another, never myself."

He felt his shoulders being covered with something. It was Taahso's wrap. "Here, this will keep you warm," Ayascho told him.

Coleman sat in his chair, rocking back and forth, holding his injured hand. "This is really starting to hurt. And to think, she was going to do this to poor Maaryah." He shook his injured hand as the pain increased. "She wanted Maaryah to get twenty like this one. That is unbelievable! I am glad I was able to stop her," Coleman said to the others. "What is this thing Ootyiah was using?" he asked, pointing to the crop bristling with tiny spikes. Just then, Maaryah entered the guesthouse.

"It's a slave-beater. It's used to punish slaves. It leaves a real nasty mark; that's so they'll always remember," Idop told him. "You amaze me," Idop admitted. "You'll even take a beating for a worthless slave."

"Counselor, no one on this estate is worthless!" Coleman growled loudly. "This is why I will not allow anyone to be beaten on my holding," he said as he exposed the wound for the others to see. It was an angry-looking laceration, swollen and bloody, and it appeared to be getting worse by the minute. He squeezed the towel into his palm, trying to relieve the pain. It didn't help much.

Maaryah, carrying a small clay pot, approached and knelt before Coleman, took his injured hand in hers, carefully removed the towel, and began applying salve on it taken from the clay pot. The balm smelled like menthol and seemed to lessen the pain, but only a little. "I'm sorry this has happened. I'm so clumsy and look what my clumsiness has come to. Please forgive me, sire," she pleaded with tear-filled eyes.

"It is not your fault. If this had to happen at all, I prefer it was me and not you," he told her.

"But why, sire? I am but a slave, and you are the master."

"I wish you would stop thinking like that. You are a person with the same feelings as any other person, whether they be a slave or a king."

She looked at him in wonder. "I can't do that, sire. It would just lead to more trouble."

He stopped and thought for a while. Unfortunately, she was right. If she started thinking as if she weren't a slave, it could lead to serious problems for the poor girl. That realization angered him all the more.

"What happened after I left?" he asked.

"I tried to clean the gown, but the stains won't come out. I will have to make Mistress Oetan a new one if I can. I've never attempted anything so special. Also, she banished me from the manor house. Teema pleaded with Lady Oetan to allow me to attend to my duties in the kitchen, and she granted Teema's request, at least for now. There's been some talk of sending me back to the Separation House, but they haven't decided what to do with me, yet."

"I will not allow it. Counselor Idop, inform Lady Oetan that Maaryah will remain." Idop nodded and left. Coleman's gaze fell upon the young woman, and he gave her a pained smile, "I enjoy your company." Her eyes brightened, and a broad smile filled her face. She continued dabbing the ointment onto his wound, occasionally glancing up into his pain-racked face.

The searing ache increased all evening. It reached a crescendo early in the morning and began to ease a little after that. He couldn't sleep, and he noticed Maaryah had fallen asleep on the bench while leaning against the wall. He got up, found a blanket, and covered her shoulders with it. He quietly walked outside and gazed at the gibbous moons. Munnari and Munnevo looked huge as they hung low in the western sky. Munnoga was directly overhead. It was a cloudless night, and even though all three moons were out, the stars glowed brightly across the sky. Coleman marveled at the sight as several meteors raced across the starfield. He clasped his wrap with his left hand and shook his shoulders. He returned to his chair and fell asleep for a segment or two.

When he awoke, he saw Maaryah was no longer on the bench. He could hear her place a pitcher of water on the washing table. He rubbed the stubble on his face and decided he wouldn't shave today. "Good morning, Maaryah. You did not get much sleep last night, did you?"

"I'll be fine, sire. Let me look at your hand," she said as she pulled a small bench in front of his chair and sat. She carefully removed the towel bandage and examined the wound. "This is amazing. It's already healing. I wouldn't expect it to look this good for at least a wernt."

"It does not hurt as much either," he said. "I think I will survive, although there was a time last night I would have cut off my hand if I thought it would have ended the pain." He looked into Maaryah's lovely golden-amber eyes and thought of the welt across her back. Compassion filled his soul as he thought about the suffering she must have endured. She watched as sadness welled in his blue eyes and wondered what he was thinking.

The next three days passed slowly. Coleman stayed near the guesthouse, not venturing off the manor grounds. His friends advised him not to go riding because they thought the samaran reins might reopen his wound. So, for once, he listened to their advice; however, he did make them continue with their workouts in the barn.

He decided to jog rather than lift heavy weights. He removed Taahso's wrap during his jogs. The only other time he didn't wear it was when Maaryah took it and sewed tie-clasps to it. Once tied, the wrap stayed in place, freeing up a hand.

It was in the late afternoon of the third day after the incident when Ootyiah made her way to the guesthouse. Coleman was sitting in his chair with Maaryah hovering over him like a mother frizzard. When Mistress Oetan entered the room, Maaryah quickly excused herself and withdrew from the house, all the while under Ootyiah's angry glare.

"Mother says I should come by and see how you are doing. She noticed you hadn't left the manor grounds since . . . since . . . " she hesitated, searching for the right words, " . . . since your injury," she finally said, avoiding any responsibility for what she had done. "I hope your wound is healing, and I'm very sorry this happened to you."

Coleman thought she sounded like a diplomat or a politician trying to obfuscate personal responsibility. "Thank you, Ootyiah. The wound is healing faster than anyone would have guessed. I will be making my usual rounds in another day or so. How have you been?"

"I have been very well, thank you. Although Mother has been very worried ever since the . . . the accident," she told him.

"What is she worried about?"

"I really don't know; she won't tell me. She has worried a lot ever since the news of Papa's crossing-over. I really miss him, too."

Coleman suspected there was more to Lady Oetan's fretting than the loss of her bondmate. "Please tell your mother I wish to speak to her. I will wait for her here."

"May I inform her of the purpose of this meeting?"

"Just tell her, it has to do with honor."

"With honor?' Ootyiah wondered.

"Yes. Just tell her that."

"Yes, sire," she said as she bent down and kissed him on the cheek. "I really do miss our walks," she admitted. "Maybe, when you're feeling better, we can do them again." She gave him a warm smile and then left the room.

Coleman shook his head and said quietly to himself in god-speak, "If she could only be that sweet the rest of the time."

It wasn't long before Lady Oetan was at the door. "Yes, sire, you wanted to see me?" she nervously said with a bow.

"Please, Lady Oetan, come in and take a seat," he said, pointing to the bench in front of him.

"I hope your wound is healing, sire. Is there anything I can do?"

"No, no, I am healing faster than expected." He showed her his open palm. The only evidence of a wound was an angry-looking red welt.

"This is amazing. You're healing so quickly. I would never have suspected such a thing," she said in surprise.

"That is what everyone tells me. Now, Ootyiah says, you have . . . how shall I put it . . . you have had *concerns* lately. Will you tell me what they are?"

"Ootyiah said you wanted to talk to me about honor, not concerns," she said a bit ruffled.

"I think the two have a direct relationship with each other. Now, tell me, what worries you so?"

He watched as fear replaced her nervous expression. She took a deep breath, "Oy, since you've asked so directly, I will give you a direct answer. I know you are going to turn us out. My daughter did a stupid thing, and you were grievously injured. Any other master would have tossed us off his holding that very instant. Is your delay just to torture me?"

"Lady Oetan, any other master would not have been injured in the first place; only the slave would have suffered. I refuse to act like other masters. I want you to remember that. What did I tell you on the first day we met? The day you learned of your bondmate's unfortunate fate, and the loss of your holdings? Do you remember the promise I made to you?"

"You said we could continue to live here as your guests."

"Yes, I did. If I turn you out, as you put it, I would be breaking that promise. I would be going back on my word, and I would dishonor myself. I will not do that, even though I am *only* an outlander. Now, put your mind at ease. You will remain as my guest for as long as I hold this estate for the king, and you desire it." He looked deeply into her eyes.

After a few seconds, she lowered her head. "Thank you, sire. I don't know what we would have done without your kindness. I am sorry I ever doubted you are an honorable man. Will you forgive me?"

"There is nothing to forgive. I know this has been a very difficult time for you. I hope I have put your mind at ease."

The two remained in conversation for over a segment. They discussed past affairs on the estate and its management. Lady Oetan was a treasure of knowledge, although she never actually took on management responsibilities. That was her late bondmate's duties, and he would delegate management of the estate to the estate foreman in his absence. He also learned, Sire Oetan wanted his daughter to become literate, so he had employed a scholar to teach her. Lady Oetan, who wasn't literate at the time, joined the sessions and was also taught.

Coleman was told that Lady Oetan's mother, father, and brother had died during an epidemic called the Black Scourge, some thirty spans earlier—a horrible illness that killed many citizens and slaves. She had no living relatives other than Ootyiah. After their discussion ended, she never again worried about being turned out.

Coleman's hand healed quickly. By the end of the tenth day, all that remained of his wound was a red welt across his palm. It no longer diminished, so he had the feeling it would always remain with him. He'd been marked for life because of his kind act.

He resumed his daily rounds of the estate and noticed that much of the acreage was left fallow. Nestor told him that there weren't nearly enough slaves to work all of the land. It seemed a waste to Coleman to let so much ground remain untilled. There was also plenty of land for herding and the growing of fodder. Lush grass grew wherever there were no fields of crops. He hoped his idea of raising thrice would work out. The thrice egg box, still stored in a safe corner of the barn, had yet to bear fruit. He wondered how much longer before the eggs would hatch, or if they would even hatch at all.

CHAPTER 21

VISITORS IN BLUE ROBES

Late one cool afternoon, Coleman heard Ayascho's call. The young man was sitting on the ground under his 'resting tree,' as he called it, staring into the distance.

"Look, Tondo, someone is coming," he said, pointing to the hillock overlooking the manor grounds. In the distance, a couple of miles away, they could see a huge wagon, pulled by two large creatures, one in front of the other, making its way toward them. As it drew closer, they noticed three little dots sitting on a bench at the front of the wagon; the dots might be men. As the wagon drew closer, they could see the wagon was drawn by two huge rasters, one in front of the other in typical raster style. The wagon reminded Coleman of something you would see in a gypsy caravan.

As it got closer, the wagon seemed to grow in size, its true scale easier to judge. It was at least fifteen feet wide, thirty feet long, and nearly twenty feet from the ground to its top. The three dots now looked like tiny men dressed in blue robes, their heads covered with cowls.

It took about half a segment for the visitors to reach them. By then, Idop had joined the other two and stood waiting to greet their visitors. Idop informed him, priests wore blue robes. When the wagon finally arrived, the three men scampered down from their perch and stretched. Idop was indeed correct, for they were dressed in the cobalt-blue robes of priests of the temple. The three priests lowered their cowls in unison. Two of the priests were at least middle-age and bore the countenance and confidence of seasoned veterans. The other priest was much younger, hardly more than a thirty-spanner, Coleman guessed.

The estate master stepped forward and introduced himself, "Let me be the first to welcome you to the Tondo Estate. I am Tondo, and these are my friends, Ayascho of the Wilderness, and King's Counselor Idop."

The young man bowed and was the first to speak, "I am Attendant Pahno. I will be handling the daily needs of my masters during your training."

"Training? What do you mean?" Coleman asked.

"The Sutro Seer, in his wisdom, guided by the hand of the all-knowing unnamed god whom we revere, has sent us to you for your testing and training. Let me introduce the masters," the young priest told the surprised Coleman. "This is Sutro Adept Varios, the temple's master scholar. He has knowledge of all the great sciences and arts. He understands the laws of man, nature, and the commandments of the unnamed god. He will teach you all you can accept about these things." Sutro Adept Varios bowed to Coleman but said nothing. Coleman returned the bow and examined the man from head to toe. The priest stood about five feet eight inches tall, which was the average height for a man of this kingdom. He had a full head of dark-brown hair and dark-brown eyes. Coleman noticed, the man's eyes were always staring at him, taking in every little movement he made, as if gauging his intellect and capacity to learn.

Idop, who was standing next to Coleman, leaned over to him and quietly spoke into his ear, "Master Varios is the greatest scholar in the land. He has an understanding of all things. It is a great honor to have him as your teacher." Coleman bowed again, this time, a little lower.

The young priest continued, "This is Sutro Adept Shergus, the temple swordmaster. He has knowledge of all methods of blade use in defense and attack. He will prepare you for all you are about to face in the coming era of threat."

A chill coursed down Coleman's spine. *What is this era of threat?* he wondered to himself. Sutro Adept Shergus bowed to Coleman and then to Counselor Idop. Master Shergus was taller than Master Varios, probably close to six feet tall, Coleman guessed.

"It is good to see you again, megatus, or shall I call you counselor?" Master Shergus said.

"Please, refer to me as counselor," Idop answered. "Master Shergus is the greatest swordsman in all three kingdoms. He teaches only those who have received a special dispensation from the Sutro Seer himself and have proven worthy of his skills. You are indeed a fortunate man to be trained by such a noted and skilled master." All three priests bowed in unison, then straightened. Coleman looked closely into Master Shergus's face. He noticed a scar on the master's left cheek. His eyes were black pools of threat. Coleman shuddered at what he saw. This was a man who had lived through much conflict. He had an air of self-confidence that exuded from his very countenance. Coleman had felt such a presence before, always coming from the most experienced and hardened combat veterans, the ones who had walked through the valley of the shadow of death and grappled with the Grim Reaper himself. These men were changed by grievous experiences, changed in a way that molded their lives forevermore. Coleman had feared no man since his arrival to this world, but instinctively, he knew this was a man he had better respect and fear.

"We were not expecting visitors, but allow me to prepare a place for your lodging," Coleman offered.

"That will not be necessary. We will abide in the wagon. All we need is a place, preferably in the shade, to place it. We will be here for some time," the young attendant informed him.

"Choose any site that suits your needs. Let me offer you water, wine, and food. Your journey must have been tiring," Coleman said, acting as the gracious host.

"Thank you, but temple code requires that we partake of only certain foods and drink. I am sure you understand," the young priest told him.

"Of course. If there is anything I can do to make your stay more comfortable, please let me know. You are my first guests, and I want your stay to be enjoyable," Coleman told them.

"Our stay here will not be enjoyable, especially for you. You will suffer much in your testing and training; you *and* your friends. The fate of the world may rest in your hands, and, as for my part, *if* you prove worthy, I will see that you are prepared," Master Shergus told him in a tone that took all three men by surprise.

"What is this all about? I have been waiting to hear from a spokesman for the temple, and now, all I get are riddles. I expect some answers," Coleman grumbled.

"We will not discuss it now. You will learn as much as we can teach you during your testing and training. We do not have all the answers you are looking for, and we are simply following the dictates of His Eminence, the Sutro Seer. He will share what you need to know when the time is right. In the meantime, we will prepare you for your meeting with him, which will occur in due course. I will learn for myself if you nurture the good seed of curiosity or the wicked seed of indifference," Master Varios advised him.

"Testing and training will begin in the morning. I suspect you have duties to perform, so sessions will begin in the third segment of daylight. Will that be acceptable?" Master Shergus asked.

"Ha, that will be okay. What will we learn first?" Coleman asked.

"You will spend the morning with Master Varios. You will be under my tutorage in the afternoon. I will determine if you nurture the good seed of honor or the evil seed of dishonor," Master Shergus said in an almost threatening voice.

The three priests bowed again, and then the young one climbed onto the wagon. The other two walked to a large tree near the barn, and the wagon was moved under its spreading branches. Coleman, Ayascho, and Idop silently watched as the wagon was positioned.

"Well, my friends, I think we are in for a very interesting day tomorrow," Coleman said as he watched the priest's wagon being positioned. "What is all this talk about good seeds and evil seeds?"

Idop looked worried and began to explain, "It comes from the temple's Tome of Life. The priests tell us that the seeds of good and evil are within all of us, and we choose the ones we wish to nurture. I think we will be nurturing the seed of pain. I've been taught by Master Shergus before when I was a megato. I still hurt from all the beatings he gave me with his wooden sword. He is right, Tondo, we will suffer much."

The three friends ate dinner as though they were condemned men partaking of their last meal before their executions. Idop could not tell them anything about Master Varios because he had never received training from the scholar. However, he told the others that Master Shergus was a harsh instructor, impatient with students' mistakes, and excessively cruel if the student wasn't focused on his training. He told them, they will be using heavy wooden swords at first, and the master will undoubtedly make them feel the bite of his many times before their training sessions ended. The master had a nasty habit of helping a student remember what not to do with a quick and stinging slash to the head, leg, arm, or chest. No one was looking forward to that abuse, but Coleman felt it was little different than some of the tough Army training he had been through in the past. He certainly wasn't looking forward to that pain and humiliation, but he was sure it would be well worth it to gain expertise with the main weapon of the land.

Coleman chuckled to himself, then said, "I am very interested in learning from the masters. I bet I can teach them a few things myself."

"That is a very arrogant thing to say, my friend," said Idop. "They are the most knowledgeable and skilled men in the kingdom, probably in all three kingdoms, and you really think you can teach them something they don't already know?"

"We will see," Coleman simply responded.

Coleman and the others didn't sleep well that night. They arose well before dawn, even before Maaryah brought in water pitchers for their washbasins. When she arrived, she apologized profusely. Coleman quickly set her mind at ease, but Idop's scowl unnerved her. They ate their morning meal in silence, and then they gathered in the barn for their morning workout. Following that, they spent some time practicing archery. This drew the attention of Master Shergus.

"What is this you are doing?" he asked.

"We are practicing with bow and arrow," Coleman explained as he held up his bow in his left hand and an arrow in his right. "I use them to bring down game, but they can also be used in battle."

Master Shergus continued to watch as the men took aim and let their arrows fly. All three hit their targets, three bales of hay fifty feet away. The men walked to the bales to retrieve their arrows. The priest followed and then examined the feathered shafts as they protruded from their targets.

"I see these weapons can be effective; however, I see no honor in killing from a distance," the master swordsman proclaimed.

"Dead is dead, and ends the confrontation, whether from close range or from a distance," Coleman challenged.

"You sound like a man who has been in battle before. Are you a warrior?" the priest wondered.

"Yes, for nearly ten spans I served my kingdom and fought in many battles."

"Ha, a mere ten spans! Have you killed only from a distance, or have you seen the eyes of your enemy?" the master asked.

"Mostly from a distance. But I have seen the dying eyes of a man I killed with a knife."

"Oy, only one?" Master Shergus wondered. Coleman nodded. The master's face soured, and then he said, "You must show me how to use this bow and arrow."

For the remainder of their practice time, Coleman instructed the master. He gave Idop a wink and said, "Already, one down, and only one to go." Idop just shook his head and said nothing.

When the third hour of daylight was upon them, they presented themselves in front of the priests' wagon and waited for Master Varios to appear. He soon stepped out of the wagon's back door carrying a satchel. "I will need a table and some benches for our study place. Can we meet in that building?" he asked, pointing to the guesthouse. Coleman nodded and led the way. The men entered, and Coleman pointed to the table.

"Ha, that will do very well. Please sit while I prepare my things," the master said. From his satchel, he pulled out ink pots, quills, paper, and a scroll.

He looked over his small class and said, "Counselor Idop,

I know you can read and write, at least somewhat. Are either of you two literate?"

Ayascho shook his head, and Coleman said, "I can read and write what the people call godspeak, but concerning world-speak, I am afraid I cannot."

"Godspeak? Ha, I've been told you can speak a tongue no one has ever heard. Before we start, I would like you to write a few things on paper using godspeak, if you can."

Coleman took quill to paper and printed, 'The quick brown fox jumped over the lazy dog's back.' "This line of words, which is called a sentence, has all the symbols, called letters, in the godspeak language," he told the master.

"It is very concise. How many symbols are in this godspeak of yours?"

"Twenty-six."

"Only twenty-six? Amazing! I have never heard of another language or a different method of scribing. It seems quite elegant, though. Unfortunately, godspeak will not help you here. If you want to be an educated man, you must learn world-speak. I can tell by your speech you are an outlander. You and your man, Ayascho, have accents. It's not too pronounced, so I should be able to help you overcome it. However, you, the Tondo, have a peculiar way of phrasing your words. It's like you haven't learned how to shorten words and combine them. That emphasizes your accent and makes it more noticeable. We will work on that together."

Coleman was a bit taken aback. He had never noticed his accent, nor had anyone ever mentioned it to him. He realized long ago he had difficulty with contractions. He just couldn't get the hang of them in this peculiar language of clicks and pops. He welcomed the master scholar's direct comments.

Master Varios continued, "If you are to learn to write in world-speak, you will need to master the five-hundred and twenty symbols it uses. We will begin by memorizing all of them."

For the next few segments, the men went over the world-speak symbols. They appeared to be a mixture of symbols representing phonics and pictographic script similar to hiero-glyphics, Coleman thought. Ayascho said it looked like funny pictures to him. Master Varios was not amused and gave the young man a quick, sharp rap on the wrist with a long, stout stick the master used as a pointer. All three students quickly realized that lighthearted comments were not welcome in the master scholar's class.

As expected, Idop did much better than the other two, for he already could read and write to some degree. In the early after-noon, they were allowed to break for their midday meal. They were told, after they ate, Master Shergus would begin teaching them the fine art of the sword. This was the class they had all been waiting for with both excitement and trepidation.

The men ate and then left the guesthouse. Coleman could see Master Shergus was still practicing with the bow he had loaned him. "He has been at it since morning," Coleman told the others as they walked over to him. They continued watch-ing the master until he stopped and addressed them.

"This is quite a device. How did you come by it?" he asked.

"I made it out of things I found in the Wilderness. It has a long history of use in my homeland."

"Your bow is more powerful than the sutro gravetum ones. Why is that?"

"Mine is called a composite bow, made with several layers of wood and animal sinew. The other two are made from sutro gravetum. I would have preferred to make them from wood, but there are no suitable trees in this area."

"Why are the sutro gravetum bows blue?" the priest asked.

"In the wasteland, we found rocks from the blue moon on our way to the Ancient City," Ayascho cut in. "They are gifts from the great god."

"You, a savage, know of the god of the blue moon?" Shergus asked in wonder.

"Yes, he guides my people," Ayascho said with a frown.

"You say the blue bows are made of rocks from Munnari? How is that possible?"

"We found a crater in the wasteland beyond the Mountains of Magheedo. I think it may have been caused by a huge rock that came from the blue moon, but it is only a guess. We collected many small blue rocks, which may have come from the big rock that made the crater," Coleman told him.

"Do you have any more of this blue rock?" Shergus asked.

"Yes, let me show you." Coleman directed the master into the barn and showed him the collection of meteorite fragments stored there.

"These could be sacred things; gifts from the great god; gifts for a righteous purpose. May I touch one?" the priest asked breathlessly. Coleman handed him a meteorite, and he hefted it.

"It is very heavy, more so than regular stone." He handed it back to Coleman.

"Would you like me to have the blacksmith make this into a bow for you?" Coleman asked.

The master's face lit with excitement, "Yes, yes, it would be a gift beyond measure. Thank you, thank you," Shergus repeated and bowed low.

Coleman thought silently for a moment, then picked up a second, smaller fragment. "Why haven't I thought of this before?" he mumbled in godspeak. He headed to the blacksmith's shop and gave Pendor instructions to make another bow for Master Shergus and a straight razor from the smaller meteorite fragment for himself. After explaining what a straight razor was, he returned, finding that the swordmaster had changed into leather trousers and a short-sleeved leather jerkin. The master quickly began his first lesson as though nothing had transpired previously.

"Since our time is limited, the first thing I must do is determine which technique suits you best. There won't be time to master more than one. Counselor Idop has already been trained, to some extent, with sword and shield. You will continue your training in that technique. Now, to begin with, you two will show me what you can do with sword and shield, as well," he said while eyeing Ayascho and Coleman. He handed each a stout wooden sword and a wooden shield. He held his wooden two-handed longsword in a defensive posture, then commanded, "Ayascho, am I pronouncing your name correctly?" Ayascho nodded. "Attack me!" The young man delayed. "Don't hesitate! You must gain the heart of a warrior. Dawdling can cost you your life. Now, attack me!" the master shouted. Ayascho charged him and swung his sword. Shergus swiftly stepped aside, and Aya-scho's wild swing found only air. "Control! You're off bal-ance. I could have cut off your arm." The master's wooden blade hovered above Ayascho's sword arm. "Now, try again. This time with control."

Ayascho was more cautious in his attack, but each time he swung his wooden blade, the master blocked it with his sword. After several attempts, he told the winded Ayascho to step aside and rest. "Let us now see how the warrior handles him-self." The master signaled for Coleman to attack.

Coleman shifted and dodged, leading with his shield and then quickly moving in for an attack with his wooden sword. The stroke found only air, but Coleman had not overextend-ed. He quickly recovered, shoved the shield at the master, stepped around it, and attacked once more. Again, his wood-en sword found only thin air.

"Very well done for someone who has never used a sword before," the master quipped. "Tell me, warrior, what type of weapon do you favor? Obviously, it's not the sword."

"SCAR2, my trusty Heckler & Koch .45, and the old, re-liable Ma Deuce," Coleman replied in godspeak, referring to Earth weaponry.

Master Shergus gave him a quizzical stare, then he sim-ply said, "Continue." The two maneuvered for the next sever-al minutes. Coleman was beginning to breathe heavily when the master told him to stop. "We will now use the two-handed sword," the master said.

They repeated the exercise using longer two-handed wood-en swords. The pupils were no more effective than before, but Coleman thought the larger sword felt more comfortable. Ayascho's feeble attempts were obviously awkward.

"I don't like this one," he admitted.

The next technique was dual swords. Each pupil was given a wooden longsword and a wooden short sword. Coleman went first this time and struggled with the left-hand short sword. All his attacks were made using the longsword in his right hand.

Ayascho did much better, but the master replaced Ayascho's wooden longsword with another short sword. The master continued the exercise. Ayascho was quick, and both wooden blades slashed through the air in a cascade of threat. Not once was the master touched, but he needed to move around more to avoid Ayascho's attacks.

"Very well," the master finally said. "Ayascho, you are very quick with the two blades. You will learn the dual sword technique. The Tondo will learn with the two-handed sword. Your long arms, height, and bulk are best suited for the powerful attacks that come with the big blade. And of course, Counselor Idop will use sword and shield. This is an excellent mix. All of you will have the opportunity to practice against the three major techniques. For the remainder of the afternoon, I will teach you the various parries you can use to defend yourselves. Follow my lead."

Master Shergus guided his pupils through a series of motions that taught his small class the important parry moves a swordsman must learn. There were no biting remarks, nor did they feel the sting of his wooden sword, much to each student's relief. By the end of the day, the master had not even worked up a sweat, but his pupils were tired, sore, sweaty, and grimy.

Shergus ended the lesson on a not so encouraging note. "I have been easy on you today. Tomorrow, we will step up the pace. We don't have much time."

"Master Shergus, how much time do we have, and what are we preparing for?" Coleman asked.

"His Eminence has told us, we have only two or three spans to prepare you for the coming cataclysm. What that is, he did not say, but believe me, if the Sutro Seer says a cataclysm is coming, you can be sure it is. Now, rest and refresh yourselves, and don't worry about things you cannot change. Now is the time to prepare and prepare we will."

The first thing the three students did after their lessons ended for the day was to head for the bathhouse. All were sore, dirty, and tired. After a good soaking, they ate dinner and talked until dark. Coleman waited for Nestor's report and then went directly to bed, falling asleep immediately.

The second day with the master scholar was similar to the first. Master Varios seemed to be a patient man, but he expected his students to pay close attention. They had already learned that he didn't tolerate foolishness, so they behaved themselves. Counselor Idop did well, and Coleman felt he was making good progress. Poor Ayascho, on the other hand, struggled; however, the master took the time to explain things repeatedly to him, trying to help him grasp the meaning and purpose of his efforts. By the end of the session, he was doing better.

Unfortunately, sword training became a brutal affair. Master Shergus demanded his students show him what they had learned during the first day. They did their best, but all fell far short of the master's expectations. Master Shergus began with criticisms, then humiliations, and by mid-session, each pupil had felt the sting of his wooden sword. By the time the shadows grew long, each man had many bruises.

Coleman was growing more frustrated by the minute. Near the end of the session, his anger boiled over, and he challenged the master's methods. "I have been through some rough training before, but what you are doing is not helpful in teaching us what we need to learn."

"Is that so?" the master quipped. "Do I anger you, my little chetzy? I don't have the time to coddle you as your mother did. If you concentrated more on your practice and less on your complaints, you might improve. Right now, you're the worst of this sorry lot. Even the savage is a better swordsman," Master Shergus's words were as biting as his wooden sword. "Now, defend yourself!"

Coleman raised his sword as the master advanced. In less time than it takes to blink, Coleman had been hit on the thigh, the shoulder, the back of the head, and an embarrassing smack across his buttocks. That was enough for him. With his anger and frustration building, a powerful wave of force emanated from his center. Unexpectedly, it felt like a brick wall hit him in the face. He flew backward more than ten feet and landed in a heap in the dust, his ears ringing, and his mind reeling. He saw stars, and he struggled to stay conscious.

The master stood above him, his two-handed wooden sword floating in front of the prone student's face. "Now, things will get interesting," the master began. "You have the inner-power, the strength of tzaah. You may be worth my efforts, after all. Of course, you must learn to control it." The master leaned forward and offered Coleman his arm.

Coleman shook the dizziness from his head and accepted the master's help. "What happened?" he feebly asked.

"I have been provoking you all afternoon. I wanted to learn for myself if what I've been told is true. You indeed have the Gift, the inner-power that grants you many abilities; however, you don't know how to control it properly. When I felt your force attack, I countered with a controlled response that sent you flying backward. I can teach you to make your attacks and your defenses much more effective. Coupled with the blade, you will be a most worthy apprentice."

"What about Ayascho and Idop? Can you teach them tzaah?" Coleman asked, his head still swimming.

"Many men have tzaah, but it remains dormant in all but a very few. For some reason unknown to us, it awakens, and the holder can wield the power his Gift grants. I already know, Counselor Idop's tzaah has not awakened. Surprisingly, I feel an awakening within the savage, and we will test him to see if he has the Gift. And as for you, I am very impressed. I have not felt such a strong influence from someone outside the temple. You may have the potential to become a master; we will see. Now, go and rest. We will resume our lessons tomorrow.

Ayascho, you will come with me. Master Varios and I will test you."

Ayascho looked at Coleman with apprehension. Coleman placed a hand on the young man's shoulder and gave him a curt smile; however, his eyes revealed his concern. He, himself, certainly wouldn't want to be under the scrutiny of the two masters, and he felt sorry for his friend. "It will be all right. Wouldn't it be wonderful if you also possess this Gift?" Coleman finally said.

"I'm not taahso. That is not my calling. I am a simple hunter, little more," Ayascho replied.

"We will quickly determine if what you say is true," Master Shergus interjected. "Now, leave us," the master commanded, looking into Coleman's face.

Coleman did as he was told. He and Idop walked the short distance to the guesthouse, both rubbing their newly earned bruises. They sat at the table and watched through the open window as Master Shergus led Ayascho into the priest's wagon.

As the p´atezas touched the western horizon, Teema and Maaryah brought the men trays of food and drink. Ayascho was still being evaluated by the two masters. Just before the glow of dusk disappeared, Ayascho entered the room. He sat on a bench, lifted the tray of food the others had saved for him, and offered a silent prayer. He then began to eat, not even looking up. He munched away, only stopping to take a gulp of wine from time-to-time. The other two just watched, waiting, hoping he would soon tell them the results of his test. He remained silent, and when he had finished eating, he leaned back and looked at the other two. A smile slowly crept across his face. The tension increased as the others waited.

Finally, Coleman could bear it no more, "What did they say?" Ayascho's smile grew larger, exposing his gleaming white teeth.

"Hurry and tell us," Idop demanded.

"They say I have a portion of what they call the Gift. They say I will make things move by thinking about it. I had no idea that was possible. I thought only a taahso or the Messenger could do things like that."

"Good for you!" Coleman shouted.

Idop looked dejected. He wondered why this savage was blessed with the coveted power, yet he, a civilized man, was not. He stood and exited the house, disappearing into the darkness.

"Master Shergus says, he and Master Varios will work with me every day after our training sessions. He says I should begin to use the inner-power with my sword training in forty days. Why does Idop look so angry?"

"He is disappointed. It will be best if you do not talk to him about this unless he brings it up first," Coleman advised.

The men heard Nestor's footsteps as he passed by the guesthouse on his way to his cabin. Coleman dismissed himself and followed Nestor, receiving his daily report.

The next several days continued as expected. Training was difficult, but the students were progressing well. Master

Shergus remained a harsh instructor. He felt no compunction about whipping his wooden blade across the flesh of a wayward student. All three men were covered in bruises and welts. One evening, after Idop and Ayascho had retired, Coleman remained sitting in his chair, weaving his basket while pondering his new life. Maaryah hovered nearby, waiting to fulfill his smallest request. He put his unfinished basket down, rubbed his left shoulder, and groaned.

"What is it, sire?" Maaryah asked.

"Today, Master Shergus hit me so hard on my shoulder; it has ached ever since."

"Let me fetch some of the ointment. It will help ease the pain," she offered.

"Okay, I'll welcome anything if it helps. I don't think I can sleep with this ache," he told her, proud that his lessons with Master Varios had improved his speech.

She moved to a table and opened a drawer, retrieving a clay jar. Coleman removed his jerkin, and Maaryah gasped. His upper body was covered with bruises and red welts. She began applying the ointment to his left shoulder, and then she dabbed some on each bruise and welt on his back, gently rubbing it in. Coleman felt a drop of liquid roll down his back, but he thought nothing of it. A short time later, he felt another. He turned and saw tears flowing down Maaryah's cheeks. She quickly wiped them away and lowered her head.

"What's all this?" he asked as he lifted her chin with his hand and looked into her beautiful golden-amber eyes.

"Forgive me, sire. I'm just a foolish girl," she said.

"What's bothering you? Have you been badly treated by someone? You must tell me," he demanded.

"No, sire. I . . . I am sad because of what they are doing to you," she admitted. "You won't let Foreman Nestor or anyone else beat us, but you allow that awful man to hit you over and over every day. Please, sire, send him away," she pleaded. Coleman chuckled and wiped away another tear that quickly ran down her cheek.

"There is a difference, my dear. I choose to allow it. You and the others don't. Master Shergus can be a harsh teacher, but we are learning things we must know. Sometimes, that requires pain." Coleman laughed again and continued, "What does not kill you makes you stronger." Maaryah stared at him with a tender look and an inviting smile.

She belongs to you; take her, an inner voice carped. He was about to reach out to her and draw her closer, but the memory of the promise he'd made to himself came to mind, stopping him. He reluctantly turned around, allowing her to continue applying the ointment.

The next morning, during their training with Master Varios, the samaran caretaker, Seemo, rushed to the door of the guesthouse. "Master Tondo, the trunk you've stored in the barn is making noises. There must be something inside; maybe an evil varmint or a viper," the young man exclaimed breathlessly.

Coleman looked at Ayascho and Idop in wonder; then, his face lit up. "The thrice eggs have hatched. I must see this!" he exclaimed as he scurried out the door heading for the barn with the others, including Master Varios, following closely behind.

The wooden trunk was stored in a dark, secluded corner of the barn. When Coleman reached it, he dropped to his knees, cocked his head, and listened. He could hear scratching sounds and an occasional chirp coming from inside. He carefully lifted the lid. Three tiny thrice had broken through the tough, leathery skin of their eggs and were wiggling around the nest. Two more eggs had been pecked open from the inside as the newborns within struggled to escape. They looked like puppies. They had no horns, and their head-plates were hardly noticeable. Coleman was transfixed by what he saw.

"Bring Lulubelle over here," he told the samaran caretaker.

"I don't understand, sire," Seemo replied.

"The thrice, bring the thrice here. I want to see what she does."

"Yes, sire," he replied, but he hesitated to move. Coleman could tell, Seemo was reluctant to handle the large beast. The estate master knew he was a marvelous samaran caretaker, but the thrice was a different matter altogether. He took pity on poor Seemo, so he rose to his feet and went to Lulubelle, who was in the corral. He scratched her behind the ear, and she cocked her head to get the full effect. The caretaker closely watched everything Coleman did with the beast. The estate master firmly grabbed her ear and led her into the barn and over to the trunk. She sniffed the nest and quickly began licking the hatchlings with her huge tongue. When she had licked them for a while, she gently placed one in her mouth, lifted it from the nest, and gently dropped it onto the springy straw scattered on the floor. The little critter landed with a plop and struggled to gain its footing. After a couple of tries, it was standing, swaying back and forth like a tiny, newborn calf.

By midmorning, seven little thrice were wobbling around Lulubelle's feet. Coleman was worried she would accidentally crush one, but she was very careful when she moved her feet. He noticed the little ones were quickly learning to keep their distance from her huge pads.

The men spent the entire morning watching the miracle unfold. By midday, ten baby thrice had hatched. The remaining two eggs showed no signs of life. All in all, Coleman felt it was a great start. Ten out of twelve eggs had hatched. Now, the question was, will the younglings survive to adulthood, and how long will that take?

"Keep an eye on all the thrice for me, Seemo. This is a great start for my new business."

Master Shergus walked in and scanned the scene. "So, this is where all of you have been hiding. What's going on here?"

Ayascho held up both hands with his fingers spread wide. "Ten thrice have hatched! That's good."

"Too bad, you missed all the excitement. I think Lulubelle will be a good mother," Coleman surmised. "Seemo, are there rats in here?"

"I'm sorry, master, I don't know what raaht´ is?"

"I mean creatures that could eat the little thrice?"

"Sometimes, master, but I will hunt for them."

"Good. It is your responsibility to see that these young-lings are safeguarded. Do whatever is necessary. Do you understand?"

"Yes, master, as you wish," Seemo replied.

By this time, Coleman had grown accustomed to being called master, and it was no longer bothering him the way it had when he'd first arrived, but that sudden realization began to concern him even more.

Sword training was more brutal than ever before. The three students let their concentration drift after the morning's surprise. Master Shergus made each one pay for his indolence. Coleman was particularly angered by the master's heavy-handedness. He thought he would try to use his taah, or tzaah as the masters called it, to ignite Shergus's wooden blade.

When the master called him forth for more master-on-pupil practice, Coleman gave Ayascho a wink, and then he focused his taah on the master's sword. Instead of the blade bursting into flame as expected, Coleman felt like he'd been doused with a bucket of water. He staggered backward a couple of steps and looked at Shergus with dismay. The master stood grinning at him, his wooden sword pointing in Coleman's direction. The student quickly took account of himself and discovered he wasn't wet at all; he was as dry as a bone.

"What happened?" Coleman sputtered.

"You thought you could fool the master, didn't you?" Shergus challenged.

"Yes, I wanted your wooden sword to burn up. I'm tired of being hit by it."

"I've been wondering how long before you'd try something stupid. You're not the first of my students to think they could outsmart me," the master said. "If you are going to use tzaah, you must not foretell your plan. I can teach you how to do that, but not today. Now, defend yourself!"

The remainder of the lesson was more punishing than the first part. Shergus was on a terror, and each student dreaded facing him. After the lesson was over, the three students limped into the guesthouse and collapsed wherever they could find a resting place.

"That's it; I've had it!" Coleman grumbled. "We need a break. I declare tomorrow a day of rest for everyone; man and beast. There will be no training, and no one works."

"You know Master Shergus will be madder than a wet frizzard, don't you? Nestor won't like it either," Idop warned.

"I don't care. I should have done this a long time ago," Coleman grouched.

He limped out of the house and paid a visit to the priests' wagon. Ayascho and Idop could hear shouts of anger but were too tired and sore to move. Soon, Coleman returned.

"Oy, what did they say?" Idop asked.

"They don't like it, but that's too bad. They will have to live with it. I told them, from now on, everyone, and I mean everyone on this estate, rests on Du-Zet."

The Anterran wernt—equivalent to a week—was ten days. The first five days were named Nu, Tu, We, Gute, and Zet. As was the custom, the following five days were repeated but preceded by Du, meaning the latter. Du-Zet was the tenth day of the wernt, and Coleman, master of the Tondo Estate, declared it a day of rest from now on and forever for everyone under his stewardship. When he gave the edict to Nestor that evening, the foreman grouched his objections, but he woefully complied.

"Fortunately," Nestor told him, "the harvest was nearly completed, and the bales of divitz would soon be transported to market." After the estate holder departed, another clay cup was shattered against the wall of Nestor's cabin.

The three men, Lady Oetan, and Ootyiah had to fend for themselves on Du-Zet. Coleman refused to grant a dispensation of his declaration to anyone. Doros, Teema, and Maaryah complained and offered their services, but he insisted that they take their day of rest, as well.

Nestor went to work, as usual, passing along the master's declaration, angrily dismissing everyone from their assigned duties. After that, he didn't know what to do with himself. He traveled from worksite to worksite, making sure everyone had gotten the word, and then he reluctantly returned to his cabin. He yelled for Teema, but she didn't respond. He sat in the shadows drinking his unfinished pitcher of wine from the previous night. He fumed and decided he could not continue working under these outrageous conditions dictated by a stupid outlander. He was not going to renew his contract. He was sure there were many other estates that would appreciate his skills, estates with stewards who weren't Munnoga-touched.

CHAPTER 22

A s the last light of Du-Zet began slowly fading, two visitors reached the estate. They were riding on a smaller version of the wagon the three priests had arrived on, except this wagon was pulled by two draft samarans. One of the men was obviously a priest, dressed in a cobalt-blue robe. The other was a black man; the first Coleman had seen since his arrival on this world, dressed in the tattered garb of an outlander. His hair was long and black, tied in a ponytail. He carried a poor-quality short sword at his side.

"We would like to talk with the master of the estate. Is he available?" the priest asked.

"I am the master, what can I do for you?"

"His Eminence, the Sutro Seer, has sent us to you," the priest said.

"More training?" Coleman asked. Just then, Master Varios, Master Shergus, and Attendant Pahno approached.

"Master T´erio," said Varios, "What are you doing here?"

"We've been sent by His Eminence. It appears that the Tondo has the means to help us," the newly arrived priest told them.

"What is this all about?" a surprised Coleman asked.

"Sutro Adept T´erio is the greatest and most skilled carpenter in the kingdom, and the Sutro Seer has sent him here for a reason. Sutro Adept, who is this with you?" Master Shergus asked.

"This is Hermanez; he wants to cross the great ocean and needs a boat. The Sutro Seer says, the Tondo can help," Master T´erio replied.

The master's statement surprised Coleman even more. "I don't want to be disrespectful, but I think the Sutro Seer has made a mistake. I have no skill of sailing, nor do I have any knowledge at all concerning the building of boats. Did he say what he wanted me to do?"

"He advised me, you would know what needs to be done," T´erio simply responded.

Coleman ran his fingers through his long sand-colored hair. "This is another mystery. I don't see what I can do to help. We are about to have our evening meal. Would you like to join us?"

"Master T´erio will prefer eating with us," Varios said.

"I will join you if you don't mind," Hermanez replied. "I've been eating the priests' food for over a detz, and it doesn't agree with me."

"You are welcome to join us, such as our meal is tonight. I have given the workers the day off, and we are fending for ourselves," Coleman told the newcomer.

"Wur-gors?" Hermanez wondered aloud.

"Slaves," said Idop in a perturbed voice.

"That seems strange. I thought the master of an estate this large would have plenty of slaves waiting to meet his every need," Hermanez said, surprised by what he had just been told.

"You will find this one to be a different kind of master," Idop warned. "He coddles the slaves and takes their beatings." Hermanez looked at Coleman with an odd stare but didn't say a word.

The three masters walked to the large wagon and disappeared inside. Pahno took the samarans by their bridles and led the smaller wagon to a place near the larger one. He then cared for the animals. Coleman, Idop, Ayascho, and Hermanez stepped into the guesthouse where a large tray of food was waiting. Coleman had raided the manor house kitchen and managed to find plenty of food for the hungry men. Maaryah and Teema had helped him select the food, but he wouldn't allow them to prepare any. He was adamant that everyone was to take a day off from their daily chores. Lady Oetan heard him in the kitchen and came in, spouting her objections to his new edict, but it did her no good. She finally relented and took a tray and piled it with food for Ootyiah and herself.

While the men ate, Coleman peppered Hermanez with questions. The poor man could hardly take a bite of food, and it was obvious he was very hungry, so Coleman relaxed and let the man eat in peace.

After Hermanez had eaten his fill, he began answering all the questions he was asked. He told them he was from a large island in the middle of the ocean. He and three other men had built a boat to go exploring. They understood the risks and knew full well the dangers of sailing a small vessel in the realm of the terrors, but they thought they would be safe if they stayed near the shoreline, remaining in shallow water.

Much to their dread, the tide and winds took their small craft northward and out to the open sea. As the days passed, they saw many terrors, but none attacked. A few actually bumped their craft and then went on their way. They attempted to sail against the wind and current, but they failed to make any headway. They finally decided to sail northward as far as they could go, seeking the legendary land where people with white skin dwelt. They caught fish and stored rainwater in the two large gourds they had brought with them.

On the thirty-fifth day at sea, their boat was attacked and torn asunder by one of the monstrous terrors. His two companions perished in the attack. He managed to cling to some debris, and he drifted for three days. Eventually, the tide and wind deposited him on the peninsula of Terratia. That was almost two spans ago. He had spent most of his time since then working at any odd job he could find. The Terratia authorities finally forced him out of the city because he was an outlander and had overstayed his welcome.

He worked on several of the farms on the Magheedo Plain, but most of the harvests were now in, and there was no more work available. He was destitute and starving when a priest befriended him. When he told the priest his story, he was taken to the temple in Anterra. The Sutro Seer interviewed him, called for Master T´erio, and sent them on their way to visit the Tondo.

When Hermanez finished, Coleman didn't know what to think. How was he going to help this man? Since the Seer had sent the temple's master carpenter with him, it was obvious they were to build a ship. But what did that have to do with him?

After his meal and his story, Coleman offered the newcomer a bath in the lukewarm water of the bathhouse. He told him he could share Idop's bed. The counselor was not happy about that.

"I share my room with Ayascho," Coleman reminded him.

"Yes, but he sleeps on the floor. Let the newcomer use his bed," Idop told him in an annoyed voice.

"The room will get too stuffy with three in it. He'll sleep in your room tonight. You can sleep on the floor if you'd like," Coleman offered with a grin. Idop stomped out of the room and went to bed.

"I don't want to be a burden. I can sleep in a barn; I've done it before," he told the remaining two.

"Counselor Idop can share his bed for one night. I'll have someone move Ayascho's bed into his room tomorrow."

Ayascho dismissed himself and went to sleep on the floor. Hermanez cautiously walked into Idop's room, and after a few gruff comments from the counselor, all was quiet.

Coleman sat in his chair and began weaving his basket. After a few minutes, he stopped in thought. He selected several flexible reed stalks from his stockpile and began forming the framework of a ship's hull. Maaryah, who just couldn't stay away, quietly entered and watched as the efforts of his labors began to form.

"What's that, sire?" she finally asked.

He hadn't noticed her standing behind him. "What are you doing here? This is your day of rest."

"I thought I would see if there was anything you need before I went to bed," she told him.

"You're not supposed to be thinking about your duties today. This is a day for you to relax."

"The day has ended, sire."

"That's not true; the new day begins at first light," he counseled.

"I really just wanted to be here in case you'd like to talk to someone, sire. I enjoy talking with you," she finally admitted.

"That's okay then."

"What is that?" she asked again.

"I am making a model of a ship's hull with these reeds," he told her using godspeak terms.

"I don't understand when you talk in godspeak, sire."

"I used to make little boats when I was a boy. I never dreamed I would build a big boat. Do we have any sticky pitch?" he asked.

"Doros has a pot somewhere. He uses it to fix broken things. I'll fetch it for you." A few minutes later, she returned and handed him a clay pot full of glue-like pitch.

"I'll need some of your sewing pins and some string, too." She scampered off and returned with a clay pot of pins and a ball of string. She waited for his next request.

"I will be working on this project most of the night. You can go."

"I'll stay in case you need something else."

He looked up from his work and gave her a smile. "Okay, that would be great. What would you like to talk about?" he asked as he returned to his work.

Coleman worked most of the night on his project. Maaryah and Coleman chatted, mostly about his homeland. Early in the morning, her eyelids grew heavy, and she fell asleep while seated on the bench and leaning against the wall. He found a blanket, covered her shoulders with it, and then continued his project. He finished a couple of segments later. He carefully placed his fragile work on a table near the wall and then fell asleep in his chair.

He awoke when a beam of light from the rising p´atezas pierced the darkness and shined on the side of his face. He squinted and stretched. Maaryah was still asleep on the bench. She rustled, awoke, and then jumped up.

"Forgive me, sire; I've slept too long."

"That's all right, Maaryah. I enjoyed your company last night." Her face lit with a huge smile, and then she scampered out of the room.

Maaryah rushed to the back of the manor house and entered through the kitchen door. Teema was busy preparing
first-meal. "Maaryah," Teema began, "your bed hasn't been
slept in. Are you all right?"

Maaryah answered as she helped Teema prepare the food,
"Yes, yes, I'm fine. Sire Tondo spent the night making something he's going to show the priests this morning. I stayed with
him, and we talked while he worked. I fell asleep on the bench
and didn't wake until it was light."

"You fell asleep? Was the master angry?" Teema asked
with concern.

"No, Teema. He even covered my shoulders with a blanket
while I was sleeping," Maaryah said with a smile.

"He did?" Teema wondered in surprise. Maaryah nodded
and continued preparing food. "You say, the master talked
with you while he worked? What did he say?"

"I learned, Sire Tondo had an older brother who was a
warrior. He died in a war far from his homeland. I could tell,
Master Tondo misses him. He also told me some things about
his homeland."

"What did he tell you?" Teema asked as she worked.

"You won't believe this, but his kingdom doesn't have
slaves. He told me, slavery was ended a long time ago."

Teema stopped her work and looked at Maaryah in amazement. "A kingdom without slaves. Is that possible?"

"Yes, he said for more than two-hundred spans; outlander
spans," Maaryah added.

"How long did you and the master talk?"

"Segments, Teema, I don't know how many. He's so friendly; I like talking to him. He makes me feel good," Maaryah admitted.

"Careful, child, don't get too friendly with the master; it's for your own good," Teema warned.

"You were right, Teema. He is a good man, and he's very kind, too."

Teema examined Maaryah's countenance and realized she needed to offer the younger woman some wise counsel. "Child, don't forget who *he* is and what *you* are."

"It seems to make no difference to Sire Tondo," Maaryah told her. Teema simply shook her head in dismay.

Maaryah soon returned to the guesthouse with pitchers of water for the men to wash the sleep from their eyes.

Idop left his room and plopped onto a bench at the table. "Hermanez snores. I don't think I slept all night," he complained.

"Both of you sounded like you were sawing logs together," Coleman told him with a grin.

"He tossed all night. If I hadn't been lying next to the wall, he would have knocked me out of bed," Idop lamented.

"I'll have another bed put in your room."

"Please, have them put it by the cliffs, where I can't hear him."

Coleman grinned. He knew he had better do something

about the sleeping arrangements, or he was going to have a full-fledged insurrection on his hands.

After the men had eaten their morning meal, they went to the barn, and Coleman checked on the newborn thrice. They were doing well, so the three began their daily workout. After that, they practiced archery. As Master Shergus had done every day since he'd received his blue bow, the one Coleman had Pendor make for him; he met them at the makeshift archery range. He was becoming quite proficient. Hermanez watched as they practiced, enthralled by what he saw. They practiced for about a segment and then stored their bows.

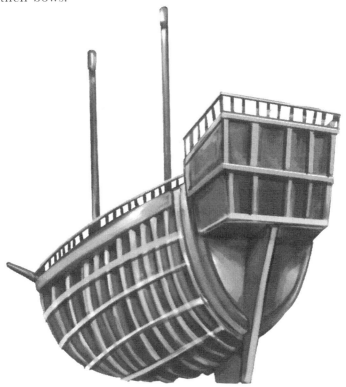

Coleman called the men together for a meeting. Attendant Pahno set up a large portable table and benches in the shade of a tree. The three masters, Hermanez, Ayascho, and Idop, sat at the table. Coleman went to the guesthouse and returned with his ship model. He placed it in the center of the table. The men stared at it in wonder.

"Do not touch it. It's very fragile, but it gives you an idea of what I have in mind," Coleman explained.

"It looks like a skeleton of some creature I've never seen before. What is it?" Ayascho asked.

"This is a model of a ship's hull. A ship is a large boat," Coleman told them.

"It's too small. What could anyone do with that?" Idop wondered.

"It's a model. A model represents what a larger version would look like. It gives you an idea of how to brace the hull, giving it strength. This will help when building a real ship—a boat as *long* as the barn."

The other men looked at him as if he were Munnoga-touched. After his surprise, Master T´erio examined the model closely, almost touching it with his nose. "Now, I understand. But you say it has to be as big as a barn? Is that even possible? No boat that big has ever been built," he asked in wonder.

"I said, it has to be as long as the barn. It needs to be twice as long as a terror. Maybe the monster won't attack something that big."

"No one has ever been able to make a boat that large. They either fall apart or sink," Idop warned.

"No one has ever tried such an unusual design as this. It

may have promise," Master T´erio replied in awe.

"What are those two sticks coming out of it for?" Ayascho asked.

"Those are masts. You hang cloth sails from them, and the wind pushes the ship through the water," Coleman expounded.

"Ha! I used to sail small boats in the bay near my home. When the tide is out, the water is too shallow for a terror to come in. The wind pushed my little boat along so fast I sometimes thought I was flying," Hermanez told them.

The men spent a good portion of the morning discussing the model, shipbuilding, and sailing. Master T´erio had one final question. "Now that we've decided to build this big boat, where will we build it?"

"The ocean is just over there. Why not right here?" Ayascho wondered.

"We'd have to build it above the cliffs because of the tides. How would we get it into the water when it's completed?" Idop asked.

"I thought about this problem last night. Getting it into the ocean is only one of the issues we face," Coleman warned. "After it's built, we will have to test it and learn if it's seaworthy. The crew will also have to be trained on how to sail her," he advised.

"Her? You refer to it as if it were a woman," Master Shergus noted.

"It's just a custom from my homeland. As I was saying, we will also have to test her and train a crew, the men who will run it. The safest place to do that is on the lake, where there are no terrors to interfere with testing and training. There will be enough problems without worrying about giant fish eating the men."

"The lake? But it's so far from the ocean. How will we get something as big as a barn all the way from the lake to the sea?" Idop wondered.

"It will be as *long* as the barn, not as *big* as the barn," Coleman clarified again. "We can put the ship on wheels and pull it with thrice or rasters or even samarans," Coleman explained.

"How far away is this lake?" Master Varios asked.

"About a march from here," Coleman told him.

The three master priests stepped away for a few minutes and held a private council while the others waited. After a short discussion, they returned to the others. "It has been decided that since the Sutro Seer endorses this effort, we will go and examine this lake. There will be no training today," Master Shergus told them.

Attendant Pahno, with the help of the other priests, spent the next half-segment putting a howdah on one of the rasters. It had been stored atop the large wagon, and with the help of a built-in wooden crane, it was fitted to the lead raster and secured. The three master priests climbed aboard.

While the priests were preparing the raster, Coleman had samarans readied for the rest of the group. Attendant Pahno would remain on the manor grounds. He had many priestly duties he had to complete.

It was mid-morning when the group departed. Coleman knew they would have to hurry if they were to make it there and back before nightfall. The samarans ambled at a fast clip, and much to Coleman's surprise, the raster trotted along so quickly that the samarans had to break into a cantor from time-to-time to keep from falling behind.

It was early afternoon by the time they arrived at the lake. The group explored the area and found a suitable place to build the ship. "Now," Master T´erio began, "we must figure out how to purchase the needed construction materials." Coleman already had anticipated this, and he had a solution. He tossed the master carpenter a small leather pouch.

When Master T´erio poured some of its contents into the palm of his hand, he was amazed at what he saw: gold nuggets. "Where did you get all this zanth?" he asked.

"That is my secret, and I will not reveal it. That should cover the expenses. I want you to keep a written record of all your purchases. I want to know all the costs in case we decide to build another ship." He was already looking ahead. The idea of creating a shipping enterprise on a world where no one had ever been successful at it excited him.

Ayascho gave Coleman a knowing look. When the others were no longer near, he spoke, "I know where that zanth came from."

"We must keep it our secret. Don't tell anyone," Coleman warned. Ayascho had learned enough already to realize how the shiny metal made kingdom men excited. He now shared Coleman's concern for his village's safety.

Coleman gave T´erio the authority to use all estate resources to build the ship. Nestor was called upon to find ten willing wur-gors—Coleman emphasized 'willing wur-gors'—to help build it. Nestor was aghast; he couldn't afford to lose ten laborers or separators at this crucial time in the season; how-

ever, Coleman insisted, so the foreman had to suffer through
another troublesome dictate from the outlander he had grown
to detest. Coleman told Nestor he wanted skilled carpenters
asked first. He knew a work camp would need to be built near
the construction site, and several more men and women would
be needed to provide support for the builders. The thought of
losing even more slaves from the divitz harvest drove Nester into a dither. He hoped he could complete the harvest and
be gone before the Munnoga-touched outlander placed any
more ridiculous demands on him.

It took nearly a detz to gather the materials needed to
start construction. T´erio had the workers erect several bar-
racks-like buildings on site, including living quarters, and a
cooking and meal building, something Coleman referred to as
a mess hall—everyone started calling it a *mezz*. On the fortieth
day, work on the ship officially began. A prayer was offered
by Master T´erio, and Coleman was asked to say a few words,
which he did. Shortly after he finished, the sound of hammers
and saws could be heard. By the time work began, T´erio had
already gone through the pouch of gold Coleman had given
him. Another pouch was soon forthcoming. T´erio wondered
where this strange outlander had gotten a seemingly endless
supply of zanth nuggets, and Coleman wondered if he would
be bled dry by the cost of building this ship.

While the shipbuilding preparations were taking place, the

divitz harvest was ending. Wagon loads of baled divitz departed the estate daily on their way to market. Coleman, Ayascho, and Idop continued with their training, and at the end
of each day, Coleman received his daily report from Nestor.
It had been a good harvest, he was told, and the trading price
for divitz was favorable to the seller, not as good as in the best
spans but better than most. Nestor had also told the estate
holder he would not be renewing his contract. Not wanting to
offend a man of rank, he sugarcoated his reasons as well as he
could, but Coleman could see through Nestor's gruff and un-
couth manner that he was fed up with the estate master's un-
reasonable dictates. It was a fortuitous development for Coleman. He was not going to renew the foreman's contract anyway. His future plans did not include a foreman, especially
one like the sadistic Nestor.

Coleman had asked Master Varios to deviate from his
lesson plan and teach the class about Slave Law. The master agreed and presented several lessons going over its finer
points. Coleman felt he had a pretty good idea of its concepts
by the time they moved on to another subject.

Shortly after that, the estate holder sent Doros into the city
to fetch an adjudicator, a scholar, and a markerman. It would
take him about ten days to travel by wagon to Anterra; at least
five days, maybe more, to find and contract with the three
men; and another ten days to travel back to the estate. No one
was really sure what the estate owner was up to, and when
questioned, he wouldn't give anyone a direct answer concerning his plans. In the meantime, Coleman had a rather large
wooden building built behind the guesthouse, near Nestor's

cabin. The carpenters had also built several odd-looking small desks and stored them in the new structure.

One morning, before Doros's return, while Coleman, Ayascho, Idop, and Master Shergus were practicing archery, they heard an outcry from inside the barn. The four rushed into the barn and found a man cornered by Seemo. The samaran handler was holding the intruder at bay with a wooden pitchfork.

"What's going on here?" Coleman demanded.

"I found this man sneaking down from the loft, sire," Seemo told him as he jabbed the pitchfork in the trespasser's direction. Coleman stepped forward and pushed Seemo's makeshift weapon down.

"Who are you, and what are you doing here?" Coleman demanded. The intruder was a young man, a teenager Coleman thought, hardly older than thirty spans. He was barefoot and clothed in worn and tattered rags. In the shadows of the barn, it was hard to tell colors, but the boy had light-colored hair, probably similar to his own, Coleman guessed. "Who are you, and what are you doing here?" Coleman repeated in an angrier tone. The boy didn't respond, his eyes wide in fear. Coleman could see he was ready to bolt, and sure enough, he tried. Master Shergus collared him and threw the boy against the barn wall so hard it nearly knocked him unconscious. "You had better answer; Master Shergus is not a patient man," Coleman warned. At the mention of the master's name, the boy's expression turned from fear to outright terror. He slumped to the dirt floor and began sobbing, his hands covering his face.

Coleman crossed his arms over his chest and waited for the boy to calm down, his companions doing the same. It took several minutes before the boy regained his composure and looked up, revealing a dark smudge on his right cheek. Coleman wondered if he had been injured by the priest's rough treatment, but he soon realized the boy had been branded with the symbol of a hand with a line through it. The hand symbol, Coleman had learned, had many meanings, but when by itself, with no context, it meant 'to take.' The line through the hand symbol meant 'to take without permission.'

"He's a thief!" Idop shouted. "Beat him and send him on his way."

Coleman stepped forward, reached down, and jerked the boy to his feet, pinning him against the hard, brick wall. He looked into the boy's dark eyes and saw despair. Coleman could feel his inner-power stirring, and soon it turned to compassion for this rascal. He stood examining the boy for a long time; then, he released the trespasser.

"When was the last time you ate?" he asked.

"I . . . I don't remember."

"You are speaking to the master of this estate and tetzae," Idop warned the boy.

"I don't remember, sire," the boy said with respect, his voice quavering in fear.

"Why were you in the loft," Coleman asked in a calmer voice.

"It was cold last night. I just wanted to get warm. I didn't mean nothing by it."

"Did it ever occur to you to ask for help?" Coleman questioned.

"No, sire," was the boy's simple response.

"Why not?"

"No one ever does. They just hit me and chase me away."

"It's because you've been branded a thief. You get what you deserve," Idop growled.

"Well, I won't send you away until you've had a chance to eat something," Coleman promised.

"What did you try to steal? I know you didn't come here just to get out of the cold. Seemo, check to see if anything is missing," Idop ordered the samaran handler.

"Yes, counselor. I'll do it right now."

Coleman stepped closer to the young man and looked into his fear-filled face again. "Did you steal anything?" he asked.

"No, sire."

"Were you going to steal something?" Idop interjected. The boy's eyes lowered.

"Ha, at least you're not a liar," Coleman said. "Come with me, and I will get you some food." Coleman led him to the guesthouse by the scruff of his neck. Maaryah had already cleaned up the remains of the morning meal, so he asked her to bring the boy a new tray of food and some water. When the food was placed in front of the boy, he ate like a famished pig. Coleman asked Maaryah to get a second tray of food. By the time the boy had eaten his fill, he had consumed more food than the three men ever did. Coleman chuckled.

Seemo came to the door of the guesthouse and told the men that nothing was missing. "Thank you, Seemo. Come in; I'd like you to stay for a while," Coleman said. He turned to the boy, "Now tell me, what's your name?"

"Numo, sire."

"Now that you have had your fill, what are your plans?"

"I don't know, sire. I have no place to go."

"I know what you're thinking, Tondo. This brigand is trouble. He's a thief. Send him away," Idop warned.

"Are you trouble?" Coleman asked.

"I stole food, but only once. I was starving, sire."

"Once a thief, always a thief," Idop warned.

"Will you always be a thief?" Coleman asked.

The boy touched the brand on his cheek. "I'll always be marked a thief."

"That's not what I asked. Will you always be a thief?" Coleman repeated.

"I don't want to steal, but what else can I do to survive?"

"There, Tondo, I told you so. Besides, he all but admitted he was going to steal something from you," Idop admonished.

"He's desperate and needs a hand up, not the back of a hand. I tell you what, Numo. You work for me, and I will see that you receive food, a place to sleep, and a few bhat for your labor. Are you interested?"

"I knew it; I knew your soft heart would reach out to this dung creeper. You're a fool, and you'll always be a fool," Idop growled with contempt.

"Maybe so, but I'll be a fool for the right reasons," Coleman countered.

Idop confronted the boy and threatened, "If you steal anything, I will hunt you down and kill you myself." He turned and stomped out.

Coleman could see the boy shudder under Idop's menacing words. He then said in a calm voice, "You will be Seemo's helper. You are to do whatever he says. Is that understood?"

"Yes, sire," he answered.

"Both of you can go. I'm sure there's plenty of work that needs doing."

Ayascho watched through the open window as the two headed for the barn. "He went inside. I thought he was going to run," Ayascho declared.

"We'll see, we'll see," Coleman said as he rubbed his chin.

"You're a curious man, Tondo. A warrior who nourishes the good seed of compassion. I have never met anyone quite like you before," Master Shergus admitted while smiling broadly, something Coleman hadn't seen the master do before.

Coleman noticed Maaryah's broad smile, too. "What?" he asked.

"It's nothing, sire," she coyly replied.

Master Varios stepped through the doorway with his satchel. He placed it on the table and pulled from it a rock, an oil lamp, and a cup. After setting each item on the table, he poured water into the cup, and then lit the lamp. He motioned for his students to gather around. Master Shergus decided to leave, and so did Maaryah.

"Today, I will teach you about the five basic elements," Varios told them. "The touchable elements are rock, water, fire, and air. The untouchable element is ether, sometimes called the spiritual. All things are made from the four touch-able elements. Ether surrounds and influences everything." His three students intently listened as he continued with his lesson, explaining where the elements came from and how they were created by the great god.

Coleman contained himself through the master's lecture, but when Varios had finished, Coleman began a retort and picked up the rock. "This is not an element. It is composed of many *different* elements." He then blew out the lamp. "Fire isn't an element, either. It is a state in which some elements are consumed by combustion. Air is also composed of sever-al different base elements. The same is true of water. I cannot speak to you about ether. It seems more mystical than any-thing else."

Master Varios gave Coleman an indignant stare. Coleman took quill to paper, but he paused in thought. He pondered whether to draw out a periodic table, but he realized that would only result in confusing the master. Besides that, he had forgotten many of the elements he needed to list. He chose to go with something much simpler. He diagrammed a hydrogen atom, a single proton orbited by a single electron, and then he went into a lengthy dissertation on atoms, molecules, and how matter is constructed. When he stopped, Idop and Ayascho were looking at him through eyes glazed over. The expression on the master's face had changed from indignity to wonder.

"What you say is a mystery to me," the master finally said, "however, it has the ring of truth to it. How did you learn all this?" he continued, pointing to Coleman's etchings on the paper.

"I was studying to become a physicist in high school. That was before I became a warrior," he told the onlookers.

"High school? Is that a school on a mountain?" Ayascho asked. Coleman smiled and shook his head.

"What is a fiz-t´iz?" the master asked.

"Phys-i-cist . . . Phys-i-cist. It is a scholar who studies matter and energy, and their relationship to each other. I wanted to learn how everything is made." Just then, Seemo and Numo appeared at the door. "What is it?" Coleman asked.

"I won't do his kind of work, sire," Numo declared.

"What kind of work is that?" Coleman asked.

"Shoveling manure. That's slave work. I'm better than that," the boy said defiantly.

Coleman thought for a moment, then responded to the young man's complaint, "Seemo was born a slave, it wasn't his choice; he is an honest man. You, on the other hand, were born a freeman, but you chose to steal. Now, who is the better?" Numo didn't respond and lowered his eyes. "Come with me," the estate holder ordered. The three men headed for the barn at a quick pace, leaving Master Varios with a question hanging on his lips.

Coleman marched into the barn, grabbed two square-ended shovels, tossed one to Numo, and said, "Bring that with you and follow me," pointing to a wooden wheelbarrow. The young man did as he was told. Coleman stopped at the first stall and entered. He began shoveling soiled straw and manure into the wheelbarrow. "Hoy! Don't just stand there; get to work!" he commanded.

The boy reluctantly began to shovel, as well. When the

wheelbarrow was full, Coleman wheeled it to the manure pile behind the barn and dumped it. He returned to the stall, and the two continued their work. When the wheelbarrow was filled again, it was Numo's turn to wheel it out, and so he did.

For the remainder of the morning, the two continued their labors as Seemo protested, "Master Tondo, please let me do it. You shouldn't be doing this kind of work," he lamented.

"Work is work, and all honest work is good and proper. Anyone who thinks honest work is beneath them should be ashamed of themselves. Am I right, Numo?"

"I guess so, sire. I would never have thought an important man like you would ever do this," the young man said, pointing to the wheelbarrow full of straw and animal waste.

During their labors, Coleman learned that Numo's father had abandoned his family about two spans ago. It wasn't long after that when his mother took up with a cruel man who didn't want Numo hanging around, so he kicked the young man out. His cowed mother didn't intervene. He'd been on his own ever since. Because he was so young, he seldom found work, and finally, in desperation, he stole food from the marketplace. He was apprehended by the Pannera and turned over to an adjudicator, who had him branded. Things got worse from there. He left the city, hoping to find work in the fields, which he did but at half-wages. Now that most harvesting was over, his situation had become dire again. His last employ was at the Penno Estate, not far from Tondo's. The elderly foreman, Wendro, had taken pity on the boy and gave him work. When Lord Penno learned that a branded thief was working his oil-tree orchards, he chastised Foreman Wendro and demanded he throw the branded boy off his holding. Numo then made his way to the Tondo Estate.

The outlander sire and the boy continued their conversation until they worked their way to the stall that held the newborn thrice. The boy immediately fell to his knees, and he started petting and holding the baby creatures.

The scene reminded Coleman of a boy with puppies. "How would you like to become a thrice handler?" Coleman asked.

"What would I have to do, sire?" Numo wondered.

"Learn everything there is to know about thrice, train them to do work, *and* clean their stalls. Do you think you can do that?"

"I'll try my best, sire," Numo promised.

"That's good enough for me," Coleman told him with a smile. The boy returned his smile, and soon, they were back at work.

It was midday by the time they finished. "Now, go with Seemo; he will see that you are fed. I don't ever want to hear you say again, Seemo's work is beneath you. Is that understood?"

"Yes, sire," the boy said with bowed head. The three then parted.

Doros returned after twenty-eight days with the three men Coleman had requested he bring to the estate, plus a woman, the bondmate of one of the men. The estate master met with each newcomer, reviewed their contracts, and gave each a handful of bhat coins as a bonus for their time and willingness to travel the long distance to the estate. He promised to pay them the full amount as stipulated in their contracts when fulfilled. All three men were very pleased to receive this unexpected boon.

They had arrived two days before the Harvest Celebration, a holiday the estate had conducted for many spans. It was a day of feasting and dancing. The slaves always participated, the Harvest Celebration being their only respite during the span, at least until Master's Day was instituted, the day Coleman had proclaimed as the day of rest at the end of each wernt.

The day before the celebration was to begin, Nestor was paid his contracted wage. Nestor had told him days before that he would not be renewing his contract. Coleman handed his departing foreman a large pouch of bhat coins. "Here you are, five-hundred and fifty bhat, more than what five men earn in a span," Coleman said.

"And I earned every bhat, especially this span, sire," came his snide and bitter response. Coleman handed him a paper scroll, secured by a leather strap. "What's this?" Nestor asked.

"It's a letter of reference," Coleman told him using the godspeak term.

"What does that mean?"

"It means I approved of the way you did your duties, and I recommend you be hired by anyone who reads this document. I know you didn't like my changes, but you did as I asked."

"Thank ya, sire. Yer very kind."

"I wish you well, Nestor. I only ask that you treat slaves a little kinder in the future. You have seen that brutality isn't always the best way to do things." Nestor cleared his throat, turned his head, and spit on the ground. Coleman resisted his urge to punch the man.

"I'll take my leave now, sire." He quickly mounted his samaran and rode off in the direction of the Ancient City.

Coleman stood pondering their final exchange for several minutes. He'd hoped Nestor would take his advice, but the ex-foreman had made it abundantly clear what he thought about Coleman's suggestion.

"Well, at least that burr in my side is gone. Now, we'll see what happens," he said worriedly to himself in godspeak.

"What did you say, sire?" It was Maaryah's voice. She had moved to his side and was watching Nestor ride away.

"Nestor is leaving. He no longer wants to work for me, and I no longer want him here."

"Who will take his place?" Maaryah wondered, looking worried. To her thinking, Foreman Nestor was a known entity. Even though his departure gave her relief, she, as well as all the other slaves, would have to learn a new foreman's temperament and way of doing things. For the slaves, this knowledge came at a price, always a painful one.

"I've decided this estate no longer needs a foreman," Coleman told her as he continued following Nestor with his eyes. Maaryah turned toward him and stared. After a moment, he felt her eyes on him and turned his head. She was literally beaming with joy, her golden-amber eyes sparkling.

When he looked at her, she asked, "Sire, how is that possible? I've been told every estate needs a foreman."

"Not this one, not anymore," he replied. He watched her countenance grow even brighter. She started hopping up and down on her toes with excitement. Her joy was infectious, bringing a huge smile to his face. He continued, "There are going to be a lot of changes coming to this estate, beginning very soon."

She stopped hopping up and down, and her joyous attitude turned to surprise. "What is changing, sire?"

"You'll have to wait until the Harvest Celebration to find out."

Nestor moved on to another estate and assumed foreman duties there. He had a well-established reputation as a good estate manager, and Coleman's letter of reference solidified it. He carried out his duties much as he had before and reveled in dispensing punishments to those he oversaw; however, he never forgot the annoying outlander and his outrageous dictates. Neither did he forget the slave girl who had refused his offering of gifts and favors, kindling a burning hatred for the tall slave.

CHAPTER 23

A NEW DAY DAWNS

The days had become cooler, and cloud fronts were coming in from the southwest, pushed by the Zerio winds, indicating a change in the season. The night before the estate's Harvest Celebration was to begin, light rain fell, but only enough to settle the dust. Coleman had the workers build a two-foot-high platform, fifteen feet long and ten feet wide. A table and chair were placed near one end. He had the word passed across the estate that all slaves were to report to the manor house no later than midmorning of the celebration day. He told Doros to make sure all could make the journey, and if anyone was ill or infirm, a wagon would be sent to fetch them. This caused quite a stir throughout the estate. The slaves kept their curiosity to themselves, only sharing their thoughts with one another. Lady Oetan and Ootyiah were especially inquisitive, but Coleman refused to tell them or anyone else what he was up to. Only Idop surmised his plan, but he kept his troubled inkling to himself.

People began arriving early in the morning. Large tables were set up, each full of an assortment of food, unfermented grape juice, and water. Everyone was invited to enjoy their fill. The slaves were stunned by the scrumptious feast laid out before them. In spans past, only flat-cakes and water had been offered to the slaves.

Lady Oetan and Mistress Ootyiah were provided chairs and sat to the left and immediate front of the platform. The priests were invited to take the benches behind the two women. Pendor, Numo, and the bondmate of one of the recently arrived men were also invited to seat themselves on the bench behind the ladies. Adjudicator Perdiz sat at a table placed at the far-left side of the platform. Markerman Zet´us sat at a table placed on the ground to the right, a small box resting on the table in front of him and an empty chair on his left side. Four chairs were set in the rear center of the platform. Idop, Ayascho, and Pammon, the scholar, sat there. The empty chair was Coleman's. The slaves sat on the ground, forming a large semi-circle facing the platform.

At midmorning, Coleman counted heads to make sure every slave had arrived. When he was satisfied that all two-hundred and fifty were present, he stepped onto the platform and began to speak in a voice loud enough for all to hear.

"As you know, I'm an outlander, and I come from a land far away. My homeland is a place where all people are free. The idea of slavery is abhorrent to me. I will not be a master over others—men, women, or children—any longer. Therefore, on this day, the detzamar of Du-Tuz, the fortieth day known as Du-Zet, I grant each and every slave held by this estate their freedom. No longer will you be called a slave. All of you will become freed-men and citizens of the kingdom. A new day has dawned on this estate, a day of freedom for all! *You* will be allowed to make *your* own way in life, to choose for *yourselves*, to set *your* own goals, to face *your* own struggles, to grow or diminish as *you* choose. Be forewarned; freedom is a two-edged sword. No one will care for you, and you will face the consequences of your own choices." Coleman stopped speaking and let the audience ponder his words.

Lady Oetan was the first to speak. "This is outrageous! You can't do that!" she howled.

"I'm sorry, Lady Oetan, but you are mistaken. I can, and I have. By royal decree, I am the holder of this estate, and I can do with it as I please. I choose to free these people, and therefore, they are freed as of this instant."

Idop soon registered his protest. "Do you realize the loss you will take for this foolishness?"

"Yes, I do—about seventy-five thousand bhat or seven-hundred and fifty regums," Coleman told him.

"How will you run the estate with no slaves?" Ootyiah chimed in.

"I will hire freed-men and commoners to do the work. I believe, in the long run, the estate will benefit more from the labor of free people working for their own gain than it will by the forced labor of unpaid slaves," he advised, making sure all could hear him.

He squarely faced the seated throng and continued, "Adjudicator Perdiz will provide each of you with the official documents you will need. Markerman Zet´us will give you the mark of a freed-man. Both Adjudicator Perdiz and Markerman Zet´us have been paid by me, so there is no cost to any of you for their services. I will also pay the royal tax for each freed slave. Do you have any questions?"

Silence prevailed for a long time; then, Deemeos worked up enough courage to ask the master a question and stood up.

"Master Tondo, what happens to my ma and pa? They's old and ain't gonna be able to do much. All they know is picking divitz and the Separation House."

"The elderly—those who are very old and frail—can remain on the estate if they choose. I will see to it that they receive food, a place to live, and a few bhat to meet their needs. They will be expected to do some chores that are appropriate to their age. Are there any other questions?"

A young man stood up. "Master, are you telling us we must leave the estate? What do the rest of us do about food and home?" he asked.

"You are your own master now. No one has to leave the estate. You are welcome to stay and work for me, earning your own bhat. I hope you do, but it is *your* choice. I need laborers and divitz growers. Those who wish to leave have forty days to do so. I will provide you with food, and you can stay where you are living now until the forty days are up. After that, if you still want to leave, you must go. If you choose to stay, you and I must come to an agreement, a contract. Are there any more questions?"

A middle-aged man stood up, "Master Tondo, if we leave, can we take anything with us?"

"You may take anything you keep in your dwelling: tables, chairs, tools, clothes, and extra food, for example. There is one other thing I must tell you." He paused and swallowed hard before continuing. "Each adult, man or woman, will receive one-hundred bhat for their labors this span. Each working child will receive fifty bhat, which will be given to their father or mother, if they have one. This payment will be made when you choose to leave the estate or come under contract with me."

An excited commotion erupted from the seated throng. One-hundred bhat was more money than any slave had ever seen. This promise worried Coleman the most. He had thought long and hard about how to handle it, and finally, he decided that if they are to be free, they must learn to manage their money. He would leave that challenge in their own hands, but he would provide a safety net for those who needed one.

Lady Oetan nearly swooned, she couldn't believe what she was hearing. "This is Munnoga-touched! We're ruined!" she cried.

"Mother, calm yourself," Ootyiah told her. In a softer voice, she whispered, "We have no say in this. Tondo is the estate holder now."

"We'll all end up destitute, even the outlander," the lady bemoaned.

"Lady Oetan, I haven't forgotten you in all this. I will grant you one-sixth of the divitz profits every span. I will tell you in private what your share of this span's harvest is." This unexpected boon seemed to placate her, and she calmed down.

Coleman waited for a while, but there were no other queries. Finally, he said, "I'm sure you will have more questions as you think about all this. I will remain available to answer any you may think of. Now, it is time to process your freedom documents, and for you to receive your freed-man mark. Who will be first?"

To Coleman's surprise, no one moved. The slaves' spiteful lives were all they knew, but there was security in it. The door to freedom had just swung wide open to them, but they feared to tread into the unknown. Coleman scanned the crowd, looking into many faces, but each lowered their eyes and head. He wondered if they thought this was an evil trick he was foisting on them, testing their loyalty to the estate master.

Finally, Coleman saw Maaryah sitting in the throng, flanked by Doros and Teema. "Maaryah," he called, "it's time for you to spread your wings like the bird you dream of. It's time to fly over the fields and the ocean in freedom. Will you be the first?"

Hesitantly, she stood. After a few moments and buoyed by the trust she'd gained in the estate master, she made her way through the crowd, stepping onto the platform. All of the other slaves' eyes were fixed upon her, waiting to see what would happen. She presented herself before the adjudicator. A few words were exchanged; she made her mark on the official document—a figure that looked like a bird in flight, it resembled a curved, open 'M' in godspeak. The adjudicator made an entry in his records, and another on a second scroll, signed and sealed the document, then he handed it to her. She looked at Coleman, and he returned a smile and a wink. She couldn't stop the expression of joy that suddenly engulfed her. She practically skipped to the markerman. It wasn't long before lines formed in front of both tables.

The processing took until midafternoon. The food tables were re-stocked, and all feasted, except the priests who retired to their huge wagon. Happy chatter filled the air. Lady Oetan and Ootyiah withdrew to the manor house. Coleman went to the door and gave a shout. Doros opened it and ushered him in. The two women were waiting for him.

"I can't believe you're doing this. The estate will collapse without slaves. You still have time to put a halt to this insanity," she warned.

Coleman raised a heavy pouch he was carrying. "This is your share of the harvest: five-thousand five-hundred and forty bhat. There are fifty-five regums and forty bhat coins in the pouch. Please count them," he ordered.

"That will not be necessary, sire," Ootyiah said.

"I insist," he told her. He took back the pouch and poured its contents onto a nearby table. He separated the coins into several stacks of regums and bhats. "This is yours, my lady. I think you can live quite comfortably on your share."

"Thank you, thank you so much. Do you really think there will be any income next span? How will the crop be sown? How will the harvest be made? How will the seeds be separated, and the divitz cleaned and baled? Without slaves, all will be lost," Lady Oetan lamented.

"Free people must work to survive. I will contract with them to do the work that needs to be done."

"In a bad year, Master Oetan made fifteen thousand bhat in profits. How much have you made?" she asked.

"I've set aside the freed slave's portion. You and I split the remaining profit. That is a little more than eleven-thousand bhat. I expect that will be typical of the profit we will see in the future; however, I hope to open more land for crops, and that will increase our income."

Idop had entered and was listening to the conversation. "Doesn't it bother you to give the slaves so much? That's over twenty-thousand bhat," he said.

"Twenty-two thousand five-hundred bhat to be exact," Coleman told him. "That's their share, gained by their labor. I'm fully satisfied with my portion. It's enough to reinvest in the estate, and hopefully increase our profits next span."

They could hear someone in the dining area; it was Teema. Coleman went to her and examined her mark. The marker-man had completed his job. Her tattoo was now a circle with four lines through it, indicating she was now a freed-man, a citizen of the kingdom, and no longer subject to Slave Law.

"Teema, tell me what you think of all this," he asked.

"I don't know what to think, sire. This has all happened so fast. I don't want to leave Lady Oetan and Mistress Ootyiah. I wouldn't know what to do."

"Maybe you won't have to leave," Coleman told her. "I'm sure you and Lady Oetan can come to an agreement that would allow you to stay here and work just like you have been doing. Only now, by your own free choice."

"Yes, I'm sure we can do that," Lady Oetan said. Teema's worried expression lifted. She continued preparing the settings for the midday meal.

Coleman, Lady Oetan, Ootyiah, and Idop enjoyed the midday meal together. They discussed the changes Coleman had instituted, and he tried to allay their fears. He succeeded but only a little. They were beginning to gain some confidence in his plan, but fear of the unknown worried them just as much as it worried the freed slaves.

Later in the afternoon, after all the slaves had received their official freedom documents and had their marks changed, Coleman returned to the platform and began speaking again. "Master Varios, please stand." The priest stood and faced the seated freed-men. "Master Varios is authorized by royal decree and sanctified by the Great Temple of the Unnamed God to perform bondings. He is willing to bond any couple who wish it."

Slaves were not allowed to marry—referred to as bonding in this culture. The slaves' masters felt it was too disruptive if they had to sell or trade a slave to another estate. Nevertheless, couples would often pair up and live together, hoping upon hope that nothing would cause them to be separated. Now that they were freed-men and citizens of the kingdom, there were no bonding restrictions placed upon them.

Coleman's announcement caused a buzz throughout the gathering. Slowly, couples stood and worked their way to the front of the platform. Master Varios stood atop the low stage and bonded each couple one at a time. It was a simple ceremony; a few words of advice from the priest, a commitment to support one another, each took a sip of wine from a brass-colored goblet held by Varios, and as a final rite, the priest wrapped the couple's wrists with a white cord, symbolizing their union.

The sharing of the goblet reminded Coleman of the shared fruit that Taahso and Atura had eaten, and so did the wrapping of their wrists with a cord. He wondered if there could be a connection between the cultures. When the ceremony was over, there was no snug, no ghizz; the couples simply returned to their places, usually with joyous expressions on their faces.

When all those who wanted to be bonded had been, Master Varios returned to his seat, and Coleman stood again. "Let me introduce Scholar Pammon," he loudly stated. The scholar stood so all could see who he was. "I have asked Scholar Pammon to begin holding classes for anyone who wants to learn to read and write. If you wish to improve your new lives as freed-men greatly, you will need to learn these skills. I especially encourage parents to send their children to Scholar Pammon's class. Scholar Pammon, is there anything you wish to say?"

Pammon cleared his throat, "Yes, just a few words. My bondmate, Wandra, and I have always objected to slavery, and I want to thank Master Tondo for allowing me to help you. We will begin classes tomorrow morning. When you hear this . . . " Pammon began ringing a large hand-held gravetro triangle, " . . . class is about to start. Don't be late. A wonderful world of knowledge has just opened to you. Please take advantage of it." He returned to his seat.

Coleman then stood and shouted, "For the remainder of the day, we will celebrate the harvest and your freedom!" The throng jumped to their feet and began shouting in joy. The chant of 'Tondo! Tondo! Tondo!' echoed throughout the manor grounds. Coleman was elated, but worry nagged at him. *These people don't fully understand what they're in for, but let them rejoice for now.*

The festivities lasted late into the night, but gradually, the hosts' number decreased as small groups returned to their homes. Coleman took a late-night, lukewarm bath, and then rested in his favorite chair, weaving a basket. Maaryah was nearby, as usual. Coleman did his work in silence, pondering the day's experiences.

Unexpectedly, Maaryah initiated a conversation. "Sire, what's to become of me?" she asked.

"What do you mean, Maaryah?"

"I already know what I want to do."

"And what is that?"

"I want to stay here and do what I've been doing. I want to serve you and the others."

"Good. I was hoping you would stay. What do you think is a fair wage for your services?" he asked.

"All I need is food and a place to sleep. Nothing more," she meekly replied.

"I think you deserve more than that. Let us take a look at all you do. You prepare our meals, you wash our clothes, you clean the house, you sew clothes for me, and you do a lot of other things with Teema and Doros I don't even know about. Don't sell yourself short. How much do you think all that is worth?"

"I have no idea, sire. I've never thought of it that way before."

"Okay, I can understand why it would be difficult for you. How does room and board plus five bhat every forty days sound?"

"Oy, that's too much, sire. I wouldn't know what to do with all that coin," she confessed.

"Well, I'm sure you will get used to 'all that coin' as time goes on. Let us agree on what I've said, and we can review our agreement whenever either of us is no longer satisfied with it. Can you agree to those terms?"

"Yes, sire, whatever you say."

"Oh, and one more thing I want you to agree to," he said.

"What is that, sire?"

"Now that you are a freed-man and a citizen, I want you to call me Tondo. Can you do that?"

A protest was about to escape her lips, but she stopped and smiled, "Yes, Tondo, I can do that."

"Good, then. Let us seal our agreement with a handshake." He raised his arm and waited.

"What do you mean?" she wondered.

"It's a custom from my homeland. That will seal the deal, meaning we both agree to the terms of the contract."

"If you think we should," she said as she lifted her left hand in front of herself.

"No, like this." He grasped her right forearm firmly, and she instinctively grabbed his. Unexpectedly, a charge of energy flowed from his center, through his arm, and into her body.

Her head snapped back, and she stared wide-eyed at him; her shocked golden-amber eyes as large as regums. "What did you do?" she asked fearfully.

"I don't know. It's just as surprising to me as it is to you."

He released her hand and asked, "Are you okay?"

"Yes, yes, I think so." She paused, then weakly whispered, "Oy, I feel dizzy," came her shaky reply as she swayed and began to collapse. Coleman quickly grabbed her by the waist and pulled her against his body for support, and he held her tightly. After a few seconds, he gently lowered her into his chair. She slowly began to recover. "What happened? I feel weak," she told him.

"I think it was tzaah, but I don't understand what happened. Stay with me for a while, and let me make sure you're okay."

For the next segment or two, he watched over her while she slowly regained her strength and began to feel normal again. After she'd recovered, Coleman gave her a zanth regum, the promised one-hundred bhat he told her she'd earned the previous span. She tucked the coin into her sash. She then dismissed herself and turned in for the night. What had happened was another mystery to Coleman.

Maaryah never spent the coin Coleman had given her. From time-to-time, she would take the shiny coin from its hiding place and sit, examining its luster, pondering the estate master's kindness and generosity, dreaming of a day when he might think of her as something more than just the guesthouse wur-gor.

The next morning, as the men completed their workout, they heard the ring of the school triangle. Coleman told the others to go to archery practice, and he would meet them there later. He wanted to see how things were going on the first day of school. He quickly marched over to the school building and counted heads. Just ten children and three adults were in attendance.

A very disappointing number, indeed, Coleman thought.

He passed the guesthouse on his way back to the barn and noticed Maaryah busy at work inside. He went to the door and loudly cleared his throat, getting her attention. "I want to amend our agreement," he told her.

"What is it, sire, I mean Tondo?" she asked.

"As part of our new agreement, I insist you spend every morning in school, learning how to read and write."

"Please, sire, there's too much work to do. I can't spend all morning doing that."

"Yes, you can, and you must. I also want Doros and Teema to attend class, as well. Now, go, tell them what I said, then report to Scholar Pammon," he ordered.

"Yes, I will do as you say," she said, recognizing his serious tone. She left the guesthouse and headed for the manor house kitchen. A few minutes later, he saw Maaryah, Doros, and Teema scurrying to the school building. Later in the morning, Pendor, the blacksmith, needed to go into the city for some supplies, so Coleman asked him to take Adjudicator Perdiz and Markerman Zet´us with him, their services no longer required.

The morning class with Master Varios took a different turn. The master asked his outlander pupil, Tondo, to continue with his explanation of matter, energy, atoms, and those other things that were impossible to pronounce, meaning molecules. Master Shergus quietly entered the guesthouse and sat on a bench near the wall, listening to Coleman's lecture. The estate holder spoke until midday; then he paused, waiting for a response from the others.

After a few moments, Master Varios stood and began speaking, "What you say is incredible. I would never have guessed such things, but they are true. I can feel their correctness," he admitted as he patted his chest, the center of his tzaah.

"The student teaches the great master. This is something unheard of in all the kingdoms," Shergus quipped.

Coleman looked at Idop and said, "That's two." The counselor only rolled his eyes.

"Two what?" Varios asked.

"Oh, it's not important," Coleman told him.

"Master Varios has the gift of learning. His tzaah is as powerful with knowledge as mine is with the sword. It is extraordinary for someone as young as you to teach a master," the swordsman revealed.

"You must tell me more, but not now. His Eminence expects me to teach you things you need to know, and that I will do. If there is any time left over, I would like to learn more of this viz-ee-zit´," Varios said.

"A physicist is a person who studies physics. I just want

to be clear on that. I will do my best to teach you phys-ics. I know it's a hard word for you to say, but that's what it's called," Coleman advised.

"So be it. I don't care what it's called; I just want to learn all you can tell me about it," the master told him.

Maaryah was a little late with the midday meal. She apol-ogized profusely to the men, but Coleman set her mind at ease. "Don't worry. From now on, we'll adjust our schedule so you'll have enough time to prepare a meal without feeling rushed. If we have to delay the start time of our lessons with Master Shergus, we will. We'll start later and end later, that's all. It's important for you and the others to be educated. I hope you understand," he counseled.

"Yes, Tondo, I guess I do. Excuse me while I get the water and wine. Teema couldn't help me because she's busy serv-ing Lady Oetan and Mistress Ootyiah. We were all in such a rush."

"That's okay; we will all have to make adjustments," he told her. She scampered off to the manor house.

"She called you Tondo. Don't tell me you're going to let her get away with that," Idop challenged.

"That's part of the agreement we made last night. She pro-vides all the services she has done in the past and refers to me by my name, and I provide her with food, housing, and some bhat on the side. Oh, and this morning I amended the agreement to include a requirement that she attend school, as well."

Idop shook his head in disbelief, and then he grouched, "What a waste of time that will be."

A few minutes later, Maaryah returned with pitchers of water and wine. She set them down, stepped back, and waited. The men ate, and Idop poured himself a cup of wine. Shortly after he set the wine pitcher down, it began to vibrate. Everyone began staring at it in wonder as it bounced across the table and stopped in front of Ayascho. He grabbed its handle and poured himself a cup.

He looked at the others' amazed faces and smiled a broad, toothy smile. "The masters have been teaching me," he finally stated to his wondering audience. "They call it tzaah. I told them it's taah, but they won't listen to me."

Coleman clapped his hands. "That is fantastic, my friend. What else can you do?"

"That's all for now. They say I might be able to knock a man down if I practice hard."

"You have two new lines. When did you get those?" Coleman wondered.

"I asked the markerman to do it. I missed the last Matti-mas, and another is arriving soon, I think. So, I thought it would be a good time to have the lines added." Coleman smiled, but all Idop did was grunt. It was obvious he was not a happy man.

After they finished their meal, Coleman noticed a man and his family waiting in front of the guesthouse. He recognized him as Bazi, and the woman with him was named Ada. They had two children, a boy of ten spans and a girl of five. Coleman couldn't remember the children's names. He went to them. "Congratulations, Bazi, Ada, on your bonding yesterday. What can I do for you?"

"Me and Ada been talking, master, and we want to stay. You been the best master we ever had, and we don't want to leave. How can we stay and work for you?" Bazi asked.

"Please, don't call me master anymore, I don't like it. Now, about an agreement for you and your family to stay on the estate: I will share some land with you. You plant, grow, and pick divitz. I will see that it gets separated, cleaned, and baled. When it is sold at market, I will get one-third of the profits, and you will get the rest. Of course, that's after I pay the king's tax, and you pay me for the seed I'll start you out with. Does that seem fair to you?"

"Yes, sire, I think so. Can we live where we are now?" Bazi asked.

"Yes, but depending on the land you're assigned, you may want to move closer to your parcel. You can build a new home there. I will provide the materials if you provide the labor."

"Yes, master, that is good," the freed-man agreed.

"Now, Bazi, what did I tell you I didn't like?" Coleman asked.

"Sorry, master, I mean, sire." Coleman smiled and extended his right hand. Bazi stared at it, not knowing what to do. Coleman took Bazi's right forearm and firmly gripped it.

"This seals our cavalier's agreement. It means we both promise to live up to what we have said. Do you understand?"

"Yes, sire; thank you, sire."

Coleman went into the guesthouse and returned with two-hundred bhat and handed it to Bazi. Coleman spent a few minutes talking with him and Ada. He dropped to one knee and said a few words to the children; Adia was the daughter's name, and Bazio was the son. He was sad because they had to carry the mark of a freed-man for the remainder of their lives, but at least they were no longer slaves.

"I think Bazio is old enough to attend Scholar Pammon's class," Coleman told his parents. "I didn't see him there this morning."

"We didn't know what to do, so we kept him with us, sire," Ada told him.

"Please, see that he goes to school tomorrow. It's for his own good. You can go, too," he reminded the adults.

"Yes, sire, we will do as you say," Bazi promised. With that, Bazi lifted his son onto his shoulders, and Ada carried Adia in her arms. They walked toward the slave quarters. Coleman would be glad when he could burn down those wretched dwellings, but for the time being, it was all the freed-men had.

Shortly after Bazi and his family left, two angry young men reported for their payout. They were brothers, Edder, the elder, and Danner, the younger. They were rude and demanding. There was a moment when Coleman thought he would be attacked. The two freed-men calmed down when Idop and Ayascho joined the group after hearing their angry shouts. As soon as Coleman handed them their coin pouches, they were off in a huff.

Day after day, families and individuals slowly trickled in, meeting privately with Coleman, and accepting either a labor or sharecropper agreement. A few, mostly young men, chose to take their one-hundred bhat and leave the estate. Coleman made it clear to those leaving, they could always find work here, with him. That was his safety net for the freed-men.

By the end of the forty days, almost all two hundred and fifty freed-men had made a decision. Coleman kept a written record of each person's choice. One-hundred and seventy-five had chosen to stay and work for him in one capacity or another. Sixty had left the estate. Ten freed-men had not contacted Coleman at all, even though he still held their payout. On the forty-first day, he closed the granary to all except five whom he'd deemed old enough to be retired. The threat of hunger motivated the remaining ten to make a decision. All chose to remain on the estate and work for him, bringing the total choosing to stay to one-hundred and eighty-five freed-men workers, plus the five retired elderly. He knew the respect and fairness he had shown them in the past was the main reason so many chose to stay.

Shortly after the forty-day period had expired, a few who had chosen to leave returned and asked if they could stay and work for him. By the end of the eightieth day, five more had found their way back and went to work for Coleman, their payout having been completely spent or cheated from them, or a combination of the two.

On the eighty-sixth day, Danner, the younger of the two angry brothers, made his way back to the estate, his money gone, his stomach empty, and his face bruised.

"Where's your brother?" Coleman asked. "Does he have any money left?"

"No, all our money is gone."

"What happened to you?" Coleman asked, lightly touching the bruise on the freed-man's cheek.

"When our money was lost, Edder wanted me to join the brigands with him. I said no; I wouldn't become a thief, so we got into a fight. He beat me like he always does, but I still wouldn't go, so he left. That was seven days ago."

"You made the wiser choice, Danner. Let me get you some food; then we can talk." The angry young man was angry no more. The reality of his newly gained freedom had humbled him. Danner and Coleman worked out a labor agreement later that day, the freed-man taking advantage of the safety net Tondo had provided.

Coleman was already beginning to feel the stress of managing the estate on his own. Keeping all the freed-men engaged in the things necessary for running the estate's business was becoming overwhelming for him. He soon organized the labor teams into squads of ten or so workers, each headed by a boss. He tried using the title *foreman*, but the freed-men recoiled at the idea of working for a foreman ever again. Working for a *boss*, a godspeak word, was more acceptable to them.

The sharecroppers were allowed to stake out their territory. There were a few squabbles over some of the choice *bottom-land*, as Coleman called it, but he managed to work out the disputes, mostly by compromises that left all parties winning and losing a little.

While all this was going on, Coleman had to continue his training. He was learning quickly under the tutelage of Master Varios. He soon realized that part of the master's Gift—his tzaah—allowed him to influence a student's ability to learn.

Although Coleman was still struggling with the written language, he felt he was learning at a very fast pace. The estate records he was keeping were all written in world-speak now; he seldom wrote anything in godspeak anymore.

Maaryah continued her studies with Scholar Pammon, but much to Coleman's disappointment, Teema and Doros exercised their new freedom by dropping out. The class itself had increased from the ten children and three adults present on the first day to twenty-two children and twelve adults. The only children not attending were too young, but their parents promised to send them as soon as they became old enough.

One evening, while Coleman was poring over his notes by the dim light of a single lamp, Maaryah joined him at the guesthouse meal table. "Every night, you seem to struggle over these scrolls. What are they for?" she wondered.

"I'm trying to keep up with all of the things going on around the estate. This one keeps track of the expenses and the progress of the ship. This scroll tracks the work being done on the road to the ocean and the floating dock. These scrolls are records that track which families are cultivating parcels of land and where that land is located. This one tells me how the tree cutting is going. We need wood for the ship and new homes for the families." He picked up another stack of scrolls, "And they just seem to go on and on. I haven't had time to rest since Nestor left. He used to handle all these things, and all I had to do was get his report every night."

"Oy! Please don't bring that awful man back. He's so cruel," Maaryah pleaded as she absentmindedly rubbed her left shoulder.

"Don't worry, I have no plans to do that, and even if I wanted to, he wouldn't come back. He didn't like my outlander-ways. How are your studies coming?"

"At first, it was so hard I just wanted to quit. When Doros and Teema left school, I was going to leave, too, but I knew you would be angry with me, so I stayed. Now, it's getting easier. I'm beginning to enjoy it."

"Good for you. If you get good at reading and writing, maybe you can help me manage this mess," he said, pointing to the scrolls littering the table.

"I'll work at it harder than ever," she promised, a large smile filling her face.

As the days rolled on, the weather changed. Rain fell often, and a southwesterly Zerio wind constantly blew, making the days cold and dreary. Sword practice was moved into the barn on most days, but Master Shergus made sure his pupils also spent time in the rain and mud, so they could learn how to deal with even the most dismal conditions. Coleman, as well as Idop and Ayascho, were covered with bruises, as usual. Master Shergus had not relented a bit. Coleman had to admit that the constant bite of the master's wooden blade had improved his concentration and his reflexes. He'd even begun to control the power of his tzaah and direct it in ways that enhanced his attacks and defenses.

Progress with the ship's construction was slow. Master T´e-

rio struggled with the concept provided by Coleman's crude
model. Coleman had advised the master and Hermanez that
the ship had to be at least as long as the barn, which Coleman
estimated to be one-hundred feet. He also emphasized that it
have an extra-strong hull. He advised them to double all hull
elements, from the keel to the planking, as well as the addition
of diagonal ribs, something he had learned during a family
vacation that included a tour of the USS Constitution—Old
Ironsides. He reasoned, his ship may be heavy and slow, but it
would have a better chance of surviving an attack by the monstrous shark-like creatures that plied the ocean's waters.

It was a difficult learning process for the two builders, and
many mistakes were made, each one adding to the cost of the
project. Coleman had to dip into his gold reserve a third time
in order to keep the enterprise funded. He was beginning to
look upon the venture as if it were a government program
from his homeland, always over budget and behind schedule.
He was starting to wonder if the Sutro Seer had misread his
crystal ball, although he would never make such a disrespectful thought public.

CHAPTER 24

AMENDING THE CONTRACT

Late one afternoon, a band of men rode onto the estate, interrupting Master Shergus's class. It turned out to be none other than Prince Teg-ar-mos and his contingent of Pannera guards, including Sestardus Titus and twenty men.

Coleman left the training session and greeted the prince. "Welcome to the estate, Your Highness," he said with a bow.

"Thank you, my friend," the prince said as he extended his hand. The men gripped each other's forearm in the traditional manner.

"May I ask the nature of your visit?" Coleman asked.

"The king has concerns about your management of this estate. Is there a place we can discuss the matter privately?"

"Right this way," Coleman said as he directed the prince toward the guesthouse.

"Seemo, see that the animals are watered and fed," Coleman ordered.

Coleman introduced the prince to Master Shergus, Ayascho, and Idop, and each kneeled. He asked Ayascho to fetch Maaryah. Just as he was about to leave, she entered.

"Maaryah, this is Prince Teg-ar-mos," Coleman told her. Her eyes widened in surprise, and she quickly kneeled and bowed. The prince nodded, and she stood. The prince stared at her in astonishment while scanning her tall frame.

"Is there anything I can do for you, Sire Tondo?" she asked.

"Please provide the prince with water and towels so he can refresh himself. Your Highness, would you prefer to drink water or wine?"

"Wine, of course. Everyone knows this estate produces the best wine in the kingdom," the prince quickly responded.

Maaryah swiftly left, as Coleman led the prince to the table, and the men sat. Maaryah soon returned with a washbasin, a pitcher of water, and some towels. The prince refreshed himself, and while he was doing that, Maaryah dashed off and returned with a pitcher of wine. The prince dismissed everyone in the room except Coleman, poured himself a cup of wine, took a long sip, and smiled at the cup. He leaned back, his demeanor becoming serious. Looking into Coleman's face as he sat across the table, the prince began to speak in an unnerving tone.

"Word has gotten around the kingdom that you have freed many of this estate's slaves. When Counselor Idop's report first mentioned it, no one took it seriously, thinking he overstated what you had done. The king has also received other reports confirming the counselor's. No one could believe you would make such a foolish and costly decision, but when several slaves came into the city, marked as freed-men and saying they came from the Tondo estate, people started believing it was true. I've been sent by the king to look into this. Now, tell me how many did you free?"

"I freed everyone, all two-hundred and fifty, and I was glad to do it."

"As you know, the king granted you stewardship over this estate for saving my life; however, he expects you to manage it wisely, remaining profitable, and paying the royal tax. How are you going to do that without any slaves?"

"If I recall, I paid more in taxes this span than was paid last. I see no reason I can't pay as much next span, depending on the weather and all."

"How will you plant, cultivate, and pick divitz without slaves? It doesn't seem possible," the prince wondered, his cold stare boring into Coleman.

"Over one-hundred and ninety of the freed-men are still on the estate. I've worked out agreements with them all for the next season. They will share in the profits. I will wager that free men will work harder for themselves than they ever did for a master. I'll be very surprised if next span's harvest doesn't exceed the last one, and the king will receive more in taxes, too."

"Since it appears you have enough laborers, I will allow you to continue with this unusual plan. But be forewarned, the king expects you to manage the estate properly, and if you don't, he will take it from you."

"Duly noted, Your Highness. If I can't make it run better by the labor of free men, then I don't want it," he affirmed.

"I must warn, you'll make many other estate holders very nervous when they learn of this. They will look upon your actions as a menace. When powerful people in the kingdom see a threat, they usually find a way to eliminate it. Be careful, my friend, I wouldn't want anything unfortunate to happen to you," the prince warned.

"I have plenty of protection. Besides Ayascho and Idop, three master priests from the temple are now here."

"I know of Master Varios and Master Shergus, but who is the third?"

"Master T´erio, the master carpenter. The Sutro Seer sent him here with an outlander by the name of Hermanez. They are building a ship, a large boat, of my design."

"That seems like a rather foolish and costly enterprise," the prince admonished. "You say the Sutro Seer sent T´erio? Why did he send him to you?"

"I had the same question. I know very little about boats and sailing, but I gave the master some ideas from my homeland, and now, he and another outlander, Hermanez, are building a large boat. If it works out, it will be one of the greatest things to ever happen here, I think."

"Indeed, it would be. No one goes on the ocean; all who do die. If you could build a boat that can withstand the terrors, you will become a much wealthier man than you already are," the prince counseled. "The king will be very interested in learning more about this project."

"I thought Counselor Idop's report had included it," Coleman wondered.

"The Court's counselors review all reports, and only the important and noteworthy items are taken to the king. People have been building boats for many, many spans, but it always ends the same way: in death. I doubt they felt it important enough to take to the king, assuming you, an outlander, were ignorant of the previous failures; however, since the Sutro Seer is involved, the king will be very interested in learning of your progress. Before I leave, you must show me this boat."

"It's being constructed at the lake. We can go there tomorrow if you'd like," Coleman promised.

"Yes, yes, that will be acceptable. Now, I wish to speak with you about a more personal matter," the prince said as he leaned forward, quickly glancing toward the door and windows, checking to see that no one was listening. In almost a whisper, he continued, "On the journey from where I was attacked by the brigands, I had the opportunity to speak with the savage, Ayascho. He mentioned that you had nearly crossed-over in his village, and you had dreams or visions of death. Will you tell me about them?"

"I was very sick, and I had a burning fever. Everyone thought I was going to die. I saw a tunnel of light, and I was floating toward it. I could feel peace and safety there. I wanted to enter, but the voice of the taahso, the village shaman, pulled me back from the brink. When I awoke, I felt sad, like I had lost something precious."

The prince stared into Coleman's eyes. "When I was dying, I had a vision, too. Only my vision was not one of comfort. Dark and evil creatures clawed at me, scratching my skin and delighting in my agony. I tried to escape them, but they pulled me down. I was about to surrender to their torment, but suddenly, I was jerked from their clutches by your shouts. Why would we have such different experiences?" The prince was almost pleading, his stare fixed on Coleman's eyes. "I have not been able to sleep well ever since. I feel a horrible doom will take me in the end."

"This sounds more like something you should share with

the priests. I doubt I can help you with such a spiritual experience."

"Ha, but you can. You are uniquely qualified. I can't share these things with the priests; they are too personal and dangerous. I cannot show weakness in any way, nor can I admit my fears to them. It would not be good for the stability of the kingdom to admit these frailties. You've had your own vision, and I'm sure you have pondered its meaning, haven't you?"

"It's not so much the vision of the tunnel of light that I wonder about. It was the accompanying vision about subjugation and war that concerns me. It's like a higher power has summoned me here to perform a mission of great importance. But I have read about trials similar to yours in my homeland. Usually, the person who had such a bad near-death experience identifies something they need to change in the way they live their lives. Is there anything in your life you think you need to change?"

"Not that I have considered. As royalty and heir to the throne, others bow to my will. My father establishes order and rules the kingdom as he sees fit. As his son, I see that his will is executed. That is my duty."

"Do you always agree with your father's dictates?" Coleman asked.

"If I didn't, I wouldn't talk about it. The sovereigns of the kingdom must present a united will. This gives our subjects confidence in the king's leadership."

"Have you ever discussed with your father the rulings he has made that you don't fully support?"

"Only once, and the king made it very clear that I was never to do that again. Since then, I have never objected to any of his edicts," the prince admitted.

"I can see this might be difficult for you, and why you have visions of demons. One day, you will be king, and I suggest you rule with wisdom and fairness, holding honor in your right hand and humility in your left."

"If I do, will I be able to sleep calmly?"

"Try it and see, then you will know for sure whether my advice has merit," Coleman suggested.

The two men continued chatting about the affairs of the estate and the kingdom. When they finished talking, they stepped out of the guesthouse for some fresh air.

It was then that Doros approached and kneeled before the prince. "Your Highness," Doros said with bowed head.

"You may stand. Who are you?" the prince asked as he examined the man's freed-man mark.

"I am Doros, servant to Matriarch Oetan. She would be honored if you joined her and Mistress Oetan for last-meal this evening."

Turning to Coleman, the prince said, "I understand you allowed her to remain on the estate, even after her bondmate's disgrace. My father may have been too harsh in dealing with Megato Oetan. The last I saw of him, he was fighting two or three brigands. I was going to his aid when I was hit from behind. I understand his body was never found." He turned to Doros again, "Tell your mistress I will be pleased to dine with her."

"She will be delighted to learn of your acceptance. She asked me to extend an invitation to you as well, Sire Tondo, and of course Counselor Idop and Ayascho."

"Tell her we will," Coleman answered.

Doros fetched the dinner guests just as darkness began to overtake the day. It was a pleasant evening for everyone, even though the prince never referred to the hostess as Lady Oetan, using terms such as 'lady of the house' or 'our gracious hostess.' Coleman could see that rank was taken very seriously, and the prince never drifted from proper protocol, even during a friendly social gathering. He asked the prince to share with the others the news of the kingdom he had learned during their afternoon discussion.

About halfway through the evening, Coleman began noticing how the prince's eyes always seemed to drift in the direction of the lovely Mistress Ootyiah. By the end of the evening, they were sharing hasty glances and smiles. When the party dismissed, Coleman and his friends returned to the guesthouse, but before he entered, he looked heavenward and noticed the clouds had parted, and the glow of Munnoga was peeking through, casting a silvery light upon the landscape. He then noticed the prince and Ootyiah side-by-side, walking slowly in the direction of the ocean cliffs, Sestardus Titus following at a discreet distance. Coleman wondered if her amazing beauty would be enough to overcome her disgraced family name in the eyes of the prince. He smiled, realizing only time would tell.

Surprisingly, the prince chose to extend his visit, so he was invited to lodge in the manor house. Coleman allowed his guards to camp in the barn. They had brought tents with them, but a dry barn was much more inviting than a cold and damp tent. Coleman and Ayascho spent some time talking with the soldiers, especially those who had journeyed with them from the Wilderness. Their morale was high, certainly bolstered by their award from the king of double salaries for a span. Titus looked the part of a sestardus, a senior non-officer. His uniform was more colorful, and his armor better crafted. He also carried with him an increased air of self-confidence that Coleman hadn't noticed before.

Coleman's old friends welcomed him into their circle around a fire that he allowed them to build on the hard brick floor of the barn's front entrance. They shared stories of their perilous journey with the other men of the Prince's Contingent. It was a grand reunion for all. Coleman took the opportunity to ask Pontus to give Numo some pointers concerning the handling of thrice. The soldier was more than happy to help the man who had saved his life more than once.

The prince delayed his departure from Tondo's estate for many days. Most of his time was spent in the manor house or on long, chaperoned walks with Mistress Ootyiah. But, with reluctance, the prince had to bid all adieu and get on with his duties. The prince still wanted to see what kind of boat was being built, so Coleman, Idop, and Ayascho rode with him to the construction site.

The prince was amazed by what he saw. "Never before in the kingdom has such a large boat been built. Even smaller attempts ended in failure when the boat fell apart; however, never has such a design been seen," he was quoted as saying. Before he departed for the city, he instructed Idop to keep the king apprised of the ship's progress in more detail.

The days slowly passed, and the wet season drenched the land. Master T'erio had a roof built over the ship construction site so the builders could stay reasonably dry. The ocean road and dock were put on hold until the land dried out, and the ocean calmed.

Early one evening, after the day's lessons were completed, and after the men had eaten, Coleman was sitting at the guesthouse table with Maaryah sitting across from him. He had created several flashcards, and he was teaching her the multiplication tables. Scholar Pammon had been teaching the class their numbers: addition and subtraction, and Maaryah had shown Coleman her progress. He soon discovered that this culture didn't know about multiplication or division. He started teaching her a way to shortcut some of the repetitious addition strings her teacher had assigned. She was quickly learning her numbers, and having discovered that she had a very keen mind and an excellent memory, Coleman decided to teach her an entirely new concept.

While they were so engaged, Master Varios entered the room, desiring to learn more from his student. When he saw that Coleman was already engaged in teaching Maaryah, he watched for a while, and then he asked, "What is this you are doing? I have never seen this method of numbers before."

"I'm drilling her on the multiplication tables. She has become quite good at it." Maaryah smiled at the compliment.

Coleman had written the numbers in the world-speak symbols he'd learned, but he had added the multiplication sign 'x,' which was godspeak.

"What is marh-parh-ga-zun?" the master scholar asked.

"Mul-ti-plica-tion, it's a faster way of adding numbers together," Coleman explained.

"What does that symbol represent?" the master asked, pointing at the multiplication sign.

"The 'x' means to multiply. Instead of adding 10 and 10 and 10 to make 30, we can multiply 10 by 3 groupings, which also makes 30," Coleman explained.

"I think I understand the concept, but can you do the same thing with larger values?" he asked.

"Of course, you can. Watch," he said as he held up the flashcard 12 x12.

Maaryah thought for a second and then answered, "144," smiling from ear to ear.

"That is correct. You can even multiply much larger numbers, for instance: if I sell 500 bales of divitz for 25 bhat each, how much would I earn? Maaryah, can you figure that out?"

Maaryah took chalk to her slate board, and in a few seconds, she scratched out the answer. "12,500 bhat," she replied.

"That's right. Excellent multiplication," he praised. Her smile grew even larger, which hardly seemed possible.

The master's face suddenly grew stern. He stared at Coleman, and then he turned to Maaryah. He grabbed her face with both hands and peered deeply into her golden-amber eyes. She gave a startled cry and tried to pull away, but the priest's powerful grip held her head motionless.

Coleman was stunned by what he saw, and after a few seconds, he intervened. "Master Varios, stop! What are you doing? You're scaring her." Varios didn't answer and continued to glare into her eyes, his nose nearly touching hers. She gave another feeble cry, but the master held her tight. "Master Varios, release her!" Coleman demanded, and then he stood, preparing to intervene forcibly if the master didn't comply. Varios finally released the girl and stepped back. Maaryah quickly scooted to the end of the bench, her eyes wide in fright. "Maaryah, are you okay? Are you hurt?" Coleman asked with a worried tone. She shook her head, indicating she hadn't been harmed, at least not physically. Coleman faced the priest and growled, "What was that all about? I demand an explanation." Coleman's anger was beginning to rise, and the others could literally feel it.

"This is not possible. Never has such a thing been recorded. I must consult with the other masters," Varios said to no one in particular as he turned and was about to exit the house.

Coleman grabbed him by the arm and spun him around, "I demand an explanation! You've scared her half to death, and as far as I can see, for no good reason."

"I feel an awakening within her. It is as if she possesses the Gift. That cannot be, for a woman has never had the Gift of inner-power, and certainly never one who carries a mark. I must consult with the others." He shook his arm free from Coleman's grip, turned, and exited the room.

Coleman and Maaryah watched him march into the darkness, and soon, they could hear him enter the priest's wagon. Coleman turned and looked at Maaryah, her eyes still wide in fear. "Did you hear what he said? He thinks you might have the Gift, tzaah, taah, whatever, the inner-power that makes a person extraordinary. If it's true, I wonder what power it is? Aren't you excited?"

"I . . . I don't know. I'm so scared I can't think," was her shaky reply.

A few minutes later, Attendant Pahno mounted the priests' lead raster and rode off in the direction of the ship construction site. Coleman knew it would take more than half the night to get there and back. To call for the other master in such a way meant that whatever Varios had discovered in Maaryah was extremely important and troubling. But it excited the estate master.

He walked over to Maaryah and held her hands. She was trembling. He talked with her until she relaxed a bit, then he went to his chair and started weaving a basket. He wondered what the morrow would bring. Maaryah sat on the bench near him, sewing a new shirt, her hands still trembling. Coleman recalled how she once feared him, but now, his presence offered her safety and security. The thought made him smile. It was very late before she dismissed herself and went to the quarters she shared with Teema at the rear of the manor house.

In the morning, shortly after Coleman and the others had arisen, the three masters came to the guesthouse. "We want your permission to examine the girl," Master Varios began.

"First of all, it's not my permission you need; it's her choice. And secondly, I suggest you approach her a bit more kindly this time. You nearly scared her witless last night. I had to sit with her until after the midnight segment before she was calm enough to retire for the night. I have no problem with you examining her, but do it in a respectful way. She has feelings, after all," he counseled.

"You're right. I will apologize to her. I was so shocked I couldn't believe what I was sensing. It was such a surprise I forgot myself. I won't let it happen again," Master Varios promised.

"Very well. Oh, here she is now," Coleman said as Maaryah entered with a tray of food. She abruptly stopped upon seeing the three priests in the room. "Maaryah, the masters want to test you to learn if you have tzaah. You don't have to do it if you don't want to, but I think you should," he advised. She detoured around Varios, staying just out of his reach, then she set the tray on the table.

She turned and looked at the three priests with a worried expression. "Will it hurt?" she asked.

"No, not at all, my child," Varios promised.

She looked at Coleman, and he reassured her with a smile. "All right, but I want Sire Tondo here with me," she said. Varios looked at the other two priests, and they nodded their approval. Idop, who had been standing near the doorway of his room, advanced, lifted the tray of food from the table, and left the house, not saying a word but bearing a stern and dour expression. Ayascho shrugged and followed him.

"I'm sorry I frightened you last night; it was not my intention. I was surprised by my inner feelings, that's all," Varios admitted.

"Are you going to grab me like that again?" Maaryah asked timidly.

"No, child, we will place our hands on your head, very gently, and wait for the tzaah within you to stir, if it is really there. You probably won't feel a thing," he told her.

Varios pulled the bench away from the table and motioned for her to be seated. She slowly walked over to it and stopped. She looked in Coleman's direction and waited, her amber eyes expressing her tepidity. He winked and gave her another smile that convinced her to sit. Varios stood directly behind her and gently placed his fingertips on her head. Master Shergus stood at Varios's right and did the same. Master T'erio took his place at Varios's left and placed his fingertips on her head, as well. They stood in silence for quite a bit of time, but slowly, imperceptibly at first, a halo of golden light began to surround the masters. The light began at their heads and descended down their arms and over their fingers. Soon, Maaryah's head began to glow, and then the light descended until it covered her entire body, surrounding her and the three masters with a glowing, golden aura.

Coleman's gaze was transfixed on the scene before him, so much so that he hadn't noticed the golden glow that was emanating from his own body. When he noticed it, he lifted both of his hands and examined their glowing radiance. He could see Ayascho peering through the open window, his eyes wide with excitement, for he, too, could see the phenomenon. Coleman waited, turning his hands from front to back, examining them. He then turned his attention back to the masters and Maaryah. The glow was beginning to fade, and soon, it was gone altogether from the masters, Maaryah, and himself. The priests removed their hands from Maaryah's head and let

them hang at their sides. They looked at each other and nodded, one after the other.

"Then it is confirmed, she has the Gift. The Gift of Learning and the Gift of the Scholar has awakened. They are the
same gifts I possess," Master Varios announced, "But there is
more. We also learned she has the Gift of Discernment, the
power to detect intent in the hearts of men. These powers are
only now awakening, and there may be more. However, there
is a catalyst, a power that awakens the Gift, an ability seen
in only one mortal before. Only one other person has ever
had the power to awaken the latent gift of tzaah that exists
in some others. He was the greatest Seer of all, Sutrum Seer
Myndron, who lived one-thousand spans ago and walked with
the unnamed god." Varios ceased speaking and looked down.
T´erio and Shergus were also looking at the floor.

After a few moments of silence, Master Shergus lifted his
head and turned toward Coleman, "You have the power that
awakens the Gift, you have the ability to awaken tzaah. That
explains how the Gift was awakened in the savage, and it also
explains how a marked woman was granted the Gift. All this
is a revelation to the three of us, but it reveals the great god's
mercy and willingness to bless all of his children. You, Tondo,
are indeed the Messenger sent by deity. Undoubtedly, Tondo,
you are the catalyst, the one who prepares the righteous for the
coming struggle between good and evil. We are honored to be
in your presence," he said with a tone of humility and rever-
ence Coleman had never heard from the swordmaster before.

The Messenger found no words to utter. He sat, dumb-
founded by the revelation. *What could it mean? How should it be*

used? Indeed, why me? Maaryah sat quietly, a timid smile on her face.

Varios gently put his hands on her shoulders. "She must join the morning class, and I will teach her in the afternoon, as well. This way, I can teach her what she must know and determine the limits of her gifts. I'm sure her tzaah has been awakened for an important purpose. In due time, we will understand why. This day will be remembered for all history as the day a woman joined the ranks of the Gifted," Varios proclaimed.

The three priests soon left, and not long after that, Attendant Pahno left the estate, riding a raster he pushed at a full trot, heading up the road toward the city, undoubtedly, Coleman guessed, to make a report to the Sutro Seer on what the masters had discovered. Master Shergus and Master T´erio borrowed two samarans from Tondo and rode to the ship site; Shergus returned late that afternoon with both mounts.

The swordmaster's absence allowed Coleman time to discuss arrangements with Maaryah. There would be little time for her to accomplish her regular duties, so he amended their contract again. She was to tend to her training and manage the affairs of the buildings and functions in the immediate area of the manor grounds. This included the manor house, the guesthouse, the school, and the barn. It meant she would be responsible for maintaining and ordering food stocks for man and beast, as well all materials necessary for the upkeep of the work that went on in the immediate area, such as the blacksmith's shop and the school. Coleman knew this would be a stretch for the young woman, but he promised to help her make the adjustment.

With trepidation and not a little hesitation, she accepted her new responsibilities. Coleman also told her, he was doubling her wages to ten bhat a detzamar, with a promise of more increases as she mastered her new duties. The first thing he tasked her with was finding a replacement for her previous chores. She tried to convince him she could continue doing them, but after a short discussion, she realized it wouldn't be possible.

A few days later, Maaryah introduced her replacement, a short, pudgy young woman with light-brown hair and dark-brown eyes, by the name of Tenny. She looked to be sixteen years old, but Coleman knew that meant she was probably twenty-five to thirty spans.

As expected, Idop grumbled and complained about Maaryah joining the morning class, but everyone ignored his complaints, and when he saw how fast she progressed, his respect for her abilities increased. It took several wernts, but eventually, he stopped referring to her as 'the slave girl.'

Coleman became aware that the living and sleeping arrangements for the former house slaves had gotten crowded. Doros had his own room tucked away at the rear of the manor house, and Teema willingly shared her small room in the manor house with Maaryah. However, now that Tenny had moved in with the other two women, Coleman learned things had gotten too crowded for comfort. He had become quite fond of Maaryah and considered her a good friend. He decided to push her abilities by having her oversee the construction of a house for the estate's newest boss. At first, Maaryah objected, saying she could do without, but he convinced her by telling her it would really be a second guesthouse, and she could live there when it wasn't in use by visitors to the estate. Surprisingly, his white lie worked, and she agreed. He put her in charge of overseeing its design and construction, and he told her to build it to her liking, using the manor house and the current guesthouse as examples. He also preferred it to be built from fired brick, so she would need to get a crew for the kiln, as well. As Coleman expected, it was another stretch for the young woman, but as it turned out, it was one of her most enjoyable responsibilities, and she learned much in the process.

CHAPTER 25

THE RISE OF THE SUTRO SHOWTON

King Ben-do-teg sat on his mount, surveying the carnage before him. A city of several thousand had been pillaged and burned. Numerous dead bodies lay scattered about, and the wail of mourning women and children filled the air, rising above the carnage along with the smoke from fires the outlaws had started.

"This is outrageous!" the king finally growled through clenched teeth. King Ben-do-teg, a man of slim build and average height, had ruled his kingdom for the past twelve spans. He had dealt with brigands and outlaws before, but nothing like this. "Lord Pendrog, when we trap these culprits, will you be able to deal with their sorcerer leader?"

Lord Pendrog, the king's champion, sat on his mount next to the king. He was a tall and muscular man of thirty spans—outlander spans. His dark-brown eyes were full of anger as he stared at the horrific scene before them.

"Your Highness, it will be my pleasure to end that evil sorcerer's life. How dare he come into your kingdom and do this."

"Are you confident you can deal with his sorcerer ways? You've heard the reports. He appears to be quite powerful," the king warned.

"I've been trained by Master Shergus, and my sword was blessed by Master Eezayhod, may he rest with calmness," Lord Pendrog reminded the king.

"Yes, of course. I see you still wear the claw from the beast you slew," the king said.

Many spans ago, King Ben-do-teg had conducted a kingdom-wide competition to find the best swordsman. Pendrog had proven himself to be that man, having bested every other competitor in one-on-one duels with wooden swords. The king then sent Pendrog to the Temple of the Unnamed God in Anterra, the Ancient City, for training by the temple's master swordsman. King Ben-do-teg was preparing the young man for a future date because the king realized that the neighboring Gor-bin-den Kingdom and his would soon be engaged in a dispute over a large, fertile valley of unclaimed land. Shortly after Pendrog returned, the dispute escalated into war. Rather than waste the lives of their subjects, the two kings decided to resolve the issue by a Battle of Champions. Pendrog prevailed, and King Ben-do-teg bestowed the title of Lord upon him.

A few spans after that, a large predator beast moved into the kingdom. Several of the king's subjects were killed by the creature, and terror gripped the kingdom. Lord Pendrog was called upon to end the threat. The king's young champion faced the snarling and growling furry beast alone. It was a desperate fight, but Pendrog prevailed again. The king rewarded him lavishly, and Pendrog was given one of the beast's huge claws as a trophy. Master Eezayhod was so grateful to Pendrog for ending the beast's threat to his flock of followers, he blessed the lord's longsword.

"Haptane," the king called.

A man quickly rode up to him and saluted by thumping his chest. "Yes, Your Highness?"

"I want these transgressors chased down and put to the sword. We can't be far behind them. If we hurry, we may be able to catch them this time."

"What shall we do about these victims?" the haptane asked.

"Delay has allowed the sorcerer to escape in the past, but not today. We'll deal with these unfortunates after we've subdued their tormentors. Assemble your men and follow me!" the king ordered.

Nevesant was observing the king and his guards from the crest of a hill overlooking the city he and the other followers of Munnevo had just plundered. Everything of value had been taken and divided amongst Tangundo's men. His master now had over five-hundred followers willing to obey his commands. With each successful raid, more men joined his band, and now, they had become a force to be reckoned with. Reports his master had been receiving said the king had about four-hundred full-time guards.

Maybe it's time to strike the killing blow, Nevesant thought. He galloped off the hill, heading back to his master to relay his observations.

Nevesant found Tangundo and the others resting and awaiting his report. The young man rode up to his master, dismounted, and excitedly rushed to his god. Hardly able to control himself, he shouted, "Master, they're coming; the *king* and his men are coming!"

Tangundo clutched him by the shoulders. Unexpectedly, a surge of energy flowed from master to servant. Nevesant's eyes grew wide, and his legs lost their strength. He fell to the ground and struggled to remain conscious. Tangundo stared down at the boy, wondering what was wrong with him.

"What happened, master?" Nevesant groggily asked.

Tangundo pulled the boy to his feet and steadied him. "I don't know. How many king's men are coming?" he asked worriedly.

"Less than four-hundred, I'd say," the boy weakly replied.

Tangundo stood silently in thought for a few moments, then he turned to the men near him and said, "Men, this is the day we've been waiting for. If we catch the king unawares, we can take the whole kingdom. Mount up and follow me!" Tangundo led his men into a predetermined gorge and stopped. "We've trained for this before. All of you take your places," Tangundo ordered. The men quickly dispersed and hid while their master remained where he was, in the center of the canyon. Nevesant staggered away and took his place with the others.

It wasn't long before Tangundo heard the sound of approaching hooves. His heart pounded in his ears as fear gripped him. If he won this battle, he'd be well on his way to conquering this alien world. If he lost, he would surely be killed, either in battle or by execution, should he survive the fight and be captured. As the sound grew louder, he comforted himself with the knowledge that his force outnumbered the king's, and he had the advantage of surprise. The king's force was undoubtedly better trained and equipped, but his men had rock-flingers, something no one else possessed. With his confidence bolstered, he awaited the king's arrival.

The king and his men rounded a bend in the gorge and stopped. King Ben-do-teg stared at the man with the veiled face standing a stone's throw away. The two men eyed each other angrily, neither saying a word. Lord Pendrog dismounted and began advancing toward Tangundo, his gleaming longsword in hand.

"So, king, you fear to face me yourself, do you? Just as well. First, I'll destroy your lackey, and then I'll destroy you. Men, attack!" Tangundo yelled. His followers rose from their hiding places and began slinging rocks at the king and his men. Lord Pendrog had advanced far enough to be clear of the turmoil and chaos going on behind him. His dark eyes were fixed upon the veiled man well to his front.

Tangundo's aura ignited. He formed a purple energy ball in his hands and flung it at his challenger. Lord Pendrog held his blessed sword in front of himself, and it intercepted the riving ball of energy. Tangundo watched in horror as his deadly mass of energy was absorbed into the blade, which began ringing. Terror and panic overtook the sorcerer, and he began to retreat, stumbling backward as he did.

When his master gave the order to attack, Nevesant jumped up from his hiding place and twirled his sling over his head. He let the fist-sized rock loose, and it slammed into the rear of King Ben-do-teg's helm. The king weaved in the saddle and then fell to the ground. Several guards dismounted and rushed to him. The guards circled the king and defended him with their bodies. King Ben-do-teg struggled to his feet, assisted by a guard, and stood swaying from side-to-side as he attempted to regain his bearings. Nevesant let another stone fly, and it took down a guard. He then noticed the fearsome-looking warrior advancing on his master.

Tangundo's dread increased. His inner-power attacks were being thwarted by his assailant's glowing and ringing sword. He raised the purrant's sword of authority in a feeble attempt to defend himself, but he instinctively knew he was no match for this king's warrior. Tangundo continued to retreat as his antagonist advanced, hatred and vengeance burning in his assailant's eyes. As Tangundo's desperation grew, a bolt of purple energy sprang from his free hand. It, too, was absorbed by the king man's sword, but its jolting power slowed the warrior's advance.

Although hindered by the evil sorcerer's powers, Lord Pendrog knew it was just a matter of time before he ended the villain's threat. His resolve stiffened, and he closed upon the tall man with the veiled face. Tangundo and Lord Pendrog grappled in a death-wrestle, the king's champion growling in pain of Tangundo's burning aura, yet he was not deterred.

Nevesant saw his master was in trouble and froze for an instant as he thought. He dare not use his rock-flinger; he could hit the wrong man. He was too far away to charge to his master's aid. Suddenly and unexpectedly, he felt a burning sensation in the center of his chest. He swept the air with his left hand, and a rock half the size of a man's head lifted from the ground near the two combatants. It flew through the air and slammed into the side of Lord Pendrog's helmed head, stunning the king's champion, causing him to release his grip on the sorcerer's sword arm. Tangundo slashed with his short sword, striking Pendrog on the left side of his unprotected neck. The king's warrior fell to the ground, and Tangundo finished him with a slashing blow to the back of his neck, severing his spinal cord.

Nevesant dashed to his master's side, a huge smile on his face. "Master! Master!" he called excitedly, "Did you see what I did?"

"Was that you, Nevesant?"

"Yes, Master, I was able to make that rock fly by magic," the young man was nearly shouting with glee.

Tangundo turned his attention from Nevesant to the continuing battle not far away. More than half of the king's men were now dismounted. Some were down, knocked senseless by the rock-men's stones. Several king's guards were charging up the steep sides of the gorge, and they became prime targets for the next volley of stones, felling several more guards. The surviving king's men beat a hasty retreat as they attempted to protect their heads and bodies with their arms. Twenty or more mounted king's guards, realizing their peril, chose to forsake their king, and ran for their lives. Their retreat was blocked by several scores of mounted outlaws.

"Alright, men, take 'em with the sword!" Tangundo ordered. Hundreds of men scrambled down the steep sides of the gorge and engaged the stunned and terror-stricken survivors of the rock-men's volleys. Tangundo blasted a few purple bolts of energy into the king's defenders, further sowing fear and hopelessness into their ranks. It wasn't long before King Ben-do-teg found himself standing alone. The king was still reeling from Nevesant's stone to his head, and he offered only a feeble last defense as several followers of Munnevo advanced on him, their blades flashing through the dusty air, biting into the hapless king's body and armor.

"The king is down!" Nevesant shouted gleefully.

"Your king is dead! Surrender or join him in death!" Tangundo shouted in warning. A couple hundred king's men were still standing, but when given the choice of life or death, they reluctantly chose life and dropped their weapons.

Tangundo turned to the young man at his side, "Nevesant, I owe you my life," he said as he reached down and grasped Lord Pendrog's sword by the grip. "Here, take this magic sword as my reward for your service." As the sword was passed from master to servant, its shiny zanth-colored blade turned a dull black to the astonishment of the two. Although it was a great sword, balanced, hard, and sharp, it never again displayed any of its magical powers.

For the remainder of the day, Tangundo and his men questioned the survivors of the king's small army. The four officers, three defetane, and one haptane were summarily executed. King's warriors were given the choice of joining Tangundo's army or facing the same fate as their officers. Only a handful remained loyal, and they were quickly executed. A few were driven into the mist, never to be seen again. The remainder were integrated into Tangundo's growing army.

Tangundo learned that a few king's men had escaped his ambush, and he was sure they would return to the king's city, Farwune, and warn others of the king's defeat. There was no time to waste. He told his men they would begin their march on the city in the morning. He didn't want to allow the remaining authorities time to mount a defense.

Four days later, Tangundo and his army arrived at Farwune. It was the largest metropolis Tangundo had seen since his arrival on this world. Surprisingly to him, it wasn't a walled city. He was told that never had a threat required the city to become walled. Now, it was too late. Tangundo rode into the city with the newly promoted Defetane Sassin at his side, carrying a pike with King Ben-do-teg's head displayed on it, giving the residents of Farwune a clear message as to who now ruled.

One of the dead king's warriors directed his new master to the palace. When he arrived, the conqueror was greeted by dour palace officials. Tangundo dismounted and strode toward them, his gait was a strut, exuding confidence and power. He stopped a couple of strides short of the officials and glowered at the ten men awaiting a pronouncement from their new ruler. After several uncomfortable moments, Tangundo growled angrily, "Down on your bellies!" The men delayed, so their new master snapped his fingers and pointed to one of the officials in the center of the group. Two of Tangundo's men grabbed the man and dragged him away from the others. "Kill him!" Tangundo ordered. The remaining officials were aghast and quickly prostrated themselves before him. "That's better," he snarled as his victim screamed in pain when a sword was plunged into his bowels.

"Master, what's to be done with the king's head," Sassin asked.

"Mount it in front of the palace and let the birds pick at it." His angry red eyes turned back to the men groveling before him. "Where's the king's family?" There was no response. He snapped his fingers and pointed to another victim. He was quickly dragged away and dispatched, just like the first official. "I am not a patient man. Now, answer my question, or you'll all feel cold gravetum."

"They fled," an official offered in a quavering voice.

"Where have they gone?"

"The neighboring kingdom," the official told him.

"Which direction did they go?"

"South," the man said, his voice still revealing his dread.

"How many?"

"The queen, the prince, and the two princesses. Four guards went with them," Tangundo was told by the quaking official.

"Sassin, take twenty men and chase them down. When you catch them, kill them all," Tangundo commanded.

"Yes, master," Defetane Sassin said as he raised his left arm with a closed fist in salute. He marched off, selected a detachment of outlaw warriors, and galloped out of the city heading south.

Tangundo glared at the officials cowering at his feet. "Kill them," he ordered his guards, "Spare this one," he said, pointing to the city official who had answered his questions. The terrified men were dragged away as they screamed hysterically, leaving only one man groveling at Tangundo's feet.

"What's your name?" Tangundo asked the lone survivor.

"Master, my name is Neehoer."

Tangundo moved into the palace and claimed the dead king's riches. With his new-found wealth, he rewarded old followers and bought new ones. His most devoted disciple was the young man, Nevesant. He revered his master and sought to become like him, for the outsider had raised him from the depths of poverty and near starvation to the heights of conqueror and overlord. All the young man could see now was success and an increase in personal power. Just like his mentor, it was this which drove him, and he grew calloused to the cries of his victims.

Yet, there was one thing Nevesant craved more than anything else. He desired the same magical power his master possessed. Somehow, he had gained it, but he knew not how to call it forth. *Could his master's touch, the day he felt lightning pass into his body, have instilled him with a portion of the master's magic?* He knew not and decided to seek his mentor's counsel.

"Master," Nevesant began, "I've been wondering, when you were struggling with Lord Pendrog, I was able to use magic to hit him in the head with a boulder. Did you give me some of your magic? Can I do the things you do? Will I be able to glow with terrible power like you?"

The realization he had activated Nevesant's inner-power had occupied Tangundo's thoughts during his recent moments of introspection. If he had indeed caused the boy's power to awaken, what did that mean for himself? *Could Nevesant become as powerful? Could he become a threat?* He had already decided to avoid future mishaps as had occurred with the boy. He had made it clear to his attendants and subordinates that he was not to be touched without his express permission. Now, what was he to do with the boy? Should he execute the young man before he became a threat and be done with it? No, that seemed too cruel, even for one whose compassion was withering.

"Nevesant, I will see to your training as you prove your loyalty to me," Tangundo told him.

"But master, what more must I do? I saved your life."

"Yes, you did, and I'm grateful. You've been rewarded with Pendrog's sutrum gravetum sword, the best one in the whole army."

"But it has lost its magic, master."

"Are you complaining about my gift, Nevesant?"

The young man hung his head. "No, master, it's a generous gift. I'm grateful."

"Good. Be patient, Nevesant, I have great plans for you. Now, go and fetch Neehoer, Sassin, and Soidentee for me. Tell them I have important missions I need them to perform." Nevesant saluted his master and withdrew.

Neehoer was the first to respond to his new master's summons. He dropped to a knee and bowed low. "Ha, Neehoer, you may stand. I've been told you designed and saw to the construction of this palace. Is that true?"

"Not exactly, Your Eminence. King Ben-do-teg commissioned me to refurbish the old palace and add two new wings. The king was quite pleased with my work," Neehoer wheedled.

Tangundo looked down from his throne on an elevated platform, glaring at his new toady while holding the deposed king's scepter, the symbol of authority. "I'm sure he did. I want you to draw up plans for a fortified palace, a walled castle impregnable to attack."

"Yes, Your Eminence, I'll begin work immediately. Where is this castle to be built?" Neehoer wondered.

"I don't know yet," Tangundo told him as he noticed Sassin had arrived. "You're dismissed, Neehoer. Keep me apprised of your progress. I will review the plans regularly." Neehoer saluted his master and scurried away. Tangundo waved for Sassin to approach, "Come here."

Sassin, his long-time follower, did as he was commanded and then dropped to a knee. "Yes, master; I was told by the boy you wanted to see me."

"I have a task for you. I've decided that my army needs an elite formation of warriors, men with strong resolve, and a willingness to serve me to the death. I remember such a force from the histories of my fatherland. They were fierce and powerful warriors, and they served their leader, the Illustrious Showton, without wavering. I want you to find men of steadfast resolve and dedication to *me* and only *me*. They will be *my* Invincibles. I am making you their leader. I have become the

Sutro Showton of this world," Tangundo declared proudly.

"How many should I choose."

"Start with one-thousand. Their numbers will grow over time. And remember, choose only the very best warriors; train them well. You're dismissed."

Shortly after Sassin was excused, Neva Haptane Soidentee arrived. He had been an officer in King Ben-do-teg's guards, and he chose to willingly shift his loyalties to the new master of the kingdom. Soidentee had a military background, and Tangundo quickly realized he needed the man's skills and knowledge if he were to build the armies he had in mind. Soidentee now led Tangundo's army, and it was modeled after the Drund, the Farwune city guards.

"Soidentee, you may approach," Tangundo announced. The neva haptane marched forward and dropped to a knee. Tangundo nodded, and Soidentee stood. "I've received a communication from King Gor-bin-den. It appears he sees the hopelessness of his situation and is willing to come to terms peaceably. I want you to take a thousand men and fetch the king and his family. Place one of your subordinates as overseer of the city along with five-hundred men. Any questions?"

"No, Your Eminence," was the neva haptane's simple reply.

"Good, you're dismissed." The neva haptane saluted and marched out.

A few days later, Soidentee returned and presented King Gor-bin-den before his master. The neva haptane dropped to a knee, and the king bowed. "Your Eminence," the Haptane began, "I present King Gor-bin-den."

Tangundo glared at the king for several moments, and then spat, "Why are you still standing?"

The king looked surprised at first, but his shocked expression turned to anger. "Royalty never kneels," the king responded with an angry and proud tone.

"My regrets, I failed to make myself clear. I don't expect you to kneel; I expect you to drop to your royal belly," Tangundo ordered.

"I refuse! No civilized ruler would expect a king to submit to such an indignity. I have come in goodwill to negotiate the terms of peace between our two kingdoms," King Gor-bin-den explained, his attitude and countenance displaying proud and resolute defiance.

"There are no terms," Tangundo answered. "I now rule the kingdom that once was yours. I will take what I please."

"This is outrageous!" the king shouted. "We will settle this dispute by a Battle of Champions."

Tangundo began laughing, and then his red eyes glared more menacingly at the king. "Soidentee, remove this man. Kill him and the rest of his family; leave none of them alive."

A shocked and pained expression darkened the neva haptane's face. He stood and signaled for two guards to take the king out. King Gor-bin-den voiced his indignation and shock, but his protests fell on unhearing ears.

After the king had been removed, Soidentee turned to his master and asked, "Your Eminence, why kill the king? He was willing to submit to your rule and follow your dictates."

"Neva Haptane Soidentee, I will explain my reasoning only this once. Just like the Illustrious Showton from my homeland,

I cannot risk leaving one who has tasted the sweet savor of ruling authority to remain a threat. No subjugated ruler is to remain alive, and that goes for those who ruled at his side, as well as his seed. Do you understand?"

"Yes, Your Eminence."

"Good. I expect you to kill the king yourself. You're dismissed." The neva haptane's expression turned sullen. He turned and began to exit. "Neva Haptane Soidentee," the self-proclaimed Sutro Showton called. Soidentee stopped and faced his master. "If you ever question one of my rulings again, I will have you skinned alive." Soidentee blanched at the threat, bowed in submission, and resumed his exit.

With his power growing, Tangundo proclaimed his new title to all. He was to be known henceforth as the Sutro Showton. As his army advanced, its ranks increased. He also culled young and healthy men from the cities and provinces he conquered, adding them to his army's rolls. It wasn't long before he had two armies, and then three. Over the succeeding spans, these armies fanned out across the known world, overpowering any and all who resisted, for never before had such a threat been encountered.

The great cities south of Farwune were unwalled. These city-states had existed in an era of peace. The land was spacious, and the populations of the established realms had seldom found it necessary to engage in hostilities. There was plenty for all. The Sutro Showton simply captured city after city as if he were plucking ripe, low-hanging fruit from a tree.

Cities to the north and east were a different matter. These older, well-established lands and richer kingdoms had walled cities. These well-prepared defenses only slowed Tangundo's armies' advances. The warning cry that the Sutro Showton was coming terrorized every peace-loving soul.

PRONUNCIATION GUIDE

b´ This low-pitched popping sound is made by pursing the lips together, rolling them inward, and releasing them, creating a low-toned pop.

p´ This high-pitched popping sound is made by pursing the lips together, extending them forward, and releasing them, creating a high-toned pop.

t´ This clicking sound is made by placing the tongue against the palate, and pulling it down, making a sharp, clicking sound.

WORD	PRONUNCIATION
Ada	ā´ dä
Adia	ā´ dī ä
Anterra	ăn tĕr´ rä
Ardo	är dō
argent	är´ jĕnt
Atura	ä too rǎ
Ayascho	ī´ ä shō
Bardas	bär´ dǎs
bataro	bä´ tär ō
Batru	bǎ´ troo
Bazi	bā´ zē
Bazio	bā´ zēō
Ben-do-teg	bĕn´ dō tĕg

WORD	PRONUNCIATION
betzoe	bĕt zō´
bhat	bhăt
Braydo	brā´ dō
Buffo	bŭf fō
Chashutza	chă shoo´ tzä
Chashutzo	chă shoo´ tzō
Dada	dä´ dä
Danner	dăn´ nĕr
Deemeos	dē´ mē ōs
detzamar	dĕtz´ ä mär
divitz	dīv´ ītz
doez	dō´ ĕz
Dondi	dŏn´ dē
Doros	dō´ rōs
Du	dū
Duba	doo´ bä
Dubo	doo´ bō
Dumaz	doo´ măz
Edder	ĕd´ dĕr
Eezayhod	ē zī´ hŏd
Eos	ē ōs
Fino	fē´ nō
Gangorno	găn´ gōr nō
gee	gē
Gheedan	gē´ dăn
gorga	gōr´ gä

WORD	PRONUNCIATION
gravetro	gră´ vĕ trō
gravetum	gră´ vĕ tŭm
Grazius	gră´ zē ŭs
Gund	gŭnd
Gute	gūt
ha	hä
habaga	hä´ bä gä
Hani	hă nē´
Haro	hä´ rō
Hermanez	hĕr´ măn ĕz
Idop	ī´ dŏp
Isse	īs sē´
Magheedo	mä gē´ dō
Matti-mas	mätē´ mäs
meashe	mē´ shĕ
megato	mĕ gä´ tō
megatus	mĕ gä´ tŭs
Maaryah	mär ī´ ä
Munna	mŭn´ nä
Munnari	mŭn´ nä rē
Munnevo	mŭn´ nē vō
Myron	mī´ rŏn
Namad	nä´ mäd
Namada	nä´ mäd ä
Nestor	nĕs´ tōr
Nevesant	nĕv ĕ sănt´

WORD	PRONUNCIATION
Nita	nē tä´
Nu	nū
Numo	nūmō
Oetan	ō´ tăn
Ootyiah	oot ī ä´
p´atezas	p´ātĕ´ zăs
p´oez	p´ōĕz
Pahno	päh´ nō
Pammon	păm´ mŏn
Pannera	păn´ nĕr rä
Pendor	pĕn´ dōr
Perdiz	pĕr dĭz´
Pershon	pĕr´ shŏn
Ponti	pŏn tē´
Pontus	pŏn´ tŭs
purrant	pĕr´ rănt
Rao	rā´ ō
raster	răs´ tĕr
regum	rĕ´ gŭm
Remmo	rĕm´ mō
rezus	rē´ zŭs
samaran	săm´ ä răn
schazu	schä´ zoo
sestardi	sĕs tăr´ dē
Shadi	shă dē´
Shergus	shĕr gŭs´

WORD	PRONUNCIATION
Seemo	sē´mō
sutro	soo trō´
t´onoe	t´ō nō
T´orbin	t´ŏr bĭn
tah	tä
Taahso	tä´ sō
Tangundo	tä´ sō
Tanzi	tăn´zē
Teema	tē´ mä
Teg-ar-mos	tĕg´ är mŭs
Teness	tĕn´ ĕs
Tenny	tĕn ē´
T´erio	t´ĕ rē ō
tetzae	tĕt´ zā
tetzus	tĕt´ zŭs
Tiro	tĭ´ rō
Titus	tī´ tŭs
Tondo	tŏn´ dō
todo	tō dō´
Tumtuo	tŭm´ too ō
tuntro	tŭn´ trō
Turve	tŭr´ vĕ
Tzani	tză´ nē
Tzeecha	tzē´ chä
Tzeechoe	tzē´ chō
Uragah	ŭr ä´ gä

WORD	PRONUNCIATION
Varios	văr ē´ ŏs
Vihi	vē´ hē
Wandra	wän drä´
We	wē
wernt	wĕrnt
Yos	yōs
zanth	zănth
Zerio	zĕ´ rē ō
Zet	zĕt
Zethus	zĕth´ ŭs
zin	zĭn
Zossemo	zŏ sē´ mō
Zossi	zŏs´ sĕ
Zue	zoo

PREVIOUSLY INTRODUCED
CHARACTERS

NAME	ROLE
Atura	Atura is assigned to Coleman by the Batru village chief. He is to become her provider, and she is charged with teaching him world-speak, the native tongue.
Ayascho	Ayascho takes an instant dislike for Coleman, the man who nearly strangled him to death. During a hunt, their hunt team is attacked by the most feared beast in the jungle, a gorga. Ayascho retreats in panic, abandoning his hunt mates. Coleman notices his act of cowardice and chooses not to expose Ayascho's shame to the village. Ayascho feels he is in Coleman's debt and won't rest until he can reclaim his honor. He follows Coleman when the visitor departs the village.
Bardas	Bardas is a guard in Titus's detachment.
Chashutza	Chashutza is the wife of Chashutzo.
Chashutzo	Chashutzo is the leader of Coleman's hunt team, who was severely injured during a gorga attack.
Coleman	Coleman, an earthling, who becomes known as Tondo, meaning the visitor, arrives on a distant planet due to a mishap while making an experimental transit from the Earth to the Moon. Coleman nourishes the good seeds and chooses to use his increasing power and influence on his new world to benefit others.

NAME	ROLE
Duba	Duba is Dubo's wife.
Dubo	Dubo, a hunter, is gored and killed by a tuntro. Village tradition requires his family to be banished. Coleman argues for ending this wicked tradition.
Gheedan	Gheedan is a sharp-eyed guard in Titus's detachment.
Myron	Myron is a merchant from Anterra, the Ancient City. Coleman learns he is more than 600 years old.
Namad	Namad is the tracker in Coleman's hunt team and Nita's father.
Namada	Namada is Namad's wife and Nita's mother.
Nevesant	Nevesant is a young orphaned delinquent who first notices the strange looking Tangundo. He comes to revere the outsider.
Nita	Nita is Namad's daughter. In a moment of weakness, she steals Tzeecha's necklace. Village law demands that she be banished, a sure death sentence. Coleman argues for a more reasonable punishment. Ayascho is attracted to Nita.
Pontus	Pontus is a guard in Titus's detachment.
Rao	Rao is a guard in Titus's detachment.
Shadi	Shadi is the scent-man in Coleman's hunt team.
Sutro Seer	The senior religious leader and follower of the Great Unnamed God.
Taahso	Taahso is the shaman of the Batru village that befriends Coleman. He possesses magical powers that intrigue Coleman and leads him to discover similar powers within himself.

NAME	ROLE
Tangundo	Another off-worlder, whose name is unpronounceable, arrives on the planet shortly before Coleman does. This off-worlder initially is named Tangundo, meaning outsider. Because he has a hairy face, the local populace considers him a beast-man, and they force him into the perpetual mist where an unspeakable horror lives. He survives that encounter and befriends the young orphan boy Nevesant. He begins to nourish the evil seeds within himself.
Teg-ar-mos	King Teg-ar-mos is the ruler of the kingdom where the Ancient City and the Temple of the Unnamed God are located. He is petitioned by the temple's Sutro Seer to send a detachment of city guards into the Wilderness to fetch the unusual outlander, Coleman.
Teness	Teness is a guard in Titus's detachment.
Titus	Sestardi Titus is a non-officer who leads a detachment of Anterra city guards to fetch the unusual outlander Myron the merchant discovered in the Wilderness.
Tzeecha	Tzeecha is the wife of Tzeechoe.
Tzeechoe	\Tzeechoe becomes Coleman's village mentor and close friend, teaching him the skills he must know in order to survive in the Wilderness.
Zoseemo	Zoseemo is a young slave owned by Myron, the merchant. He is the first slave Coleman meets. Coleman is shocked to learn that the youthful-looking slave is more than seventy spans old.

GLOSSARY OF TERMS

TERM
Anterran calendar and daily time
A typical span is four-hundred days. Every third span is a leap-span, which is four-hundred and one days.
Detzamar
Also referred to as detz, a period of 40 days. There are four wernts in a detzamar, and there are ten detzamars in a span. Detzamars have the following names:

1.	Ant	6. Du-Ant
2.	Zue	7. Du-Zue
3.	Dzaah	8. Du-Dzaah
4.	Tuz	9. Du-Tuz
5.	Mot	10. Du-Mot

Wernt
A wernt is a period of ten days. Days have the following names:

1.	Nu	6. Du-Nu
2.	Tu	7. Du-Tu
3.	We	8. Du-We
4.	Gute	9. Du-Gute
5.	Zet	10. Du-Zet

Anterran daily time
An Anterran day is twenty-two segments, equivalent to twenty-two hours. A segment is ten intervals long, equivalent to sixty minutes. An interval is equivalent to six minutes.
Anterran measures of distance

march ≈ 15-20 miles
margher ≈ 1 mile
rad ≈ 100 yards
radett ≈ 100 feet
radi ≈ 1 foot
radneva ≈ 2 inches

TERM
Arjent
The standard monetary unit of Anterran commoners and the lower-classes, cast from eez (copper). One-hundred arjents equal one bhat.
Batru.
The native villager's god; also, the name used by the villagers to refer to their tribe
Bhat
The standard monetary unit of the Anterran gentry, cast from zin (silver).
Creeper
An insect; also, slang for a pest.
Cross-over
To pass away; to die
Detzamar
A 40-day period; refer to Anterran calendar and daily time
Divitz
Cotton
P'oez
Honored slayer of prey
Eez
Copper
Gant
A diluted wine-like drink
Ghizz
The world-speak rendering of kiss
Godstone
The world-speak rendering of loadstone

TERM
Gravetro
A metal similar to low-grade iron
Gravetum
A metal similar to iron, having the color of brass
Groundshake
An earthquake
Gumpass
The world-speak rendering of compass
Ha
World-speak for yes; also, an exclamation similar to okay, oh, or well
Hoy
A world-speak exclamation of surprise or despair
Meashe
Food; meal
Megato
A junior Pannera officer
Megatus
A senior Pannera officer
Munnoga-touched
A person who has become insane or is deluded
Oy
A world-speak exclamation of surprise similar to oh or ah
P'atezas
The planet's source of light and life; equivalent to the Earth's sun
Panerra
The Anterra city guards

TERM
Purrant
An authority appointed by King Ben-do-teg to oversee local affairs; a hamlet constable
Regum
A monetary unit primarily used by the Anterran gentry, cast from zanth (gold). One-hundred bhat equals one regum
Span
The duration of the planet's orbit around its star, which takes 400.33 days. One day is added to every third span at the end of the first detzamar, Ant. Refer to Anterran Calendar and Daily Time
Sutro
Greater; senior, superior
Taah
The inner-power; see tzaah
Tzaah
The inner-power, also known as taah
Weak-ground
Quicksand
Wernt
A period of ten days; refer to Anterran Calendar and Daily Time
Wur-gor
The world-speak rendering of worker
Zanth
Gold
Zerio
The southwesterly wind
Zin
Silver

MAPS

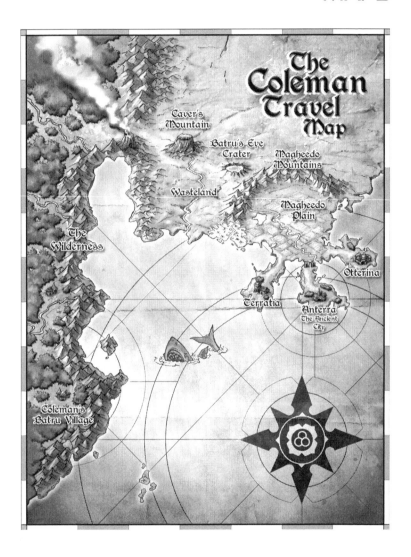

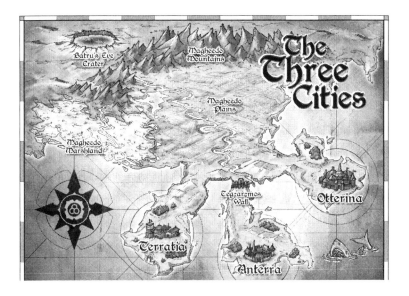

THE
MUNNARI
WAR

NOVEL THREE

While a powerful evil grows in the southland, Coleman continues his fantastic adventure as temple masters prepare him for the coming era of threat. He also teaches them wondrous mysteries from his homeland.

The huge boat is completed and sets sail. Can it survive the deadly challenge of the deep as terrors pummel the wooden craft? Maaryah's unrequited love for the outlander continues to grow. *Will he ever think of her as more than a friend?* She is shocked when he buys a healthy, well-trained slave. What would motivate him to do such an unexpected thing?

The clouds of war have formed, and the devastating storm breaks when an unexpected event brings armed conflict to Anterra, the Ancient City. Coleman faces a new threat that places the life of every kingdom slave at risk. Can he find a way to save their lives and also save the kingdom?

Coleman finally meets with the Sutro Seer after passing in astonishment through the Hall of the Guardians. He is permitted to draw upon their awesome power, unnerving friend and foe alike. He battles to the death in a contest of kings' champions. An epic struggle erupts and rocks the world as thousands of warriors struggle in a duel to determine who will rule this corner of the world, good King Teg-ar-mos or the wicked rulers of the neighboring kingdoms. Who will succeed?

The Munnari Chronicles continue with *Novel Three, The Munnari War.*

MunnariChronicles.com
MLBellanteBooks.com

Made in United States
Orlando, FL
06 June 2022